# ST. CLAIR FAMILY

## THREE IN ONE

PLAN B
HOME TO YOU
BAIT AND SWITCH

ERIN STEVENSON

# ERIN STEVENSON

## Plan B

St. Clair Family
No. 1

1

"SO, KELSEA DENISE, what's your Plan B?"

I rolled my eyes and grabbed another tissue.

"And don't roll your eyes."

My head flopped back on the pillow. How could my mother know I was rolling my eyes, over the phone, from two hundred miles away? I rolled them again to see if they made any noise. No sound whatsoever.

"I'm working on it, Mom, I'll be fine."

"You have to have a Plan B, sweetheart. You can't just pick up and move on without a plan." I tuned her out. I had heard this more times in my almost three decades than I could count. My brain rejoined the conversation a few moments later.

"...and if I hadn't had my teaching degree to fall back on, you and Morgan and I would have starved when your father died," Mom said softly.

I stopped my eyes just as they began to roll. Dad had been well insured, but I knew it gave Mom a sense of purpose to have gone back to teaching.

"I know, Mom, but Ryan didn't die." *However, that could be arranged.*

"Breaking your engagement four days before the wedding! I never would have believed it from that boy. He was so nice."

"Yeah, I know, Mom. He had everyone fooled." *Most of all, me.*

A maternal sigh rippled through the miles into my ear. "And *so* handsome! Both of you with that gorgeous dark hair and brown eyes. You would have given me beautiful grandchildren."

*Would you like some cheese with your whine, Mom?*

My mother was desperate for a grandchild, and that task rested completely on my slim shoulders. All of her close friends had about seventy-five grandchildren apiece. My sister, Morgan, was off the hook. She'd breezed through college, motored through a master's and Ph.D., and was now Assistant Professor of Art Therapy at the Midwest Art Institute in Chicago. She wasn't even thirty yet. Morgan was too busy with her teaching and her patients and her research to think about dating or marriage or children, but because of her sparkling success, Mom never harassed *her.*

*Time to shut this down.* I tossed the crumpled tissue into the overflowing wastebasket and rose up from my messy day bed, where I'd spent the last day and a half sobbing my soul out. I walked through the living room into the kitchen (which took a full five seconds), grabbed the plastic container from the bottom shelf of the pantry, and shook dog food into a bowl.

If masked men with automatic weapons burst into my tiny apartment to abduct me, my dogs would sleep through it and never see or think about me again. But the tinkling sound of their food landing in the ceramic bowl was all that was needed for the barkfest to commence.

"Mom, I've got to let the dogs out," I yelled over the din. "I'll talk to you later."

"All right, Kelsea, remember your Plan B. I'll check in with you tomorrow. Love you."

*Oh, joy.* "Love you, too, Mom." I hit *end* and tossed my phone down on the counter.

I *did* love my mom, but I was nothing like her. Morgan was like her. Morgan always had a Plan A, B, C, and D. If, on the other hand, flying by the seat of one's pants was an Olympic sport, I would win the gold medal.

I shuffled to the fridge and pulled out the milk. According to the date stamp, it would expire today. *How does the milk know to just give up on the 29th?* I decided to take my chances. It wasn't like *Ryan* or anyone would know or care if I died from milk poisoning or whatever happens when you drink expired milk.

I grabbed the Oreos and sat down at my small table. Penny and Sheldon were still scarfing down their food. The two Poms came into my life about four years ago when I first started volunteering at the animal shelter. They were the best thing to ever happen to me.

I looked at the clock and decided that this was dinner. After polishing off a few—all right—a lot of Oreos (and the milk, which tasted fine), I wiped my hands on a napkin and opened my laptop. I had ignored all the notifications and messages of shock and awe about the canceled wedding. I had no desire to talk with anyone about it.

Thank God we had kept things relatively small and local, despite Ryan's mother's attempts to make this the social event of the season. Morgan was my only attendant, and Ryan's best friend was his best man. It should have been easy enough to cancel the church, photographer, flowers, cake, and the restaurant where we were going to have the reception. Since Ryan's mother arranged all of it, I suppose she canceled all of it.

A new message popped up in my e-mail. *Flight itinerary for Ryan Patrick Singer and Kelsea Denise Anderson.*

I groaned out loud. The honeymoon! How could I have forgotten? The tears began to flow again, and I reached into my pocket for a rumpled tissue.

It was the only aspect of the entire event in which I had any say. The moment we announced our engagement, Jasmine Singer morphed into the monster-in-law-slash-wedding-planner-from-Hades.

She even chose the wedding date. New Year's Day.

I finally convinced Ryan to let me arrange the honeymoon and pay for it. And keep it a complete surprise from everyone, including him.

I blew my nose with a loud honk. In exactly three days, I would have been with the love of my life on a plane to a Caribbean island for a week at a romantic honeymoon resort. Just the two of us and approximately one hundred other bridal couples. No single lotharios, no families with noisy children, no old people.

I took one more drink of milk and, just to punish myself, clicked on the link for the resort at the top of my *Favorites*. I already had the pictures memorized. All that sand and surf and romance! I stamped my feet and let out an angry squeal. Sheldon and Penny looked up at me, and Penny padded over. "Come here, baby," I cooed, picking her up.

Her large, innocent eyes stared at me, and she rubbed her head under my chin as I hugged her close. Penny always knew when I needed comforting.

Tears blurred my vision as I looked at the screen again. *Wait a minute...*I perked up and started clicking. *What if...?*

I already knew that there were absolutely no refunds in the event of a cancellation. That had been spelled out loud and clear in several places throughout the resort's website. After a thorough search, I made up my mind. There was nothing whatsoever that stated that I couldn't still go there *alone*. I had scrimped and saved for it, and painstakingly rearranged my schedule and gotten coverage to be gone for the week. A shiver rippled through me. Most of all, I had looked forward to a break from the St. Louis winter.

Who would care? All those couples would be staring into one another's eyes. No one would even notice me. I could still read and take walks and swim and soak up the sun. *I deserve this.*

I kissed Penny and held her up in front of me. "That's it, girl, I'm doing this! I'm going on a honeymoon!"

Her reply was an enthusiastic yip.

I stared out the window as the jet began its descent into St. Jardin International Airport. I was completely mesmerized by the blue and turquoise waters, the sun sparkling on it like diamonds. In the distance, on the island itself, I could see foliage in myriad shades of green. The effect was incredibly soothing. "Nice job, God," I whispered. Then I began to think about what it must have been like during Creation week. Did He get everything right on the first try? Probably, because He's—well, God. But what if even He didn't get it right every time, and occasionally had to come up with a Plan B? What if He realized that the giraffe's neck was too long, and instead of shortening it, decided to add some taller trees?

I collected my luggage and climbed aboard the first of two shuttle buses that were waiting just outside the terminal, as promised. Even if I hadn't been directed where to go, the two-tone pink bus with the sprawling words "St. Jardin Honeymoon Resort" in silver script would have been the first clue.

"Kelsea, um, Anderson," I said in a low voice to the petite, young woman with the clipboard standing at the top of the steps. She was dressed from head to toe in the same colors as the bus, and her bright pink nametag read *Molli*, with an *i*. How appropriate.

"Anderson, Anderson," she murmured, a frown creasing her brow.

"It might be under *Singer*," I whispered. "But Ryan Singer isn't coming."

Her head snapped up, and her blue eyes popped wide open. "Isn't coming?"

"Correct," I replied. "I'm here alone. I paid for our reservation."

"This is highly unusual," Molli stated. Her blond ponytail danced as her head shook back and forth. "We've been open for almost three years, and we've never had—"

I interrupted her, trying to sound authoritative without being mean. "It may be unusual, but your website didn't say a thing about not being able to come alone. I've paid for the week." I kept my gaze even and steady.

"Well, all right, Mrs.—Miss Anderson." She pointed to the empty seat behind the driver. "Take a seat. You'll have to talk with the owners when we get to the resort."

"Thank you," I managed to croak as I pushed by her and slid into the seat. At least she didn't throw me off the bus.

I set my purse and carry-on next to me, turned my head toward the window, and swallowed the lump in my throat. *Breathe, Kelsea, you can do this.* Once I got to the resort and into my room, I could hide in there, order room service, and figure out ways to keep to myself, especially to avoid the advertised "newlywed games" and other social mixers.

The palm trees swayed in the warm, tropical breeze as I stared out the window. Even if it was uncomfortable to be at the couples' resort alone, it was worth it to be away from the snow and ice at home. I could spend the week figuring out my Plan B. My mother would be so proud.

Happy, smiling couples boarded the bus two-by-two, just like Noah's Ark. I averted my gaze and tried to tune out their laughter as they began socializing with one another.

"Miss Anderson?" It was cute little Molli-with-an-i, all efficiency. "We have a situation. A couple of our entertainers missed their flight last night and just arrived, and we need every seat on both shuttles." Her gaze flicked to the items sitting on the seat next to me.

"Oh, okay," I mumbled, gathering my things onto my lap. I turned my attention back to the scenery outside the window.

A moment later, the seat shuddered as a weight landed on it. A solid arm pressed into my shoulder, then shifted away.

"Sorry," a deep male voice growled. He didn't sound sorry at all.

Gosh, this guy was big. Not fat, just—well, big. Muscular with long legs that stuck out into the aisle. Still, his knees were nearly touching his chest. This shuttle bus wasn't made for someone his size, and he more than filled his half of the seat. I scooted closer to the window and snuck another look at him.

A blond Adonis. Not bad looking, if you liked the type, which I didn't. My type was TDH—tall, dark, and handsome. *Ryan.*

I opened my mouth to offer a sharp retort, then thought better of it. If this guy was one of the entertainers, he might be one of the few people at the resort that I could talk to or even hang out with a little, just to pass the time.

I pasted on a smile. "So, are you a singer, or dancer? Wait, let me guess. A magician?"

His amber eyes blazed. "Mind your own business, lady," he snapped, and turned away.

2

LANDON ST. CLAIR stared into the crystal clear liquid and lifted the glass to his lips. As soon as the liquor entered his mouth, he fought to swallow it, and sputtered. He rubbed a hand over his eyes. "Ach, what am I doing?" he muttered to himself, and set the glass down on the bar with a hard clink. He stood, took out his wallet, and tossed down some bills.

Landon had never been a big drinker, even in college. He enjoyed a couple of beers at a party or at a sports bar with friends. He never liked the taste of the hard stuff, and once he had experienced his first hangover, decided that it wasn't worth it.

Only being left at the altar would drive him to even consider crossing that line.

He left the resort bar and walked through the pink-themed lobby to the dining hall, but his mind was miles away. The image of standing in front of five hundred guests waiting for his bride to enter was burned into his memory. The music began to play, the six bridesmaids entered one by one, and then the doors closed. The members of the string ensemble held their instruments still, poised to launch into the bridal march. Silent seconds turned to minutes. The mother of the bride sat wild-eyed on the front row, her head swiveling between the bridal party in front and the door in back. Landon stared at the door, willing Nicola to enter.

And then he knew with certainty what he had felt in his gut for the last two days. That she wasn't going to go through with it. She wasn't going to marry him.

Now, almost exactly twenty-four hours later, Landon was alone on the Caribbean island of St. Jardin—the *Island of Gardens*. Well, *alone* as one could be with approximately two hundred honeymooners. He'd carefully checked all the legal disclaimers and decided to keep his reservation, hole up in his room, and figure out a Plan B.

Other than giving his name to the pink-clad girl on the shuttle bus, and snapping at his perky, nosy seatmate, he hadn't said a word to anyone until he'd arrived at the resort.

The check-in process had been uncomfortable, and when Landon announced that he was here alone and that *no, Mrs. St. Clair would *not* be joining him, the owners were immediately summoned. Rosie and Ike Goldman clucked sympathetically and assured him that they would do everything in their power to make his stay tolerable if not enjoyable.

Landon squirmed in his tux as he waited to meet the Goldmans as instructed. He'd been loath to put it on again, but had little choice, since tonight's dinner was black tie. For once, he wished he was closer to average height. It was hard to fade into the woodwork when you were six foot four.

Everywhere he looked, there were couples entwined, or holding hands, or staring into each other's eyes, sending loaded messages. Landon fought the urge to bolt from the building. *What was I thinking? I wish hadn't come.*

3

I CHECKED MYSELF in the full-length mirror one more time. *Eat your heart out, Ryan.*

The emerald green chiffon dress certainly made a statement, along with the three-inch black platform peep toe heels that I'd snagged at a vintage shop for a fraction of their worth. I do love a good bargain.

My hair had even cooperated tonight. I'd fashioned it into a surprisingly elegant updo with the help of several small, glittering clips, and thanks to the humidity, tendrils framed my face in a way that looked both effortless and chic.

All the clothes I'd bought for the honeymoon were back home, the tags still on them. At least I could return them. The lingerie, however, had been offered up as a burnt offering to spinsterhood in my metal trashcan. So I landed on St. Jardin with a suitcase full of mostly sloppy, comfortable clothes. But I couldn't part with the green dress, and it wouldn't hurt to make a good first impression tonight. It would be all downhill from here.

I swiveled my hips, first one way and then the other, and watched the skirt gently float out and then settle back just above my knees. "Not bad for a dog walker from Kirkwood, Missouri," I said to the glamorous woman in the mirror.

*Small business owner,* the voice in my head corrected me. I'd survived the first year, and my client list was growing. I was still astounded at the vast sums that people would shell out to have their dogs walked, played with, fed and watered, taken to the dog park, and even to the doggie day spa for pampering. Due to referrals from my happy dog owners, I was branching out to care for cats, birds, rabbits, and the occasional gerbil and ferret. I drew the line at reptiles.

I drew my black silk shawl around my shoulders, picked up my clutch and, out of habit, looked for my phone. I didn't have a very good plan, and now that I was flying solo, I couldn't afford to indulge in international minutes. Before I left for the airport, I sent a text to Morgan. *Leaving my phone at home. I just need to unplug. You have the contact info for the resort. Will you explain to Mom? I know, I owe you! Love you* ☺ Then I powered it down and left it on my kitchen table.

My stomach let out a growl, and even though I wasn't looking forward to having to socialize with people tonight, there was no other option. I wasn't happy during the check-in process when Molli informed me that there was no room service for meals.

"Can you imagine? If we allowed that, our staff could never deliver two hundred meals to a hundred rooms. No one would want to come out," Molli had lamented dramatically. "Dinner is at eight o'clock sharp. The first night is formal, and the owners will be there to meet everyone. They're busy right now, but they're particularly looking forward to meeting *you,* Ms. Anderson," she added with a lift of her right eyebrow. It looked mysterious and exotic.

I turned to the mirror and tried to lift one eyebrow, and then the other. It didn't look mysterious or exotic on me, it looked like I was having gastric issues. I guess independent eyebrow mobility is like having double joints, you either have it, or you don't.

It was a quick walk to the main lodge. I got in line in the lobby and stood there among—what else?—loving couples, and kept my head down. I had no desire to draw attention to myself. When I got to the check-in table, there was Molli—now decked out in a formal in the same shade of pink that she wore previously, that matched the bus and all the signage and decorations at the resort. There was another girl sitting next to her whose pink nametag read *Haley.* She wore a formal in a paler shade of pink.

I had a feeling I was going to see more pink over the next week than I'd seen in my entire life, although I had to concede that someone had done a fantastic job of making it all look very elegant.

"Name, please?" said Haley.

*You have every right to be here. State it loud and proud.* "Kelsea Anderson."

Molli had just finished with another couple and perked up when she heard my name. "Oh! This is the one I was telling you about," she said to Haley. "She's the one who *came here ALONE.*" Her voice rose in volume until she was practically shouting those last three words. *Say it a little louder, would you, Molli? They couldn't quite hear you back in St. Louis.*

Haley nodded solemnly. "Oh-h-h-h." She drew the syllable out for several seconds. "Rose wants to talk to you," she said, her eyes growing wide.

"Rose is the owner," Molli clarified. She stood. "Come with me."

My stomach churned. Was Rose the owner going to throw me out? My mind conjured up a dark, menacing creature pointing a long, crooked finger toward the door. *Off my island!* her evil, witchy voice roared. I trailed after Molli through the middle of the room, which was filled with round tables that seated eight. Romantic candlelight illuminated each table, and there were twinkly pink and white lights everywhere. *Where in the world does one find pink lights?*

Molli arrived at what looked to be the main table, front and center. "Here we are," she said. "Rose, this is the woman you wanted to meet. Kelsea Anderson, this is Rose Goldman."

Before me stood a tiny woman with white hair with pink highlights, swept up in a bouffant à la 1965, topped off by a glittering pink and white tiara. *Surely those aren't real diamonds! And what gemstone is pink? Topazes?* She wore pink rhinestone-encrusted cat glasses and a hot pink vintage satin formal that looked brand new. I thought I had seen everything until my gaze landed on her feet, which were encased in—wait for it—pink Converse!

It should have been a totally ridiculous look, but somehow, she pulled it off. She was just adorable.

The elfin woman followed my gaze, which remained fixed on her feet, and shrugged. "Bunions."

She couldn't have been more than five foot two, and that included the poufy hairdo. She was seventy if she was a day, but her smile lit up the room, and melted my heart. The evil witch vacated my head, and my knees nearly went weak with relief.

"Kelsea Anderson, I'm so happy you're here," she said sweetly, encasing my hand in both of her soft, wrinkled ones. "I'm Rose, but my friends call me Rosie, and I hope you will, too." With me in my platform heels, she had to tip her head way back to look up at me. I felt like she could see straight into my soul. She spent a long moment appraising me, then lowered her voice to a conspiratorial whisper and patted my hand. "I can tell you're one of the strong ones. Good for you for coming. You're going to be just fine."

I swallowed the lump in my throat as she shooed Molli away with a bejeweled hand. "Molli, dear, Kelsea will be just fine with me. You go on back to the lobby now." Her bracelets tinkled as her arm waved.

Two couples were already settled in at the main table, totally into one another and oblivious to everything around them. That left four empty chairs. I assumed three were for Rose, her husband, and me. As I eyed the remaining chair, a feeling of trepidation washed over me.

"Those are the Wilders and the McFaddens," Rose said, pausing briefly. "I'll introduce you later. Come with me." She smiled and nodded at people as she dragged me behind her. "Oh, there's my Ike. Yoo hoo, Ike!" Her face lit up and she waved. "Here he comes with your dinner companion."

I stopped dead in my tracks. I needed a dinner companion like I needed a third eye. I could barely manage shadow, eyeliner, and mascara for the two I already had, not to mention the hassle of the accompanying eyebrows. "Oh, Rosie, no. I don't need—"

She tugged on my hand. "It will be fine, dear. Trust me."

This would *not* be fine. My stomach gave a painful spasm and I took a deep breath, sending up a prayer for patience. I would have stayed in my room and skipped dinner altogether, but I'd hardly eaten over the last four days, and suddenly found that I had an appetite, which had now vanished.

Rose stopped as a white-haired man with bright blue eyes approached us. My stomach dropped when I realized who was with him. My seatmate from the bus, Mr. Rude Seat Hog.

4

LANDON COULDN'T BELIEVE it when Ike Goldman turned to him with a bright smile and said, "Will you look at my lovely bride? Fifty-three years last June, and she's still as beautiful as the day I made her mine."

Landon almost blanched, not because of Rose Goldman's outrageous pink ensemble, but because of the woman that she was pulling along behind her.

He fought the urge to groan out loud. *Is that Miss Perky?* It was hard to tell. The woman on the bus looked small and miserable, hunched down in the seat. This woman stood proud and tall, though not as tall as Nicola. The green dress was the perfect complement for her upswept, dark brown hair, not to mention a welcome respite from all the pink surrounding them. She had a nice figure, and wasn't bad looking, if you liked the type, which he didn't. Landon had always preferred blondes or redheads.

Then her eyes flashed with recognition, and her full, shiny lips twisted as if she'd sucked on a lemon. Yes, this was definitely the woman from the bus. *Great.* Where was her husband, anyway? Probably hiding out in the bathroom, if he had any sense.

Rose beamed and looked up at her husband. It was a short

distance, since he was only a few inches taller than her. "Ike, this is Kelsea Anderson. My husband, Ike Goldman."

Kelsea Anderson's features relaxed, and her face was transformed. "It's a pleasure to meet you, Ike," she said warmly, and reached for his wrinkled hand with her smooth, elegant one. *Wow.* She was almost pretty.

Rose took a breath and gestured toward Landon. "And this gentleman is Mr. St. –"

"St. Fair. Brandon St. Fair." Landon interrupted, hoping he didn't sound too forceful. He didn't offer his hand. This had been his one request when he met the Goldmans, that they permit him to use an assumed name for the duration of his stay at the resort. He didn't want anyone wondering why he was here alone and then googling his name. Landon was certain that the leading news story in St. Louis was that a partner of the city's most prestigious law firm had been left at the altar by the daughter of one of the top families on St. Louis' social register.

Rose smiled. "Yes—Mr. St. Fair. This is Miss Anderson."

*Miss?* Landon's eyes flicked to the woman's bare left hand. He saw the gleam in Rose's eye, and smelled a set-up coming. And by the look on the brunette's face, she smelled it, too.

"Miss Anderson finds herself in the same unfortunate predicament as yourself, Mr. St. Fair," Rose explained. "She is here alone. In the almost three years that Ike and I have owned this resort, we've never had anyone come here on their own, and now we have you two." She smiled brightly at them. "Obviously, a single person here upsets the balance, and we don't want any of our guests to feel uncomfortable. If the two of you would, say, sit together at meals, you'll just blend in with everyone else, and attract less attention."

"I really don't think—" Landon began.

"I'll be fine on my own—" Miss Anderson's words came out on top of his.

Rose smiled up at them. "I'm so glad that's settled," she said sweetly. "Let's find our seats." And before Landon knew what had hit him, Rose had placed Miss Anderson's hand in the crook of his elbow, and they were following the Goldmans through the dining room to the head table.

He glanced down at the woman. She looked like she'd just eaten a prune, and walked stiffly next to him, her hand positioned in such a way as to have as little contact with him as possible.

Landon smirked at her. "I don't have cooties, you know."

Her head snapped up. "What are you, like twelve?"

Landon pasted on a smile as they arrived at the table. *Let the games begin.*

5

*COOTIES? HEY, THE seventies called, they want their word back. What a dweeb.*

Staying in my room and starving would have been far preferable to this farce, although I had to admit, the food was delicious. So Mr. high-and-mighty Brandon St. Fair wasn't one of the entertainers. He was just a jilted groom, apparently. *No surprise there. That woman sure dodged a bullet.*

"How long have you two been together?" This question came from the chatty Mrs. McFadden.

The dweeb looked at me, and his gaze softened just a bit. "Oh, it seems like minutes, really. Time just flies when you're having fun." He took a sip of his water.

My heart skipped a beat. His eyes were the dreamiest shade of amber I had ever seen, like fine cognac. *Wait, how would I know that? I've never had cognac.*

"Where are you from?" Julie McFadden chirped.

I wasn't about to let him answer all the questions directed to us. "Kirkwood, Missouri. A suburb of St. Louis," I quickly replied.

A shadow crossed Brandon's face. "Ike, could you pass the rolls, please?" he asked. "These are the best rolls I've ever had."

The bread basket made its way over to us. "We have a wonderful baker, as well as a top-notch chef," Ike said proudly.

Brandon held the roll basket out to me. His eyes held a threat of challenge. "You want one, pumpkin?" *Those eyes.*

"I'm fine, honey bunny," I replied, adding an adolescent giggle for fun. His eyes narrowed slightly and darkened a shade. *Ooh, this could be fun.*

He gave me an ingratiating smile. "You're so disciplined, sugar plum," he said as he slapped about a cup of butter on his roll. "You know how those carbs go straight to your hips."

The utter nerve of this man! I suddenly had the urge to smear the front of his tux with butter.

Mr. McFadden and Mr. Wilder both suppressed a laugh. Brandon smiled and winked at me. "Just kidding, sweet cheeks."

*I'll show you my sweet cheeks, buster!* No, I couldn't do that to Rose and Ike.

Mr. McFadden turned to the Goldmans. "You say you've owned this resort for three years? How did that come about?" I was happy that the conversation was no longer on my hips.

Rose and Ike shared a loving look and laughed. "Oh, we won the lottery!" Rose exclaimed.

"We played the same numbers every week for over twenty years, and finally hit the jackpot." Her big blue eyes, magnified by her cat-glasses lenses, darted around the table. I could tell that she couldn't wait to answer the question on everyone's minds. "Fifteen million!" she announced. We all responded with happy amazement.

Ike picked up the story. "Up until that time, we'd hardly been out of Brooklyn. But we sold our apartment and headed for the Caribbean. Never looked back. We threw a dart at a map, ended up on this island, and this resort was for sale. We had no idea what we were going to do with it, but we bought it lock, stock, and barrel, and moved in."

"And about a month later, I saw a Hallmark movie about a

honeymoon destination resort, and that was that. It was fate!" Rose's hands waved animatedly, and her bracelets jangled happily.

"Did you leave family behind in New York?" Mark Wilder asked.

Ike took Rose's hand. "No. It's always just been the two of us. God didn't choose to bless us in that way."

"But we've had a long, wonderful marriage and now, all of you couples are our children!" Rose exclaimed. "And we so enjoy giving all of you the best start to your marriages that we can! It's our mission now."

I felt Rose's gaze boring into Brandon and me, and tried to send her a telepathic message. *If you have designs on fixing me up with this baboon, you're in for a disappointment, Rosie.*

# 6

LANDON RAN A finger under his collar. Ike and Rose had just finished their welcoming announcement to hearty applause. Despite his chagrin over the whole arrangement, Landon had to admire the older couple. What he had seen of the resort so far was beautiful, and they seemed in their element.

He found himself standing with the men and, too late, realized that the others were helping their wives to their feet. Miss Anderson stood on her own.

"We're going to take a moonlight walk through the gardens," Mark Wilder said. He looked at the two of them. "What about you?"

"I think we'll—ah, go back to the room," Landon responded quickly.

Mark produced an exaggerated wink and took his wife's hand. "I get you, man," he said to Landon. "This will be a short walk."

*Great.* All Landon could think about was getting out of this blasted penguin suit and relaxing in his room, *alone.* But he'd given a completely different impression. He felt hot anger radiating off the woman next to him.

The Wilders and McFaddens murmured their goodbyes, and Ike and Rose materialized beside him. They were about a foot shorter than him, and really cute together. Landon was already developing a soft spot for them.

"Your rooms are on the same hallway," Rose said. "Alphabetical by the husband's last name. Singer and St. Fair. You're practically neighbors. The Smiths are between you."

Landon glanced down at Kelsea, who looked close to tears. *Her married name would have been Singer.* He felt a pang of sympathy. "Then let me walk you home," he offered. It was the least he could do in light of the carbs remark. Landon had no idea what had come over him.

Kelsea looked at him with a mild expression of surprise. Well, he *had* been pretty much an ogre to her to this point. This was no more her fault than his, and there was no reason to be unchivalrous. They said their goodbyes to the Goldmans and thanked them for their understanding and hospitality.

As soon as Rose and Ike were out of earshot, the lemon-sucking woman was back. "I can find my own way back to my room," she snapped.

*For the love of Mike.* "Since we're right next to each other, we may as well walk there together."

Her beautiful, dark eyes shot daggers at him. "Are you sure there's room? My carb-laden hips won't push you off the sidewalk?"

He felt lower than a dachshund. "I—"

"My hips are just fine. I'm perfectly proportioned and work hard to stay that way."

*You sure are,* he thought appreciatively. But that probably wasn't the right thing to say right now, either.

They began to walk. Kelsea looked up at him through her long, dark lashes. "I'm not sleeping with you, so don't get any ideas," she hissed.

Landon came to a full stop, and his jaw dropped. The nerve of the woman! *No wonder she's here alone.* "Don't flatter yourself, Miss Anderson!" he said through clenched teeth.

"I'm just making sure we're perfectly clear on that matter, Mr. St. Fair," she retorted.

Landon rolled his eyes. She sounded like a schoolmarm from the 1800s. "Believe me, that's the furthest thing from my mind," he muttered.

They walked in silence, and Kelsea kept her distance from him (no doubt to avoid catching his cooties). Landon imagined himself walking next to Nicola, who was nearly his height when she wore heels. Their arms would be wrapped around one another's waists, and they would probably stop every few steps for a kiss. Landon could hardly believe that all of that was in his past. He glanced down at Kelsea and, if the look on her face was any clue, figured that she was having similar thoughts.

"What's his name?" Landon asked softly.

Kelsea blinked, her deep brown eyes shiny with tears. *She really does have beautiful eyes,* Landon thought to himself. She swiped a hand across them. "Ryan," she whispered, barely audible.

They stopped at her door and she pulled a key card out of her little purse. Landon paused, and tried to think of something encouraging to say. "Well, it may not seem like it now, but you're probably better off without him."

Kelsea gasped, and her eyes flashed fire. "Says who? You don't know *anything,* Brandon St. Fair!" She swiped the key card and opened the door with an angry push.

"Hey, I'm sorry," Landon offered. "I didn't mean—"

The door closed in his face with a loud slam.

*WHO DOES HE think he is?* I threw another wadded tissue toward the wastebasket, and missed. *Who cares?* I couldn't even muster up the energy to get off the bed to pick it up.

Brandon St. Fair was by far the most exasperating human being on the face of the planet. As if he knew *anything* about my hips, or Ryan, or—just *anything!* And now it looked like I was going to be stuck with him for the next week, at least for meals. Maybe tomorrow I could find some food at a market and eat in my room. I looked around. No refrigerator, no microwave, no coffeemaker, no utensils of any kind. I wondered if I could subsist on fruit, nuts, and crackers for a week.

I let out a sigh. The owners were just the sweetest couple, and they could have refused to let me stay, or made things uncomfortable. I suppose I could put up with their one request and sit through meals with the insufferable man.

I changed into comfy sleep clothes and climbed into the king-sized bed. Compared to my single daybed at home, it felt as big as Texas, and compounded my sense of loneliness. I tried in vain to chase images of Ryan from my mind, to forget how cherished I felt when he kissed me, and how safe and content I was when he held me. Now, I felt alone and bereft. I needed a distraction, but none of the books I'd brought held any interest.

I fired up my tablet and started absentmindedly surfing the net. The promotional info on the resort's website stated that internet service on the island was spotty, so I'd only brought it to watch movies on the plane, or so I told myself.

Before I knew it, my fingers had typed *Brandon St. Fair*. I clicked on some more keys and frowned. It appeared that he didn't have an online footprint. I found four men with that name, none of them remotely close to being him. None of them had his impressive height, his broad shoulders and trim waistline, the deep cleft in his chin, or his golden, dark blond hair. I had to admit that he filled out a tux in a way I'd seen on no other man.

*Brandon St. Fair*. For some reason, the name didn't sit right with me. He didn't really seem like a Brandon.

Why was I wasting time thinking about him? I started to go to Ryan's page, then remembered that I had made a pact with myself to stay off social media this week. He rarely updated it, anyway, and I had already unfriended him. I closed my computer and turned off the light.

I lay awake for a long time, unable to shut off my brain. I was still steaming about Brandon's carbs comment at dinner. Maybe I'd turn the tables at the next meal. Surely there was something…I ticked through his physical attributes and to my chagrin, couldn't think of anything that wasn't perfect. And of course I didn't know him well enough to come up with anything else.

Why did this guy get under my skin? *Stop thinking about him.*

I rolled over and punched my pillow. With nothing else to think about, my mind wandered back to Ryan. What had I done to make him cancel our wedding? Why did he stop loving me? How would I go on? I was almost thirty years old. I would just join a convent and become a nun. *Oh wait, I'm not Catholic.*

I started to cry. *Drat.* Now I was all stuffy and wouldn't be able to sleep. I switched on the light and went to find my nasal spray. It was with my toiletries on the bathroom counter.

As I reached for it, I spied the little black velvet box that held my engagement ring. Another piece of my splintered heart fell away. *My beautiful ring.* I opened the box and gently fingered the diamond. It wasn't an extravagant ring, but we'd chosen it together. Memories of that day flooded my senses, and tears rolled down my cheeks.

# 8

LANDON THREW HIS tux on the closet floor and hoped he wouldn't have to wear it again for a long, long time. The rest of the meals for the duration of the week were casual dress, and only the final night was formal. He had a pair of black dress slacks and a white dinner jacket that would do.

He scowled to himself. Miss Anderson was from the St. Louis area. What were the chances? She probably lived less than thirty minutes from him. Landon picked up his laptop and hopped online. He would have to be very careful not to give any clues away about himself. No way did he want her or anyone else knowing where he was from, or anything else about him.

Before he realized it, he had typed in *Kelsey Anderson, Kirkwood, Missouri.* One hit, but it sure wasn't her. But what was this? *Kelsea* Anderson. There she was, holding two Pomeranians. That was an unusual spelling of the name, but a pretty one. It suited her. *No relationship info to show.* She'd shed her affiliation with Ryan Singer quickly, as Landon had with Nicola. Hometown, Kankakee, Illinois. No college listed. *Worked at St. Louis Zoo.* That was impressive.

He scrolled down. *Owner of Kelsea's Kritter Sitter Service.* In one click, he was on her business website. Dog walker and companion, pet (and/or house) sitter, plant waterer, personal shopper, errand girl. She'd been doing it for about a year and had a five-star rating from seventy-two clients. Well, that was just about the cutest thing he'd ever seen.

Landon found himself smiling as he scrolled through dozens of pictures of Kelsea with various animals, mostly dogs. She looked carefree, relaxed, and absolutely beautiful in her element, nothing like his shrewish dinner companion from tonight. Her long, luxurious dark brown hair hung in graceful layers, and her eyes sparkled with joy. This woman was clearly a compassionate animal lover.

And, as he had seen tonight in person, she had a tall, perfectly proportioned athletic figure and *really* nice legs.

Landon shook his head, and closed out of the website. *What am I doing? She's prickly as a cactus, totally exasperating, and after this week, I'll never have to see her again. St. Louis is big enough for both of us.*

He was just about to power down his computer when a thought flew into his mind. After a few clicks, he easily found Ryan Singer. He had dark hair and eyes, not unlike Kelsea's. Probably a couple of inches taller than her, and skinny. Software salesman for a national firm. Lifelong St. Louis resident. Graduate of SLUH (St. Louis University High) and UMSL. There was nothing remarkable until a few words jumped off the page. Landon winced. *In a relationship with Jenna Harmon.*

## 9

THE BREAKFAST BUFFET opened on the main patio at seven o'clock, and I had every intention of being there, even though I'd gotten little sleep. There was no reason why I couldn't come alone. I didn't need a babysitter, or Mr. Know-it-All's annoying company. It was unlikely that I'd run into Ike or Rose here. The resort owners would surely have things to keep them busy early in the day.

I gazed out over the expanse of white sand to the aqua waters beyond. *Perfect.* I'd go for a walk along the beach after breakfast, and then maybe go back to my room and take a nap.

The patio was nearly empty. *Well, duh, Kelsea. If you were here with Ryan, you'd probably find a reason to stay in the room, too.* My heart gave a painful squeeze. I wondered how long it would take to get over him.

*Maybe it isn't really over*, I mused as I sat down with a toasted English muffin and a bowl of fruit. I popped a bit of juicy mango into my mouth and closed my eyes. *Heavenly.* I hadn't had real fresh fruit in months.

I replayed my last conversation with Ryan in my head as I'd done a thousand times since. He'd come to my apartment last Tuesday night, and the moment I saw his face, I knew something was horribly wrong.

"I can't do this. I'm just not ready to settle down, Kels," he'd finally said.

"You're dumping me? We're through? Almost three years down the drain?" I'd practically screamed.

"No, no, not at all," Ryan said. "Just taking a step back. I don't know, maybe I'll be ready by next summer, or next year." His foot bounced nervously. "You had your heart set on a fall wedding anyway."

*Yes, I did. It was your mother who wanted a winter wedding.*

"Why, Ryan?" I'd begged, tears running down my cheeks. "Why are you doing this?"

He couldn't even look me in the eye. "I'm not even thirty yet, Kels. I just—I'm just not ready."

"So this is about the age difference again?" I was two and a half years older, and Ryan always found a reason to bring that up.

"No, it's not. I just need some space."

I've always hated that phrase. Along with *I'm taking a step back.*

He insisted that I keep the ring. "Who knows, we might, you know—need it in the future." That sounded lame, even to me.

As we stood at my door, tears ran down my cheeks, and my heart splintered into a million pieces. "Ryan, just tell me—is there someone else? Have you met someone else?"

He took my hands in his. "Kels, no, absolutely not. No way. Listen, I'll—I'll have my mom make all the calls, cancel everything, and I'll call you tomorrow." And with a dry, emotionless peck on my cheek, he was gone.

He never did call. But maybe I just need to give him some space.

"Good morning, Kelsea!" Rose's chipper voice brought me back to the present. She gave my shoulders a squeeze. "How did you sleep, dear?"

She was a pink ball of energy. Her pinkish-white hair was

perfectly coiffed, sans the tiara. She wore pink capri pants, a brightly flowered shirt, and her Converse.

"I slept fine, Rose," I lied.

She sat down. "Remember, my friends call me Rosie."

"I slept fine, Rosie," I said, trying in vain to keep my voice steady.

She took my hand and squeezed. "And friends don't lie," she said softly. She pressed a paper napkin into my other hand.

I swiped it across my cheeks. "The room is beautiful, and the bed is so comfortable. I just—"

"You don't need to explain anything, dear. You've suffered a terrible loss. Just give yourself time to mourn, and before you know it, things will be better."

I couldn't speak, so I nodded, and drew in a deep breath.

"And you've chosen the best place to recover," she said. "The climate and the restorative power of nature will work its magic on you."

I gazed out at the pristine beach and sat up a little straighter. I was feeling better already. "I'm going to walk along the beach after breakfast. Thanks, Rosie."

"Did I ever tell you that I almost married another man before I met my Ike?"

I smiled to myself. When would she have told me that? I'd been in the woman's presence for less than two hours, surrounded by a group of people. "No, you didn't."

"His name was Tommy O'Houlihan. A Black Irish. You know what I mean by that, don't you?"

I nodded. "A TDH—tall, dark, and handsome."

Rose's laugh tinkled like a waterfall. She patted my hand again. "Oh my dear, yes. *Very* TDH, with jet black hair and the most piercing blue eyes that seemed to see all the way to my soul." She sighed. "So handsome. I met him at a dance, and it was love at first sight, for both of us." She giggled like a schoolgirl. "I was just eighteen, and he was twenty-five. Such a man of the world!

31

We saw each other every day for the next two weeks, and he had grand plans. He wanted to marry me and take me back to Ireland with him!"

I gasped. "How romantic! But how could you have left your family?"

"Oh, honey, I would have gone to Mars with that man!" she chuckled.

I laughed with her. "But obviously, something happened," I ventured.

"Yes, well." Rose's expression turned serious. "Like I said, we were inseparable after we met. But Tommy was always busy at night. And he would never tell me what he was doing, just said he had to work."

"Uh, oh," I said.

"Uh, oh is right." Rose shook her head. "Turns out he was involved in a theft ring with a bunch of other Irishmen. They'd been riding high for almost four months, and were planning to culminate things with a huge robbery and then flee back to Ireland."

"How did you discover this?"

"My brother, George," Rose said. "He was a brand new beat cop, just twenty-three years old. To make a long story short, the Irish gang was already on his radar when I told him about Tommy, and it made George very nervous. Tommy called me one afternoon and said he needed to see me that night. He would be working but needed my help with something. George smelled a rat and followed me. It was a good thing he did. Tommy was going to use me as a decoy on their 'job' that night."

"Oh my, you could have been hurt, or even arrested."

She nodded. "It could have turned out very badly."

I squeezed her hand. "You must have been devastated."

"Oh, I was, my dear, I was inconsolable."

"Were you angry with George?"

"At first, yes, but then once I started thinking with my brain instead of my heart, I realized the amazing work he'd done to solve the case. I was so proud of him." Her face glowed. "He was promoted to detective the next year. My brother had an amazing and successful career with the NYPD for over forty years. He achieved the level of Assistant Police Commissioner." There was no mistaking Rose's pride in her brother's accomplishments.

"That's wonderful, Rosie."

"So you see, dear Kelsea, Ike wasn't my Plan A for marriage. He was my Plan B."

I just about jumped out of my seat. "Plan B? Did my mother put you up to this?" The words shot out of my mouth before I could stop them.

Rose's clear blue eyes reflected confusion. "Your mother? I've never met your mother, dear."

"No, no, of course you haven't, Rosie. I'm sorry. Forget I said that."

"I just meant that Tommy was Plan A, and after that fell through, I met Ike, and he was my Plan B, and so much better."

"I'm sure. You two seem very happy together."

"We are, and I'm sure you'll meet someone, too, and he'll be your Plan B, and it will be much better."

*Or maybe Ryan will come to his senses, and I won't need a Plan B.* "Well, I'm not ready for that just yet—"

Rose was looking past my shoulder. "Yoo hoo!" she trilled. "Over here, Mr. St. Fair!" She stood and waved.

*Oh, no. My lovely morning, ruined.* "Rosie, you don't need to go. Please, stay and tell me how you and Ike met."

"Oh, my dear, we'll save that for another time." I felt a dark cloud hovering behind me.

"Good morning, Mr. St. Fair!" Rose greeted him. "Isn't it a beautiful morning? Please, take a seat and keep Miss Anderson company. She looks so lovely this morning, doesn't she? We wouldn't want any of the married men to be tempted!" She giggled at her own joke.

"Good morning, ladies," Brandon's voice had an edge to it.

"Miss Anderson was just telling me that she wanted to walk along the beach," Rose said. "I'd appreciate it if you'd accompany her. We really don't want our female guests wandering around alone. You never know what kind of sharks are lurking about." She gave a little shiver.

*What makes you think he isn't one of them?* I bit my tongue. Brandon set his plate down but remained standing.

"I promise I'll do my best to protect her from harm," he said, taking Rose's hand and bending over it with a gallant kiss. It appeared the baboon had some manners, after all.

Rose giggled like a schoolgirl. "Oh, Mr. St. Fair! It's so rare to meet a real gentleman these days. Your mother must be so proud. Well, you two have a wonderful walk!" She pointed to her left. "Be sure to go all the way down to the cove. It's about two miles there and back, but well worth the walk. There are some beautiful shells there."

"Thank you, Rose. That sounds delightful," Brandon said. His voice had warmed up considerably.

Rose nearly skipped away. "Toodles!" she sang out.

# 10

LANDON HAD PURPOSELY come late to the breakfast buffet, secretly hoping that Kelsea would have already come and gone. She seemed like an early morning person, but obviously he rubbed her the wrong way, and he wasn't in the mood for her grousing. He'd filled his plate with all kinds of delicious looking food, but now that he'd seen her, he'd lost his appetite.

As soon as he sat down, she stood up. "I'm going for more fruit," she muttered.

*Good.* At least he could eat in peace, for a few minutes, anyway. He tucked into his eggs and waffles and nearly groaned with pleasure. He would need to make time to run every day if he wanted to fit into his clothes when he got home.

Miss Prickly Cactus returned, sat down, and dug into a bowl of berries without a word to him. She wasn't very chatty this morning, which was fine with him. Landon snuck a glance at her every once in a while, wondering if she had any idea that the man she was planning to marry less than a week ago was already with someone else. It made him feel just a little bit sorry for her. *I should lighten up on her just a bit.*

They continued eating in silence. Finally, she spoke.

"You're a gopher?" She gestured at his University of Minnesota hoodie. *Go, Golden Gophers!*

He didn't want to get into a bunch of personal details. "I'm from Minnesota." That was technically true.

"Figures."

He looked at her questioningly, and there was a mischievous light in her eye. "Gophers are rodents."

"And your point is?"

"Gophers are underground pests. In some tribal cultures, they're seen as a symbol of death."

"Charming, Miss Anderson. I wonder which animal *you* best represent."

She gave him a full-blown smile. *Beautiful, like the photos of her with the dogs.* "A lovely, graceful swan, of course!" She struck an elegant pose with her long, slender arms extended. "You heard Rose. I'm sure she would agree with me."

"Ha!" Brandon finished cleaning his plate, leaned back, and stretched out his legs. "You're a porcupine."

"A porcupine!"

"Yes. Also a rodent. One that has sharp quills or spines to keep predators away." He grinned at her. "They also have a fat, flat nose."

Kelsea's hand flew to her face. "I have a nice nose!" She ran her fingers over it.

Landon couldn't help but laugh. "Yeah, you do. But you've got some prickly quills, too." He looked at her evenly.

She stood. "Well, if I do, then I don't need a protector to walk along the beach."

Landon got to his feet. "No way are you going by yourself. With my luck, you'd get attacked by some hungry sea animal and Rose and Ike would never forgive me." He rubbed his stomach. "Besides, I've got to walk off that breakfast."

# 11

THERE WAS SOMETHING different about Brandon this morning, but I couldn't put my finger on it. He seemed a bit softer around the edges, less annoying. The banter about the gopher and porcupine was almost a little fun.

The walk down to the cove was beautiful, and I felt the stress ebbing away. I'd been wound tight as a coiled spring for the last five days. I knew Rose was right. This lovely setting was going to restore my equilibrium, or at least put me on the right path. Despite all the drawbacks, I was starting to think I'd made the right decision to come.

Brandon seemed lost in his thoughts as I was in mine, and neither of us said very much during our walk. It was a relief to not have to defend myself or put out the energy to make conversation. Best of all, the beach was deserted. None of the bridal couples was out this morning. I shouldn't have been surprised.

I wondered what Ryan was doing right now. If I had my phone with me, I'd be tempted to text him. I was so disappointed that he hadn't called me before I left St. Louis. He'd promised. *He also promised to marry you, but didn't.*

I looked over at Brandon. His hands were jammed in the pockets of his cargo shorts, and his expression was vacant. I wondered what he was thinking. "Have you talked with her since it happened?" I asked.

"Her? You mean *her?*"

I nodded. "What's her name?" I figured he knew Ryan's name, why shouldn't I know hers?

His eyes grew cold. "It doesn't matter. She's in my past now."

"I'm sorry," I said. I couldn't think of anything else to say.

"Did Ryan leave you standing at the altar?"

"No," I replied. "We were supposed to get married Saturday afternoon, on New Year's Day, and he backed out the Tuesday night before."

Brandon didn't respond to that. We kept walking. When we got to the cove, we decided to take off our sandals and put our feet in the clear, turquoise water.

"Oh, it's so warm!" I exclaimed. "It'll be even better later when the sun starts to heat up." I did a little jig in the water and twirled around and around. "This is heaven!"

That elicited a smile from Brandon. Then he just stood there, looking out at the ocean. Pretty soon, the smile faded from his face.

"She left me at the altar."

"Like, literally standing at the altar, waiting for her? Like in the movies?"

"Exactly. In front of five hundred guests."

I gasped. "Oh, my. That's—that's—terrible. I can't even think of a word for it."

"Humiliating," he said, his voice flat.

"Did you have the slightest notion beforehand?"

He kicked up one foot and splashed a little water. "Not up here," he said, pointing at his head, "but yeah, in here." He tapped his fist over his heart. "We'd—things hadn't been great since Thanksgiving. I just chalked it up to the holidays and all the stress of the wedding. I thought it would be fine after all of it was over. She and her mother were—*are*—pretty high-strung women."

"I'm not high strung," I said. "At least I don't think I am. Our wedding was pretty small. Nowhere close to five hundred guests."

"Was it hard canceling all your arrangements? I'm sure you lost all your deposits."

For the first time in a while, I smiled. "I have no idea. Ryan's mother made all the arrangements, so I suppose she canceled them. Any lost deposits are hers."

Brandon's mouth tipped up in a small smile. "Sounds like you dodged a bullet."

I rolled my eyes. "You have no idea. That's the one silver lining in this cloud." But then I sighed. "I still have no idea why Ryan backed out. He insisted there's no one else, just said he needs some space. So I'm going to give it to him, and then hopefully we'll work things out."

"I wouldn't count on it," Brandon mumbled.

"There you go again!" I threw up my hands. "Expressing an opinion about something that you have *no* idea about!" I marched up the sand and grabbed my sandals. "I'm going back to my room."

I walked away without another word. After about a minute, I turned and looked over my shoulder. Brandon was still standing ankle-deep in the water, exactly where I'd left him, staring out to sea.

# 12

LANDON KNEW HE should have kept his mouth shut, but he couldn't help it. He was actually hoping to guide Kelsea to a frame of mind where she might be open to the possibility that her Ryan wasn't the model boyfriend, or fiancé, that she thought he was.

*Why do I even care?* He walked around in the little cove for a while, then collected his footwear and started up the beach. Kelsea was nowhere to be seen in front of him. *Good. She can take care of herself.*

Landon went back to his room and lasted about ten minutes. It was one thing to say that he'd just keep to himself there, but he found that he couldn't stay cooped up in the pink, romantic-themed room. And after more than two months of bitterly cold weather, he craved being outdoors in the warm sunshine and gentle breezes.

He wandered outside to a cobbled path meandering through some gardens. Soon, he rounded a corner and almost smacked into a couple entwined in a passionate embrace. *Great.* Landon scooted around them and kept going.

He went around another corner, and there was Kelsea sitting alone on a bench. Her face twisted into a scowl when she saw him. "Oh, it's you."

Landon figured that somewhere in the universe, someone must be praying for patience on his behalf. He decided to take the high road. "I tried to stay in my room, but couldn't. It's just too beautiful out here."

She shrugged. "Yeah, me, too."

Landon looked up as he heard male and female laughter approaching. *Oh no.* It was the McFaddens.

"Top o' the morning, St. Fairs!" Julie McFadden cried. She acted like they were long-lost best friends. Both hers and her husband's eyes darted between Landon and Kelsea. They were no doubt wondering why they weren't wrapped around one another like every other couple. "Isn't this beautiful! We're beginning to see why this is called the Island of Gardens."

Landon stepped over to the bench and sat down next to Kelsea. *In for a penny, in for a pound.* He wrapped his hand loosely around hers. If she was going to protest, she'd have to make a public spectacle of it.

"Yes, we enjoyed a walk on the beach earlier," Landon said. "If you head west for about two miles, there's a beautiful cove." *And it'd be great if you went there right now.*

"We'll have to remember that!" Julie's head rested on her husband's chest, and his arm held her close. "So, what's your favorite thing about the resort so far?"

"The food," Kelsea responded quickly. "Except of course that I have to watch my carbs."

Landon gave her hand a little squeeze. "I apologized for my insensitive remark, love bug." He tried to laugh lightheartedly, but it came out sounding strained.

"Yes, you did, sweetness," Kelsea said through clenched teeth.

Brian McFadden looked at Landon. "I think this one's gonna cost you a piece of jewelry," he said with a laugh.

His wife's normally happy eyes flashed. "Not every problem can be solved with a piece of jewelry, dear."

To Landon's shock, Kelsea scooted closer, laid her head on his shoulder, and laced her long, slender fingers through his. "I shouldn't have brought it up again. He already made it up to me last night, in all the ways that count," she sighed.

Landon felt heat crawling up his neck. "Ah—well, let's just keep those details in the, um, family." He cleared his throat. If the McFaddens weren't going to leave, Landon would take control. He hauled Kelsea to her feet and stood, keeping a grip on her hand.

"Well, then, we'll let you enjoy your walk. Nice talking with you," he murmured, and set off, dragging Kelsea with him.

Once they were well out of earshot, she stopped, and peeled her hand from his. "You can give me my hand back now," she said in a flat voice.

"Gladly," Landon retorted. "Why did you have to bring the carbs comment up again? Can we just let it rest?"

"You started it," she shot back.

"And I said I was sorry," he retorted.

"When? I don't remember that."

Landon rolled his eyes and crossed his arms in front of him. "Fine. I'm sorry."

"Thank you." She looked so prim and proper. An evil little voice whispered into Landon's ear.

"I'm sorry carbs go straight to your hips," he said. "Kidding! I'm kidding!" He immediately added with a laugh.

But it was too late. Kelsea's eyes boiled over with anger. "You're—you're insufferable, Brandon St. Fair!" she shouted. "If they crossed a gopher with a baboon, *you* would be the result!" She spun on her heel and marched off.

# 13

THE NEXT MORNING, I was one of the first ones down to breakfast again. No matter what, I was going to eat a meal without the odious company of the Gopher Baboon. I couldn't decide whether to call him a *Goboon* or a *Babpher*. Neither one really rolled off the tongue.

The weather was exactly the same today as it was yesterday, that is to say, it was perfect. The temperature, the breeze, the sun. Absolutely perfect, and mesmerizing. I would find a way to spend every moment outdoors.

"Are you finished?" I came out of my reverie to see a guy looming over me, a towel slung over his shoulder, one arm balancing a plastic tub on his hip.

I took the last sip of freshly squeezed OJ and nodded. "Yeah, that's fine." I stood to leave.

"I'm Todd." He took a step closer into my personal space, and I felt his eyes roving over me. He lowered his voice to a whisper. "I heard that you're here alone, without a husband." Then I noticed his dark, good looks. His coloring was similar to Ryan's, but he was broader, more muscular, a little like Brandon. He had arresting blue eyes.

43

I glanced around, but it appeared that we were alone. My heart rate sped up, and I took a step back. "I'm—"

He touched a fingertip to my left hand and tossed out a lazy smile. "Looks like you're not wearing a ring. There's no reason for you to be lonely here, sugar." I recoiled as his fingers trailed up my arm. Todd didn't know it, but a vital part of his anatomy was about two seconds away from a decisive encounter with my knee.

"Is there a problem here, sweetheart?" A voice came from just behind me, and Brandon's arm came firmly around my shoulder. He wore tennis shoes, khaki shorts, and a long-sleeved navy cotton pullover with the sleeves pushed up. As much as I didn't want to, I felt myself leaning into his solid, muscular strength.

"Ah—no. No problem at all." I laid my palm lightly on his chest and did my best to smile and look casual. "I was just finishing breakfast." My heart slowed down a little. "And— waiting for you." He moved his hand down to settle around my waist and pulled me a little closer.

"Well, that's good," Brandon said, his gaze locked on Todd, "because I know Ike and Rose wouldn't be happy if they heard there was a problem." His words were innocent enough, but the message was crystal clear.

"I must have been mistaken," Todd said to me. Then he pasted on a brittle smile and began to back away. "You two enjoy the day."

Brandon's annoyed gaze followed the man as he nearly ran back inside the building. "What was that all about?"

I dropped my hand and took a step back. "Nothing to concern yourself with," I said, aiming for a light tone. "He was just being friendly."

"He was leering at you," he muttered.

"I can take care of myself, Brandon. I'm not your responsibility." I crossed my arms in front of me.

He ran a hand through his hair. "I know you're not my

responsibility. It just looked like—that he was—you know, trying to—" He let out an audible sigh. "You know what? I'm done." He held out one arm like a stop sign and began to back away. "Best of luck to you, Kelsea. I won't bother you again." He turned and strode away, his long, muscular legs eating up the distance.

I was so stunned, I couldn't speak, couldn't move. *You're really making a mess of this.* I ran after him. "Brandon, wait!" He slowed as I caught up with him. I tugged on his elbow and scooted around to face him.

"I—yes, he was—invading my—personal space," I said haltingly. To my embarrassment, I felt my eyes begin to well up, and I wrapped my arms protectively around my middle. "I—he, he asked if I was here alone, and told me that he'd be happy to appease my loneliness."

Brandon's hands rested loosely on his hips. I don't know what kind of reaction I expected, but it sure wasn't the devastating smile that transformed his face. "Well, I'm one ahead of you. A maid greeted me when I came out of my room this morning and made me a similar offer. Then, before I even got down here, another woman cornered me in the hallway." He shook his head. "I'm pretty sure *her* proposition is illegal in some states. And if you can believe it, I think she's one of the happy newlyweds." His voice dripped with irony.

I was so miserable, but the absurdity of it hit me, and I couldn't help but giggle. I brushed away a tear. "The last thing I expected when I came here alone was to have to fend off some creep. So, what did you say to those women?"

"I neither confirmed nor denied the allegation that I was here alone," Brandon said, and then seemed to back pedal. "I mean, I didn't say anything. I walked away from both of them."

It's always hard for me to admit when I'm wrong, but I needed to step up. I took a breath. "Thank you for coming to my rescue. I mean it. I don't think he really meant me any harm, but it was getting uncomfortable."

Brandon's gaze flicked down to my feet and back up to my eyes, but for some reason it didn't bother me the way it had when I felt Todd appraising me. "I'm sure you would have handled it," he said firmly, "but I couldn't help myself. I'm too old-fashioned. I can't resist a beautiful lady in distress." He smiled again, and I felt the breath leave me.

He looked around, and gestured toward the shore. "I was just going to take a walk along the beach, in the other direction," he said. "Join me?"

For once, words escaped me, so I simply nodded.

When he smiled, Brandon St. Fair was really a very handsome man, if you liked that type. Which I didn't.

# 14

BY THE TIME they returned from their walk, Landon and Kelsea had made a pact. In his mind, Landon knew it made sense, like a good business deal. After the tumult of the last several days, both of them craved solitude to lick their wounds and sort through their feelings. But in the present setting, even the hint of being there unattached was apparently going to attract the wrong kind of attention, so they decided to stick together in public. Pretty soon, the rumors would die down.

They made it back just before the buffet closed. Landon ate every bite of his breakfast, which, like every meal, was superb.

Kelsea nibbled on some grapes. "You know, I was thinking about what you said about knowing 'in here' that your fiancée was going to back out." She tapped her fingers on her chest. "I was completely shocked when Ryan came to see me, but in retrospect, things had been a little off since Thanksgiving."

"Did you ask him about it?"

"Yeah, and he said things were just wild at work with year-end stuff, and he was trying to get ready to be gone on our honeymoon."

"You want more coffee?" Landon asked. Kelsea shook her head.

"I still can't believe you threw your watch in the ocean," she said.

He shrugged. "You were right. We're on island time. No watching the clock."

She laughed. "But I didn't mean that you should destroy a perfectly beautiful watch! It looked brand new."

"It *was* brand new. It was an early wedding gift." He pushed back his chair and stood.

Kelsea stopped and looked at him, a grape in midair. "Oh...I get it."

Landon nodded, and slipped his hands into his pockets. "There was no reason to keep it. So thanks for ridding me of it. You ready?"

She nodded and stood, and they started walking.

"You could have sold it, you know. Made some money off it."

He frowned. "It was engraved."

"Oh." Kelsea didn't seem to have a response for that. A movement ahead caught her attention, and she pointed. "Hey, what's going on over there?" Rose and Ike were just outside the entrance to the main building. Ike handed Rose a bullhorn.

"Good morning, lovebirds!" her cheery voice rang out. "For anyone who wants to go shopping in town, the shuttle buses will leave in ten minutes. We'll be back in time for lunch." She began to put the bullhorn down, and then spied them. "Yoo hoo! Kelsea and Brandon! I hope you'll come shopping with us."

*Great.* Landon would rather have his teeth pulled out without Novocain than go shopping. Hopefully Kelsea would want to go back to her room, so he could go hide in his.

To his great disappointment, she waved gaily and called out, "We'd love to come, thanks!"

# 15

"WHY'D YOU DO that?" Brandon glowered at me. "I don't want to go shopping."

I grimaced. "Oh, I'm sorry," I said. "I just thought of something I really need to get. You don't have to come."

He threw up his hands. "It'll draw attention if you go alone," he said. "Remember, the whole point is to stick *together* so we don't stick *out*."

"You're right, you're right," I said. "My mind is somewhere else. I need to get something out of my room before the bus leaves." I hurried toward the door that led to our corridor, and Brandon followed.

"I'll grab my wallet," he muttered.

We made our way back to the shuttle buses, which were filling up quickly. I slipped into a seat, and Brandon lowered himself down beside me. The day was starting to heat up, and he'd shed his cotton hoodie. He wore a dark gray t-shirt that clung to his athletic torso.

*Holy guacamole.* Ryan ran some and rode a bike occasionally, but didn't lift weights or anything. He was more soft than hard, and I always said I didn't really like muscles on guys. I was going to have to rethink that.

"So, what do you need to buy?" Brandon asked. The aroma of wintergreen floated over on his breath.

"I'll tell you later," I whispered.

The scenery on the drive was beautiful, and we enjoyed looking at it together out the window. Brandon's arm rested lightly on the seat back, and I found that I wasn't completely repulsed when he leaned closer occasionally to get a better look.

When we reached the center of town, Molli announced that the shuttle buses would depart for the return trip in exactly two hours.

Brandon and I loitered on the sidewalk until the others had moved away. "Where to?" he asked.

"The nearest pawn shop."

"Pawn shop? What do you need with a pawn shop?"

"I'm selling this." I drew out the black velvet box and opened it.

"Wow. You want to sell your engagement ring?"

I nodded. "Ryan said I could keep it. What am I going to do with it? If he comes crawling back, he can buy me another one. A bigger one." Everything that seemed so heartbreaking at night felt different in the morning sun. "And, I need the money to buy a wedding band."

Brandon's features twisted in confusion. "Wedding band?"

"Yes, just a cheap one." I held up my left hand. "Sleazy Todd pointed out that I wasn't wearing a ring."

Brandon nodded. "Good thinking. I should get one, too."

"You don't need one. Lots of married men don't wear a ring."

He smiled. "Just the one through their nose."

"Ha, ha," I retorted, and punched him playfully on the arm. It was rock solid. *Wow.*

Brandon started walking. "Come on. Let's find a jewelry store. You'll get a better deal there than from a pawn shop."

The proprietor of the fourth store finally met Brandon's high standards, and made a more than fair offer. Once that transaction was finished, we asked to see the least expensive wedding bands.

"Cheap? Why you want cheap?" The man pointed to me and smiled broadly at Brandon. "Your woman worth the best gold."

Brandon and I looked at each other and laughed. "She's not—it's a long story," he said.

"Trust us, cheap ones will be fine," I added with a smile.

The man held his hand up and pointed. "You no want fingers turn green," he said in his parlance. "I have what you need, make you good deal."

"You can show us something a little nicer." Brandon looked down at me. "I'm buying both bands."

"You are not!" I exclaimed. "I'm buying my own."

Brandon looked at the store owner. "Would you excuse us for a moment?" He took my elbow and guided me away.

"Look, Kelsea, let me buy these. I can afford it, and they won't be that much."

I crossed my arms. "I'm not poor, Brandon." *Liar.*

He raised his eyebrows. "You said you had to sell your engagement ring to buy this."

"I'm not taking charity." *I'm poor, but proud.*

Brandon sighed. "Look, just consider it an investment on my part. I'll buy the pair, then sell them back in the States after this week is over. I won't lose any money on them, I'll probably even make a little."

I tapped my foot nervously and considered it. I could really use the ring money to make up for the commissions I was losing from being gone this week. I had spent nearly every penny of my savings on this trip, and I didn't get a paid vacation like Ryan would have, or no doubt like Brandon was getting. I had no idea what he did for a living, but it seemed like he was doing just fine.

I nodded curtly. "Oh, all right."

"Good." Brandon smiled and led me back to the counter, where the man waited. Ten minutes later, we left wearing matching tri-gold bands. I had never seen rose gold and thought the combination was lovely.

We did some window shopping for the duration, and Brandon waited patiently while I picked up a couple of pairs of nicer shorts and shirts to replace the slouchy clothes I'd brought from home. Not that I was trying to impress...anyone, but the bargain prices were too good to pass up.

When we sat down on the bus, Brandon leaned over and touched my ring. "You know what this means, don't you?"

I eyed him warily. "I'm still not sleeping with you." I gasped. "Is that why you bought these? So I would sleep with you?"

He looked around nervously. "Shhh!"

I looked around, too. "No one is listening to us. They're literally wrapped up in each other," I said crossly.

"Of course that's not why I bought these. I was just kidding around," he said. The bus pulled away from the curb. "Pull in your quills, Miss Porcupine."

"Mr. Gopher, harbinger of death," I muttered.

# 16

LANDON AND KELSEA met a nice couple from San Francisco at dinner the next evening. Steve Isaacs turned out to be a big sports fan, and Landon thoroughly enjoyed their discussion. Every once in a while, he caught snippets of the women's conversation about fashion, cooking, and reality TV. At least Missy Isaacs was talking. Kelsea was making monosyllabic comments, and appeared to be more interested in his and Steve's conversation.

"Whoa, whoa there," she interrupted when Landon commented how impressed he was with Denver's new quarterback. "That guy wouldn't have had a snowball's chance in the devil's man cave of getting any playing time if Thompson hadn't been injured. He can't hit the broad side of a barn. JoJo Collins is the only one who can catch him. JoJo's the only reason the Broncos are still in the running."

Landon looked at her in amazement and hardly heard Steve's comment. Kelsea cited some stats, and Landon challenged her. She held out her hand. "Give me your phone."

Landon started to hand it over, then raised one eyebrow and raised his chin a notch.

"Pretty please?" she replied with a saccharine smile and flutter of eyelashes.

At that point, Landon would have given her anything she asked for.

She snatched the phone from his outstretched hand and searched until she found what she was looking for. "Ha! Read it and weep!" Landon had to admit that she was right.

She, Steve, and Landon sat chatting for another half hour, moving from football to hockey, and finally baseball. Having grown up in northern Illinois, Kelsea was an avowed Cubs fan. She said she didn't know much about hockey, but had been to a Blues game in St. Louis and enjoyed it more than she thought she would. Landon wished he could take her to a game. He'd grown up playing hockey, and imagined that once he shared his expert knowledge with her, she'd really get into it, screaming her head off. Landon watched as she said something to Steve about her beloved Cubbies. Her voice was animated, her eyes sparkled, and her hands waved around excitedly.

Missy didn't have anything to add to the conversation, and sat admiring her nails and looking bored. She was a beautiful blonde and reminded him a little of Nicola. Then it occurred to Landon that if Nicola had been sitting next to him tonight instead of Kelsea, she would have been chatting Missy up about fashion and reality TV. She didn't care about sports at all. He took her to a Blues game once, but she complained about the noise so much that they left after about thirty minutes.

Missy Isaacs had finally had enough. "I'm ready for a walk in the moonlight, Steve," she pouted as she leaned up and kissed his cheek.

He jumped up and helped her to her feet. "Sure thing, honey." Landon stood to shake Steve's hand. "It was great meeting you folks," Steve said with a smile. "I hope we'll see you again."

"Likewise," Landon said. He waited until the Isaacs left and then looked at Kelsea. "You're quite a sports fan." He sat down again.

"I am," she replied. "Does that surprise you?"

"I never really thought about it one way or the other until you joined the conversation."

She frowned. "Did that upset you?"

"No. Why would it?"

She didn't respond. Landon smiled at her. "You made some really great points. I've just never— I've never dated a woman who could hold her own talking about stats and players and all of that. Not that we're dating," he quickly added. "I just, well, you know."

Kelsea still didn't say anything. Her mind seemed to be somewhere else. "Ryan wasn't into sports as much as I am. If we were out with friends and a discussion like this one tonight started up, he didn't have much to contribute, so he'd just play on his phone and then after we'd get home he'd sulk and accuse me of trying to show him up in public." She pursed her lips. "I think he wanted me to just sit there and look gorgeous like Missy."

Landon let out a soft snort. "Missy isn't gorgeous. She wears too much makeup. She'd be prettier if she stuck to her natural look, like you." He scooted back his chair. "You ready?"

"Like me?" Kelsea looked surprised as she stood. "Don't men want their women looking sexy and exotic?"

Landon frowned at her. "Well, yeah, on special occasions. But if she looks that way all the time, it's not special. And the time it takes to put all of that on! My fiancée would take an hour and a half to get ready to go out for thirty minutes. She didn't have to look like a goddess to make a Target run." They were outside now. "You wanna go for a walk in the moonlight?"

Kelsea eyed him warily. "Sure, I'll walk with you. But we'll talk about the last time the Twins and the Cardinals were in a playoff series. No romance, because, you know, I'm not—"

"Yeah, yeah, I get it. You're not sleeping with me. You don't have to keep saying it. My ego has been beaten down enough lately."

She crossed her arms in front of her. "I'm not trying to beat down your ego," she said with an edge to her voice. "I just don't sleep around."

"And you think I do?" Landon shot back. He'd had just about enough of this.

"I don't know. I don't know you well enough. But you're a man."

"You're right. I'm a man. A man who was literally dumped in the most humiliating way possible, in front of five hundred people, most of them strangers. But some of them were my family, friends, and professional contacts and colleagues. And you don't know me well enough to form an opinion about my sleeping habits, or anything else."

Kelsea had the grace to look embarrassed, and truly repentant. "I'm sorry, Brandon. You're absolutely right, and that was insensitive of me. I'm sorry."

He stood there with his hands jammed in his pockets. "Thanks." He looked at the ground and then back to her. "Could we--would you just walk with me for a little while, please? And just not say anything?'

She nodded, and followed him.

It was a beautiful night for a walk on the beach. The sights, sounds, and smells were intoxicating. Landon was finally starting to relax. They walked for almost fifteen minutes without talking.

"Nicola."

"What?"

"Her name was Nicola." We met a little over two years ago at a social event."

"You mean a party?"

"Well, it was a kind of—you know, a business thing. They really don't call them parties." Landon didn't want to reveal that he attended most of these events as a representative of the law firm. Or that he'd made partner after landing the DiCarlo Luxury Motors account.

"Well, I wouldn't know about that," Kelsea said. "Anyway, go on. What did she look like?"

"What did she look like?" he parroted.

"Yeah, you know. Is she a blonde? Brunette? Redhead? Tall? Short? Skinny? Fat?"

"Um, well, she's blonde. Taller than you. And skinnier." Before Kelsea could react, he corrected himself. "Too skinny, I told her that all the time. She could have used some of your curves."

Kelsea's eyes narrowed just a bit. "I think there's a compliment somewhere in there. Eyes?"

"Yes, she has eyes."

"Ha, ha."

"Dark eyes. She's Italian."

"Ah, Italiano, very interesting."

"Yes. Her family—they're very well off, her father is a very successful businessman. Owns a whole fleet of luxury car dealerships."

"What do you drive?"

Landon laughed. "Nothing close to a luxury car. I think I was getting one for a wedding gift, though."

"I thought she got you that watch."

"She did. The car would have been from her parents."

"Bummer."

He couldn't help but laugh. "Yeah, bummer."

"Is she older or younger than you?"

Landon frowned. "Two years younger. I'll be thirty-one in a few weeks."

"When?"

"On the 28th."

"No way! That's my birthday, too!" Kelsea winced. "It's the big three-oh for me."

*What were the chances? One in about 365.* "You're kidding, right?"

"Why would I kid about that? My birthday is January 28."

Landon couldn't think of anything to say.

"Ryan's younger than me. He said that he wasn't even thirty yet and wasn't ready to settle down. Do you think the age difference had something to do with it?"

Landon thought a moment. "It shouldn't. I've dated older women before—not by much, but a year or two. I think culture is more a factor than age."

"Culture, how so?"

"Well, I think that was one thing that drove Nicola and me apart. Her Italian heritage was so important to her, to all of them. It was just one more way that I didn't fit in. I always felt like an outsider."

"That's interesting," Kelsea said. "That was never the case for Ryan and me. I guess we're both just Heinz 57, you know, a mix."

Landon smiled at that description. "Nicola has a twin brother, Francisco, and he never accepted me, never thought I was good enough for her. If I'd been Italian, I might have stood a fighting chance. He was always telling her how this friend or that friend of his would have been a better match for her."

"And all his friends are Italian?"

"Oh, yeah. There's a very tight Italian community in—where we live."

Kelsea frowned. "And where is it that you live?"

"I didn't say." Landon smiled.

"I know, that's why I'm asking." She smiled back.

Landon wasn't ready to play that card yet. Maybe he never would be. "It doesn't matter. Anyway, when I realized Nicola had left the wedding, I knew she'd gone with Francisco. Her father confirmed it. It was probably Francisco's idea."

"They're really close, then?"

Landon nodded. "Oh, yeah. I guess it's that twin bond."

"I have a sister, Morgan," Kelsea said. "She's two years younger than me. We're close, but not crazy close like twins. What about you?"

"You mean siblings? Well, I'm not a twin, but I'm an *Irish* twin."

"You don't look Irish!" Kelsea laughed. "Wait! I've heard of Irish twins. But I can't remember what it means."

Landon smiled. "Yeah, I'm not Irish, I'm mostly Scandinavian. Irish twins are siblings born less than a year apart. *True* Irish twins are born in the same calendar year, and that was the case for us. I was born on January 28, and my brother arrived on December 24."

"Wow, that's crazy! Is it just the two of you?"

"No, we have an older sister and a younger sister." Landon was through giving personal information. "You ready to head back?"

Kelsea nodded, and they walked the whole way back in companionable silence, lost in their own thoughts. Landon couldn't believe it. They'd spent the whole evening together without one argument.

**17**

WHEN I GOT back to my room, I got ready for bed and opened my computer. Brandon St. Fair was certainly an enigma. I typed in *Nicola* and *Francisco*. Nothing. Then I entered the names with various permutations of *luxury car,* but that didn't get any hits either.

I typed his name in with the birthdate and year, and still nothing. There were websites where you could pay to find out more information about someone, but it sure wasn't worth it to me to fork out any dough.

*Why do you even care?* I scolded myself. After this week, I'd never see Brandon again. I looked at the background on my screen, a picture of Ryan and me that I hadn't bothered to change. *My mother was right. We would have given her beautiful grandchildren.* This made me even more melancholy. I quickly got back online and substituted it with a generic picture of a sunset.

After we'd finished lunch, Brandon and I had met Ike in the lobby. He was pinning a photo up on a bulletin board. "This is our brag board," he said with a chuckle. "Rosie likes to put up letters from all our couples, and Christmas cards that they send us, and baby announcements. We just got a Christmas card from the

Jensens. Look at that, they were here just over a year ago, and now they have a little boy."

A tear rolled down my cheek. I'd probably never be able to send Rose and Ike a card with my children's picture on it.

# 18

THE NEXT MORNING'S walk turned into a run. Landon was impressed that Kelsea kept up with him, and told her so.

"I'm not short," she protested. "I'm five seven."

"I know, but I've got nine inches on you. Did you run track?" They were now back at the patio, enjoying the last of the breakfast buffet.

She nodded. "In high school. And I played lacrosse."

"I've never played lacrosse," he said. "But I played—"

Kelsea held up her hand. "No, no, wait. Let me guess." She eyed him. "Football and hockey."

Landon was surprised. "How'd you know?"

She shrugged. "You totally seem like a football jock, but you've had a broken nose, and you're from Minnesota, so I put two and two together."

"Good thinking. Why didn't you guess basketball?"

"You don't have the build," she said without hesitation. "Basketball players are tall, but lean."

"Oh, so now I'm fat?

"No, but you're—you have muscles."

She averted her eyes and was suddenly all into her cup of yogurt. And was she a little pink? Landon wanted to laugh out loud, and at the same time he was extremely flattered. He'd let it pass, for now. "I also swam," he said.

"Competitively?"

"Yes."

"What were your events?"

"Butterfly, breaststroke, and relay."

Kelsea chewed and seemed to be thinking about something. "I challenge you," she finally said. "Butterfly."

"Really? You won't mind getting your hair wet?"

Kelsea sputtered. "Are you kidding? Brandon, it's water. It dries." He couldn't believe it. Nicola couldn't even stand to be splashed with a few drops at the pool.

"You're on," he said with a smile.


Landon beat her in each of their three races, but she was good, and it was by no means a steal. It turned out she had been on the swim team in high school. He liked her competitive spirit, and she was a gracious loser.

They were now sitting in lounge chairs by the pool. Kelsea was wearing a one-piece red suit that was, in Landon's opinion, hotter than any bikini he'd ever seen. Red was definitely her color.

"If you don't mind my asking, where did you and Ryan meet?"

"Hmm. It's kind of a complicated story, and there are still some things about it that bother me."

"Maybe talking about it would help you sort it all out in your mind."

She stared at him for several seconds and then nodded. "Well, about three and a half years ago I moved to St. Louis. It was the first time I'd ever left home. I'm from Kankakee, Illinois."

"You didn't go away to college?" Of course, Landon already knew this from looking at her online profile.

Kelsea shook her head. "Well, I tried it, but it didn't stick.

After dropping out of community college, I worked at a daycare—no thanks! —and went to beauty school." He couldn't help but smile.

"I cut hair for two years and got tired of standing on my feet in one place all day, so I gave that up. Next was a string of office temp jobs—*yawn*. After that, I started volunteering at a local animal shelter, where I adopted two Pomeranians, Sheldon and Penny."

"Cute."

"They are! They're my babies. But volunteering didn't pay—literally—so I got a job at a library. I'm an avid reader, so I thought that would be fun. It wasn't. Turns out I can't go hours on end without talking."

Landon looked at her with amusement. "You don't say?"

Kelsea smiled. "Well, yeah. So, I was still living at home. My dad died when I was twelve, and my sister Morgan had already gone away to college and then to grad school, and hadn't lived at home in years. So it was just Mom and me, and she was constantly harping on me about getting married and giving her grandchildren, and she's an elementary teacher, and she tried to set me up on a blind date with a second-grade teacher at her school, Percy Parker."

Landon laughed. "Sounds like a winner."

Kelsea shook her head. "Desperate times call for desperate measures. I was still volunteering at the animal shelter, and saw an ad in a trade magazine for an entry-level opening at the St. Louis Zoo. I did a Skype interview and got hired."

Of course, Landon already knew this, too. "Wow, that's impressive. That's one of the best zoos in the country."

"I know. I couldn't believe that I was going to work there. So Sheldon and Penny and I moved to St. Louis to get away from my mother and Percy Parker, and after a few months, I started working in the petting zoo area, you know, where all the little kids get to come in and pet the animals. I totally loved it. It was so much fun talking with the kids and seeing them get so excited about the animals. And one Saturday afternoon, this family came in, a mom and a dad and their little girl. She was about three. Absolutely adorable."

Landon cringed. "Don't tell me."

"Yes, it was Ryan. But it wasn't what it looked like. Anyway, she was really into the animals and I probably spent about ten minutes with them, and they asked a lot of questions, and *he* asked a lot of questions, and asked my name, and was really nice, and said that their names were Ryan and Ashley and Brooke. And then they left." I sighed. "And then it got kind of sketchy."

Landon decided not to comment.

"So about a half hour later, I hear a guy call my name, and I turned around, and it was him. The dad of this little girl, or so I thought. And I said something like, 'Oh hi, did you forget something?' and he said, 'Well, yeah, I forgot to ask you what time you get off, and to ask if you would have dinner with me.' He was a total flirt."

"Yikes," Landon said. He couldn't wait to see how the story ended.

"So I was *completely* blown away, just in shock, and I said, 'Well, don't you think your *wife* would mind?' and then he said, 'Oh, she's not my wife, she's my girlfriend, and the kid's not mine.'"

Landon didn't say anything, he just raised an eyebrow.

"So then I said, 'Well, I don't go to dinner with guys who have wives *or* girlfriends,' and I walked away."

"Good answer."

"Anyway, I didn't see him again, and then the next Saturday, he showed up. And he told me that he had broken up with his girlfriend, and wanted to take me out. He was like, 'Well, things weren't going that great, and she wanted more than I was willing to give, and I didn't really want a ready-made family, yada yada yada.' And then he told me that he thought it was fate that we had met, and he couldn't stop thinking about me all week.

"The whole thing made me so uncomfortable, because I felt like maybe I was the reason he broke up with Ashley, and I hadn't done *anything* to encourage him, and I felt sorry for little Brooke if she had bonded with him, you know? So anyway, I told him I was busy and couldn't go out that night, and wasn't sure if I wanted to go out with him at all, and he just—well, Ryan's a salesman and he can be really persuasive. He ended up leaving that day, but he kept coming back almost every day, just being nice and real flirty, and he finally wore me down. So I went out with him, and it just—yeah, it just kept going."

"When did you get engaged?"

"Last July 4. We wanted a real simple wedding, and I'd always had my heart set on getting married in the fall, but his mother sort of took over and insisted that we needed more time to plan everything and make sure it was just right, so she picked New Year's Day."

"Why fall?" For some reason, Landon wanted to know.

Kelsea smiled. "It's my favorite season. I love the colors of fall."

He would file that away. "So, Ryan's mom picked your wedding date?"

I nodded. "I know, I should have run for the hills then. I just—well, I loved Ryan, and he always said things like, 'it's not the wedding that's important, it's the marriage,' and 'it's one day, we don't need to focus on that, we need to focus on spending the rest of our lives together.' He always defended her, said that it was just her way of showing her love. And he also went on and on about how she didn't have a daughter and would never get to plan a wedding."

"That wasn't *your* fault," Landon said. "For people that follow the tradition, the mothers with sons just don't get to plan a wedding."

Kelsea rubbed a hand over her eyes. "Anyway, it's over, and I'm so relieved that I won't have to put up with her for the next fifty years. But I think I still have doubts over how Ryan and I met. Right after we got engaged, I met someone who worked with Ashley, and she made me think that there was more to the story about hers and Ryan's break-up than he was telling me."

"Did you ever ask him about it?"

She nodded. "He always stuck to his original story. But now, I'm not so sure. I'm seeing more character flaws in him, and it wouldn't surprise me a bit if things weren't as they seemed."

Landon didn't say anything for a while. Then he asked, "Do you still work at the zoo?" He wanted to hear her talk about her pet-sitting business.

"No, and I'm super sad about it. I loved every minute of it, and I think I would have been happy to stay there forever. But I'd been there about a year when my supervisor, a really nice gentleman named Rich who had worked at the zoo since just before I'd been born, called me into his office and gave me the bad news. Budget cutbacks. Deep cutbacks. He said he'd fought hard for me, but I didn't have seniority, and he had no choice."

"I'm sorry," Landon said.

"Thanks. No way was I going home to Mom with my tail between my legs. I like St. Louis—I live in one of the older suburbs, Kirkwood. So anyway, I took Sheldon and Penny to the dog park the next day, and I saw another dog mom there, Maggie, and we got to talking and I told her about being laid off, and told her I really wished I could get a job working with animals in some way. Then she had this great idea. They were going away for two weeks at the end of the month, and she said she'd rather pay me to take care of their dogs than board them. Do you have a dog?"

Landon shook his head. "I live in a condo in the city," he said. "Maybe someday."

"Well, you would not believe how much it was going to cost them to board their dogs. Maggie said she'd pay me the same amount, and then she paid me more to pick up their mail and keep an eye on the house. So I did that, and before I knew it, she helped me get other clients, and they referred me, and now I have a nice little business."

"Wow, that's impressive. Not everyone can run their own business."

"It works for me," she said. "And it's growing. If I get many more clients, I may need to think about hiring a part-time helper. I was thinking maybe a young teen. You know, they can't get a real job until they're sixteen, and it'd be nice to help one of them learn responsibility and earn some spending money."

Landon was impressed with her ingenuity and generous heart. "Sounds like a plan. Hey, I think you're starting to get a little pink," he said. "Where's the sunscreen?"

"Here," Kelsea said, handing it to him. She sat up and turned her away from him. "Would you get my back?"

*With pleasure.*

# 19

THE NEXT MORNING, Brandon and I ran again after breakfast, and then walked through some of the gardens around the resort. They were just beautiful, with gorgeous tropical flowers in more colors than I had ever seen in one place. The Queen's Garden, the destination for a special excursion on our last night on the island, was touted as the most spectacular garden on St. Jardin, and we agreed that we couldn't imagine anything being more beautiful than what we were seeing now.

After lunch, we decided to change into our suits and hit the beach. We swam for a while and then spread our towels on the pristine white sand.

I slathered sunscreen on and handed the bottle to Brandon. He knew without my having to ask that I wanted some rubbed on my back. I closed my eyes as his large, smooth hands went back and forth, up and down. *I could get used to this.*

When he stopped, I opened my eyes and he was putting sunscreen on himself. He handed the bottle to me and turned his back. I was happy to have an excuse to touch him.

*What in the world are you thinking, Kelsea? You're hoping to get back with Ryan.*

Then we both lay down on our stomachs. We chatted for a little while about inconsequential things, and then he went quiet. I turned my head one way, then the other, but couldn't relax. My mind kept going back to Brandon. The first time I saw him without a shirt, I nearly melted. I was really going to have to rethink my entire opinion about the male physique. Anyway, I couldn't believe that we'd spent the entire day together and hadn't fought once so far. *Maybe I'm losing my edge.*

I finally turned my head toward him, and opened my eyes. He had flipped onto his back. I took a moment to study at this man who both exasperated me and made me feel vibrant and alive. His hair was burnished gold from the sun, as were his eyebrows and long eyelashes. His nose marred what was otherwise a perfect, tanned face. I smiled as I recalled Brandon's story about breaking it in a hockey brawl. Actually, I think the crooked bump made him more attractive. I resisted the urge to sigh. He had a strong, defined jaw and a day's worth of growth that barely hid the deep cleft in his chin. I had the strongest desire to kiss it.

That left his lips. What would they feel like on mine? They looked firm but soft. Ever so slowly, I found myself leaning in a little closer, holding my breath.

Suddenly, his beautiful amber eyes popped open, and a slow smile spread across his face.

"Like what you see?" he said huskily.

I jumped back and quickly sat up. My heart pounded. "What are you talking about? I'm not looking at anything!" But my protests sounded lame, even to my ears.

"Hey, would you guys like to play volleyball?" I shielded my eyes from the sun and looked up to see Mark Wilder. *Saved by the ball.*

"Sounds fun!" I exclaimed, and popped up, brushing the sand from my legs.

Brandon raised up on his elbows. "I'm game."

Mark grinned. "You'll be on our team. Husbands against wives. Then we'll switch things up."

Brandon stood, and I boldly gave him a playful punch on his

rock-hard stomach. *Oh, my.* "Did I tell you my nickname in high school was Spike?" I skipped away, ahead of them.

Brandon chased after me and caught me around my waist. "Don't forget, sweetheart, I've still got nine inches on you!"

I squealed with laughter. *Sweetheart.*

## 20

THE NEXT MORNING, their last day on St. Jardin began with a thunderstorm. Landon hoped he and Kelsea could get some private time inside today. He really needed to come clean with her about who he was, and maybe he'd even tell her that he lived in St. Louis.

Landon was so nervous that he nearly cut himself shaving, twice. He also went through three shirts before he changed back into the first one he'd had on. *Get a hold of yourself, man. This is ridiculous.*

He knocked on Kelsea's door. When she opened it, his breath caught. She looked bright and fresh and beautiful in white shorts, a cobalt blue top, and sandals. Her dark hair fell in damp waves past her shoulders.

"Hi," she smiled. "Wait, let me grab an umbrella—" She stopped when Landon held up his. "Oh, you've got one."

"Yep, I grabbed this one from my room."

They got to breakfast none the worse for wear due to huddling together under the umbrella between buildings. Kelsea let him pull her close as they ran through the rain, laughing and splashing. Landon had never done anything like that with Nicola.

They got their food and looked for a place to sit. Everyone

seemed to have arrived at the same time this morning. "Are you thinking what I'm thinking?" she asked.

"Yeah, I am," Landon replied. "I've got the bird's eye view. Ah, there they are." They made a beeline for where Rose and Ike were sitting.

"Good morning, Brandon and Kelsea!" Rose called out. "It's good to see you. Isn't it a lovely day?"

Landon laughed. "It's raining, Rose."

"Yes, it is," Ike said. "But even the rainiest day on St. Jardin is better than the sunniest day in Brooklyn!"

Everyone laughed. "I agree, Ike," Kelsea said. "That goes for St. Louis, too."

"Besides, it'll move on, and we'll have a perfect day and more importantly, a perfect night for our closing festivities at the Queen's Garden," Rose said.

"Ooh, that sounds beautiful," Kelsea said.

"Is the Queen's Garden really the most extravagant one on the island?" Landon asked.

Rose and Ike nodded. "It is. There's no way to describe it," Rose exclaimed. "You have to see it to believe it."

"We were saying the other day that we couldn't imagine anything prettier than the gardens we've already seen," Kelsea commented.

"You're in for a real treat. We'll take everyone there by boat—it's on the other side of the island," Ike said. "Too far to walk, and our shuttle buses can't make it all the way there."

"Wear your walking shoes, Kelsea! You'll want to see every bit of the garden. We'll get there in time to watch the sunset, and then we've got some special surprises in store for all of you."

Landon could hardly keep his eyes off Kelsea. He couldn't wait for tonight to arrive.

# 21

WE HAD BEEN instructed to dress for tonight, and for the women to wear white (but not a formal wedding dress), and comfortable shoes for walking. My dress was tea-length and strapless, with lace trim. I had a golden tan, and felt beautiful. I wore silver jewelry and high, glittering wedge sandals that were really quite comfortable.

When the knock came at the door, it startled me, even though I was expecting it. I adjusted my lace shawl and gave myself one last once-over in the mirror, smoothed my dress over my hips, grabbed my clutch, and walked to the door.

I let out a breath, and opened it.

I don't know what I was expecting, but it wasn't this.

Brandon's broad shoulders filled the doorway. He wore black pants and a white dinner jacket with a crisp white shirt and a black bow tie. His hair had lightened a little more with each day in the sun, and gleamed golden. Like me, he had a great tan.

Forget TDH. Now *this* was handsome.

He seemed a little tongue-tied, too. "Wow, you look absolutely gorgeous," he said. His golden amber eyes glittered. He held out two red roses and a white one tied with a ribbon. "These are for you."

"I love roses!" I said appreciatively as I smelled them. "They're just beautiful."

"In the interest of full disclosure, they—Rose and Ike— provided these bouquets for everyone. But they were all a little different, and I chose these for you."

My heart did a little flip. "Thank you, Brandon."

"Kelsea, where's your ring?" he pointed to my left hand.

"Oh, I took it off before I got in the shower." I went over to the dresser and picked it up.

Brandon motioned to me. "Bring it here."

I walked over to him and laid it in his outstretched palm, and he slid the ring on my finger. As I watched, everything went into slow motion, like in a movie. It was a very intimate moment, and my stomach fluttered.

Had Ryan's hand ever felt like this on mine?

"There, all set," he said lightly. "Let's go."

He offered me his arm and we set off. I was so nervous. This felt like a date. Was I ready to move on? I didn't know a thing about Brandon, not about his family background, or what he did for a living, or even where he lived. What if this turned into something and I had to move thousands of miles away to be part of his life? I enjoyed my independence in St. Louis, but it was nice to be within a few hours' drive of my family.

I took a breath and was assaulted by his woodsy, masculine scent. It was perfect, just what a man should smell like. I snuck a glance at his profile. It was one thing to smell and look incredible, but he still got under my skin at times. I wasn't sure we were a good match at all. But I was getting way ahead of myself.

One part of me yearned to reunite with Ryan, because he was safe and secure. But that wasn't a given, and the other part kept telling me that I couldn't trust him. There were still too many unanswered questions. I knew that it would take me a long time to trust anyone again. And if and when I was ready for a new relationship, I wasn't at all sure that I would choose someone like

Brandon. And to top it off, we were both on the rebound. Not the best recipe for long-term happiness.

*Slow down, Kelsea, just slow down.* I was ready to get home tomorrow, back to my tiny, manageable apartment, my dogs and my business and my life. I needed to get back in my routine, and wait for Ryan to come around.

But first, I had to get through tonight. Something told me that this was going to be a very special evening.

Brandon and I joined a line of other couples and followed them through the main garden toward the beach area. I could feel him standing behind me, and occasionally his body brushed against mine, sending little currents of electricity racing down my spine. At the dock stood a massive white yacht. Everyone chattered with excitement. The line slowed as we got closer to the ramp. When we got within sight of the entryway to the yacht, we discovered why.

Ike and Rose were standing at the top of the ramp, greeting everyone personally. Brandon gently rested his hands on my shoulders and leaned down to murmur in my ear, "Look at that, aren't they something?" I shivered involuntarily.

"They sure are." Ike was handsome in his tuxedo with a pink shirt and tie, but it was Rose who was the belle of the ball. She wore a sparkling, pale pink tulle ball gown that glittered in the late afternoon sun, reminiscent of Glenda of the North in *Wizard of Oz*. Her bouffant hairdo was topped off by sparkling clips. As her hands waved around, more pink and white jewels reflected the light. I thought I caught a glimpse of her Converse.

"You know, theirs is the kind of marriage I'd like to have," Brandon mused. "I don't think I could have ever had that with Nicola." He gently squeezed my shoulders.

For a moment, I wondered what kind of marriage I might have had with Ryan, and might still have, if things worked out.

"Oh, Kelsea and Brandon!" Rose exclaimed when we reached her and Ike. She reached out and enfolded me in her arms.

"You look beautiful, my dear! Just like a bride!" Ike and Brandon shook hands warmly.

I felt myself blushing. "Thank you, Rosie," I murmured.

Rose's arms fluttered around. "It's just perfect! You are the most beautiful woman here, isn't she, Brandon?" Rose stepped forward and reached up, wrapping her short arms around Brandon's waist as far as they could reach. He tenderly returned the hug, and I could tell that she and Ike had become very special to him.

They released one another, and Brandon gave both Rose and me an approving look. "I think it's a tie between you two ladies, Rose, but I'm honored to be Kelsea's escort tonight." He looked at both Rose and Ike. "Thank you both for everything. When I got here, my only goal was to survive the week." I felt his hand come lightly around my waist, and he looked down at me. "But it's been a great time instead."

"And it's not over yet!" Rose trilled, clapping her hands together.

"We'll see you later," I said, and we walked through the entrance onto the yacht.

A steward indicated where we should go. "Please, take the first empty spots you come to."

We sat, and Brandon rested his arm on the back of the seat. "This is a beautiful boat, isn't it? Have you ever been on anything like this?"

"Ah, no," I said. "What about you?"

He smiled. "No, nothing like this." I held my roses in my lap, and occasionally lifted them to my face. They were just heavenly. Before we knew it, we were underway. I felt like Brandon and I were alone, encapsulated in a lovely bubble, gliding through the water. His full attention was on me. It was like we were the only two people on the yacht.

I felt myself falling, and I was afraid he was falling with me.

# 22

KELSEA WAS FAR and away the most gorgeous woman here tonight, and she *did* look like a bride. The electricity hummed between them. Landon couldn't wait to get to the garden, where hopefully they could find a private spot to be alone for a few moments. There was so much he wanted to say to her. For one thing, he had to tell her his real name, and explain to her why he had deceived her and everyone else.

And Landon wanted to kiss her more than he'd ever wanted to kiss any woman in his entire life.

But for now, sitting close to her was enough. Deep down, he sensed that she was skittish, and didn't want to scare her off with the intensity of what he was feeling.

The trip around the perimeter of the island took less time than he thought it would. Landon felt the purring engines cut back, and soon they went completely silent, and the crew guided the yacht next to a large dock and began to tie up.

Everyone was murmuring about the scenery. This side of the island appeared to be somewhat rockier. The cliff that faced the water sloped sharply upward, and there were two symmetrical staircases winding up in gentle curves. On both sides, foliage in myriad hues of green covered the slopes with brightly colored flowers interspersed throughout. It was simply enchanting.

As they pulled up to the dock, Rose's voice came over the PA system. "Yoo hoo, brides and grooms!" Everyone laughed. "Welcome to the Queen's Garden, the most splendid spot on all of St. Jardin. When you exit the yacht, you may ascend by either staircase. Ladies, I hope you brought your Converse!" More laughter. "Hold on tight to the handrails, and gentlemen, hold on to your woman!" That brought the loudest laughter of all.

"When we arrive at the garden, there will be hors d'oeuvres and champagne, fruit punch, and sparkling water, and then a dinner buffet when we return to the resort. You may go anywhere in the garden, except the Majestic Meadow at the far south end, which is being prepared for the finale later this evening. The entrance to that will be roped off. There are benches everywhere that you may sit on. And I'm sorry, but the government of St. Jardin does not allow photography of any kind in the garden." Murmurs of disappointment rippled through the crowd.

"It is our national treasure, and most areas are considered sacred ground and are not permitted to be photographed. When we return to the resort, there will be photographs that you may purchase."

"Now, let's synchronize our watches. It's exactly 5:30. You will have ninety minutes to enjoy the garden, and promptly at 7:00, we will assemble at the entrance to the Majestic Meadow. Welcome to the Queen's Garden!" she concluded with a flourish.

Landon and Kelsea filed off with the others, and when they reached the staircase, she placed her elegant hand on the black filigree railing and began to climb. He was happy to follow her and enjoy the view—and not just of the flora and fauna, either.

When they reached the top, the garden stretched out before them. There really were no words. Landon looked down at Kelsea, and her hand flew up to her cheek. He heard soft gasps from many of the others.

"Can you believe this?" she exclaimed. I've never seen so many shades of green in my life! And the flowers!"

Landon could hardly form a coherent thought. He was certain that this was the Garden of Eden come to life. They would have to descend more stairs to reach the meadow—probably half the number that they had just climbed. As far as the eye could see in front of them were flowers of every color of the rainbow, trees of every kind imaginable—even flowering trees in pinks and purples—and cobblestone paths winding through the lush grass. Far beyond the tallest trees at the opposite end of the garden were sloping, tree-covered blue-green hills. The sky above them was a deep sapphire, dotted with white clouds.

Gazing upon this amazing beauty was almost a spiritual experience. Landon wanted so badly to be connected to Kelsea during this moment, and held out his hand. He wanted to make the offer and let her decide.

When she slid her fingers through his, Landon knew that this was, without a doubt, the most perfect moment of his life. Without speaking, they started down the staircase. When they reached the garden, they kept walking. It seemed that every flower in existence was there. Landon thought the tulips were the most beautiful he'd ever seen. The rose-covered arbor was Kelsea's favorite.

There were areas dripping with moss, waterfalls, and ponds with lily pads, with a shooting fountain in the middle of one of them. Every time Landon thought he'd seen the most beautiful thing ever, something else topped it around the next corner.

One of the best things about sharing this experience with Kelsea was that they hardly spoke. It was almost like being in one of the cathedrals of Europe, where it was sacrilegious to speak. But Landon felt that they were communicating in ways that went beyond words.

When they returned to the main garden, they got a few things to eat, and cups of fruit punch. Kelsea was glowing. "Are you enjoying yourself?" Landon asked her.

She nodded, her eyes alight with wonder. "I could never have imagined this place! Doesn't it remind you of the Garden of Eden from the Bible?"

Landon grinned at her. "That was the first thing that came into my mind when we saw it for the first time." They walked together on the path up to a little rise that somehow they had missed before.

Suddenly, she grabbed his arm. "Brandon, look!"

He followed her finger, which pointed out toward the way from they'd originally come, up the stairs from the yacht and then down into the garden. Beyond the top of the stairs, they could see clear out to the view of the turquoise sea. It was beyond breathtaking.

"I feel completely at peace," Kelsea said quietly as she stared toward the incredible view. "Rose said that the beauty of the island would restore my soul, and she was right. I don't know what will happen when I get home, but I know God has a plan, and there was a reason all of this happened." She looked at Brandon. "I don't know whether Ryan and I will get back together, but I can accept whatever happens."

Landon was relieved to discover that they were alone on the rise. It was the perfect place and time. "Kelsea, there's something I need to tell you," he said, and took both of her hands in his.

"Attention, brides and grooms!" Rose's voice blasted out through a speaker system loud and clear. "It's time to line up for the procession to the Royal Marriage Ceremony."

*Royal Marriage Ceremony?* Landon had a hard time concentrating on the rest of what Rose was saying, his heart was pounding so hard. Kelsea withdrew her hands from his.

"This ceremony has been a custom on St. Jardin for over eight hundred years. It is a beautiful ritual with a symbolic connection to nature and the universe, but it is not legally binding, since none of you are citizens of St. Jardin."

Landon relaxed, but couldn't bring himself to look at Kelsea.

"Please proceed to the entrance to the Majestic Meadow and line up, brides on the right, grooms on the left. Stay with your partner until you reach the Grand Rose Bower. Grooms will file in first, and line up in a large semi-circle in the meadow. Then the brides will follow and stand facing their groom. Brides, I hope you still have your small bouquets. Everyone, stay in your place in line so you will end up with the right partner when you reunite in the Meadow!" There was laughter all around, but Landon wasn't laughing.

He positioned himself on Kelsea's left and they walked to the south end of the garden with the other couples. The line stopped, and they waited. Landon had no idea what to expect. *Maybe we can get out of this.*

# 23

I COULD HARDLY believe my ears as I listened to Rose's instructions. Even though she said it wasn't legal, it seemed that Brandon and I were going to have to participate in some kind of ritualistic marriage ceremony. I felt a growing connection between us, but this made me uncomfortable.

When the line stopped, we just stood there. I had a hyperawareness of Brandon right next to me, but I was afraid to look at him. What was he thinking?

Soon, I heard Rose's voice coming closer and, sure enough, she was parading down the line on the brides' side in her Converse, holding her skirt up with both hands. As soon as I saw her, I waved as inconspicuously as I could. Her eyes lit up when she saw me.

"Kelsea and Brandon!" she said when she reached us. I grabbed on to her hands.

"Rosie, I—um—" *Oh, this was awkward.*

I steeled myself and glanced up at Brandon. Right away, I knew that he was feeling exactly as I was. I swear he sent me a telepathic message. *I like where we're headed, but I'm not ready for this.*

"Ah, Rose," Brandon said. He looked at me, and I tried to

message him back. *Please, let her down gently.* "We aren't really, that is—could we just sit on one of the benches—"

"Oh, no, that wouldn't do at all. This is a very sacred ceremony, and it would offend the native St. Jardinians who have worked so hard to prepare this for us." Rose squeezed my hands. "You two are going to be just fine. I promise, once you've experienced this, you'll be so happy that you did."

She let go of my hands and moved on.

Brandon leaned down and said in a stage whisper, "Did you ever do theatre or drama in high school?"

"No," I said, shaking my head.

"Me, neither," he said. "I was going to say something about just pretending like we were in a school play."

Despite my nervousness, I giggled. "Oh, gosh, how did we end up here?"

Brandon nudged my arm with his. "We came in a boat!" Then we both started laughing.

The grooms' line began to move forward. "Well, here we go," he said. "See ya!" He smiled and gave me a little wave as he walked away.

I was probably the only "bride" that was nervous at the prospect of this ceremony. Really, the source of my unease was due to only one unanswered question.

Whether Brandon and I would be expected to kiss at the conclusion of the ceremony.

# 24

LANDON BENT DOWN for a native woman to drape a long, colorful lei around his neck, then filed through a fragrant archway of red and white roses.

When he stepped into the Majestic Meadow, he felt like he was in a cathedral, on holy ground. The meadow stretched out before them, sloping downward, a carpet of pristine, green grass. On the other side was a backdrop of trees and flowers and just in front of them, a sparkling, clear stream running the entire width of the meadow.

A group of men and women in native costume were gathered at one end of the meadow, playing drums, hand-held percussion instruments, and several instruments of various sizes that Landon thought might be ukuleles. A sweet melody danced on the air, unlike anything he had ever heard.

The sun was just beginning to set, but the meadow was awash in firelight, the result of one hundred tall torches set in a perfect semi-circle. As the men quietly filed in, they were instructed by one of the ceremonial participants to stand in front of the next torch when the line stopped.

All of Landon's reservations about the ceremony evaporated, and were replaced by a feeling of peace. The incredible sights, sounds, and aromas floated around him, and somehow, he knew God was here, and that everything was going to be all right.

He didn't know how long they stood there, but suddenly he realized that the music had stopped. About ten seconds later, he heard the faint tinkling of bells, which grew louder as the brides entered, and he realized that each woman was holding a small set of metal chimes. Then some flute-like instruments began to play, and finally, all the brides had arrived.

Kelsea faced him, and Landon knew he had never seen a more beautiful woman. She was a vision of loveliness in the white, lacy dress, and wore a crown of flowers that matched the ones around his neck. There was a serenity surrounding her that Landon was sure he hadn't seen in the week that they'd been on the island.

A male voice came over the PA system. "Brides, please turn around and stand directly in front of your groom." All two hundred participants were now facing the same direction, looking out over the stream to the backdrop of tall trees. The meadow was so vast, even a crowd of that size felt dwarfed. And as Landon laid his hands on Kelsea's waist, he felt like they were the only two people there.

Three men dressed in elegant, traditional costumes stood before them on a raised rock dais, visible to everyone. One stood in the center, higher than the other two, and Landon assumed he was the priest. His costume was more extravagant than the others. He began to speak in French, and the two men on either side of him translated in both English and Spanish.

*The symbol of love is the beauty of nature,* the English translator said. Landon leaned forward and clasped Kelsea's arms lightly, and she rested her head on his chest.

The ceremony continued with prayers and beautiful native dances by the musicians. Then, the brides were directed to turn and face their grooms, lay their bouquets down, and everyone was asked to remove their shoes, and in the case of the men, their socks. When Landon's bare feet touched the grass, he swore it was the softest he had ever felt.

The priest asked for brides and grooms to clasp hands. "You wear matching leis and crowns," he said, "to symbolize harmony. The seven flowers that comprise them represent seven aspects of marriage: friendship, fertility, passion, loyalty, faithfulness, partnership, and everlasting love." As he heard the words of the translator, Landon relished the feel of Kelsea's soft, feminine hands in his, and was surprised that it wasn't awkward for either of them to look into one another's eyes.

When the priest finished the litany, the musicians broke into a lyrical, mesmerizing song and dance, this one with flowing ribbons. Following its conclusion, women dressed in a different kind of native costume circulated among the couples, offering everyone plastic flutes of crystal-clear water. When everyone had been served, the priest spoke.

"You now hold in your hand, water from the Fountain of Marital Bliss. Link arms with your partner, and drink deeply from the cup that they hold." Landon held Kelsea's gaze in his as they drank.

"This water now flows through your body and will saturate every cell. You are bound for life. What God has joined together, let nothing separate. I now pronounce you husband and wife."

The priest smiled. "Now, as I'm sure you have all been anticipating, we will conclude with a western custom, the bridal kiss, with an added piece of St. Jardinian folklore." Laughter rippled through the crowd.

"Husbands, draw your wife to you, and loop your lei around her neck, so that it surrounds both of you, representing that the two of you are one. Then, wives, step up onto your husband's feet. It will be necessary for you to work together, to hold on to one another to stay balanced, symbolic of how you should approach every step of your marriage journey. Husbands, you may now kiss your wife."

Landon thought his heart might stop. He drew Kelsea close as she stepped up onto his feet. She fit perfectly in his arms. Where Nicola was sharp angles, Kelsea was soft curves, and filled all the empty spaces of his heart. Her dark brown eyes glowed in the waning twilight and firelight, and she looked like a woman who deeply desired to be kissed.

Still, he wanted to be sure. "May I kiss you now?" he whispered for her ears only.

Without hesitation, Kelsea nodded, and Landon lowered his lips to hers.

# 25

DEEP DOWN, I knew a kiss would be part of the ceremony and that I would have to endure it, but when the time came, it was something I wanted, not an obligation. I felt covered by a cloak of serenity and peace. Everything about this ceremony made me want to be connected to the man whose feet I stood on, whose strong arms were around me.

When Brandon's lips touched mine, I melted clear down to the tips of my fingers and toes. The world around me ceased to exist, and all I cared about was being with him. He held me tightly, but I didn't feel trapped in any way.

This was, without a doubt, the softest, sweetest, most sensual kiss of my life. It was a long kiss, but there was no urgency about it, and I sensed that Brandon felt that he could go on kissing me like this forever. I could, too.

When we finally pulled apart, he rested his forehead on mine. "Wow," he whispered.

A soft giggle escaped. "Yes, wow," I whispered back.

He looked at me, his expression solemn. "There's so much I want to say to you, Kelsea, but right now, I just need to hold you."

I didn't hesitate, and wrapped my arms around him, resting my head on his shoulder, breathing him in.

Rose's voice over the PA system brought us back to reality.

"Congratulations, everyone! We hope you enjoyed this most special display of St. Jardinian tradition and culture. Would you please thank our hosts with a round of applause?"

I stepped out of Brandon's embrace and we both clapped heartily along with everyone else. When it died down, Rose spoke again. "You may put your shoes on now, and return through the garden to the staircases that will take you back to the yacht. Please proceed as quickly as possible. We have one more surprise for you after we board!"

We donned our shoes, and I picked up my bouquet. Brandon took my hand and we walked silently to the yacht. There was little talk on anyone's part. I think we all were still under the spell of the touching ceremony.

When we found our seats, Brandon slipped his arm around my shoulders, and I snuggled into him. The boat's engines started up, and we pulled away from the island. Suddenly, to everyone's surprise and delight, the sky before us lit up with an explosion of fireworks.

It was the perfect end to a perfect evening.

# 26

LANDON FELT LIKE he was in some kind of parallel universe, and never wanted it to end. As the yacht slid away from the island, the spectacular fireworks display got smaller and smaller in the distance. He knew that couples all around them were kissing, and he wanted nothing more than to join them. Only one thing held him back.

He was afraid that if he kissed Kelsea again, that he wouldn't be able to stop.

His heart beat an erratic rhythm. Rose was right. Landon *was* glad that they participated in the ceremony. He couldn't imagine having gone through it with Nicola, but couldn't put his finger on the reason why.

Now, all he could think about was how he and Kelsea would move forward from here. He thought the beautiful wedding ceremony was a great foundation from which to begin. But first and foremost, he *had* to tell her who he was, and more importantly, that he lived and worked so close to her in St. Louis. Landon imagined her ecstatic reaction to hearing that news. He also needed to be truthful with her about how he knew what her former fiancé had been up to, and that he'd put an investigator on the case to dig up all the dirt on Ryan.

Kelsea scooted a little closer to him, and he tightened his hold on her. His heart took wing as he thought of holding her like this for many years to come. He loved that they could just sit like this without having to talk.

It had been just one week since he was left at the altar, and now he had a future with a woman whom he already loved in a way that he'd never loved Nicola. Landon's heart was filled with gratitude.

The yacht arrived back at the resort, and they filed off with the other guests. Landon smiled down at Kelsea and took her hand, and her answering smile made his heart swell.

"Do you want to go to the buffet?" he asked quietly. He wasn't sure he could eat anything, his stomach was so jumpy.

She tucked a strand of dark hair behind one ear. "I'm not really hungry," she said, "but I didn't eat much at the garden, so I should probably get something."

Landon didn't think he could eat anything either, but changed his mind when they arrived in the main dining hall and the delicious scents of the buffet enveloped them. They filled their plates and sat with three other couples and made small talk about the incredible Queen's Garden.

The others left, and Kelsea and Landon started the walk back to their rooms. He didn't want things to get awkward. "Would you like to take one last walk on the beach?"

Kelsea's eyes lit up. "I'd love it! Who needs to sleep? I can sleep tomorrow night when the tropical breezes and sounds of the sea are just a memory."

They stopped at her door. "I'll change and be right back," he said.

"I'll be waiting," she replied with a smile.

Landon quickly changed and freshened up. As he looked in the mirror, he wondered if Kelsea would be in his arms when the sun came up. He fully intended to tell her tonight that he was in love with her, but had no idea where it would go from there. *I'd appreciate a little help here, God,* he prayed.

# 27

I WAS SO relieved when Brandon suggested a walk on the beach. I didn't want to arrive in our hallway and have some awkward conversation about what would come next. I had almost decided to invite him to my room, but didn't want to send the wrong message. I couldn't believe we would be going our separate ways in the morning, and wanted to spend every moment of this last night with him, just talking and looking into his gorgeous dark amber eyes, and hopefully be on the receiving end of a few more of his bone-melting kisses.

The problem with that is that with very little encouragement, I was sure it could lead to a lot more, and I didn't know if I was ready to take that step. I wasn't a virgin, but it had been about a decade since I'd made the decision to wait for marriage, and I still believed that was right for me.

I quickly brushed my teeth and started to brush the tangles out of my hair. My heart skipped a beat when a knock came at the door. I opened it, hairbrush in hand. Landon wore his University of Minnesota hoodie with the flowered lei from the ceremony. The combination of those two items made me giggle.

"Come on in. I'm just putting my hair up." I didn't want to have to fight with it in the seaside wind. I didn't want anything to distract me from being with Brandon. Maybe he would finally tell me where he was from and more about himself. If he was from Minnesota, maybe he lived in the Midwest. Maybe it wouldn't be so bad, if we decided to move forward together. I looked at the harried woman in the mirror. *One step at a time, Kelsea.*

When I came out of the bathroom, he was standing just where I'd left him. "You're so beautiful," he said as I approached. I felt heat rise to my cheeks. I was wearing shorts and a hoodie, hardly the definition of *beautiful.*

"Thank you." He took my hands and we just stood there, smiling at one another. Then he looped the lei around my neck, and I took a step closer.

"Could I—" Brandon closed his eyes for a second and took a breath. Then he opened them and exhaled loudly. "Could I please kiss you again?"

*He's adorable when he's nervous.* I laid my hands on his shoulders. "You don't have to ask," I said softly. His hands came securely around my waist, and his heart-stopping grin made my stomach flip.

Just as Brandon lowered his head, a loud knock on the door made us jump apart. Brandon lifted the lei off of both of us. *Of all the lousy timing.* My heart pounded as I opened the door to one of the resort's employees holding a large floral bouquet.

"Kelsea Anderson?"

"Yes, that's me."

"These were delivered for you while you were gone."

"Thank you." I took the vase, and closed the door. I smiled at Brandon. "These are beautiful! Are you responsible?"

"I wish I could take credit, but they're not from me. Maybe Ike and Rose sent them to all the brides."

"If they wanted to do that, they could have left them in our rooms while we were away. He said they were delivered for me. No one knows that I'm here."

"No one?" Brandon echoed.

"Just Morgan," I replied.

I set the vase down, tore open the envelope, and read the card. My heart pounded. I looked up at Brandon. I read the card again to make sure that I wasn't dreaming. "They're from Ryan," I whispered, in shock.

He frowned. "How did he know you were here?"

"He must have called Morgan." I held the card out to him.

"You want me to read it?" Brandon asked. I nodded.

He read out loud the words that were already engraved on my heart. *"Dear Kels, I know I screwed up bad. I want to try to make this work. Counting the minutes until you come home. Love, Ryan."*

I fingered the petals of the beautiful flowers and bent to inhale their delicious scent. "He wants me back! He still loves me!"

I began dancing around the room and, next thing I knew, I had thrown my arms exuberantly around Brandon. "Oh, Brandon, I was right! He just needed some space! It's all going to work out!" I untangled myself from him and sat down on the couch.

I pressed my hands to my cheeks to find that they were wet with tears of joy. "I knew he would come around."

"Kelsea."

I released a pent-up breath. "He just needed some time."

"Kelsea." This time Brandon's voice was a little louder, a little firmer.

"What?" I stopped and looked at him. His arms hung limply at his side. "Brandon, what's wrong? Aren't you happy for me?"

He rubbed a hand over his jaw.

"I guess I'm just—after what we shared at the Queen's Garden, and everything—I thought—"

My heart began to pound. *Oh, no.* "Brandon, it was—special. Really, I've learned a lot from you this week. But I've invested almost *three years* of my life with Ryan. If there was a chance of making it work with Nicola again, wouldn't you jump at it?" Then

I saw the look on his face, and realized how insensitive I'd been. "Brandon, I'm sorry—"

"I'm sorry, too," he said, his voice clipped. He rested his hands on his hips, and a tic worked in his jaw. "What would have happened if that delivery person hadn't knocked on the door just now?"

"I, I don't know," I whispered. I looked down at my hands for several silent seconds. Then I removed the beautiful tri-gold band and held it out. "Maybe you should take this back now."

"Kelsea—" He looked at me for a long moment, his expression unreadable. Finally, he reached out and took the ring, and put it in his pocket. "You need to be open to the possibility that things with Ryan may not be what they seem."

"What do you mean? It couldn't be any clearer." I held the note up.

"I just—I just don't want you to get hurt."

He wasn't making any sense. "How can I get hurt? Ryan *loves* me! He wants to make it work!" I scowled at him and crossed my arms in front of me. "Why can't you be happy for me? I'd be happy for you if the tables were turned."

Brandon hesitated, then came and sat down next to me. "Get your computer. I need to show you something."

I didn't move. "Why? What are you talking about?"

"Just go to Ryan's social media page."

This made no sense at all. "What are you talking about? Why would you care about Ryan's page? He hardly ever goes on there." Really, I was beginning to get annoyed.

But the look on his face made me think again. I got my computer, signed on, then navigated to Ryan's page. I scanned it, but didn't see anything. It looked like he hadn't updated anything in a while. No surprise there.

"What? What am I looking for, Brandon?"

"Right there—" he pointed, then dropped his hand. "It was there, but now it's gone."

"What was there?"

"There"—he pointed again—"it used to say *in a relationship with Jenna Harmon.*"

I looked at the screen. *No relationship info to show.* "What are you talking about? Who's Jenna Harmon? And what were you doing on Ryan's page, anyway?"

"I came on his page the first night we were here, after you told me his name, and it was right there in black and white." His expression turned serious. "Kelsea, there's more."

I slammed my computer shut and jumped up. "I don't believe you! And you had no business stalking him, anyway! What in the world is wrong with you, Brandon? Do you hate me so much that you'd try to ruin my chance to get back with the man I love?"

He stood. "Kelsea, I had an investigator look into it—"

I was horrified. "You what?" I shouted. "This was none of your business!" I was seriously starting to get creeped out. Who was Brandon St. Fair, anyway? What if he reached out to Ryan and told him that he'd met me this week, and that we'd pretended to be married, and even kissed? I knew nothing about Brandon, and yet, somehow this week, in my weakened emotional state, I'd fallen under his spell.

My heart pounded. What if that delivery person *hadn't* interrupted us? My mind began to go in all kinds of wild directions.

"Kelsea, let me explain—"

I needed time to think. "Get out!" I screamed. Tears coursed down my cheeks. "Please, just go. I have to think."

"You're making a mistake, Kelsea. Let me help you."

"Get. Out. NOW!"

Brandon walked to the door and opened it. Then he turned and looked at me.

"OUT!"

He closed the door quietly behind him.

# 28

LANDON WENT BACK to his room and paced. He felt like a caged animal, and decided to go for a run on the beach, *alone*.

That lying weasel, Ryan Singer. He must have taken Jenna Harmon's name off his page for some reason, maybe when he decided that he wanted to try to make up with Kelsea. Landon's stomach churned. She deserved so much better than this guy. Singer had bigger problems, and Landon desperately wanted Kelsea to be spared from all of it.

Landon couldn't tell her that after first seeing Ryan's page, he'd made a call to one of his firm's investigators and asked him to do a little more poking around. Ben Nelson was a young, tech-savvy guy, and this was right up his alley. It was all over social media, thanks to Jenna Harmon. And thanks to her young friends sharing every moment of their lives online, Ben was easily able to catch up with them at their favorite bar, pose as a co-worker of Jenna and Ryan, and get all the sordid details of their fling.

It was much worse than Landon could have imagined. When Ben had called and filled him in, Landon was relieved that Kelsea was free of Singer. But now it was all going to blow up in her face.

Landon ran hard, reveling in the feeling of pushing his body to its physical limits. His heart pounded, and the endorphins flowed as his long legs pounded along the sand. He ran to banish the memories of the entire evening at the Queen's Garden.

But as long as Landon lived, he knew he would never forget that kiss, and every other detail about the most magical evening of his life.

He ran like he was being chased by the devil, and he knew what he was really trying to run from. Finally, he finished, exhausted, then cooled down and walked up from the beach and through the garden to the main building.

He needed to talk with Rose and Ike.

## 29

I WAS LIVID. Brandon St. Fair was the lowest human being on the planet, and I wouldn't spend one more second in his presence. Not one more! Thanks goodness I was leaving first thing in the morning. I didn't even want to be in the same hemisphere as him.

The nerve of him, making up some story about Ryan being in a relationship with some non-existent person named Jenna. What was he trying to prove, anyway? That I had to stay jilted just because he was? I meant what I'd said, that I'd be happy for him if Nicola had taken him back.

But then I thought of the magical time at the Queen's Garden, of the moving ceremony, and of that incredible kiss. It seemed like weeks ago instead of hours. As soon as I read Ryan's words, everything changed. And now I was so confused.

I spent some time packing so I wouldn't have to do anything in the morning. Then I sat down with my computer and looked at Ryan's page. I started clicking, and then had another idea. What if there was another Ryan Singer in St. Louis, and Brandon had just been on the wrong page? I could settle this, once and for all. I typed *Jenna Harmon St. Louis* into the search engine and held my breath. There were two entries. I clicked on the first. This Jenna was at least 40 years old, was married, and had three kids and a Dalmatian. *Whew.*

I clicked on the second one, and my heart stopped. This Jenna was in her mid-20s, with long, luxurious blonde curls and big, expertly made-up blue eyes. This Jenna worked for the same company as Ryan. And this Jenna was *in a relationship with Ryan Singer.*

I pressed my hand over my mouth. *Okay, maybe it's another Ryan Singer.* So I did a little searching and found a headshot of her and Ryan nestled together.

My jaw dropped. It was definitely *my* Ryan. It looked like they were in a bar. They were both smiling and honestly, they looked a little drunk. The date listed was the night before Thanksgiving. I'd gone home to my Mom's to spend one last holiday with her and Morgan, just the three of us. Ryan insisted he'd be fine without me. He said he'd have dinner with his mom and use the time to get ahead on some of his work in preparation for being gone for our honeymoon.

But it was obvious he had found other ways to occupy himself in my absence. I hadn't seen him for a few days after I returned. He said he was getting over the flu.

There were no more pictures of Ryan and Jenna. I kept scrolling and stopped at a post that was dated the day Ryan broke up with me. My stomach heaved. There was a selfie of an ecstatic Jenna holding one of those home pregnancy test wands. *Best way to begin the new year! I'M PREGNANT!* the caption screamed.

# 30

LANDON WALKED INTO the dining hall, where the buffet was just winding down. His eyes scanned the room and to his immense relief, he saw Rose and Ike.

"Brandon! Or can we call you Landon now?" Rose said. "What did you and Kelsea think of the ceremony?"

Landon sat and tried to dredge up a smile. "Ah, we enjoyed it very much. It really was an incredible experience."

"But something's happened." Rose and Ike both looked at him with concern.

"Kelsea received some news from home. It's complicated." He looked down at his hands, at the ring on his finger, and felt sadness. He looked at Rose. "She could use a friend tonight, if you could check in on her."

Rose's gaze speared right through him. "Seems that you two have become pretty good friends, *Mr. St. Clair.*"

Landon winced, then nodded. "We have, but there was never a good time for me to tell her why I lied about my name. And now, it would—" He rubbed a hand over his face. "It just wouldn't work. She's not speaking to me right now, and she's planning to go back to her fiancé."

"Is this news from home about him?" Rose asked.

"Yes, yes it is. But there's more to the story than she knows, and she may figure it out soon. If not, I think I have to tell her. And it's just going to kill her." Landon looked down and was surprised to see that he was twisting the wedding band around on his finger.

Rose and Ike exchanged a look. "It seems that when she gets more bad news, she'll need more than a friend to turn to," Rose said. "She'll need someone who loves her."

Landon went completely still, his head still down. When he finally lifted it, he met Rose and Ike's tender gazes. "It's nothing to be ashamed of, son," Ike said softly.

"I'm not ashamed," Landon said, "it's just bad timing, I guess. She's still in love with Singer."

"She *thinks* she's in love with him," Rose corrected. "Remember, she's known him a lot longer than she's known you. When anyone has emotional upheaval in their life, they grab on to anything familiar and comfortable. The only thing you can do right now is wait for her, and be there when she gets to the bottom of everything and realizes that she's in love with *you.*"

Landon shook his head. "She's not in love with me," he said.

Rose and Ike smiled at one another. "She is," Rose said emphatically. "She's just not ready to admit it yet."

Ike reached for Rose's hand. "Sounds like another beautiful young lady I knew once," he said with a smile. Then he looked at Landon and raised an eyebrow.

"Really?" Landon looked between the two.

Rose sighed. "Oh, yes. It took me a long time to come around. My Ike was the soul of patience."

"From the time I fell in love with her, I waited for ten months," Ike proclaimed.

Landon rubbed a hand through his hair. "I've only known Kelsea for six days. And exactly a week ago, I was fully prepared to marry someone else."

"That was my situation when I met Ike," Rose said. "I'd been dating this dashing Irishman—really, it was a whirlwind courtship—and he had promised to marry me and take me back to Ireland with him. But then he was arrested for being part of a theft ring, and off to prison he went."

"Were you still carrying a torch for him?" Landon asked.

"Was I ever! I told myself that I would wait for him no matter how long it took."

"My family owned a deli and market in Rose's neighborhood," Ike said. "I worked there, and she came in quite a bit and really caught my eye, but I was too shy to speak up."

"He was quiet as a mouse," Rose said. "My brother George was a beat cop, and knew the Goldmans well."

"We always gave the cops free coffee and pastries," Ike said with a smile. "George was a friendly sort, and I finally got up the nerve to ask him about his sister. He told me that she had been planning to marry someone, but the guy went to jail, and was going to be deported back to Ireland to stand trial there."

Rose shuddered. "It turns out he and his gang had fled to New York from Ireland after a botched robbery there that resulted in the deaths of two men," Rose said. "So anyway, I was just moping around, and I was only eighteen, and I was *sure* that he would write to me and send passage, and then I would go to Ireland and marry him and visit him in prison. I was so naïve. After about six months, I still hadn't heard a word from him, and George had finally had it with my sackcloth-and-ashes routine, and told me that I should let Ike Goldman court me. My response was, 'Ike Goldman? Who in the world is Ike Goldman?'"

They both laughed, and Landon laughed with them.

"I'd made no impression whatsoever on her!" Ike said. "I was just plodding along, trying to work up the courage to say hello to her, and lo and behold, one day she came into the store with George and he introduced us, and she suggested that we go for a walk the next afternoon."

Landon smiled. "Once you figured out who Ike was, you must have liked what you saw," he said to Rose.

"I did, but I was still carrying a torch for Tommy O'Houlihan," Rose sighed. "I wasn't interested in anything but friendship with Ike, but he stuck with me and I finally came around."

Landon looked at Ike. "Was there ever a time that you doubted her? Did you think the two of you might not ever get together?"

Ike shook his head. "I knew deep in my soul that this was the woman God chose for me." He squeezed Rose's hand. "And I was willing to wait as long as it took. Just having her friendship was more than I'd had. I was happy enough for that."

Landon shook his head. "I admire your patience, Ike. I feel like I've been through a hurricane. But I know that I love Kelsea, and I'll wait as long as it takes."

Rose patted his hand. "She'll come around, I'm sure of it."

"Well, I know she won't open the door to me tonight," Landon said. "So would you be willing to check in on her?"

"We'll do better than that," Rose replied. She picked up the two-way radio sitting on the table next to her. "Front desk, we need an extra key card for Miss Anderson's room. Mr. St. Fair will come by to pick that up in a few minutes."

"Yes, Ma'am," came the reply.

Landon rested his hands on his knees. "I'm not sure that's a good idea."

Rose smiled. "It is. Trust us."

Ike stared at Landon, his gaze steady. "You can't leave her like this."

Landon looked at them for a long moment.

"You're right. Thanks, both of you. I can't thank you enough." He smiled. "If we get through this in one piece, we'll name our first son and daughter after you."

He was happy that this elicited a hearty laugh from the couple. He stood and squeezed their hands. "We'll be praying for you, son," Ike said.

When was the last time anyone had prayed for him? The thought lightened his footsteps.

Landon got the key card from the front desk and went straight to Kelsea's room. He took a deep breath, then knocked.

"Kelsea, it's me. Please, can we talk?"

No answer.

He knocked again, a little louder. He didn't want to roust any of the neighbors, but it was important to make it clear to her what he intended to do. "Kelsea, if you're there, please open the door. I just want to make sure you're okay."

Landon stood there in silence, willing his breathing to slow down. It was possible that she'd gone out on a walk, but he felt deep in his bones that she was in the room.

He took a cleansing breath. "Kelsea, Rose gave me a key card. I'm coming in now." He swiped the card and slowly opened the door.

The room was dark except for one of the bedside lamps. Landon saw water reflected on the floor, broken shards of glass everywhere, and crushed, wilted flowers.

Kelsea sat in a corner of the sofa, rolled up in a ball. Rumpled tissues littered the area around her, and her laptop was open on the table. Landon stepped closer and glanced at the screen. He wasn't at all surprised at what he saw.

Slowly, he lowered himself down and sat next to her, leaving some space between them. Neither of them said anything, and Kelsea seemed to be staring at some faraway spot. After several minutes, Landon began to grow concerned that she was in some kind of catatonic state or something.

"How did you know?" She finally said in a low voice. She still wouldn't look at him.

*Oh, this was going to be sticky.* "Well, um, I—that first night after you told me Ryan's name, I went on his social media page."

"You stalked him." She crossed her arms in front of her chest and continued to stare straight ahead.

"I was just—curious. And that night, on his page, it said that he was in a relationship with Jenna Harmon. So then, I went to *her* page, and it said that she was in a relationship with someone else, not Ryan."

"*Not* Ryan?"

"Correct." Now came the hard part, and due to Kelsea's state of mind, Landon didn't feel that this was the right moment to reveal that he had lied about his identity. This was a mine field, and he had to step carefully. "So. I'm—in my line of work, I use the services of private investigators, so I contacted one of them and asked him to poke around a little. And he reported back to me about the pregnancy."

Kelsea jumped up and began to pace. "So then, you thought you would just flirt with me, spend time together, get me into your good graces, get me to go along with some fake wedding ceremony, and then sleep with me."

Landon leapt to his feet. "Are you kidding me, Kelsea? How could I have had any idea about the ceremony tonight? None of us knew anything about that."

She came and stood right in front of him. "Empty your pockets, Brandon," she ordered.

"What? What are you talking about?"

"Empty your pockets, now." Her eyes flashed at him.

"I don't know what you're looking for, but here you go." He took out his key card and slapped it down on the table. He pulled the linings of both of shorts pockets out, stretched his front hoodie pocket out, and stuck his hand through it so she could see that it was empty.

"No cell phone?"

"I didn't want any distractions."

"No wallet?

He was completely confused. "Why would I need my wallet for a walk on the beach?" Suddenly, the light bulb went on. "You want to see if I'm carrying any protection! Well, I'm not. Because as I've told you, I don't sleep around. That's a big step, and one I don't take lightly."

She threw up her hands. "Then why did you spend all this time with me this week, and kiss me tonight like—like no other man ever has?"

He picked up the key card and jammed it in his pocket. "Maybe it was because I fell in love with you, Kelsea. Did you ever consider that?"

Landon walked out the door and slammed it behind him, closing the door to his heart.

# 31

BRANDON *LOVED* ME? I couldn't believe it. That was the last thing in the world I expected him to say. The words ricocheted around in my mind all night. I hardly slept, and welcomed my last sunrise on St. Jardin with a hundred-pound weight on my shoulders. I called housekeeping and asked for a broom and dustpan, cleaned up the flower mess, then tossed my last few items into my suitcase.

My stomach was in knots and I had no interest in breakfast, but I had to find Rose and Ike and say goodbye to them. It was a conversation I wasn't looking forward to.

I didn't see them anywhere in the main dining hall, and went back to the front desk. "Yes, they're in their office," the clerk said when I asked about them. He indicated an unmarked pink door across the lobby that stood slightly ajar.

"Hello?" I peeked in, and Rose's face brightened. I went in, and she greeted me with a hug. Today, she wore a flowing pink flowered muumuu and her ever-present Converse. Ike sat at his desk.

"Oh dear, Kelsea, I take it things didn't go well last night."

*That's right, Brandon said Rose had given him the key card to my room.* "How—did Brandon talk to you?"

"He was very concerned about you, dear."

"Well, it doesn't matter. Whatever did or didn't happen between us this week is over, and I'm going back to St. Louis, and he's going back to wherever he's from."

Rose and Ike exchanged a glance. "He didn't tell you anything about himself?"

I frowned. "No. What is it that you're not telling me?"

Rose rubbed my arm. "Kelsea, you've had a terrible couple of weeks, and your life has been turned upside down—what? About three times?"

Ike got up and came to stand beside his wife. "These things have a way of working out," he said. "Mine and Rose's path to the altar wasn't a straight one."

I smiled dimly. "Yes, she told me about it, Ike." I looked at these two people who had become so very dear to me, and reached for their hands. "Thank you so much for this week. I'll never forget it, and I'll never forget you." Tears rolled down my cheeks as I realized how much I would miss them. I knew I would never set foot on St. Jardin again, and the thought made me immensely sad.

Rose grasped both of my hands. "You are going to be fine, dear," she said. "Ike and I will be praying for you, and we *know* that we are going to see you again." That made me cry even harder.

They reached their arms around to hug me, and Rose whispered in my ear. "Remember, Kelsea Anderson, you're one of the strong ones."

# 32

LANDON STARED OUT the window of the plane. The first-class seat next to him sat empty, just as it had on the trip down. Then, it mirrored the empty space Nicola had left in his heart, but now, it hurt much worse because of the gaping hole left by Kelsea.

How could a woman whom he'd known only eight days turn his life so upside down?

When he discovered they were booked on the same flight, Landon had planned to arrange for Kelsea to sit next to him on the trip home. Instead, he'd pulled on a baseball cap, sunk into his jacket, and turned his face toward the window while the other passengers boarded. The fact that they were on the same flight to St. Louis was supremely ironic. *So near and yet so far.*

When they landed, he was the first one off the jet. He was hungry, so he went for a leisurely early dinner. He didn't want to chance running into Kelsea at baggage claim. When he was convinced enough time had passed, he went down and collected his bag.

He took an Uber home and walked through the frigid air to his front door. When he put the key in the deadbolt, he realized it wasn't engaged. He tried the knob and was relieved that it was locked. That could mean only one thing.

Landon walked into the entry and his gaze went immediately to the hall table. In the dim light he could make out a key, an envelope, and the ring that would be on his left hand now if things had gone differently. He looked at his bare ring finger. Both his and Kelsea's tri-gold wedding bands rested in his shirt pocket, next to his heart.

He set his bag down, picked up the envelope, and took out the notecard. Nicola's small, feminine script flowed across the page.

*Dear Landon, I know you can never forgive me for leaving you at the altar. It was a cowardly way to handle things, and you deserved better. I think you know that things between us weren't what they should have been for a couple about to commit their lives to one another. That was my fault, too. I loved you, but I'm not sure I was ever in love with you, if that makes any sense. I always suspected that I was part of the business deal between my father and your firm, and that's not a good foundation for a lasting relationship.*

*I hold nothing against you, and wish you every happiness. Someday, I know that you will find a woman who loves you with her whole heart, and who is deserving of yours. Please, take this ring and my bridal set, and put them to good use. Have the engraving removed and then give them to someone, or sell them and use that to buy another ring when you meet that special woman.*

It was signed simply, *Nicola.*

Landon took the note and the envelope, walked over to the gas fireplace, turned it on, and threw them in. Nicola had called her actions cowardly, but he realized that he'd been the coward by not being willing to confront her when he had serious doubts about their approaching marriage. He watched the paper burn until it was no more, and felt a weight lift from his shoulders. This chapter was completely closed. There was no need to meet with Nicola. There wasn't anything to say.

He walked into the kitchen and opened the fridge. He knew

there was virtually nothing there, but came up with a can of soda. He popped it open and sat down at the counter on one of his bar stools, then made a call.

"Hello? Is that you, Landon?"

"Yeah, Dad, it's me. Just wanted you and Mom to know that I'm home."

"It's good to hear from you, son. Are you okay? We've been praying for you."

Landon smiled. "Thanks, Dad. I appreciate that."

"I hope it was a time of healing for you."

"In some ways it was, but something very unexpected also happened this week, Dad, and that's what I need to talk with you about."

Landon spent the next several minutes pouring out his heart about Kelsea. He told his dad how he felt when he was with her, how colors were more vivid, the air was fresher, and that he felt more alive than he ever had with Nicola. Landon said he couldn't explain it away by being in the tropical setting, he knew that it went beyond that. He told his dad about their common interests, about the things that he and Kelsea argued about, about her sharp wit and her strong opinions, and how just being around her made him feel like a better man.

He left out any reference to the ceremony at the Queen's Garden, or their kiss.

"It sounds like you're in love, son, for real this time," his father finally said.

"But it seems impossible," Landon protested. "What if it's not real, like a shipboard romance?"

"Trust your heart, son, despite the circumstances, despite how bad the timing is, despite how impossible it seems."

"But now, it looks like her former fiancé wants her back," Landon said, and shared everything that he knew about Ryan Singer, and about his and Kelsea's fight. He found himself choking up. "Dad, I can't lose her."

"I know you want to protect her, son, but she's got a lot to work through right now, and she needs to do it on her own. If you love her, you have to step back and give her the time and space to do that, so that when she comes to you, it will be with her whole heart."

Landon felt some of the burden lift. "Thanks, Dad. Someone else gave me similar advice. It won't be easy, but I know it's the right thing to do."

"I'll be praying for you, son, and you pray, too."

"Thanks, I will, Dad. I love you." Landon disconnected and sat where he was for quite a long time, not moving.

Finally, he admitted to himself that he couldn't be in control of this, and that he needed to leave it up to God.

# 33

WHEN WE LANDED in St. Louis, it was ten degrees and overcast. When the plane broke through the clouds on our descent, the sight of the stark, gray and white landscape settled around my heart like a heavy blanket. *Back to reality.*

I sat staring out the window while the other passengers filed out. I wasn't in a hurry to go anywhere. I was one of the last ones off the plane. By the time I hit the restroom in the terminal and shuffled down to baggage claim, most of the crowd had cleared. I grabbed my bag and headed for the door.

The subzero wind hit me like an icy freight train, and I sucked in a breath. *Would I ever feel warm again?* Fortunately, the shuttle to long-term parking was idling at the curb. I climbed aboard and found a seat.

"Oh, Myrtle," I said to my green VW bug when I reached it. "Let's get this ice scraped off." I started the engine to warm up. Myrtle was one of the new beetles, not a classic one. Her full name was Myrtle the Turtle.

My first stop was the kennel. I couldn't wait to see Penny and Sheldon. I hadn't ever been away from them longer than overnight, and was afraid they had forgotten me. But I needn't have worried. Their enthusiastic welcome assured me that my dogs still loved me. It was a wonderful reunion.

We went straight home, and the first thing I did was turn up the heat and make a cup of tea. Then I changed into my softest, comfiest sleep clothes and my thickest socks.

*I'm home,* I texted to my mom and Morgan. That was our rule, anytime any of us traveled, that we'd notify the others when we were safely home. Almost instantly, my phone vibrated with a text. I really hoped it wasn't Mom. I wasn't up for a big conversation.

I breathed a sigh of relief when I saw Morgan's name. *Can we face time? Call me.* I sat down on my daybed, pulled the comforter up, and speed dialed her. "Hey Morgy, what's up?" I adjusted the screen and took a sip of my raspberry tea. *Perfect.*

"Hi. I just want to know how you're doing, Sissy." Morgan was the only person on the planet who was allowed to call me that. And I was sure that Dr. Morgan Anderson would *never* let anyone else call her Morgy. "I felt bad that I didn't come after the wedding was canceled. I was between semesters, so I could have."

"It's okay, really. I was such a mess, I wouldn't have been good company."

"How was St. Jardin?"

Sheldon and Penny hopped up to snuggle. "It was—not what I expected." *Understatement of the year.* "It's unbelievably beautiful, though." An image of the Queen's Garden in all its glory filled my senses. But that inevitably led to an image of Brandon and the fake marriage ceremony, and I needed to banish that.

"So, are you and Ryan getting back together?" Hesitancy filled my sister's voice.

"No," I said. "But I'm not mad that you told him where I was," I quickly added.

Relief showed visibly on her face. "Oh, that's good. But there must be more to the story. If you're not ready, I understand." I knew she was sincere. One of the best things about our sister relationship was that we had established firm boundaries years ago, and we both honored them.

I launched into the whole story, starting with general comments about the resort, Rose, Ike, and even a nameless jilted groom, then moving on to the details about Ryan's flowers and the drama that ensued—although nothing about Brandon's involvement and our fight. Morgan gasped when I told her about Jenna being pregnant.

"Kelsea! That's horrible! I never would have thought Ryan could do something like that!" Her long golden-brown hair, pulled high into a ponytail, bounced as she shook her head back and forth.

"I know. He had everyone fooled."

"Have you talked with him? Are you going to?"

"No, not yet. But I will. I want him to look me right in the eye and explain it, no matter how much it hurts. I'll text him tomorrow and set up a time to meet."

"So, tell me about this guy, the jilted groom that you got thrown together with on the island," Morgan said. Her eyes danced with anticipation. "Is he cute?"

*Cute* wasn't the thought that came to mind. *Try gorgeous, ripped, sexy, and overwhelmingly masculine, for starters.* "No, not really. And we were like oil and water. Not a good mix."

"Rose and Ike sound like a trip," she said with a laugh.

"Oh Morgy, they're just the cutest, sweetest people. Best friends and so in love after fifty-three years of marriage."

"Eww. I can't imagine being with one person for that long," Morgan groused. My sister was very career focused. I couldn't remember the last time that she dated anyone.

"When you meet the right guy, you'll change your tune," I said.

"Well, I don't see that happening." Morgan said. Something in her voice alerted my sister radar. There was something she wasn't saying. I just knew it.

"Because?" I prompted.

Silence settled in around me. Her eyes welled up. Then I heard her breath catch, like a little sob, and she began to cry.

"Morgan, what's wrong?"

"I, um, I've been having some issues," she said. My heartbeat accelerated. "Female issues. I haven't said anything to Mom about it, because, well, you know, she's Mom."

"I understand. I'm so sorry." I was really at a loss and didn't know what to say. "How serious is it?"

"It's not cancer or anything," Morgan reassured me, and I felt a wave of relief wash over me. She wiped her tears with a tissue, and her green eyes glistened like spring grass in the morning dew. "But the doctor says I probably won't ever be able to have children." I could hear the heartbreak in her voice.

My heart fell. "Oh, Morgan, I don't know what to say. I'm so sorry. Are they sure?"

"Pretty sure," she sighed. "I have to decide if I want them to do a procedure where they look around to know for sure. Right now I just need to get my pain under control. That was the main reason I didn't come to St. Louis when you canceled the wedding. I'm so sorry."

My eyes spilled over with tears. "You don't have anything to apologize for. I'm just so sorry that you're going through this. Is the pain bad?"

"It's getting a little better. I had to cut way back on some of my extra-curricular activities in the fall. They're adjusting my meds and hopefully I'll see a bigger improvement by the end of the month."

"Listen, Morgan." I cleared my throat. "You already have a very fulfilling career. If it *does* turn out that you can't have children, you can still meet a wonderful man and be very happy together. My friends Rose and Ike never had children." There was adoption, too, but I didn't feel that now was the time to get into that.

Her voice sounded small and scared. "I know, but it's hard to find a guy like that, you know? And I don't even know how that would work. I can't see myself on a first date saying, 'Hey, I'm damaged, I can't ever give you a child,' but if it starts getting serious, then how would I tell him? If I fall for a guy and then he walks away—"

"Hey, you're getting way ahead of yourself," I said. "Don't borrow trouble, like Mom always says."

"I know," she sighed, and swiped at her eyes again. "I just— I feel so old."

"I'm older than you!" I exclaimed, and we both laughed. "And now I'm back on the shelf, as they used to say."

"You'll be fine," Morgan said emphatically. "You'll end up marrying a great guy and have a whole houseful of kids."

"Well, I don't know where I'm going to meet any great guys. Not in my line of work, anyway. And the clock is ticking," I muttered.

"Maybe you'll meet a cute vet," she said. I was happy to hear the lilt in her voice again. "And the one silver lining in my situation is that I'll have a valid excuse when Mom starts bugging me for grandkids."

"Ugh," I said. "I've got a lot of years before I'm off the hook for good."

"Well, sis," Morgan said, "go and let Ryan have it with both barrels, and then move on. If I can't be a mom, I want to be an aunt!"

"I love you, Morgy," I said.

"I love you, too, Sissy." She grinned. "Hey, we should do something during spring break. I know! We could go to St. Jardin! But not to that resort. There must be others."

"No thanks! I mean to St. Jardin. I'll always associate that place with honeymoons." *And a certain blond hunk who kissed like a dream.* "But we can go somewhere else. That would be fun."

"Awesome! I'll check out some ideas and e-mail you."

I told Morgan I loved her one more time, and disconnected. Penny and Sheldon had fallen asleep curled up in my lap. I buried my face in their soft fur, and thought about my sister. As successful a career as she had, I knew that she wanted to be a mother, to have a family. Both of us had held that deep desire for many years. It looked like that dream had slipped away for me, but it didn't have to for her.

"Dear God, please make a way for Morgan," I prayed.


I really meant to get up and unpack and do some laundry, but Sheldon, Penny and I ended up falling asleep. An incoming call shook me awake, and I hit decline when I saw that it was Ryan. It was after six o'clock. I had no desire to talk with him. In a few seconds, he sent a text.

*Are you home? I've been thinking about you all day.*

I took a deep breath. I wasn't ready to drop my bombshell on him, so I would need to appear cordial.

*Yes, I'm back.*

*I can't wait to see you. Dinner tonight at eight? Le Bistro?*

I snorted. The romantic French restaurant that we called *our place?* Not on your life. *I can't. Coffee, tomorrow morning at 11, Tillie's. I'll fit you in between appointments.* That was a bald-faced lie, but he didn't need to know that. I needed to make the point, now, that he was no longer first in my life. Tomorrow he would know in no uncertain terms that he no longer had *any* place in my life.

*Can I please come over tonight?*

*No, I'm going to bed now. Super tired. See you tomorrow.* I turned my phone off, and went to the kitchen to figure something out for dinner. Ritz crackers and peanut butter counted as a two-course meal, right?

I went straight back to bed, slept fitfully, and woke up with a headache. A cup of peppermint tea and massaging peppermint oil on my temples took care of it, but I was jumpy and didn't feel like eating anything. Not that there was anything to eat in my apartment. The grocery store would be my first stop after meeting with Ryan.

Since I hadn't gotten to it last night, I decided to unpack and start a load of laundry. As soon as I unzipped my suitcase, the aroma of tropical flowers wove itself around me. My eyes filled with tears. Right on top where I had wrapped them in a plastic bag lay my crown and Brandon's lei, and the little nosegay of red and white roses that he had chosen for me. They were crushed and wilted, but still amazingly fragrant. I buried my nose in them and closed my eyes. Memories of being with Brandon at the Queen's Garden assaulted me, and I was filled with a deep sense of sadness.

I spent the morning trying to keep busy but not accomplishing anything, willing the clock to move along, and finally left my apartment at 10:45. I hadn't taken any pains with my appearance. I didn't want Ryan to think that I was trying to impress him. I wore jeans, boots, and an oversized teal cable-knit sweater. My hair was up in a messy bun, and my makeup consisted of a little mascara and my favorite vanilla mint lip balm.

I cruised into Tillie's and chose a table near the door. I wanted to be able to make a quick exit. A swirl of heavenly scents surrounded me, and my stomach rumbled in protest. I ordered comfort food—a cup of hot chocolate and a blueberry muffin.

As soon as I got settled, Ryan came through the door. He leaned down and tried to kiss me, but I turned my head just in time for his lips to make awkward contact with my cheek.

He shrugged out of his coat and sat down. "Wow, Kels, you look good. You got some sun."

Ryan's dark, good looks suddenly didn't seem so attractive to me. The descriptor *smarmy, oily cheat* leapt to mind.

"Yes, a week in the Caribbean usually does that." I took a bite of muffin and it all but melted in my mouth.

"Well, um, I—wow, Kels, I've missed you."

I kept chewing and stared at him, but stayed silent. I wanted to see what kind of trouble he'd talk himself into. If there was one thing I knew about Ryan, it was that he couldn't keep quiet for long.

He didn't disappoint. "So, I guess you've been wondering about me, about us, about—" he laughed nervously. "About how we're going to pick up and go on. Because I really do want us to, you know, go on." He seemed to be waiting for me to say something.

*This is kind of fun.* I took a leisurely sip of my cocoa and kept quiet.

"I guess you're waiting for me to say I'm sorry. I really am sorry, Kels. I know my timing was terrible, but I just got cold feet, you know? So, ah, if you still want to get married, let's go ahead and plan that. I'm ready now. I'm really ready. We can have the fall wedding you always wanted."

*When pigs fly.* I wanted to spin this out. I wiped my mouth with my napkin, picked up a spoon, and stirred my cocoa. Then I took another bite of my delicious muffin, chewed, and swallowed.

"Who's Jenna Harmon?" I said matter-of-factly.

I really wish I'd taken a video of his reaction. Ryan's face blanched white, and he put his head in his hands and groaned. Then, he quickly recovered. "Kelsea, I can explain. It's not what it looks like."

I took another sip of cocoa. "That's interesting, Ryan, because it *looks like* the minute I left town for Thanksgiving, you hooked up with Jenna. And now she's pregnant."

He ran his fingers over his face and up through his dark brown hair, then let out a loud breath.

"I—Kelsea, I, yes, it was a huge mistake, and I really didn't know what I was doing. A bunch of us went out on Wednesday night after work, and I, you know, drank a little too much, and somehow ended up going back to Jenna's apartment with her. I never stopped loving you, it was just—a big mistake."

Ryan reached for my hand, but I pulled it away before he could make contact. "You never stopped loving me." I drenched every syllable with sarcasm. "Gee, Ryan, how does that work, when you're in bed with another woman? You're thinking, 'I love my fiancée so much, even though I've never slept with *her*.'" I crossed my arms over my chest and stared at him. "Please, tell me how that works, Ryan." My voice was cold and clipped.

"Kels, I'm—I'm so sorry. I know we said we would wait. I just—"

"You said that it would make our marriage more sacred, more meaningful."

"It still can be," he implored, his voice low and impassioned.

I wanted to scream, but after all, we were in public. "Are you kidding me, Ryan? You think I'm going to plan a wedding to you while you're *in a relationship* with Jenna? While she's carrying your child?" I was done here. I started to push my chair back.

He sat up straighter and reached out his hand again, and found nothing but air. "But that's just it, Kelsea. I—it happened *just that one time.* Then she put on my page that we were in a relationship. I took it down as soon as I saw it. It wasn't even up there for thirty minutes."

*Wow.* How serendipitous was it that Brandon happened to click on Ryan's page during that short window of time.

I crossed my arms in front of me. "But it's up on *her* page."

"That was all a big—plan on her part to make her boyfriend jealous. She never cared anything about me," Ryan spat. "We're *not* in a relationship. I don't know why she won't take it down. She put his name back up, and now it's back to mine, but I don't know why. She won't answer any of my calls or texts."

*Oh, poor, poor Ryan!* Cue the violins.

"Is the baby yours?"

He shook his head, looking more miserable. "I don't know. Right after we—right after Thanksgiving, he came running back to her, and then she turned up pregnant just after Christmas." He swallowed. "She doesn't know who the father is, but she says she has some of my DNA from when I was at her apartment, and she's going to have a paternity test done when the baby's born."

I didn't want to even contemplate what comprised the DNA sample.

"So if the child isn't yours, you're off the hook. And if it is, she'll stick you for half of all her medical bills, and child support for the next eighteen years."

He nodded, looking utterly miserable. He hung his head. "I know I don't deserve another chance, Kelsea."

"You're absolutely right, and you're not getting one, Ryan. You had *one job*. To be faithful to me. And you failed. I could never, *ever* trust you again."

"Kels—" his tortured eyes begged.

I was completely disgusted with him. I collected my jacket and stood. "Goodbye, Ryan. I kind of hope the baby is yours. Maybe parenthood will force you to grow up."

"Kelsea, wait. I—"

If he was going to beg again, I might lose my cocoa and blueberry muffin.

Ryan clambered to his feet. "Well, if you're not going to— could I—" He scratched his head. "Well, I was wondering, could I have my ring back?"

I stood there frozen, unable to move. "*Your* ring? It's *my* ring," I said in the iciest voice I could dredge up. No way was I telling him that I sold it.

"Well, I think there's a legal—law or something about that. And it would help, um, pay my mom back for some of the deposits—"

I wasn't listening to another word. "Don't ever try to contact me again, Ryan, or I *will* take legal action." I'd never hired an attorney and had no idea how I would afford one, but he didn't need to know that. I enunciated each word, turned my back to him, and walked away, holding my head high.

I spent the rest of the day running errands in an attempt to stay busy. Every time I thought about Ryan and his outrageous demand that I return the ring, I got steamed up all over again.

The next day, I went back to work. It was good to be back in my routine, and I almost had more work than I could handle. I was too busy to think about Ryan and what my life would have been now as a married woman.

We always have a January thaw in St. Louis, and a couple of days later, the temperature soared up to the high fifties. I knew it was a temporary reprieve, so I moved my schedule around so I could go to the dog park. I took Sheldon, Penny, and two client dogs with me, and was happy to see my friend Maggie there with Duke the Scottish terrier and Lucky the golden retriever.

We exchanged a hug. "How are you doing, Kelsea?" she asked, tucking her auburn hair under her cap as the temperate breeze played havoc with it. She was probably ten or twelve years older than me.

I shrugged. "I'm okay." I said. "Believe it or not, I went on our honeymoon, alone." I explained how I'd come to that decision, and a little bit about St. Jardin.

"Good for you, girl!" Maggie said, squeezing my arm. "I've heard that island is beautiful, but I never knew anyone who went there."

"It's unbelievably gorgeous," I said. "And it was so good to get away from winter. My mom thought I should use the time to figure out a Plan B, but I never really got around to it."

Maggie nodded. "Are you going to keep doing your pet business?"

"Definitely," I said. "I'm thankful I have a great place to live, and I get to work with animals. I almost have more business than I can handle, thanks to you."

She waved her hand. "Oh, I didn't do anything. Just sang your praises to a few friends. You're the one who earned your good reputation."

We chatted for another little while and watched the dogs frolic. "Let's walk," Maggie suggested. There was a beautiful paved trail next to a pond. We made one loop around, and as we were getting ready to go our separate ways, a stocky man with medium-brown hair approached us. "Is one of you Kelsea Anderson?" he asked pleasantly.

"That would be me," I said.

"The one with the pet business?"

Maggie and I exchanged a smile. A client was seeking me out! "Yes. Do you have a dog that needs walked or something?"

"Yeah, I might," he said, taking a piece of paper out of his pocket. "Could you just write your name and phone number on this?"

I scribbled the information down and handed it back to him. "Great," he said. Then he drew out an envelope and handed it to me. "Thanks, Kelsea Anderson, you've been served."

My jaw dropped, and Maggie and I stared at each other as the man turned and left without another word. "What was that all about?" she exclaimed.

"I have a bad feeling about this," I muttered, tearing the envelope open. It was worse than I feared. "Ryan is suing me for the engagement ring, or its fully appraised value in cash, and—" I gasped. "I don't believe it." I thrust the papers at Maggie.

She gasped. "He's suing you for *half* the cost of everything associated with the wedding? He's the one who pulled out!"

"*And* the reception!" I stomped my foot furiously. I couldn't believe this. "That lying scumbag—you don't even know the whole story!" I felt tears pricking at my eyes.

"I've got time to listen if you want to talk."

I looked at my phone. "I'd love to, but I've got to get these guys back to their house." Tears threatened to spill.

Maggie patted my arm. "Why don't you come to my house after? I'd really like to help you figure this out, Kelsea."

I was so thankful for Maggie's friendship, and nodded. "That would be—nice, thank you. What was your address again?" It had been over a year since I'd looked after Duke and Lucky.

"We're on La Bonne Terrace, 169."

"I'll take these dogs home, and then drop Sheldon and Penny at my apartment."

"Great, see you soon." She gave me a hug.

"Thanks so much, Maggie."


The first time I came to Maggie's house, I was surprised to discover that she lived right across the street from *The Victorian*. That's what I called it, anyway, a gorgeous home that sat on an acre of land. There were other beautiful homes in this eclectic neighborhood, but The Victorian outshone them all. It became my dream home from the moment I saw it when I'd first moved to Kirkwood and started taking Sheldon and Penny on walks.

I rang Maggie's doorbell and she answered almost immediately. "Come in, come in," she said. "I'm so glad you came. I just made tea. Would you like some?" She took my coat and hung it on the coat tree. I followed her into a cozy breakfast nook just off the kitchen, where I could smell bread baking.

"You live across the street from *The Victorian*," I commented as we sat and fixed our tea. "That's what I call it. That's my dream house."

Maggie smiled. "Have you ever been inside?"

I nodded. "Yes, about two years ago when it was for sale. I went to one of the open house events. I couldn't resist."

"That's when I went inside it, too, when we were looking at houses." Maggie and I spent several minutes talking about all the things we both loved about the house.

"Did you consider buying it?" I asked.

Maggie shook her head. "Melissa was already off to college by then, and Mike and I knew that it was too much house and yard for just the two of us. This one was perfect for us."

I looked around the warm room. "It's beautiful," I said. "I still have every square foot of the Victorian memorized." Maggie laughed. "I always told Ryan that he could buy that house for me for our tenth anniversary. I figured we would have a couple of children by then and would need the space." To my surprise, a deep sense of melancholy washed over me.

Maggie took a sip of her tea. "So, tell me the rest of the story about Ryan, if it will help."

I dove in, and didn't leave out any details. She was aghast, and repeatedly assured me that as painful as it was, that I was better off without him, and I knew she was right. My heart was completely over the louse.

"But now, this lawsuit," I said. I put my head in my hands. "I have no idea what I'm going to do about it. The court date is in a little over a week, on my birthday." *Brandon's birthday.* I tried to push that thought out of my mind.

"Oh, no! That's adding insult to injury!" Maggie exclaimed.

"I suppose I should hire a lawyer," I said, "but I have no idea how to go about that. And the timing is terrible. I haven't had time to replenish my savings after paying for the honeymoon. I don't know what I'm going to do."

"Listen," Maggie said. "My husband is an attorney. He specializes in corporate law, so he doesn't work directly with things like this, but maybe he'll have some ideas." She looked at the clock. "Oh, it's almost six."

I pushed my chair back. "I'm sorry, I didn't realize it was so late. I'll be going now."

Maggie put her hand on my arm. "Kelsea, no, that's not what I meant. Mike will be home soon. Please stay and have dinner with us, and we can tell him all about this and maybe he can think of a solution."

"Are you sure?" I asked.

Maggie stood and went to the stove. "Absolutely. We're just having soup and bread tonight."

I followed her, and leaned against the island. "The bread smells delicious."

We kept chatting, and before long, a man came through the door from the garage. He was in his late forties, balding, with glasses and an engaging smile. Maggie greeted him and made the introductions. "This is Kelsea Anderson. My husband, Mike Porter. Kelsea's staying for dinner."

"That's great," he said. I liked Mike right away. "I'm happy to meet you, Kelsea," he said with a warm smile.

We all chatted while I helped Maggie get dinner on the table in the little nook, and we held hands. Mike prayed, thanking God for His provision, for the food, and for the privilege of having their friend Kelsea in their home. I realized that I couldn't remember the last time anyone had thanked God for me, and a peaceful feeling settled over me.

We made small talk for a while, chatted about dogs and the neighborhood and my business. The soup and bread were amazing—I told Maggie she should open a restaurant! And then she told Mike about my dilemma—leaving out the dramatic parts—and encouraged me to talk, which I did.

When I finally got to the part about the lawsuit, Mike asked some thoughtful questions. "The ring could go either way," he said, "depending on who he hires to represent him. I think you've got the advantage on the costs for the wedding and reception, if you didn't have a hand in actually making those arrangements."

"I didn't," I insisted. "His mother chose everything and managed all the details. She even set the date."

Maggie had gotten up and was dishing up ice cream at the island. She rolled her eyes. "She sounds like a nightmare."

Mike rocked his hand back and forth in so-so motion. "The problem is, you'll get mired down in a "he said/she said" scenario. He could say that his mother made the arrangements, but *you* were the one who chose everything, and insisted on everything, so you should be responsible for half the cost."

"Even though *he* was the one who called off the wedding?"

"That doesn't seem fair," Maggie murmured. She set down bowls of ice cream for everyone.

Mike patted her hand. "Honey, you know the law isn't always about what's fair." He looked at me. "It depends on whether or not there's some dirt there, and if you want to find it. About the reason he backed out."

Maggie and I exchanged a look. I didn't know if I wanted to go down that road, or even if there was enough of a road to go down. "How does that work?" I asked Mike.

"Well, you hire a defense attorney, who hires a private investigator to dig into what Ryan's been up to for the last six months or so—or you could hire a PI on your own."

I felt hopeless. "The real problem is, I don't really have any money saved to hire either one." I asked Mike a ballpark idea of what a defense attorney might cost, and almost fell out of my chair at the figure he quoted. I had been thinking of *maybe* asking my mom for a loan, but it was completely out of the question.

"The other option you have is the Public Defender's Office." He explained how that would work, and I saw a dim glimmer of hope. I didn't really have another option. "When's your trial date?"

"January 28."

He grimaced. "That's coming up quickly. They didn't give you much time. Probably part of their strategy. You don't know who he hired to represent him?"

"No idea. If his mother's behind it, probably a big, tough law firm."

Mike pulled a pen and a business card from his shirt pocket. "I know a guy over at the PD's office." He scribbled on the back of it and handed it to me. "Here's my card. Ask for him and tell him I referred you. I can't guarantee anything, but maybe it will help. And if you run into a wall, call me and I'll see if there's anything else I can do."

I thanked him sincerely, and asked Maggie if I could help her clean up.

She gave me a hug. "Absolutely not. This will take five minutes to get in the dishwasher." They walked me to the front door.

"Thank you so much," I said. They told me to keep them updated, and to stop by any time. I felt warmed by their friendship and the simple home cooked meal that they'd shared with me. I should really learn to cook real food, but when you live alone, it's hardly worth the trouble, and then you have all those leftovers.

Maggie stepped out onto the porch with me, and looked around in the darkness. "Where's your car? Did you walk?"

"I did," I said. "The weather was so nice today."

"Oh, let Mike run you home, Kelsea."

"No, absolutely not. Really, Maggie, I want to walk. I have some thinking to do."

"Do you have your mace?"

I grinned and held up my key ring. "Right here."

"Okay then, that makes me feel better. I'm so glad you came." She waved goodbye and I headed down the walk.

*The Victorian* was right in front of me, beautifully lit up. It looked utterly peaceful and so perfect. I stopped at the end of the sidewalk and stared at it. This was a home for a family, and I imagined a loving mom and dad inside with their children. They had probably just finished dinner. They would be helping the kids with their homework in the great room with the fireplace, or maybe playing a game together before baths and story time and then bedtime.

A tear trickled down one cheek. Earlier today, living in a studio apartment with Sheldon and Penny and walking dogs had seemed like enough. Suddenly, my life felt very empty.

# 34

LANDON FINALLY GOT the last of the boxes out to the curb. He was relieved to be done with moving. Hopefully, this would be it for a while.

When he'd arrived back from St. Jardin, his condo no longer held any appeal for him. It was right downtown, too noisy, and reminded him of Nicola. He swore her scent still lingered.

He contacted a realtor and put it on the market, fully furnished. A sale was already pending. He ended up finding a great starter home in a suburb just west of Kirkwood. Landon wanted to be closer to Kelsea and intended to make her a much bigger part of his life. He'd thought about looking right in Kirkwood, but didn't want to chance running into her yet, especially if she decided not to make a future with him. The house was a good investment and he could fix it up and flip it if necessary. *Stop thinking that way.*

Landon paused for a few moments to look at the front of his house. It was a foreclosure, which was why he was able to close on it so quickly and move in. Once spring arrived, he couldn't wait to get busy in the yard. There was a lot of work to do, and he hoped Kelsea would be by his side.

He still didn't know how or when he was going to contact

her, but an idea had occurred to him just last night. Landon wanted to think and pray about it before making a decision.

Just as he walked into the kitchen, his cell vibrated on the counter. It was his brother. "Hey, man," he answered.

"Hey, man," Brandon echoed. Landon felt a twinge of discomfort. He hadn't shared yet that he'd "borrowed" his brother's name when he was on St. Jardin, and wasn't sure if he ever would. "What's shakin'?"

"Not much. I was just thinking about you, and thought I'd give a call. How's the new house?"

"It's good. Feels good to be out of that condo. Too many memories."

"Yeah, she decorated it and all, didn't she?"

"Um-hmm." Landon started sorting piles of clothes to put in the dresser drawers.

"When you have a big break-up like that, sometimes it's good to just start over again with a clean slate."

Landon chuckled. "Like you'd know?" Brandon had married his high school sweetheart, Darla.

"Well, that's what I've heard," Brandon replied with a laugh. "How's my niece?"

"She's great." Landon could hear the deep pride in his brother's voice. "I love being a dad. Can't wait for our second daughter to get here." Darla was about seven months along now.

"You guys are gonna have your hands full," Landon said.

"I know, but it's okay. We got started late." Brandon and Darla were both doctors and had waited to start a family until they'd gotten through med school and residency.

Landon smiled. "I'm happy for you, bro."

"Mom would be happy if you gave her some grandchildren, too," Brandon said.

"Yeah, I'm sure, but she's going to have to wait now." Their older sister, Reagan, was completely career-focused and had no interest in a husband or children, and their younger sister, Sara, was in college and trying to figure out what she wanted out of life.

"And one of us needs to make sure the St. Clair name will go on." Landon snorted. "That's your department, bro."

Brandon laughed. "We'll see. So, anyone on your radar?"

"What do you think?" Landon retorted. He was certain that his father wouldn't have broken his confidence. His brother wouldn't believe it if he said that he'd already fallen in love and picked out his next bride, and after the debacle with Nicola, Landon didn't think he'd let a word slip to a soul until the marriage was legal. But how would that work, to give Kelsea the wedding she deserved with no one in attendance? *Slow down, man. Take it one step at a time. She's not even speaking to you.*

"Hey! Bro, you still there?"

"Sorry," Landon squeezed the bridge of his nose. "I was just looking at something in the backyard."

"Well, I'll let you go. I just wanted to check up on you. Come for a visit when you can." Brandon and Darla lived in Minnesota, where it was winter for at least six months of the year.

"Yeah, maybe in the summer," Landon replied.

"And don't hesitate to call if you need to talk, anytime," Brandon said.

Landon laughed. "When? You work a hundred hours a week."

"Not so much anymore," Brandon protested. "I'm down to eighty. Love ya, man."

"Love ya, man."

Landon had a great family and was very fortunate for their support at this time in his life. He couldn't wait for Kelsea to meet them. He stuffed his phone into his pocket and went to tackle the bedroom that was going to be his office. Soon, he had his desk organized and fired up his laptop. It had been a couple of days since he'd checked his personal e-mail.

*Aww...look at that!* Landon chuckled and opened the e-mail, and his entire world shifted on its axis.

# 35

MY PHONE WOKE me up at 6:30, and for a moment, I was disoriented. For the third time this week, I had dreamed of walking hand-in-hand with Brandon along the sea shore. And this time, he was just about to kiss me.

I looked at my phone. *Mom.* This was my birthday call. It was the last thing I felt like celebrating, but she had no idea about the lawsuit, and I had no intention of bringing it up. Depending on the outcome, I might never have to.

I've always thought that someone's birthday should be as much about their parents as about them. After all, it was one of the most joyful days of their life. With every passing year, I missed my dad more and more. And even though my mother annoyed me to no end at times, I loved her, and was truly thankful for her.

I took a breath. "Hi, Mom," I said cheerily.

"Happy Birthday, Kelsea Denise!" she cried. "I can't believe my baby girl is thirty!"

I winced. "Me neither," I said. "It sounds so old." *Especially when you're a spinster with no prospects.*

"Then what does that make me?" Mom lamented. We chatted for a while, and she wrapped up the call saying that she had sent me a check "to buy yourself a little something special." She didn't mention anything about my present circumstances, and I appreciated that.

After I hung up, I grabbed my coat and slippers to take the dogs out. Our January thaw was completely over. We'd gotten snow over the past two days, and the overnight temps were back in the single digits.

When I opened the back door, I almost tripped over something. A cardboard box? I couldn't imagine who had left that. It was long and narrow, but not too heavy. There were no markings on it.

I stuck it inside and hurried down the stairs with Sheldon and Penny to do their business. When we got back inside, I tossed off my coat and carried the box to the table and opened it. Inside was a Styrofoam container. I pulled it open and was shocked to see two dozen beautiful red and white roses.

I picked them up and inhaled their scent. *Oh, heavenly. These didn't come from the grocery store.* I searched for a card, and finally saw it. If they weren't from Mom, they were probably from Morgan. But how did it get delivered, and by whom? I looked carefully at the outer box again, but there were no markings on it.

I opened the card, and the blood rushed to my head. The neat, block printing swam before my eyes. *Happy Birthday, Kelsea. You know who this is. I've thought of no one and nothing but you since we left St. Jardin. I know it seems impossible, and it doesn't make sense, but I knew even before we went to the Queen's Garden that I had fallen in love with you. I know I made a lot of mistakes, the worst one being that I lied to you about my name, and never told you anything about myself. I had my reasons, and had every intention of doing that on our last night there, but we both know that didn't happen.*

My heart pounded, and I began to cry. *Lied to you about my name?* This was impossible. It seemed that I could only fall for men who were allergic to the truth. I read on. *Will you meet me tonight at 7pm at Union Station, at the entrance to the indoor lake? I promise to tell you everything then—everything about me. You can ask any questions you want, and I'll answer them. Please, wear the beautiful green dress that you wore the first night we met at the resort. I hope this is the first of many birthdays together. I love you. Please, come tonight.*

My eyes roamed over the page again, but kept going back to two phrases, *I had fallen in love with you,* and *I love you.*

I closed my eyes and thought about our kiss on St. Jardin. I'd relived it hundreds of times over the last three weeks. I missed Brandon—or whoever he was—so much.

I dried my tears and jumped up. I couldn't think about this right now. I had dogs to walk and two houses to check on, fish to feed (not to mention cleaning the aquarium), a cat to take to the groomer's, and then the blasted court case at two o'clock. So much was riding on it. Maggie was coming over at noon to do my makeup. If I couldn't be confident about the case or my defense, at least I would be dressed for success.

I fingered the card again. I couldn't seem to let go of it. How did he get the roses here? Of course he knew my name, so he could find out where I lived. But did he deliver them himself, or have someone do it for him? If he was hoping to meet me tonight, he must be in town, or on his way. This was crazy. I had no idea who he was, or where he lived, or what he did for a living.

Could I commit myself to a man that I knew so little about? And was I ready to trust someone again? I tucked the card into my purse. I couldn't think about this now.

**36**

"HAPPY BIRTHDAY, BOSS." Landon's executive assistant, Pam, greeted him when he arrived at the office. "There's bagels and pastries in the break room."

"Thanks, Pam," he replied with a smile. She was his right arm and always honored Landon's wish not to make a big deal about his birthday.

He'd felt like a cat burglar when he snuck up the back stairs to Kelsea's apartment at o'dark hundred and left the box for her. He was worried about alerting her dogs. If Sheldon or Penny had started barking, he had no idea what he would have done.

Thankfully, his schedule for today was jam packed. He had about twelve hours until he would know whether Kelsea was willing to move forward with him. But he had a lot to do before then, and settled into his large, leather chair to begin the workday. He had two meetings and a conference call, and managed to power through the morning, which helped pass the time. He ate a salad for lunch at his desk and started working on a brief that was due next week.

Landon looked at his watch and sighed. It was three minutes later than the last time he had checked. He rubbed a hand over his face. *Tonight, I'll see her. I've missed her so much. Please, God, let her come. Let her heart soften so that we have a chance at happiness. I love her more than I ever thought possible.*

He had to get this brief done, but his mind wasn't on it. It kept straying to ways that he could get through to Kelsea if she didn't show. Had she liked the roses? He could buy her a hundred dozen more. Maybe he would take them right to her apartment and refuse to leave until he could get through to her.

Landon got up from his desk and walked over to where he'd hung up his brand new suit jacket. He'd never spent so much on a suit, but tonight would be the most important night of his life, the first of many birthdays that he hoped with all his heart that he and Kelsea would celebrate together.

Landon slipped his hand into the inner pocket and drew out their tri-gold wedding bands, and a 1.75-karat solitaire diamond in a rose gold setting. The brilliant, flawless stone sparkled in the early afternoon sun. Landon intended for it to blind every man who came within a mile of his woman.

The phone on his desk rang, and he quickly returned the rings and reached for the receiver. "Landon St. Clair."

It was the top second-year associate on his team, Sean Busch. "Landon, it's Sean." He sounded out of breath. "Olivia's water just broke. Her mother is driving her to the hospital. I'm in the car, on my way to meet them."

Landon thought the couple's first baby wasn't due for a while yet, and Sean's next words confirmed his fears. "She's only at thirty three weeks," he said, his voice cracking. "I'm due in court at two o'clock, but I have to go."

"Of course you do, Sean, don't worry about it. Are you sure you're okay?"

"I sure could use some prayers right about now."

"You got it. And I'll take your case. Where's the file?"

"On my desk. I'm working on three cases right now. This one is Singer vs. Anderson. We're representing the plaintiff, Ryan Singer."

139

# 37

I WAITED OUTSIDE the courtroom for my attorney. I didn't have a clue what to expect. I just knew it would be someone from the Public Defender's office, whoever had been assigned to my case. I was thankful that Mike had referred me, but I wondered if I should have taken out a loan or figured out a way to hire a better lawyer. Oh well, it was too late now.

I wore a black pencil skirt, black-and-white polka dot pumps with a sweet white bow on top, and a red cashmere sweater over a white shell. I'd spent more than I should have last night to have my hair trimmed and styled. It fell past my shoulders in shiny, perfect layers, and Maggie's magic with a makeup brush had produced phenomenal results. I looked good and I knew it.

"Ms. Anderson?" a male voice cracked on the last syllable. I looked up to see a painfully skinny thirteen-year-old dressed for his first dance, right down to his slicked-back hair. Actually, I feared that this was my attorney. My heart dropped to my feet. This was probably his first case.

I stood, looming over him in my heels. I stuck out my hand, and he pumped it with his clammy one. "I'm Anson Greene," he said. "Your lawyer."

I wanted to ask him if his mother had dropped him off at the courthouse, but instead, dredged up a smile. "Pleased to meet you, Mr. Greene."

He laughed nervously. "Oh, no one has ever called me that. You can call me Anson." He just stood there.

I looked around, then glanced at the clock, which read 1:54. "Should we go in?" I asked.

Anson Greene looked startled. "Sure! I mean, yes, we should. Go in." He rushed over to the door, and we did an awkward shuffle as he stepped in front of me, opened it, and gestured for me to enter.

This was it. I was about to go to battle with Ryan. Rose's voice played in my head. *You're one of the strong ones.*

I threw my shoulders back and stood tall and proud. My mind went back to the days when Morgan and I would spend rainy afternoons practicing walking like queens with a book on our heads. I sailed down the main aisle of the courtroom as if it were Westminster Abbey, with my page—er, lawyer—trailing along behind me.

Suddenly, I realized that I didn't have a clue where to go. I called on my expertise, formed by many years of watching TV courtroom dramas, and decided that we would be on the left side of the courtroom, the judge's right.

I was so proud of myself for figuring this out that I didn't see Ryan approach. He inserted himself between Mr. Greene and me and tugged on my arm.

"Kelsea, can we talk?" he whispered.

I looked down at his hand, and back at his face. "Remove your hand, now." I said in a cold voice. "I have nothing to say to you, now or ever."

"Kelsea, please. It was my mom. It was all my mom."

"Your mother got Jenna pregnant? I'd love to have seen that."

Ryan's face twisted and he closed his eyes. "No, of course not. I told you, that was—a huge mistake. And one way or another, I'll be paying for it the rest of my life."

"Yeah, some actions have long-term consequences, Ryan. Goodbye."

He held fast to my arm. "Kelsea, this lawsuit was all my mom's idea—"

"Mr. Singer! Unhand my client at once!" Anson Greene shouted. His face was...well, I never understood what the color *puce* was until now. Ryan jumped back, startled.

I ignored the murmurs rippling through the courtroom and resumed my regal walk to our table. *Who are these commoners, anyway, and why do they care about this case?* I sat down, crossed my ankles in what I hoped was the picture of demureness, set my purse on the table, and folded my hands in my lap. The epitome of calm. I turned to my lawyer, who was a hot mess, and dipped my chin. "Thank you, Mr. Greene," I murmured. Maybe there was some steel in him, after all.

On the inside, I seethed. Of all the—how could I have not seen how much of a mama's boy Ryan was? I suppose I'd been blinded by love, to the point I didn't see through Jasmine Singer's controlling machinations. I thought she was just being generous and kind to manage all the details. I fell for it hook, line, and sinker.

I couldn't wait for this to be over. I rubbed some peppermint oil on my pounding temples and spread another drop inside my mouth to freshen my breath. I still had to decide whether or not to meet what's-his-name tonight. Part of me wanted to, but part of me was still so confused and scared. I just needed to get through this afternoon, and then I could make a final decision.

"All rise," the bailiff intoned. "Call to order the Court of the City of St. Louis. The Honorable Lawrence D. Williamson presiding."

After we sat, Anson Greene splashed water into a plastic cup and took a gulp. His face had faded to tomato red. "Want some?"

"No, thank you." The judge was looking through some papers and seemed to be waiting for something. "Who's the plaintiff's attorney?" I whispered.

Anson opened his briefcase, which was full of papers. He started pulling them out haphazardly, and several fluttered to the floor. He gathered them up, rifled through them, and frowned.

"Jacoby, James, and something, I think," he said. Then he held up a sheet of paper. "Ah! Here it is." I took the paper from him.

*Jacoby, Jamison & St. Clair.* I nearly groaned out loud. Anson Greene must not be from the area. JJS was the very best law firm in St. Louis, a legal powerhouse with an astonishingly high success rate. That's all. Of course Jasmine Singer would have hired them. What was I doing, sitting here with Beaver Cleaver? This was a David vs. Goliath match-up if there ever was one.

The legalese swam before my eyes. None of it made a lick of sense. I glanced at my attorney, who was already sweating. I was doomed. JJS was a huge firm with lots of resources, even though I was sure this little case would go to one of their junior associates. I scanned the partners' names at the top of the letterhead. *Jeffrey M. Jacoby. Paul R. Jamison. Landon P. St. Clair.*

Something sounded familiar about one of those names. I read them again. Hmm…Landon St. Clair. Why did that ring a bell?

*Brandon St. Fair.*

No. It couldn't be.

The judge looked at the clock. "Mr. Singer, it's now 2:05. I don't know where your attorney is, but we can't wait any longer. We'll have to reschedule." I had refused to look at Ryan and was surprised to see him sitting alone at the plaintiff's table.

"But Your Honor—" Ryan sputtered.

I heard the door in the rear of the courtroom open, and strong, resolute footsteps echoed on the tile floor.

"Landon St. Clair, JJS, for the defense, Your Honor. I apologize for being late."

*That voice.* I would know it anywhere. That voice had lived in my head and filled my dreams since I had left St. Jardin. That voice had moved me to joyous laughter and to tears of frustration.

143

That voice had shouted at me in exasperation and whispered sweetly in my ear. My heart went into wild palpitations.

Brandon St. Fair was really Landon St. Clair? He was the S in JJS? He lived and worked in St. Louis? My head was spinning. Anson Greene looked like the proverbial deer in the headlights.

Ryan was incredulous. "What do you mean, for the defense? I don't know who you are, or where my attorney is, but JJS is representing me!" he shouted. Then my brain caught up with reality. The tall, outrageously handsome attorney had stated he was *for the defense.*

"Actually, we're not." He strode confidently through the bar and approached the bench, addressing the judge in a loud, clear voice. "Mr. Singer is no longer our client. I'm here to represent the defendant."

I waited for my lawyer to do something. But he just sat there, his mouth opening and closing like a fish.

I almost stood to object. *Can the defendant do that?* I didn't have a prayer of being able to afford an attorney from JJS, let alone a partner. He probably made more in an hour than I made in two weeks.

"You can't do that!" Jasmine Singer screamed as she shot to her feet just behind Ryan. Her Botox-infused face twisted into one big grimace.

"Sit down, Mrs. Singer," Judge Williamson ordered.

"Yes, I can." Landon St. Clair said calmly. He handed a thin, tidy sheaf of papers to the judge. "It's summarized in this brief, Your Honor. There's precedence for extenuating circumstances."

Judge Williamson perused the papers and frowned. "I understand the allowance due to extenuating circumstances, but this is highly unusual, Counselor. Why would you change your representation from the plaintiff to the defendant?"

For the first time since entering the room, the man I knew as Brandon made direct eye contact with me. No more baboon, no more gopher, no more dweeb. He was the most handsome man I had ever seen in my life. Tall and tan, broad and blond in an impeccably tailored charcoal gray suit, he looked every inch the successful, respectable lawyer, but his eyes were sending me a different message.

One side of his mouth tipped up. "Because I'm head over heels in love with the defendant," he announced.

"And because she's my wife."

The courtroom erupted. I heard a cacophony of shouting and the judge's gavel banging repeatedly, but I only had eyes for—Landon. I don't remember getting to my feet, but by the time he had walked over to our table, I was standing next to Anson Greene.

"Thanks, Counselor, I'll take it from here," Landon murmured, towering over Anson and shaking his hand. The young man's head bobbed up and down. He stuffed his papers into his briefcase and raced out of the courtroom without a word.

Landon took his place beside me. When his arm brushed against mine, an electric current shot clear down to my toes.

I looked up at him. "We're married?" I managed to croak out.

He nodded. "The ceremony at the Queen's Garden was legal." His eyes crinkled with amusement. "You really should check your e-mail more often, Kelsea."

My legs suddenly turned to spaghetti, and I collapsed into my chair. I grabbed my phone and pulled up my e-mail. There! That had to be it. *PinkLady@StJardinResort.com.*

*Yoo hoo, Kelsea and Landon! (I hope you've come clean about your identity, young man. If you haven't, now would be a good time.) Imagine our shock when we were notified by the St. Jardin Historical Society about a change that went into effect on January 1. Because of new protocols outlined in the trade agreement between St. Jardin and the United States, any rituals conducted on our soil—ceremonial or otherwise—are legal and binding in both countries. The marriage ritual in which you participated is as if it took place in the US. You're legally married!*

*Now, I know you may be panicking right now, dear Kelsea, but don't you see? This is your Plan B! We know that Landon is crazy about you, and if you'll be honest with yourself, you'll admit that you feel the same way, too. Give him a chance. He'll show you, in more ways than you can count, how deeply he loves you.*

*I knew the moment I met both of you that you were meant to be together. Did I tell you that when we lived in Brooklyn, I had a bit of success as a matchmaker?*

*Ike says to come back to St. Jardin for a real honeymoon! It'll be on us! Love, Rosie*

My mind floated back to the present to hear Landon addressing the judge.

"Your Honor, request a recess to confer with my client."

"Fifteen minutes, Mr. St. Clair." The gavel sounded.

Landon lifted me to my feet and propelled me through a side door into to a small conference room. The moment the door closed behind us, he dropped his briefcase and pulled me into his arms.

And kissed me the way I'd been dreaming of for almost three weeks.

Our kiss on St. Jardin was amazing, but this one was a thousand times better. He wasn't holding anything back this time, and neither was I.

When we finally came apart, he held me close and we just stood there, breathing heavily and rocking back and forth. "Mmm...you taste incredible," he murmured.

*Thank you, Lord, for peppermint essential oil.*

Landon kissed my forehead and moved his large, smooth hands to bracket my face. He lifted his head just enough to smile into my eyes.

"Happy Birthday, Kelsea."

"Happy Birthday...Landon." I loved saying his name. I had a feeling this was going to be the best birthday ever, the first of many together.

"I didn't think I'd see you till tonight, but since we're here now, I have a question to ask you."

My heart thudded. *He was going to propose!* I held my breath and swallowed a squeal.

"Will you... sleep with me now?" His smile filled his entire face, and his beautiful amber eyes danced.

I burst out laughing, and he joined me.

I smoothed my hands over his lapels and tried to calm my thundering heart. "Well, if we're married..."

"We absolutely are. I double-checked."

"Then, of course," I whispered, and he kissed me again. I looked deeply into his eyes. "I love you, Landon," I said for the first time. I whispered his name as I trailed kisses along his jawline, his cheeks, even the bump on his nose and the cleft in his chin. "I love your name. You never seemed like a Brandon to me."

He locked his hands behind my back, and I slid mine up to his broad shoulders. He looked at me sheepishly. "Well, just don't ever slip and call me that, especially around my family."

Understanding dawned. "You mean—? Your brother?"

"Yeah." He laughed and shook his head. "I don't know what got into me when I came up with that."

"I'm very glad that you're Landon," I murmured.

"So am I." His lips devoured mine in a kiss that completely curled my toes. Then he took a step back and gazed at me, his expression solemn. "I will never, ever lie to you again. Not outright, or by omission, for any reason. You have my word on that. I love you to the bottom of my soul, Kelsea."

I couldn't even speak, I was so overcome. I nodded.

His eyes searched mine. "Do you want a wedding? A real one? You never got a wedding. We could do it next fall."

*He remembered.* I swallowed past the lump in my throat.

"You'd go through that again? You'd stand up in front of five hundred guests for me?"

He didn't hesitate. "I'd stand up in front of five *thousand* guests for you. Because I know without a doubt that you would come through that door. You wouldn't leave me standing at the altar."

*Rose was right. That's how much he loves me.* I swallowed. "You're right. I absolutely would come through that door. But I don't want another wedding, Landon. The one at the Queen's Garden was perfect, and it's all I want. You're all I want."

"In that case, I have another question for you," he said, his gaze steady.

Without breaking eye contact, he dropped to one knee. I wanted to memorize this moment forever.

"Kelsea Denise St. Clair." He smiled, and my soul sang at the sound of my new name. "Will you stay married to me?"

*I can't resist.* "We'll fight, you know. I'm full of sass."

"We will." He squeezed my hands. "And then we'll make up." His voice had gone husky.

My heart exploded with joy. "Yes, yes, yes! Of course I'll stay married to you."

Just when I thought things couldn't get any better, he stood, reached into his pocket and pulled out my tri-gold wedding band, along with a stunning diamond solitaire. "Oh, Landon," I breathed. He lifted my hand, slipped the rings on, and kissed them.

His gorgeous amber eyes melted into mine. "With this ring, I thee wed," he whispered.

I had noticed in the courtroom that he wore his ring. I kissed it and whispered the same timeless, sacred words.

Landon pulled me close. "Now, Mrs. St. Clair, we're going to go back in that courtroom, and you're going to watch your husband mop the floor with the plaintiff."

*Mrs. St. Clair. My husband.* I might die from happiness. "Can I afford you?" I giggled.

"Probably not, but we'll think of a way that you can pay me," he said in a completely sexy way. *Oh, my.*

As I lifted my lips for another delicious kiss, a loud rap came at the door, and we sprang apart like two teenagers caught necking.

The bailiff stuck his head in. "Time's up."

Landon picked up his briefcase and flashed me a devastating smile. "To be continued. Let's get this over with so we can start the honeymoon."

# 38

IF LANDON DIDN'T see for himself that the soles of his shoes were hitting the floor, he would have sworn that he was walking on air. All the doubts about his and Kelsea's relationship were settled. *She loves me and wants to be my wife!* He felt like he could take off and fly around the courtroom.

Landon was completely in his element, and the stars had aligned. He shuddered to think what might have happened had Olivia Busch not gone into labor. Sean was a good lawyer, and he would be here right now pleading Ryan's case. But he wouldn't have had any of the information that Landon was about to reveal, and with Kelsea's fate in the hands of the bumbling public defender, the case would likely have gone Ryan's way.

Landon never would have known, until after the fact, that his own firm had represented the man who had already broken Kelsea's heart and was on a self-serving mission to inflict more pain. She would have been completely devastated, and who knows if she even would have come to meet Landon tonight?

Despite all that, Sean and Olivia's situation weighed heavily on Landon's heart. He sat down next to Kelsea at the defendant's table, took her hand, and leaned in to whisper, "Say a prayer for my colleague, Sean. He's at the hospital with his wife. She's in premature labor. I'll tell you more, later."

"Of course," Kelsea whispered back, and gave his hand a squeeze.

"All rise," the bailiff announced. "Call to order the Court of the City of St. Louis. The Honorable Lawrence D. Williamson presiding."

Judge Williamson sat down and put on his glasses. "Hello again, everyone. First order of business." He looked in the direction of the plaintiff's table. "Mr. Singer, it appears that you are without counsel. If you wish to retain another firm, we will grant a seventy-two-hour continuance for you to make arrangements."

Ryan stood and cleared his throat. "Not necessary, Your Honor." He threw a smug smile toward the defendant's table and puffed out his skinny chest. "I will be representing myself."

Landon slid a glance at Kelsea and fought the laughter that bubbled in his throat. Among the many things he admired about Abraham Lincoln was his assertion that *he who represents himself has a fool for a client.*

Judge Williamson shook his head and mumbled something to himself. Maybe he was thinking of Lincoln, too. "All right then, Mr. Singer. Please proceed with your opening statement."

Landon stood. "Your Honor, I'd like to move for a dismissal."

Jasmine Singer shot to her feet. "Dismissal? Are you crazy?" she shouted.

Judge Williamson banged the gavel sharply and pointed it in her direction. "One more outburst from you, Mrs. Singer, and I will have you removed from my courtroom! Is that clear?"

The woman's face flushed bright red, and her lips settled into an angry line as she plopped down into her seat.

Landon continued. "The plaintiff is suing my client for the engagement ring or its estimated value in cash. Ms. Anderson asserts that Mr. Singer told her the ring was hers to keep. So it's a case of 'he said, she said.'

Landon strolled to the front of the courtroom, one hand in his pocket, and turned to face the gallery. "Mr. Singer has also requested that my client remit to him one half of the value of all the deposits that were lost when he canceled their wedding and reception, in the amount of $8,400. He claims that he and Ms. Anderson wanted a very small, simple wedding, but once his mother graciously offered to pay for everything, Ms. Anderson began expanding the scope of the event, contacted vendors directly without Mrs. Singer's knowledge, and drove up the costs."

Landon looked at Kelsea, and a look of disbelief washed over her face. He knew that this was the first she was hearing any of this, and did everything in his power to send her a message.

*Trust me.*

He continued, "Ms. Anderson maintains that she had nothing whatsoever to do with making the arrangements, that they were completely made and paid for by Mrs. Singer."

Landon shifted his gaze to Jasmine Singer and waited for her reaction. She crossed her arms in front of her and speared him with a hateful look, but kept quiet.

Landon walked back to his table and picked up a folder. "May I approach, Your Honor?"

Judge Williamson nodded. "Yes, Counselor."

Landon went through the bar and strode confidently to the bench. "We have signed statements from eight vendors that Jasmine Singer contracted with for various services to be provided for the wedding and reception. All of them are willing to testify that they did business only with Mrs. Singer, and not one of them ever had any contact, by phone, e-mail, or in person, with Ms. Anderson. Copies of the original orders, placed by Mrs. Singer, are also provided. In every case, the original amounts contracted for were never amended."

Landon clasped his hands behind his back and waited for the judge to look over the papers. Thanks to Sean's meticulous preparation, all the vendors' names and contact information had been listed, with the intent of bolstering Ryan's claims. All Landon's paralegal team had to do was call them this afternoon, and the truth quickly came out.

Judge Williamson took off his reading glasses and set them down. "What about the plaintiff's claim that the decision to cancel the wedding was mutual, and that there was no alienation of affection on his part?"

Landon handed another folder to the judge. "We have sworn affidavits from three of Mr. Singer's co-workers. In summary, they state that he was a notorious flirt in the office, and one of them is willing to testify that two weeks before Thanksgiving, she discovered Mr. Singer and a co-worker, Ms. Jenna Harmon, in a, shall we say, compromising position in a storeroom. We are also prepared to compel Ms. Harmon to appear as a witness to confirm documented posts on social media that she and Mr. Singer had a brief affair in late November, approximately one month before Mr. Singer and Ms. Anderson's engagement was called off."

Singer's face went white, and he jumped in his seat when his mother cuffed his shoulder from behind.

Landon had purposefully left out any reference to the pregnancy. That would be the ace in his sleeve if they ended up calling Jenna as a witness.

He couldn't stop thanking the fates that he'd trusted his instincts that first night on St. Jardin, when he'd looked on Ryan's social media page and asked his investigator to check into Jenna Harmon. With that information, his paralegal team had been able to quickly obtain the affidavits just this afternoon. Landon was already planning to give each of them a nice bonus.

Judge Williamson closed the folder and handed all the materials back to Landon. "I don't think there's any question that this is a frivolous lawsuit," he growled. "Mr. Singer, you're lucky that I'm still in the holiday spirit, and I'm not going to fine you for providing false information to your attorney. But if I ever see you in my courtroom again, all bets are off. Case dismissed." The gavel banged.

Judge Williamson stepped down from the bench, his robe billowing behind him. When he reached the door, he turned and raised his hand. "Mr. St. Clair?" he called out.

"Yes, Judge?"

"Congratulations to you and your bride."

# 39

LANDON CAME RIGHT to me and pulled me into his arms, and I looped my arms around his neck. "You were amazing!" I exclaimed. My heart skittered as his hands came around my waist.

"Larry Williamson is a fair judge. This may not be the most challenging case I've ever tried, but this victory is definitely the sweetest." His gorgeous amber eyes glittered and he pulled me a little closer. "Are you ready to get out of here, Mrs. St. Clair?"

"Definitely." I gave him a quick kiss, then stepped out of the circle of his arms and gathered my purse and coat while he packed his briefcase. He glanced over at the plaintiff's table and then back at me.

Landon lowered his voice. "Unless you want to wait until they're gone."

I looked around him. Ryan was slumped at the table with his head in his hands. His mother stood over him. I couldn't hear what she was saying, but it was obvious that she was spitting angry words at him.

"No way," I said with determination. "In fact, don't you need to tell Ryan when to expect your bill? That way, he can be on the lookout for it," I said innocently.

He grinned. "Remind me to stay off your bad side."

I took his arm, then switched to the other side. I looped my left hand through his elbow and wiggled my fingers. "This way they'll see my rings," I whispered.

Landon laughed softly and winked, and we set off. When we stopped in the aisle, Ryan looked up miserably, and Jasmine Singer glowered at me.

"I'll send you a bill," Landon announced. "It will include both my billable hours and Sean Busch's. Mine are at partner rate, of course. And you'll be responsible all court costs." He turned to me. "Ready to go, sweetheart?"

"More than ready, darling," I replied, and without a backward glance, I sailed back down the aisle of the courtroom on the arm of my hero, my Prince Charming, my husband.

The solid, wooden door of the courtroom closed behind us, completely shutting down that chapter of my life. I can't wait to see what God has in store for Landon and me.

He pulled me into a jubilant hug and smiled down at me. "You know what their problem is?"

I shook my head. "No, what?"

"They didn't have a Plan B."

# EPILOGUE

## *THREE YEARS LATER*

EVERY NEW YEAR'S Day, Landon and I send up an extra prayer of thanks that we both escaped what surely would have been disastrous marriages. About a year after Ryan's ridiculous case was dismissed, I heard through the grapevine that a DNA test proved that he was indeed the father of Jenna's son. I don't think either of them was ready to be a parent, and occasionally I send up a prayer for that little boy. And just a few months after that, we read in the society pages of the St. Louis *Post-Dispatch* that Nicola had married Giovanni Mancini, who had just been named manager at one of her father's luxury car dealerships.

After Landon's victory in court, we began a honeymoon that started at the Ritz Carlton and finished back on St. Jardin, where we participated once again in the ceremony at the Queen's Garden. It was the most romantic week of my life.

I asked Rose once if she and Ike knew about the change in legal status *before* the first ceremony—the one they kept insisting was just *a ritual,* and she acted as if she hadn't heard me, and changed the subject.

January is always a big month for Landon and me. The 2nd is the anniversary of the day we met, and the 8th is the anniversary of our wedding at the Queen's Garden. We always celebrate the anniversary of our engagement on the 28th, along with our birthdays. Not many couples can say that they were married for almost three weeks before they got engaged.

We go back to St. Jardin every year for our anniversary, and Rose and Ike are just the same—more in love every year, just like Landon and I are. We hope and pray for a marriage as long and as happy as theirs. Their friendship has become so very precious to us, and they're just like family.

But this year, there are two reasons that we can't go to St. Jardin, and that's okay. They're nestled together in their cradle in our bedroom. Rose Elizabeth and Isaac Anderson St. Clair arrived on January 4. Rose has my dark hair, and Isaac is a perfect little replica of Landon, right down to the cleft in his chin. Their photo and birth announcement will be in tomorrow's mail to the resort, where we've been assured a prime spot on the lobby bulletin board is ready and waiting.

Morgan, my mom, and Landon's parents have already been here and gone, and are the proudest grandparents and aunt on the planet.

Rose and Ike are coming in May to meet their namesakes, after any danger of snow and ice is long gone. After all those years of living in Brooklyn, they avoid winter at all costs. Our families are coming, too, and we're going to have the babies dedicated when everyone is here, at the little community church where Landon and I are members. I can't wait.

I heard the front door open, and my husband, the love of my life, the father of my children, met me in the front hallway. He grows more handsome with each passing year. There are still times when I can't believe that he's all mine.

"Hi! Are they awake?"

"Hi! Happy Birthday, Kelsea," I mocked. "I'm so glad I asked you to marry me three years ago today." I tried to peek around him to see what he was hiding. "If those are roses, you *might* be off the hook."

"I'm sorry," Landon said with an endearing grin. "I just love them so much. But I love you more." He produced a huge bouquet of gorgeous red and white roses, my favorites, and my heart melted at the sight of his smile.

"Thank you," I said, breathing in their delectable scent. "They're beautiful."

He laid them on the hall table and took me into his arms. I still have a long way to go to regain my flat stomach, but it was wonderful to be able to stand toe-to-toe with him again and pull one another close. "They're nowhere near as beautiful as you. Happy Birthday, my love." His gaze drifted downward and he nuzzled my neck. "Thirty-three looks amazing on you, babe."

I took his face in my hands. "Landon," I said, trying not to laugh, "It won't look so amazing in a few months. They'll deflate once I stop nursing the babies."

His eyes sparkled. "I'll still adore you," he whispered.

I sighed dreamily, running my hands over his broad shoulders and into the hair at the base of his neck. "Just for the record, thirty-four looks absolutely incredible on you. Happy Birthday, Landon." Then he treated me to one of his magic, toe-curling kisses, and I forgot about everything else for a few moments.

"Come here." Landon took my hand and led me into the living room. "I have another gift for you," he said. "And you probably need to be sitting down for it."

I couldn't imagine. I sat down on the sofa, and Landon lowered himself down next to me. He grinned, reached into his inside pocket, and laid a key in my hand. *A house key!*

"The house? We got the house?" I squealed. "Oh, Landon!" We had put in an offer just after the babies were born on a large, beautiful home about two miles from our present one, which we were rapidly outgrowing. It wasn't the Victorian, but sometimes, you have to go with your Plan B. And sometimes, it ends up being better.

"No, we didn't get the house. Not that one, anyway."

My heart plummeted, and I looked at him in confusion. "I don't understand."

"What would be better?"

There could only be one thing. I couldn't believe it. "The Victorian?" He nodded, and I squealed and threw myself into his arms. He knew that was the home of my heart. My mind was short-circuiting. "Landon, how? I can't—you—it wasn't even for sale!" I couldn't believe it. He'd bought me my dream house?

He laughed. "It *was* for sale, for the right price. Happy Birthday, my love. Happy engagement, happy anniversary, and happy arrival of our babies." I pulled his head down for a happy kiss.

I couldn't believe it! *The Victorian* would be our home. Landon and I would raise our children there, and Mike and Maggie would be our neighbors. "It all worked out," I bubbled. "My Plan A house went away, and then we found Plan B, and then you turned Plan A into Plan B. Or would that be Plan C? Plan B went away, and you turned Plan C back into Plan A, I think."

"Huh?" Landon's eyebrows knit together. He really should be used to this by now. "Kelsea, just kiss me."

And so I did.

ERIN
STEVENSON

St. Clair
Family
No. 2

Home to You

# 1

"DADDY, SHELBIE DROPPED her sippy!"

If April hadn't announced it so clearly, Shelbie's ear-piercing scream would have alerted Brandon St. Clair that something had gone very wrong in the back seat. He tried to make eye contact with his daughters in the rearview mirror, but could only see their shadowy outlines in the darkness.

"April, honey, we're almost to Uncle Landon's," he said. "Can you—" then he stopped himself. *You were about to ask a 4-year-old to climb out of her car seat to get her sister's sippy cup off the floor, while you're whizzing along the interstate at 65 miles an hour? What kind of lousy dad are you?*

Brandon switched the windshield wipers to *high* as the rain pelted down even harder. He could barely see, and it was pitch black. He consulted his phone in its dash holder, guiding him to his brother's house in suburban St. Louis. Thank God, they would be there in sixteen minutes. It was almost midnight.

He had fully intended to be there long before now, but everything that could go wrong at the hospital had gone wrong today. He'd had to cover for another doctor, and the surgical schedule was backed up. So much for Fridays being a lighter day.

By the time he'd picked up the girls from the sitter's, gotten them fed (with yet another fast-food meal), and arrived home to pack for the trip, they were already well behind schedule. Then Brandon realized he hadn't put the last load of the girls' laundry into the dryer last night, so he had to make a decision: delay their start by another hour, or take the damp clothes with them?

A trash bag filled with damp clothes rested next to their suitcases in the back.

A flash of lightning and simultaneous crash of thunder shook the vehicle, and Brandon tightened his grip on the wheel while easing his foot from the gas.

"Daddy, I'm scared!" April cried.

"I want Mommy!" Shelbie screamed.

*I want Mommy, too,* Brandon thought as he blinked back tears. *Oh God, why, why did you take her?*

# 2

MORGAN ANDERSON RESTED her chin on her hand and gazed at her sister. "Motherhood totally suits you," she said with a smile.

Kelsea St. Clair lifted her sleeping daughter up to her shoulder and rubbed her back. "It's the most exhausting thing I've ever been through, but I love every minute of it."

Her husband, Landon, entered the room. "I'm not so sure we love it at three in the morning," he quipped, with an affectionate squeeze of his wife's shoulder. He held out his arms. "You want me to take her?"

"Sure, thanks," Kelsea replied, and Morgan watched as they made the seamless transfer. She tried to ignore the way that her sister and Landon operated as one mind, one heart. Morgan swallowed, and turned her attention back to the baby.

"She's really out," she commented. Little Rose hadn't made a peep.

Kelsea yawned and looked up at her husband. "How's Isaac?"

"Fine. Hopefully he'll sleep a few hours before he needs to eat again."

Morgan was so proud of her sister. "You're really brave, nursing twins. But it's the best thing for them. Good for you."

Kelsea looked at Landon. "Have you heard from Brandon?"

"Yeah, they should be here in about fifteen minutes." He left the room with the baby.

Morgan glanced at her phone. "Oh, gosh, is it that late already?" She'd lost track of the time, as was usually the case when she and Kelsea got together. Morgan had driven down from Chicago and thankfully arrived before the spring storm.

She had never met Landon's brother, but knew about the tragic car accident that had taken his wife early last summer. "You know, it's kind of weird that I've never met Brandon," Morgan mused. "You and Landon have been together over three years now, and I've spent some holidays with you."

Kelsea put her chin in her hand. "Well, we really haven't seen him that much, either. When Darla was still alive, one of them was always on call, or she was pregnant with one of the girls or had just given birth, or something."

"So, what's the schedule for the weekend?" Morgan asked. "Or have you figured that out yet?" She stifled a laugh.

Kelsea feigned indignance. "Hey, I'm getting better! But I don't have a printed itinerary like you would," she teased. They both laughed. Kelsea was famous for flying by the seat of her pants. Morgan and their mom were the planners in the family.

"Mom will arrive sometime tomorrow afternoon," Kelsea said. "Landon and Brandon's parents will be here sometime then, too. We'll all go to the Spaghetti Factory for dinner tomorrow night, and then church on Sunday, and a barbeque back here."

"Don't forget the babies' dedication service," Morgan said.

"Of course! The whole reason you're all here," Kelsea said with a smile. "I *love* the outfits you got them to wear. They're just precious."

"Well, they're the most beautiful babies in the world, and I'm the proudest aunt ever!" Morgan had discovered that she absolutely loved shopping for baby clothes.

Kelsea reached over and squeezed Morgan's hand. "Thank

you." Her expression turned serious. "Be honest with me. Does it bother you at all—you know—"

"What? To see you being a mother? Kels, no! Not at all. I'm so happy for you and Landon. I adore the babies, and *love* being an aunt." Kelsea had been her rock when Morgan discovered that she would probably never be able to have children.

Silence settled itself over the two sisters like a warm blanket, and Morgan's heart began to quicken. *I guess this is as good a time as any.* "Kels, I, um—I need to tell you something." She took a deep breath. "I—oh wow, this harder than I thought it would be."

Worry settled over her sister's dark brown eyes. "Morgy, what's wrong? Are you sick again? Are you—"

Morgan shook her head adamantly. "Oh, no—I'm fine. I didn't mean to scare you. It's just—" she took another breath. "I've been thinking about maybe adopting a baby."

Kelsea's jaw dropped, and her eyes grew large. She grabbed Morgan's hand. "Oh, Morgy, that's fantastic!" Her eyes teared up.

"Yeah, well—" Morgan gave a nervous little laugh and tucked a strand of hair behind her ear. "It's such a big step, but I'm not getting any younger, and I'll probably never get married, and even if I do, I still can't—well, you know."

Kelsea squeezed her hand. "You don't know that, Morgan," she said softly. "But what got you thinking about this?"

Morgan wiped a wayward tear from her eye. "Well, you know I've been working with that arts program with preschoolers in Chicago," she said. Kelsea nodded. "There are so many children who need a loving home. A lot of the children in the program are orphans, and it just got me thinking. You and I are both big advocates for adoption." One of their best friends from high school was adopted, and they both knew other families who had adopted children.

Morgan shrugged. "Anyway, you know me and my planning." The two sisters laughed together. "So just pray for me, that God will make His will clear on this. It's a huge decision."

"I sure will," Kelsea said warmly.

Morgan chewed her lower lip. "And keep it to yourself for now, okay?"

"Of course."

"Now, back to this weekend," Morgan said, closing the door on that subject. "When do the guests of honor arrive? I can't wait to meet them."

Kelsea's eyes lit up. "Rosie and Ike's flight gets in at eleven-thirty tomorrow morning. I can't wait to see them. It's been more than a year." Rose and Ike Goldman owned a resort on a Caribbean island where Landon and Kelsea had met, and had become like family to the young couple. "I hope you're okay staying at Maggie and Mike's with them," she added, referring to hers and Landon's best friends who lived across the street.

"Of course," Morgan said. "They have plenty of room for all of us, and I'll be there to help Rosie and Ike if they need it."

"Maggie practically begged me to house some of you there! I wanted you here, but Landon thought it would be better for his brother and the girls to be close to us." She looked at Morgan apologetically.

Morgan reached out and touched her sister's hand. "Kels, you don't need to apologize. I know it's a difficult situation. How's he doing, anyway?"

Kelsea shook her head. "Not great. He's super-doctor-in-control at work, and a hot mess otherwise."

"Does he have any help with the girls, other than daycare?"

"No, he's determined to handle the home front on his own. And he's still so broken and lost without Darla. I think Landon and their parents are going to try to talk with him this weekend."

"Well, I should probably get back to Mike & Maggie's," Morgan said. "They gave me the front door code and said to stay here as long as I wanted to." She stood, and Kelsea got to her feet and held her arms out. The two sisters hugged.

"I'm so glad you're here, Morgy," Kelsea whispered.

Morgan snorted softly and pulled back. "You know you're the only one who's allowed to call me that, don't you?" She looked into her sister's dark brown eyes and smiled.

"Yes, and you're the only one who can call me Sissy," Kelsea replied with a smile.

A bright bolt of lightning flashed outside, illuminating the living room window, and the women held their breath, bracing themselves. Still, they both jumped when a crack of thunder boomed a mere second later.

And then, the lights flickered out.

"Gosh, that's close!" Morgan exclaimed, her hand on her chest.

Landon's voice called out, "Honey, don't move. I'm coming with flashlights." The sisters huddled together until he arrived.

"Are Penny and Sheldon okay?" Kelsea's Pomeranians had been a big part of her life even before she met Landon.

He came into the room. "They're fine. They're completely zonked out on our bed."

Kelsea looked at Morgan. "Maybe you should stay here," Landon held out a flashlight.

"I'll be fine. It's just across the street," Morgan replied. She put her hand up. "Guys, I'll be fine."

Kelsea walked with her to the front door, and opened it. "Oh, wow, it's pouring!" She quickly reached into the hall closet. "Here, at least take this," she said, and handed Morgan a big umbrella.

"Thanks, I think I'll need it." She squeezed Kelsea's hand. "Love you, see you tomorrow."

"Yes, come for pancakes around nine. Oh! Would you babysit so Landon and I can go to the airport?"

*You can do this.* "I'd love to!" Morgan grinned.

"Thanks! Sleep well, Morgy."

# 3

BRANDON COULDN'T THINK of anything but getting off the road and out of the rain. He was so tired, and he had a headache. That last crack of thunder ushered in a chorus of wailing from his young daughters, which only added to the pounding in his head. The lightning must have hit a transformer, because all the lights around them went out.

He'd turned his phone off because it was almost dead. *LaBonne Terrace,* that's what he was looking for. Had Landon told him it was the first house on the left, or the right, after the road curved? Brandon came to an intersection and slowed to try to read the sign. He couldn't really see it, but it looked like it might begin with an *L,* so he turned right. He knew he was probably going a little too fast, but there were no other cars on the road, and he just wanted to get there.

"Big Victorian house with a circular driveway," he repeated his brother's instructions to himself. Brandon looked left, hardly able to see anything in the downpour.

As he looked right, a sudden movement flashed in the headlights, and he instinctively slammed on his brakes. Was it an animal? Brandon's mouth dropped open and his heart leapt into his throat. He clutched the steering wheel as his heart pounded in his ears.

An indistinguishable figure, hunched under an umbrella, dashed across the road just in front of the SUV.

*I almost hit someone. The idiot just ran out in front of me, didn't even look!* The realization sent white-hot anger racing through his veins. Without thinking, he rolled down his window.

"Hey!" He screamed. "What is WRONG with you?"

The figure slowed, but didn't stop, and the person's head was almost totally obscured by the umbrella. He was medium height, but that's all Brandon could make out.

"Where do you think you are, the Indianapolis Speedway?" a woman's voice shouted.

*I almost hit a woman.*

Water poured in through the window. Brandon quickly rolled it up, his breath coming in short bursts. April and Shelbie continued wailing.

"Girls, we're almost there," he said over his shoulder, *I hope,* he added to himself. Brandon wished he could get them out of their car seats to comfort them.

When he looked back to the front windshield, the woman was gone. Surrounded by the darkness and the pouring rain, he had no idea which way she had gone. Brandon rested his forehead on the steering wheel. "Oh, God, help me." He put his foot back on the gas pedal and inched forward, struggling to see.

Almost immediately, he glimpsed a driveway on the right, and swung out in a slow, wide arc. His headlights illuminated a big, Victorian house. *Finally.* Brandon's grip on the steering wheel loosened, and he pulled up to the front door. He put the car in park and closed his eyes. "Thank you, Lord," he whispered.

The door opened, and there was his brother with a big umbrella. Landon came right up to the car, and Brandon lowered the passenger window. "Hey, man," he said, relief flooding his veins. The girls had finally stopped screaming.

"Hey, man," Landon answered back. "Sorry, I just have the one umbrella. How can I help?"

"Maybe get the girls in the house first?" He turned in his seat and reached over to unbuckle April. "This is Uncle Landon, April, remember him?"

With his brother's help, Brandon had both girls and the car unloaded in minutes. As soon as he crossed the threshold into the house, the lights flickered back on.

"Hey, perfect timing!" Landon exclaimed.

Kelsea came into the entryway and held out her arms. "I'm so relieved you're here! I've been praying that you'd arrive safely." Brandon gave her a hug, and she stooped down to greet the girls. "April and Shelbie, you're both getting so big!" She held out a hand to each girl. "Why don't you come with me and have a snack while your daddy and Uncle Landon put your things upstairs?"

Brandon was amazed at his sister-in-law's ability to assess a situation and do exactly the right thing. He picked up his roller bag, the girls' suitcase. His brother reached for the toy bag and another bag of the girls' things.

"What's this?" Landon said, pointing to the black trash bag.

Brandon winced. "Oh, it's clean laundry that didn't make it into the dryer."

"Okay, we'll leave it here and take care of it when we come back down," Landon replied. Brandon was relieved that his brother didn't judge him.

Landon led him up the stairs, down the hall, and into a large blue and white bedroom with a queen-sized bed and an inflatable mattress on the floor, piled with blankets and pillows. "You can figure out the sleeping arrangements," he said.

Brandon had never been so happy to see a bed in his life. "The girls will probably want to sleep with me tonight," he said. "This is terrific, thanks."

"You have your own bathroom," Landon said, pointing to a door. He paused and studied Brandon as if seeing him for the first time. "You okay? How was the drive?"

Brandon let out a breath and rubbed a hand through his dark

hair. "It was a long day. I did four surgeries this morning." He stretched and stifled a yawn. "The drive was okay until the last hour. It kept raining harder and harder. And then I almost hit one of your idiot neighbors. I don't know what she was doing out in the middle of the night, but she ran right out in front of the car."

Landon frowned. "Neighbor? Just now?" Brandon nodded. "Oh, that wasn't a neighbor. That was Kelsea's sister, Morgan. She's staying across the street with our friends Mike and Maggie. She left just before you got here." He turned and began walking toward the door into the hallway.

Brandon followed him. "Well, she's an idiot," he muttered.

"Do you want to see your niece and nephew?" Landon said with a smile.

"You bet!" Brandon answered. He couldn't believe his brother had both a son and a daughter now. He followed Landon into a softly lit nursery where two white cribs resided.

"This is my son, Isaac," Landon said proudly, resting his arms on the first crib.

Brandon felt his chest swell on his brother's behalf. "Oh, man, he's so little!"

Landon laughed softly. "He's huge! Four months old now."

Brandon felt a wave of sadness wash over him. "I can't remember the girls being this small." He turned to the other crib with Landon.

"And here's Rose Elizabeth," Landon said tenderly.

"Look at all that dark hair," Brandon murmured. "Like her mama."

Landon smiled. "She has her mama's personality, too. Sassy." He leaned down and rested his hand on the baby's head. He looked at Brandon. "There's nothing like it," he whispered.

Brandon nodded and swallowed past the lump in his throat. "They're beautiful, bro."

They went back downstairs into the kitchen and found the girls enjoying bowls of cereal with Aunt Kelsea.

"We're having breakfast, Daddy!" April exclaimed.

"I like the marshmallows," Shelbie said around a mouthful of cereal.

"Wow, that looks good," Brandon said.

Kelsea laughed. "Help yourself," she said, indicating several assorted boxes on the counter. Landon got out a bowl, a spoon, and the milk.

"Are we having cereal for breakfast in the morning, too?" Brandon asked with a smile.

"No, we're having your brother's famous pancakes," Kelsea said. She sidled up to Landon and looked at him lovingly, and their arms went around each other. A jolt of pain sliced through Brandon's heart.

They chatted for a few more moments and then he took the girls upstairs and got them ready for bed. Brandon wished he could take a long, hot shower, but being in a strange place, it was more important for him to be there for April and Shelbie. He'd take his shower after they fell asleep.

Brandon climbed into bed with them, still in his clothes, and they snuggled in, one on each side. Shelbie popped her thumb in her mouth. What would he ever do without them? They were his world now. His thoughts went to Landon and Kelsea, their arms entwined around each other, and he missed Darla more than ever. Would the pain ever go away?

The next thing Brandon knew, it was morning.

# 4

MORGAN KNOCKED ON her sister's front door and poked her head in. "Knock, knock!"

Kelsea was just coming down the stairs, holding Isaac. "Good morning!" The dogs ran ahead of her, greeting Morgan with enthusiastic barks and yips.

"Morning, Sissy, morning, Penny and Sheldon." She patted their heads, deposited the umbrella in the corner, and held out her arms. "Come to Aunt Morgy, Isaac!"

Kelsea laughed as she handed the baby over. "Whatever happened to *'no one else can ever call me Morgy!'*?"

Morgan kissed the little boy's silky-soft cheek. "My niece and nephew can call me whatever they want." She tipped her head toward the umbrella. "I'm returning that. Thanks."

Kelsea put it in the closet. "Did you get soaked anyway? It was pouring so hard."

"No, but I almost got hit," Morgan replied.

"Hit?" Kelsea began walking toward the kitchen, and Morgan followed her.

"Yeah, some moron in an SUV came flying around the corner. I don't know what he was thinking."

Kelsea stopped. "Right when you left here?"

Morgan nodded.

"Oh gosh, that must have been Brandon. They drove in just after you left."

Morgan rolled her eyes. "Well, he's a moron." She followed Kelsea into the kitchen, and stopped.

Two adorable little blond girls sat at the counter, eating pancakes. Rose sat happily in the baby swing.

Landon stood at the island range top, over a griddle. A dark-haired man stood next to him, and they looked up in unison when the two women entered the room. Morgan's breath caught in her throat.

Kelsea had told her that they were always mistaken for twins, even though Landon was eleven months older. But Morgan had never seen anything like it. The two were like matching bookends. They were exactly the same height and build, with the same facial structure, the same amber-brown eyes, and even the same cleft in their chins that little Isaac had inherited. They had nearly identical haircuts, but whereas Landon's hair was blond, Brandon's was dark brown, almost black.

Both men had the same smile, showing perfect white teeth. "Morning, Morgan," Landon said.

His brother's smile dimmed noticeably. *Great.*

"Good morning," she managed.

"This is my sister, Dr. Morgan Anderson," Kelsea said cheerily. "Meet Dr. Brandon St. Clair."

*That's right, he's a surgeon. So he's* Dr. *Moron.* Morgan shifted little Isaac in her arms as she watched the wheels turning in Dr. St. Clair's head. His smile warmed up a little.

He dipped his head in acknowledgement. "Doctor," he murmured. He held out a plate on which Landon piled a half dozen golden pancakes.

"Nice to meet you," Morgan said softly. Suddenly she felt very self-conscious, like she always did in the presence of a good-looking guy. *Stop it,* she scolded herself. *He's not that handsome.*

*Liar!* Another voice in her head shouted. *He's totally hot, and you know it!*

There was no doubt that Kelsea's husband was handsome, but in Morgan's opinion, his brother's dark hair took him to a whole new level. She had a real weakness for tall, dark, handsome men. Before Kelsea met Landon, she did, too. *TDH* was their code, and Brandon St. Clair had it in spades.

Morgan tried not to stare. She was so self-conscious and wanted to thrust her nephew into his mother's arms and bolt from the room. But she managed to stay where she was, rocking back and forth on the balls of her feet with Isaac and—hopefully—looking calm.

Kelsea held her arms out for the baby. "Let me take him so you can eat," she said.

"Um, oh, sure," Morgan said. She tucked a strand of her caramel-colored hair behind one ear and turned to the counter where she saw plates, silverware, and napkins.

As soon as she picked up a plate, Brandon materialized beside her with a spatula and plate of steaming pancakes. *Wow, is he ever tall.* Morgan was taller than average, but he dwarfed her.

"Here you go," he said, placing three pancakes on her plate.

"Oh, no, thanks, two is plenty," she said, and felt her face heating up. *Moron, moron,* she repeated to herself. She tried to ignore his sculpted chest and broad shoulders.

"You sure?"

She nodded.

He took one pancake back. "Okay, then," he said with a smile. Morgan swallowed.

Penny and Sheldon ran into the room, their expressions expectant. "No pancakes for you two," Landon scolded with a smile.

"Oh, they're so cute," the older girl said.

"Eat your breakfast, April," Brandon said. "You can play with the dogs later."

As Morgan picked up a fork and napkin, the smaller girl

looked up from her pancakes and stared at Morgan. "You look like my mommy."

The plate that Brandon was holding clattered to the countertop, and it seemed as if the air went out of the room.

Morgan didn't know what to say. She glanced at Brandon, whose face had blanched white. Landon froze where he was.

Kelsea, still holding Isaac, moved to stand next to the little girl. "Shelbie, that's Morgan," she said matter-of-factly. "She's my little sister, just like you're April's little sister. She looks a little like your mommy, doesn't she? But she's taller, and her eyes are green instead of blue." Kelsea looked at her brother-in-law. "Brandon, could you get Shelbie and April some more juice?" Then she made eye contact with her sister. "Morgan, come and eat your pancakes before they get cold."

Morgan walked quietly to the table while holding her breath, and sat down.

"I want apple juice this time, please," Shelbie said. Morgan glanced at Kelsea and Landon, who seemed to be holding their breath as well. It appeared that the awkward moment had passed.

Brandon cleared his throat. "Sure thing, Shelbie. And good job saying please."

Morgan was sure the pancakes were delicious, but she didn't taste a thing.

Brandon took the carton of apple juice out of the fridge and turned to the counter. He frowned. "Where's April?" he asked.

The other adults looked around. "She was just here," Kelsea said. She looked at her husband and Morgan. "Did either one of you see her leave?"

"No," Morgan and Landon said in unison.

Brandon set the carton down on the counter. "I have a feeling I know what this is about," he said, his face grim. He turned and abruptly left the room.

When he returned a few moments later, he didn't say anything, just fixed a plate of pancakes and sat down.

"Is everything okay?" Landon asked.

Brandon didn't reply. He motioned to the butter dish on the other side of Kelsea. "Would you please pass the butter?"

"Sure," Kelsea murmured. She glanced at Landon and then at Morgan and Brandon. "So, you're both doctors," she said brightly. "Brandon is an orthopedic surgeon."

Brandon took a sip of his juice and looked at Morgan. "What's your specialty?" he asked.

Morgan swallowed. *Here it comes.* She sat up a little straighter. "I'm a PhD. I'm an art therapist."

Brandon stared at her for a moment. He chewed a bite of pancakes and swallowed. "So, what's that? Painting and drawing?"

Morgan started to open her mouth to retort, but her sister jumped in. "Morgan is an Assistant Professor at the Midwest Art Institute in Chicago. She's one of the youngest faculty ever hired there, and has published tons of research."

Brandon gave Morgan what felt like a placating smile. "Well, that's impressive," he said. Everyone continued eating for several moments.

"Honey, these pancakes are amazing," Kelsea said. It sounded to Morgan that her sister was trying to fill the awkward silence.

"They sure are, bro." Brandon stood, put his plate in the sink, and picked up his younger daughter. "Let's get you cleaned up and dressed," he said.

"Thanks for breakfast," he tossed over his shoulder as he carried Shelbie out of the room.

Landon let out a breath. "Morgan, I'm sorry—"

Morgan shook her head. "It's okay, Landon."

"He's just—he's not himself." He sighed. "I think I know what's up with April. She's not handling the loss of her mother well. I'm sure Shelbie's comment upset her."

Morgan's heart gave a painful squeeze. "She's only four. Of course she's not handling it well." She rested her chin on her hand

and sighed. "Poor little thing." She looked from Kelsea to Landon. "Do I—do I really look like their mother?"

Landon frowned. "I don't think so. But then again, I've known Darla since we were all teenagers. Your hair color is similar, though."

Kelsea nodded. "Yes, it's really close, and it's long and straight, too. In the grand scheme of things, you look a lot more like her than I do. I could see where a three-year-old would make the connection." She lifted Rose out of the baby swing and kissed the top of her head. "April has always had a more sensitive spirit. She's a thinker. Shelbie is more easy-going. And she doesn't remember Darla as clearly as April does. She just has a general impression of her. "

The three adults sat silent for a moment, each lost in their own thoughts. Landon stood and began gathering the breakfast dishes. "I'll get everything cleaned up here."

"Hey, Morgan," Kelsea said, "could you get Isaac out of his swing and bring him upstairs? I'll get these two fed before we have to leave for the airport." She paused. "If you're still willing to babysit?"

*As long as I can steer clear of Dr. Moron.* Morgan pasted a smile on her face. "Are you kidding?" she said, "I can't wait!"

# 5

BRANDON SAT DOWN on the bed and ran a hand through his hair. *Great.* He was stuck here for a family weekend with a woman who reminded Shelbie of her mother, and was a PhD to boot. He had never had a good impression of people with doctorates. He'd met several over the years—among them his cousin, Mark—who thought they had the biggest brains in the room. He had a PhD in Psychology and insisted that everyone call him "Doc." Brandon sneered. Mark probably made his wife call him that, even when they were alone.

He and Darla used to have good-natured arguments about it. Her best friend had a PhD, so she didn't have the same bias toward them. And Dar loved everyone and always wanted to give them the benefit of the doubt—even Mark. Brandon squeezed his eyes shut. How were he and the girls ever going to get over losing her?

When April had disappeared from the kitchen, Brandon found her upstairs on the bed, curled up in a ball. She wasn't even crying. She was just lying there, staring into space. His heart broke for his older daughter. What was he going to do? His beautiful, sunny, and gentle April Dawn was losing her spirit. She would take one step forward and two steps back.

Brandon didn't have a clue how to help her. Heck, he was

barely holding himself together. He and Darla had agreed that no matter the demands of their careers, that they would raise their children themselves. No nanny or au pair, like most of their friends and colleagues had. Since Darla's death, Brandon's folks kept telling him to hire someone to help, but he stood firm. Putting his daughters in daycare five days a week and leaving them with neighbors when he was called in on emergencies was bad enough.

For once, he wished that he had family close. His parents lived in Wisconsin, about four hours away. Darla's folks lived in Arizona, along with her two sisters and their families. His and Landon's younger sister, Sara, was in college in Michigan. Their older sister, Reagan, lived in Miami.

The girls were looking out the window at the backyard. "Daddy, I want to swing!" Shelbie shouted as she jumped up and down. Brandon stood and looked over their heads to the large yard below. Even though his brother's twins weren't ready for it, a large, colorful play structure sat in the middle of the lush green grass.

"Let's get you dressed, then," Brandon said, and lay Shelbie down on the bed to change her diaper. That was something else he needed to figure out, how to potty train her. Darla had taken complete charge of that with April. He'd heard somewhere that summer was the optimum time to attempt it, so he was waiting.

April dressed quietly, and Brandon asked if she wanted him to fix her hair. She shook her head no, and he decided not to press her about it. He handed her a brush, which she ran haphazardly through her hair while he got Shelbie's up into two pigtails.

"I hafta have the purple bows, Daddy," she instructed with all seriousness.

After he got that detail taken care of, Brandon ushered the girls into the hallway and toward the stairs, but Shelbie stopped and pointed the opposite direction. "I wanna see the babies," she said in a loud whisper.

Brandon smiled. "We have to be very quiet. I think they're sleeping."

"I be quiet."

April nodded, too. They tiptoed into the nursery, and Brandon picked both of the girls up to peer into the cribs. "Here's baby Rose," he whispered.

"Baby Wose," Shelbie parroted. "I wuv you, Baby Wose."

He turned to the other crib. "And baby Isaac."

"Brother?" Shelbie asked.

"Yes, Isaac is Rose's brother."

Shelbie's little forehead wrinkled up as she frowned. "My brother?"

"No, you don't have a brother. Isaac is your cousin."

"I wish I had a brother." Brandon was surprised to hear those words come out of April's mouth.

Then he felt Shelbie's little hands on his cheeks.

"I want brother, too, Daddy," she ordered.

A little piece of Brandon's heart broke off. He adored his daughters, and had hoped someday to have a son, too. Now he knew he'd have to let go of that dream.

He forced a smile. "Maybe someday God will give you a brother," he said. He didn't know what else to say. Then he gave each girl a peck on the cheek and set them down. "Come on, let's go check out the backyard."

# 6

MORGAN SAT IN the family room looking out at the backyard. She'd seen and heard everything that had just transpired in the twins' room over the baby monitor.

Shelbie skipped into the room ahead of her father and sister. "We're going to get a brother someday!" she cried. *Oh, to have the faith of a child.* Shelbie stopped in front of Morgan and put her hands on her hips. "I forgetted your name."

Morgan took in Shelbie's purple shoes, pants, and hair ribbons. Her shirt was white with purple and lavender hearts. She was just the cutest thing, with her blond pigtails bobbing up and down. Morgan smiled. "I'm Morgan. And I'll bet your favorite color is purple." She looked at April. "What's your favorite color, April?"

Brandon stepped forward. "Ah—we don't call adults by their first name, girls."

Morgan stood up. "Then you can call me Dr. Anderson."

Brandon frowned. "You can call her *Miss* Anderson." He quickly stepped to the French doors and slid the screen door open. "Girls, go on and play for a few minutes. I'll be right there."

*Really? Miss?* This guy was unbelievable. Morgan mentally prepared herself for battle. "You're kidding me, right?" she said as Brandon turned to look at her.

"No, I'm not kidding. I want to raise my daughters to respect adults."

Morgan itched to cross her arms over her chest, but forced them to stay down at her side. "And what's disrespectful about calling me by my title?"

Brandon smiled in a way that bordered on a grimace. "I don't want them to be confused. I'm a doctor. Their mother was a doctor. In their world—our world—a doctor is someone in the medical field."

Morgan felt her blood boiling. *Of all the*—she'd met a few doctors like this in her practice. Fortunately, they were more the exception than the norm. She let out a huff. "How—how are you even Landon's brother?" Landon was a partner at the largest, most successful law firm in St. Louis, and he was still one of the kindest, most down-to-earth people she had ever met.

Brandon looked completely confused. "What does Landon have to do with this?" He parked his hands on his hips. "I'm one of the top orthopedic surgeons in Minneapolis—in the Midwest, in fact—and I worked extremely hard for over a *decade* to earn the title of *doctor*. It just riles me that anyone who goes to college for a few years and publishes a couple of articles can run around making everyone call *them* 'doctor' and misleading everyone."

Morgan could hardly believe what she was hearing. She drew in a deep, cleansing breath through her nose and straightened her spine. "*Dr.* St. Clair, I know that medical doctors pride themselves on the depth and breadth of their knowledge. But in the hour and a half that I've known you, you've shown me that you're really very ignorant. You possess little to no knowledge about what it means to be a doctor of philosophy, or anything about the widely recognized and *respected* field of art therapy."

A squawk from the baby monitor cut her off. She marched out of the room, her back ramrod straight. Then she stopped and turned to him. "And you obviously don't have any kind of a degree in *driving*," she added.

She stomped up the stairs to the nursery, her breathing coming in angry spurts. *TDH* or not, Brandon St. Clair had an abrasive, unpleasant personality. Morgan had no idea how she was going to survive the weekend without punching his lights out.

She crept into the nursery, and both babies were sleeping soundly. Morgan stood for a long time over Isaac's crib, and then over Rose's. As she stared at her sister's children, a wave of tenderness washed over her. She fingered one of her niece's dark curls. Kelsea and Morgan had been so very different growing up, but the one dream they always shared was to be mothers. Morgan had taken their father's death especially hard, and dreamed of having a husband and children of her own someday. But that day hadn't yet come, and she felt that dream slipping away, especially after her diagnosis.

Morgan heard a child laughing, and stepped to the window that overlooked the backyard, where Brandon was pushing his daughters on the swings. He looked exhausted and it was only mid-morning. Morgan felt a pang of sympathy for him. She couldn't imagine what it would be like to lose your spouse and have to raise two young children alone, especially juggling a demanding, high-pressure career.

Then she remembered his haughty, condescending words and attitude, and her sympathetic thoughts dissolved. She crossed her arms and continued staring down at him. He'd probably love it if she stayed in the house the whole time Kelsea and Landon were gone so he wouldn't have to deal with her.

Morgan turned on her heel and went back downstairs. She knew exactly what she was going to do.

# 7

BRANDON PUSHED SHELBIE and April on the swings. "Higher, Daddy!" Shelbie shouted. This girl was going to love roller coasters once she discovered them. He had a feeling Shelbie's teen years would be one long, wild ride.

He tamped down a feeling of guilt. He had no idea why he'd come down so hard on Morgan Anderson, or why she got under his skin. He thought about her. Maybe she did remind him a little bit of Darla. Morgan was quite a bit taller, and was a completely different body type, but their coloring was similar. All he knew was that he didn't want to be around her. Thankfully, his parents would arrive later today, along with Kelsea's mom and their other special friends, and that would make it easier to avoid Morgan.

"I want to get down, Daddy," April said. He slowed her swing to a stop, and she hopped off and wandered off toward a plot of dirt that looked like it might be a future garden.

*Great.* Here came Morgan. The two Poms trailed after her. Why couldn't one of the babies have needed something so she could stay inside, out of his hair? She smiled, sat down in one of the patio chairs, and set the baby monitor on the table.

"It's beautiful out here, isn't it?" she called. She lifted her face to the sky and drew in a deep breath. "I love the days after big storms have moved through and cleared the air."

Brandon grunted and continued pushing Shelbie. Morgan was apparently planning on staying out here. He wondered if he should take the girls into the house.

April was crouched in the grass near a plot of moist dirt, playing with a stick. Last night's wind had littered the yard with them. Morgan got up and went over to her, and sat down on the grass with her. "Whatcha doin'?" Brandon heard her ask.

"Drawing," April replied in a soft voice.

"Do you like to draw?" April nodded. "I do, too," Morgan added. She picked up another stick and Brandon saw her start to doodle in the dirt.

They just sat there, and Brandon thought they talked occasionally, although he couldn't hear what they said. He was lost in thought when he heard Shelbie say, "Daddy! I said stop!" He stilled her swing and she jumped off and ran over to join her sister and Morgan.

"Hi, Shelbie," Morgan said. "We're drawing. Would you like to draw, too?"

Shelbie shook her head and placed her hands on her hips. "No, I'm going to pick up all the sticks." She dramatically drew out the word *all*. Shelbie started skipping through the yard, singing and gathering sticks as she went. Penny and Sheldon trailed after her, and she babbled to them and threw sticks for them to run after.

Brandon smiled to himself. April was like Mary in the Bible, content to immerse herself in quiet reflection for long periods of time. Shelbie was Martha, all busyness, all the time. His gaze swept across the large yard. Picking up sticks could keep Shelbie busy for several hours, but she'd soon tire of the task and look for something else to do.

Feeling awkward, Brandon sat down at the round patio table. After a few minutes, Shelbie ran over to her sister. "April, you hafta help clean up the yard!" she exclaimed.

"I'll come in a minute, Shel," she said.

Shelbie huffed and skipped away, resuming her task. Pretty soon, she was back, and April agreed to help this time. Morgan got up and headed his way. "You have quite a little artist there," she said as she sat down.

Brandon ignored her comment. "Just for the record," he said sternly, "I have an impeccable driving record. I do just fine until some—" he almost said *idiot* but tried to temper himself. "Some person with no common sense comes running out in front of me."

"I have plenty of common sense. You were driving too fast. End of story." She plowed on. "That's in the past, so let's put it aside and talk about your daughter's artistic flair."

Brandon frowned. "Artistic flair?" he looked at Morgan evenly. "She was messing in the dirt with a stick."

"She drew a picture of your family at the mountains," Morgan said. "It was quite good and it was meaningful to her." She paused. "Did you take a trip to the mountains?"

Brandon swallowed. Memories overtook him and he wondered if he could draw his next breath.

"Yes," he croaked. His voice broke, and he cleared his throat. They had gone skiing in Utah last spring. It was their last trip together as a family, but no way was he going to share that. He needed to take control of this conversation right now. He had no intention of breaking down in front of Morgan Anderson.

Brandon sat up straighter and leveled her with a hard look. "How do you determine that something scratched into the dirt with a stick is 'quite good'?"

"The level of detail, both what I could see and what she told me. Her fine motor control is remarkable for a child of that age. I'd love to see what she does with colored pencils or crayons."

Brandon stood. "Well, that's nice, but she's not your research subject." He turned his back on her and began to walk away.

"Just what do you have against me, Dr. St. Clair?" Morgan called out sharply.

He turned back and blew out a breath. "Look," he said, "we have to get through this family weekend, so let's just coexist peacefully and shelve the attitude for the sake of your sister and my brother. Deal?"

Morgan jumped to her feet and put her hands on her hips. "Shelve the attitude?" she said in a voice laced with disbelief. She narrowed her eyes at him. "Physician, heal thyself!"

Morgan watched the high-and-mighty *Dr. St. Clair* pick up some larger branches and interact with his daughters, laughing with them and giving them an occasional hug or pat. She crossed her arms over her chest. Really, it wasn't fair that such an insufferable boor should be so handsome and so…masculine. She had to admit that he seemed to be a good dad. She recalled Kelsea's comment about him being a control freak at work, and totally falling apart at home.

Many doctors that Morgan had dealt with were alpha personalities who felt the need to be in control, some to the extent of having a "god" complex. She'd gone on one dinner date with one handsome, charming resident who insisted on ordering for her as if she were incapable of doing it for herself. Morgan had quickly set him straight on that, and he never called her again.

The baby monitor continued to show that all was well upstairs. Morgan sat contentedly in the sun until she heard Landon call out, "hi, we're here!" That sent Penny and Sheldon into full bark mode.

"Hi, Unca Landon!" Shelbie squealed. She ran to him and launched herself up into his arms.

Morgan stood, and Landon laughed as April and Brandon joined them. Morgan stared at the older couple who stood next to her brother-in-law, dwarfed by him, Brandon, and even herself. They couldn't be more than a couple of inches over five feet.

"Meet Rose and Ike Goldman." Landon made the introductions, and everyone shook hands.

Shelbie looked at Rose. "My favorite color is purple," she said. "And I think your favorite color is pink!"

Everyone laughed. Kelsea had told Morgan about Rose's penchant for pink. Today, she wore a tie-dyed pink shirt with hot pink capris and her trademark pink Converse. Ike seemed quiet and pleasant, but Morgan could tell that a vibrant *joie de vivre* oozed out of Rose's every pore.

"Yes, indeed it is," Rose agreed, all smiles.

"You even have pink hair! Shelbie exclaimed, eyeing the pink highlighted tips of Rose's white hair. "Daddy! Can I get purple in my hair?"

Everyone laughed again. "Ah, not now, Shelbie. Maybe when you're all grown up, if you still want to do that."

Shelbie wriggled out of Landon's arms, and he set her down. "Unca Landon, we cleaned up the *whole* backyard!" she said, sweeping one little arm in a wide arc in front of her.

"You did a great job, girls! Thank you," Landon said.

"Daddy helped with the big branches," April added.

"Let's go wash our hands, girls," Brandon said, ushering them into the house.

They heard Shelbie chattering happily as they walked away. "She has pink glasses, too! Daddy, can I get purple glasses?"

The Goldmans and Landon laughed along with Morgan. Rose reached up to adjust her pink-encrusted rhinestone glasses. "Your nieces are delightful," she said.

"They sure are," Landon agreed.

Everyone's attention turned to the baby monitor as it began to make noise, and Kelsea's voice came over. "Landon, could you or Morgan come help me?"

"I'll go," Morgan said, and quickly left.

She helped Kelsea dress the twins, and carried Rose downstairs while Kelsea took charge of Isaac. Everyone was in the family room, and Morgan handed her niece to Landon. Rose and Ike got settled on the couch, and she felt her eyes well up as her sister and brother-in-law tenderly laid the babies in their arms. She knew how much the older couple meant to them.

Morgan was so focused on the touching scene that she started when she heard Brandon's soft voice near her ear. "Do you have your phone? Mine's upstairs. Could you get some pictures of this?"

His aftershave or cologne smelled wonderful, and Morgan resisted the urge to draw in a deep breath. *Moron, moron.*

She drew her phone from her pocket. "Of course, yes. Good idea." For once, Brandon had a pleasant, even tender, look on his face. Of course, he was focused on the babies, not Morgan.

Morgan spent the next several minutes taking pictures of the Goldmans with the babies and Landon and Kelsea, and tried unsuccessfully to forget that Brandon was there. Morgan hadn't ever let a man's physical attributes outweigh a sincere and kind heart and pleasant personality, things that meant much more, and that appeared to be totally lacking in Brandon St. Clair. Morgan was totally disgusted and frustrated over her hyperawareness of him.

Rose Goldman beamed as she looked down at her namesake. "This girl is going to do great things," she announced. "She may even grow up to be president."

"What about Isaac?" her husband countered with a smile. "Look at that strong profile. I think he'd make a great president, too."

"He can be Rose's vice president," she replied firmly. Everyone laughed.

After a few moments, Ike looked over at baby Rose. "I'm ready to hold that little beauty," he said, and Kelsea and Landon got the babies switched.

"Landon, this little boy is the spitting image of you—and your brother," Rose said. "You two aren't twins, though?"

"No, I'm almost a year older," Landon said.

"And I have a perfect nose," Brandon said with a smile aimed at his brother. *He really is perfect,* Morgan thought to herself. *Why can't he have a tooth missing, or a big wart on his nose, or hair sprouting out of his ears?*

Landon burst out laughing and touched the bump on his nose. "Kelsea thinks it gives me character." He looked at the Goldmans. "I got it in a hockey brawl in my misspent youth."

After a little while, Rose looked at April and Shelbie. "I think these girls would like to hold their little cousins. If it's okay with their parents," she added.

"Of course," Kelsea said, and they got the girls settled in with the babies. April and Shelbie were so excited, and Morgan took lots of pictures. Both girls got a turn at holding each twin with help from their dad.

Shelbie touched a gentle finger to little Isaac's cheek. "God is going to give us a brother someday." she announced.

Isaac began to fuss, and Brandon picked up his nephew and stood, gently bouncing him in his arms. He looked totally at home holding a baby, but a look of discomfort took over his features. "I don't know why she's obsessed with having a brother," he said softly.

"Sometimes, children know these things," Rose said.

"Well, it's not going to happen," Brandon said. He handed Isaac off to Landon. "Excuse me," he said as he left the room.

# 8

BRANDON WALKED QUICKLY through the family room, down the hallway and out the front door. He paced back and forth on the porch and rammed his hands through his hair, drawing in deep breaths.

*Why, God? Why, why, why?* Shelbie's talk of wanting a brother filled him with desperation for all that he had lost, for all the years ahead that he and Darla should have had. Raw anger and deep, piercing pain radiated through his chest. He braced his hands on the porch railing and hung his head. *God, how will I ever survive? I could easily be on this earth for fifty more years. Alone. I can't do it, God, I can't.*

Suddenly, Landon materialized at his side. Brandon hadn't even heard the door open.

"You okay, man?"

Brandon couldn't speak around the lump in his throat. Even if he wanted to sugar-coat things, this was the one person on this earth who could see straight through him. He shook his head and swallowed. "No, no I'm not," he whispered. Landon reached over and gave his shoulder a comforting squeeze. Brandon swiped at his tear-filled eyes. "I can't do this. I can't."

"I know," Landon said. "You can't. Not on your own." He sighed. "We're all worried about you. Let us help."

Brandon gave a mirthless laugh. "I'm sure Mom has some kind of intervention planned for this weekend. Are the girls coming, too? Strength in numbers?" He knew that Landon caught the reference to their sisters.

"No, Sara's got finals next week, and Reagan's tied up, the way Reagan always is." Their older sister worked at the *Miami Herald,* and was totally career-focused. Landon squeezed his shoulder again. "How are things with you and God?"

Brandon shook his head. "I talk with Him a lot. I talk *at* Him a lot," he corrected. "I keep asking *why,* but I never get an answer." He thought for a moment. "I'm still angry."

"That's normal." Landon's eyes were filled with compassion, not condemnation.

"But I'm stuck in the anger phase," Brandon said. "I can't get past it."

Landon moved on his other side and propped his hip against the porch railing. "Try this. You're angry because you can't change the outcome."

"Hmph," Brandon mused. "The physician's god complex?"

Landon nodded. "And you're still consumed with guilt. Am I right?"

No one else could have said that to Brandon and gotten away with it. He felt the same sick sensation that he'd wrestled with for almost a year bubble up in his stomach. He pressed a fist to his mouth. "I could have gone to the store that night, I *should* have—"

Landon looped a long arm around his shoulder. "You could have. But you didn't send Darla out because you were a bad husband. You had a rare night off and wanted to stay home and put your girls to bed. And you can't change that. Bro, You. Can't. Change. It." Landon removed his arm. "You'll never move on until you leave the land of would-a could-a, should-a."

Brandon rubbed his eyes and let out a huge breath. "We've

gotten through all the 'firsts.' First Thanksgiving, Christmas, birthdays, anniversary without her. This will be our first Mothers' Day," he said. He felt his eyes filling up again. "I don't know what to do, how to handle it. I don't know what's best for the girls." He looked at Landon.

"I know," Landon said. "So let your family handle it. Let us be there for you. We'll get you through it. I think Kelsea has some ideas."

Brandon managed a weak smile. "Your wife is very special," he said.

"Don't think I don't know it," Landon replied. "I'm very blessed. And you're blessed, too, even though you're still overwhelmed by grief. It's hard to see."

Brandon nodded. "I'm so tired of being tired. And discouraged. And not having any hope of getting past it."

Landon squeezed his shoulder. "You'll get past it. One step at a time, bro." He tilted his head toward the door. "You ready to go back in?"

Brandon shook his head.

Landon looked at him. "Could I pray with you?"

*Like that will do any good,* Brandon thought to himself. But this was his best friend in the world, so he nodded, and bowed his head.

# 9

"DO YOU HAVE a platter or something I can set these on?" Morgan was helping Kelsea with lunch. She was in charge of the sandwiches, and Kelsea was putting the finishes touches on a relish tray.

Rose walked in, and Morgan couldn't help but smile. Even after two days of travel, she was a pink ball of energy.

"I wish you girls would let me help," she said. "I'm not as old and feeble as I look."

Morgan and Kelsea laughed. "Okay, Rose, get the chips out of the pantry," Kelsea said, pointing to a door. She set tubs of potato salad and pasta salad on the counter.

"She's adorable. They both are," Morgan whispered to Kelsea.

"I know," her sister whispered back.

Rose laid the bags on the large island counter and climbed up on a stool. "Tell me about yourself, Morgan."

"Well, I live in Chicago, and I'm an art therapist."

Rose smiled brightly. "Oh, Ike's nephew is from Chicago." Then Rose asked her some questions about art therapy, which Morgan was happy to answer.

"You're such a lovely young woman, Morgan," Rose said. "Are you dating anyone?"

*Not another matchmaker.* Morgan was used to this from well-meaning people. No doubt Rosie thought she was the perfect match for Ike's nephew. "No. I have extremely high standards, and the right man hasn't come along."

Rose nodded. "David isn't at all your type," she commented. Morgan and Kelsea exchanged an amused glance. "But there's someone out there for you. God will put him in your path when you least expect it."

"What about that doctor you went to dinner with a few weeks ago?" Kelsea asked.

Morgan made a face. "Dud," she said, giving a thumbs-down.

"What about Landon's brother?" Rose piped up. "He's a handsome man, and he needs someone."

"No. No, no, no," Morgan shook her head vehemently. She stopped when she saw the frown on Kelsea's face. Her sister had no idea that she and Brandon had clashed multiple times in the few hours they'd known one another.

"I mean," she back-pedaled, "He's not really my type." She felt her face growing warm.

"He's exactly your type, Morgy," Kelsea drawled.

Morgan looked at Rose. "Well, we live hundreds of miles apart," she said.

Rose waved a dismissive hand. "Oh, that's nothing to God," she said.

Morgan carried two platters of sandwiches to the kitchen island. "I'm really not interested," she said firmly. "I'm focused on my career right now." She looked to Kelsea for help, and fortunately, her sister radar was in good working order.

Kelsea brought out pitchers of tea and lemonade from the fridge. "Anyway, Rose, Brandon is still in deep mourning for his late wife. I don't think he's ready to move on yet."

Rose nodded. "He still needs time. But God will work it out so those sweet little girls can have a brother." She looked at Morgan again. "I'm sure of it."

Morgan really wanted this conversation to end. Even if she and Brandon St. Clair lived in the same city and somehow got past their intense dislike for one another, her fertility issues would ensure that April and Shelbie's wish for a brother would never come true.

Thankfully, the men and girls came in then, and things got wonderfully lively as they had lunch, and Morgan was happy that she could avoid Brandon. When they were cleaning things up, Landon went to take care of the laundry, and Kelsea asked Brandon if he would go out to the garage and get the extra tables and chairs that were out there, and take them out to the deck for tomorrow's barbeque.

"Sure thing, Kels," he said.

"Morgan can help you."

Morgan seethed inwardly. She gave her sister *the look* behind Brandon's back.

Brandon looked at her and then at Kelsea. "I'm sure I can handle it," he said as he walked toward the door to the garage.

"No, you can't. It'll take two people," Kelsea said.

"Then Landon can help me," Brandon said.

Kelsea stopped and looked between him and Morgan. "Is something going on with you two?" she asked.

"No!" Morgan and Brandon said in unison.

Morgan quickly walked to Brandon. "Let's go." He opened the door and she placed her hand on his back and shoved him through it.

When it closed behind them, he pulled away from her. "What is wrong with you?" he scowled.

"Nothing's wrong with me! You are the most exasperating person I've ever met!"

"I get along just fine with everyone else, which means that you're the problem!"

Morgan marched past him. "Let's just get the tables and chairs out of here and be done with it." She spied them behind some things and started to figure out the easiest way to get to them. She moved a lattice panel out of the way and began to move a stack of boxes, and caught a rake just before it fell over.

Brandon stood behind her with his hands on his hips. "What are you doing? You're going to get hurt."

"Well then, it's good that there's a *real doctor* here to take care of me!" He didn't reply, and she glowered at him. "Well, are you going to help, or not?"

Brandon closed his eyes and muttered something to himself. "Come on, move out of the way and let me get it."

The bickering continued for several minutes and they finally got one table free and carried it around the house to the back deck. Then they went back for the other table and the chairs, never speaking.

Morgan went back into the house and joined Kelsea, who was standing at the sink. Morgan squirted soap on her hands and began to vigorously wash them. "Kels, if that was some kind of cute trick to throw Brandon and me together, give it up!" she hissed.

Kelsea's mouth dropped open. "What are you talking about?"

Morgan tilted her head. "Seriously?"

"Sheesh, Morgan! Chill."

# 10

BRANDON HUGGED HIS brother and sister-in-law and got into the car. "Thanks for everything. We had a great time." They had stayed over until Monday morning and were headed back to Minneapolis. Fortunately, Morgan left yesterday afternoon to go back to Chicago. Brandon felt that he could finally relax without her there.

They had finally reached a truce and agreed that the girls could call her *Miss Morgy*. In his opinion, it was the silliest name on earth. He still couldn't figure out why April and Shelbie were so drawn to her. It annoyed him that they trailed after her all weekend, and insisted that she sit with them in church yesterday.

Even worse, when they were milling around after the service as Landon and Kelsea received congratulations from their church family, a woman greeted him and Morgan and remarked on what beautiful little girls "they" had. Without thinking, he'd replied curtly, "They're not hers, they're mine." The woman's face turned beet red and she slunk away. Brandon managed to hold his tongue when the second similar comment came. After that, he'd taken the girls to the car.

They had nearly cried when "Miss Morgy" left after the barbecue. Kelsea saved the day by suggesting that her friend,

Maggie, take April and Shelbie across the street to her house to meet their new puppies. But that presented a new set of problems. It was bad enough that they'd already fallen in love with Penny and Sheldon, but when the girls came back, they begged Brandon to let them *each* take a puppy home.

Brandon had to be the bad guy and put his foot down. He could barely manage the household, the girls, and himself. The thought of adding one animal, let alone two, to the chaos that was his life was completely impossible.

They got through Monday morning traffic, cleared the city, and got on the interstate. The girls were content in the backseat with games, books, and snacks that Aunt Kelsea had supplied.

Brandon loved getting out on the open road to clear his head. As Landon had forewarned him, his parents had sat him down for a long talk yesterday afternoon. Brandon had gotten so used to carrying his heavy load alone, and their tender concern finally caused him to break down. His dad, Jim, was still working at his engineering job, but his mom worked part-time, and offered to come to Minneapolis for a week each month over the summer to help Brandon out. It was a pretty easy trip from their home in Wisconsin.

"What if Sara came to live with you for a while, like a nanny, to help with the girls?" Janice St. Clair suggested.

Brandon shook his head. "I can't ask her to do that." He refrained from adding that he already had two children and didn't need a third. Sara was twenty, but still a kid, in Brandon's eyes. "Mom, she can't even cook," he added, trying to lighten the moment.

His mother started to open her mouth again, and Brandon's dad laid a hand on her arm. "Don't press, Jan. Give him some time to think it over." Then Jim St. Clair leaned over and kissed his wife's cheek. "Why don't you go find a grandchild or two to spoil?" he said with a smile.

Brandon's mom sniffed. "I know, I know, you want to have a

man-to-man talk," she said. She stood and bent down to hug her younger son. "I love you, Brandon. Please let us help you," she whispered, and then she was gone.

"Thanks, Dad," Brandon said, wiping his eyes. "I really do appreciate your support, and Mom's."

Jim St. Clair wasn't a big talker, and they sat in companionable silence for a few moments. Finally, he spoke. "Maybe a change of scenery would do you good. Have you ever thought about taking a job in a different city?"

Brandon was surprised at his dad's suggestion. "No, that's never occurred to me," he said. "I like my work, and Minneapolis is home." He couldn't imagine himself living anywhere other than his and Darla's home, or raising the girls anywhere else.

His dad clasped his shoulder. "Something to think about, then. I know it would be hard, but maybe it would be good for you in the long run. Pray about it," he added.

Brandon thought about it as he drove. He wasn't praying much these days. He decided to challenge God. "If you have a different plan for me, I'm not going to go looking for it, so you'll need to bring it to my doorstep."

# 11

MORGAN CALLED HER sister. "I'm home," she said.

"Oh! Good. You usually text," Kelsea said. "I wasn't expecting you to call. How was the trip?"

"Okay," Morgan said. She grunted as she wrestled her suitcase up the stairs of her townhouse.

"Are you hurting, Morgy?"

Morgan stopped. Her sister had an uncanny ability to know when she was in pain.

"I'm okay. I'll get everything organized here and then take a pain pill." The condition that was at the root of Morgan's infertility issues was under control, and only flared up on occasion, usually when she'd overdone. It had been a big weekend.

"Me getting organized takes five minutes," Kelsea said drily. "It will take you two hours. Take it slow."

Morgan smiled. "Yes, mama." She changed the subject. "It was such a great weekend. The babies are so precious, and I loved every minute of it." *Well, except when Landon's conceited, detestable brother was around.*

"It was perfect. I'm so glad everyone was able to come."

"Rose and Ike are just adorable," Morgan said. She couldn't

get the amusing picture of Rose in her Converse out of her mind. "They were so sweet with the babies."

"I know! They really are like family to us. I'm so glad all of you got to meet them." Kelsea giggled. "Promise not to get mad?"

"Mad? About what?"

"Before they left, Rosie took my hand and whispered into my ear, 'Your sister and that handsome doctor are going to make a beautiful couple.'"

"Aargh!" Morgan shouted. She rolled her eyes. "Not. Happening."

"Was something going on between you two?" Kelsea asked.

"No!" Morgan insisted. "Kels, I know you and Landon think he walks on water, but he was totally rude to me all weekend."

"I never saw that," Kelsea murmured.

"Well, that's how those kind of people are. They act one way to one person, and then show a completely different side to everyone else." Morgan unzipped her suitcase and started putting things away.

"You sure got along well with April and Shelbie."

Morgan's voice softened. "They're so precious. I enjoyed them so much." She sighed. "April has an amazing artistic ability, and I think art therapy could really help her sort through her feelings about her mom, but Dr. Moron wouldn't hear of it."

"Dr. Moron?!" Kelsea sputtered.

"Oh," Morgan said, "Sorry, that's just what I call him in my head."

"You sure have some strong feelings for him," her sister murmured. "You know, they say the line between hate and love is pretty thin."

"Not in this case! It's a brick wall. Make that a brick wall encased in steel. Case closed."

"Okay, I get it," Kelsea said. "So, what's your next step with looking into adoption?"

Morgan stilled. "I don't know, I just said I was thinking about looking into it." Suddenly, the idea seemed overwhelming. She sat down on her bed.

Her sister seemed to sense her hesitancy. "I'm sorry, Morgy, I shouldn't have brought it up. I'll be praying for you."

"Thanks, Sissy." They talked for a few more minutes, then said goodnight.

Morgan opened her laptop and transferred all the pictures from her phone onto it. Then she started scrolling through them. Her eyes teared up unexpectedly when she saw pictures of herself with her niece and nephew that Kelsea had taken. "I'd be a good mom, I know I would," she whispered to no one.

Then, her breath caught as the screen filled with a close-up shot of Brandon holding Isaac. *Who took this picture?* As far as she could tell, it had been taken out on the deck at lunchtime earlier that afternoon before Morgan had left. Morgan let out a huff and shook her head. It had to have been Kelsea, but Morgan wasn't going to call her out about it. Her sister would just deny it.

She continued to stare at the picture, and her heart skipped a beat. *This* Brandon St. Clair was unbelievably handsome. All traces of the negative emotions that Morgan had witnessed on his face throughout the weekend were gone. He looked completely relaxed and happy, holding the baby close. Rose Goldman was right; little Isaac looked as much like his uncle as he did his dad.

Brandon was looking directly into the camera, and Morgan felt like he was looking straight into her soul. She closed the computer screen and walked away.

# 12

*THREE MONTHS LATER*

"CHICAGO? YOU'RE MOVING to Chicago?" Landon's jaw dropped.

Brandon laughed and adjusted the screen so he could unload the dishwasher. He and his brother were video chatting. "Sure am. You're talking with the new Medical Director of the Chicago Professional Sports Medicine and Orthopedic Center."

"Wow, bro. Well, congratulations."

"Thanks. It's brand new, the only one of its kind. The five professional sports teams in Chicago came together to plan it, build it, and fund it to serve all of their athletes. It's state of the art. Believe me, they've spared no expense."

"I hope they didn't spare any expense when it came to your salary," Landon said drily.

Brandon smiled, and named a figure.

"Are you kidding me?" Landon grinned. "That's almost the annual operating budget at the firm!"

Brandon laughed. It was an amazing salary, but he knew his brother was exaggerating. "Yeah, it's a game changer. I'll run the whole place, and get to pick my surgeries. They said I could do as few as three or four a week. I wasn't about to tell them that most days, I've usually done that many before noon."

"Any travel involved?" Landon asked.

Brandon nodded. "Some. I'm pretty sure I'll get comp tickets to attend championship games and the like."

"Wow, man. Take me to the Super Bowl with you."

"You got it, man." Brandon laughed.

Landon shook his head slowly. "I never thought you'd leave Minneapolis."

Brandon let out a breath. He was leaving the life that he and Darla had built together. "Yeah, when Dad floated the idea to me at your house, I was dead set against it. But about a month later, the attorney representing the Center called me out of the blue. I have no idea where he got my name. They gave me everything that I asked for. I really think this is the right move. The change will be good for the girls and me. And we'll be closer to Mom and Dad."

"And to us. I know that'll make Mom happy. Have you told them yet?"

"Nope." Brandon smiled. "You're the first. Always."

"So, when are you moving?"

"I start the day after Labor Day. Movers are coming on Thursday."

"Wow, that's fast. Have you sold the house yet?"

"I just listed it with an agent. My employers said they'd cover the payment for a year if it doesn't sell. But it will. It's a sellers' market here."

Landon whistled softly. "Hey, is Peanut going with you?" Their younger sister, Sara, had moved in with Brandon and the girls a couple of months ago. Their mother's suggestion had turned out to be a good one.

"Yeah, she's excited about it."

"How's that working out, her being the nanny and all?"

Brandon smiled. "Great, as long as she stays out of the kitchen." Landon laughed.

Brandon saw his brother's attention move away from the screen. Then Kelsea appeared, holding Isaac. "Hi, Uncle Brandon," she said.

"Whoa! Look at that linebacker! Hey, big boy!" Brandon laughed when Isaac's little face broke into a wet grin.

Landon picked up his son and bounced him in his arms. "Maybe one of those teams you're gonna work for will give Isaac an early tryout." His eyes darted to his wife. "Can we tell her?" he said in a stage whisper.

"Tell me what?" Kelsea said.

"Sure," Brandon replied. Landon made the proud announcement and Brandon supplied the details.

Kelsea beamed at him. "That's fantastic! I'm really happy for you, Brandon. Congratulations. Oh, my goodness, Morgan lives in Chicago! You'll have to get together."

Brandon tried to look enthusiastic at the prospect. "Yeah, we'll have to do that," he said.

There was a long, loud squawk off-screen, and Landon smirked. "Your daughter is calling you," he said to Kelsea.

"Gotta run, Brandon. Congrats again!" She waved at him and disappeared.

"Great," Brandon muttered. "I forgot that she was from Chicago." That really wasn't true, but he didn't want his brother to know that. Every once in a while, he thought about Morgan. About how her beautiful green eyes lit up when she was with the girls, and her gentleness with them. How intuitive she was about the best way to talk and deal with them. Then he would think about how she rubbed him wrong, and how he didn't want to examine the possible reasons why. And then, he would feel guilty for having treated her so badly. Since Brandon didn't deal well with guilt, he'd just shove her out of his mind. And until now, he thought the only time he'd ever see her was at some random and infrequent family event.

Landon peered in the direction his wife had gone, waited a

beat, and then looked at the camera, right into his brother's eyes. "Don't worry, bro," he whispered. "I think the Windy City is big enough for both of you."

# 13

BRANDON LOOKED UP and did a full three-hundred-sixty-degree turn in the two-story foyer of his new home in one of Chicago's northwestern suburbs. They'd been here for three weeks and were finally settled in. The girls were asleep in their bedrooms upstairs. There were six, so there was no need for them to share. Still, most mornings he woke to find them in his bed, or curled up together in one of their beds.

He wandered into the formal living room, which was nearly empty. He'd bought new furniture for the family room, but Brandon had no idea what he would do with this enormous space.

"Hey," Sara said from behind him.

"Got any bright ideas for this room?" he asked, hands on his hips.

His sister mirrored his stance and looked around. "You could turn it into a game room."

Brandon shook his head. "There's already a game room. And a home theater. And another bonus room." The house had over 6,000 square feet.

Sara's dark brown eyes stared back at him. "Well, I sure can't complain about my rooms. They're really an apartment," she said with a smile. She had a large bedroom, a sitting room, a kitchenette, and full bath on the main floor. "I think they were meant as servants' quarters, but don't get any bright ideas," she added.

Brandon walked over and gave her shoulders a squeeze. "I know, Peanut," he said, using the name he and Landon had tagged her with twenty years ago when she was born. Sara was a foot shorter than him. "You're here to take care of April and Shelbie, nothing more." He gave her a mock grimace. "Certainly not to cook."

"I know," she said with a laugh. "But maybe even I could turn out an edible meal in that kitchen."

The kitchen was a chef's dream. Brandon enjoyed cooking, but never really had the time. Darla had loved to cook and bake. A familiar pain flared in his heart. He wished that he'd been able to give her this kitchen.

He and Sara wandered back into the kitchen. Brandon pulled up a stool to the counter, and Sara got a pitcher of iced tea out of the fridge. "Want some?"

"Sure."

"So, how's the new job? How many famous athletes have you met?" Sara's long blond ponytail swayed behind her.

Brandon laughed. "A couple of Blackhawks' players you probably wouldn't recognize."

She made a face. "Yeah, I don't follow hockey." Brandon fiddled with his phone, brought up a picture of him with the two players, and held it out. Sara cocked an eyebrow. "Maybe I'll start following hockey." She took a swallow. "You got any trips coming up?"

Although it would take him away from his daughters, this was one aspect of his new job that Brandon was really excited about. A doctor always accompanied the team, but as the top orthopedic surgeon at the center, Brandon would have the privilege of going on trips to various championship games, to be on hand to consult and do surgery, just in case. "Yeah, probably with the Cubs this week if they make the playoffs," he said.

"Do you get to ride on a private jet?"

He nodded and smiled. "Sometimes."

"Cool," Sara said.

They sat in silence for a moment. "Sara, I really do appreciate this," Brandon said. "Most sisters wouldn't take a year off college to care for their brother's children."

She shrugged. "It was good timing for me, too." Sara had been studying music at the University of Michigan. "I'm not convinced I was in the right major, and that's an awful lot of money to waste if you don't know what you want. When Mom suggested this, it felt right, and I wanted to help you, too." Her eyes took on a sheen. "I still can't believe Darla's gone. I was so little when you started dating. I don't remember a time when she wasn't there." Sara's voice shook, and a tear escaped and rolled down one cheek. "I still miss her so much."

"Come here," Brandon said, holding out an arm. Sara slipped under it and laid her head on his shoulder. He found himself fighting tears as well. Would the pain ever stop?

"I was closer to her than to my own sister," Sara whispered.

Reagan was almost two years older than Landon, and then Brandon came along less than a year later. Jim and Janice St. Clair thought their family was complete, but God had other ideas. Sara came as a total, although joyful surprise when their children were in their teens. By the time Sara was three, Reagan was off to college, and never lived at home again. And in recent years, the further she climbed up the career ladder, the more holidays she missed.

Sara sniffed and swiped a hand across her cheeks. "I'm going to bed," she said.

"It's only 8:45," Brandon said. "You wanna watch a movie in the home theater?"

Sara shook her head. "Maybe tomorrow night. I'm tired." She kissed her brother's cheek. "'Night."

"Good night, Peanut," Brandon said softly. He looked around

and finished the last of his tea. He didn't feel like watching a movie, either. He picked up his phone, pushed a button, and soon his brother's face appeared on the screen.

"Hey, man," Brandon said.

"Right back atcha," Landon replied.

"Is this a good time?"

"Yeah. Babies are down, and I was just finishing up some stuff. What's up?"

Brandon stood. "You want a tour of a multi-million-dollar house?"

Landon laughed. "Heck, yeah. One of my partners has a house like that, but it's not brand new."

Brandon gave him the kitchen tour, and decided to skip Sara's apartment. "Peanut's room is down that hall," he said, "but she already went to bed."

"Before nine?" Landon looked surprised.

Brandon shrugged. "She was tired."

"Hold on." Landon was walking now, too. He opened a door. "Everybody decent?" he called out.

Brandon could tell exactly where he was. "Hi, Kelsea," he called out.

"Oh, hi, Brandon." She laughed. "Yes, I'm in slob mode, but I'm decent." She was propped up in bed, reading.

Landon lay down next to her and adjusted the screen. "We're going on a tour of a million-dollar house," he said "Go back to the kitchen, bro."

"Ooh, awesome!" Kelsea closed her book.

Brandon walked through the house, pointing out all the amenities. He skipped the girls' rooms since they were asleep. Kelsea and Landon thought it was a spectacular home, and agreed with Brandon that there was a lot of space to fill.

"You know, Brandon, Morgan has all kinds of contacts with decorators and artsy people. You really need to call her," Kelsea said.

"Um, yeah, I'll try to do that," he said.

"Do you have her number? I can text it to you."

"Yeah, I'm pretty sure I do." He changed the subject quickly. "Well, guys, I need to do some stuff to get ready for the week. Talk to you soon."

After they'd signed off, Brandon went up to his room. When he turned on the light, the sight of his and Darla's bed sent a fresh wave of pain washing over him. The large dresser looked barren without her things on it. He could see into the enormous walk-in closet that was about a third full of his clothes, but otherwise empty. He was beginning to wonder if this was too much house for them.

Brandon sat down on the bed and sighed, rubbing his eyes. He'd almost sold the bedroom furniture when he left Minneapolis. After all, he was trying to make a fresh start. But in the end, he simply couldn't part with it. He remembered the day that he and Darla had picked it out together.

And how they'd celebrated the first night after it had been delivered.

Brandon stripped to his shorts and t-shirt and tumbled into bed. But it was a long time before sleep found him.

# 14

MORGAN RACED UP the steps and into her assigned classroom. She still had lots of prep to do before that afternoon's class. She'd overslept this morning—only by ten minutes—but had been playing catch-up all day long.

Her fall semester was fuller than she'd like. Morgan had a heavy teaching and advising load, and she was preparing an article for publication, plus she had her private patients.

She opened her e-mail and scanned them to make sure there wasn't anything there that couldn't wait until tonight to answer. Then Morgan's breath caught. There was an e-mail from Joyce Sheldon, the woman she'd recently talked to about what was needed to begin looking into fostering a child. Morgan had done some more research and thought maybe this would be a better way to go for now.

She quickly read through Joyce's e-mail, and her heart dropped. *So many steps to go through, so much red tape.* She would have to read it more thoroughly tonight.

Her phone pinged with a text. Morgan picked it up and rolled her eyes. *Not again.* Would her sister never give up? She read the text: *Hey Morgy! Texted Brandon last night and he still hasn't had a chance to get a hold of you. Why don't you call him at his office?* Kelsea had conveniently provided the number.

Morgan couldn't believe it when Kelsea called her a month ago and told her that Brandon and his girls were moving to Chicago. She brushed off her sister's suggestion about helping him figure out how to decorate his house, and gave her busy schedule as an excuse.

That night, Morgan had pulled up the picture of Brandon holding his nephew and stared at it for a long time. It wasn't the first time she'd looked at it since returning home from the family Mother's Day weekend in St. Louis. *Get a hold of yourself. That isn't the real Brandon St. Clair.*

Morgan didn't have time for distractions today. She had two classes to teach, three patients to see, and finally, a group session to observe conducted by one of her doctoral students. It would be a late night. And as soon as she got home, she would delete that picture from her computer.

Morgan thought tenderly about April and Shelbie. She would love to see them, but had no desire to even talk with their father. Chicago was a big enough city. Millions of people lived here, and with any luck, hers and Dr. St. Clair's paths would never cross.

# 15

BRANDON SAT AT his desk, answering e-mails. He'd been in his new position for almost a month and was settling in nicely. So far, he loved the job. He'd been on one trip and done five surgeries, all on top-tier athletes with household names. Besides that, he also managed the sports medicine clinic day-to-day, and did a lot of high-level work. He had directives from the board and was working on long-range planning and strategic initiatives. The work challenged him in a way that was different than just performing surgery, and he loved it.

Although Brandon wasn't convinced he liked the suburbs, he was getting used to the house and the neighborhood. He hadn't met any of the neighbors yet, but his sister had. Sara took the girls to the neighborhood park and arranged play dates with (in most cases) the nannies of their little friends. She had enrolled the girls in dance lessons, and as expected, April was taking more to ballet than tap dance, and Shelbie vice versa. They went to activities at the library and even though Sara couldn't boil water, no one was going hungry. The girls adored their Aunt Sara.

Landon had asked him a couple of times if he had found a church home yet, and Brandon kept fudging on that. Although his pain over losing Darla had lessened a bit, and even though he prayed occasionally, he still wasn't on good terms with God and hadn't decided yet what he was going to do.

Brandon got up and took his coffee mug for a refill. When he passed his assistant's desk on the way back, she waved at him. "Oh, hold on. He's here now," she said into the phone.

"Who is it, Giselle?" he asked softly.

She pushed a button that he assumed put the call on hold. "Morgan Anderson," the middle-aged brunette replied.

*Oh, no.* "Ah—I'll have to call her back," he said. "Just take a message." He went into his office and closed the door.

He walked over to the bank of windows that overlooked Lake Michigan and stared out, nursing his cup of coffee. What was it about Morgan that troubled him so?

His intercom beeped. "Brandon," Giselle said, "they want you down in the clinic. JoJo Collins just arrived." JoJo was one of the NFL's premier players that the Bears had acquired from Denver in the off season. He had a knee that was beginning to act up.

Brandon set his mug down and grabbed his stethoscope. "On my way," he said. Any thoughts about Morgan Anderson would have to wait.

# 16

TWO DAYS LATER, Brandon played his voicemail messages at the office. "Dr. St. Clair, this is Morgan Anderson." Brandon sat up. Her voice was crisp and businesslike. "My sister tells me that you've moved to Chicago and bought a home. She's decided that you need my help finding someone to help you decorate it, or at least get things up on the walls. You may know that when Kelsea gets an idea in her head, she doesn't let it go. She keeps asking if you've called me, or if I've called you. Now I can tell her that I have. Goodbye."

Brandon listened to the last remaining message and then replayed Morgan's. There sure wasn't any warmth in her voice.

*Well, what did you expect? A ticker-tape parade welcoming you to town?*

Brandon sighed. Last Sunday, Sara had convinced him to come with her and the girls to church. Although Brandon felt uncomfortable at first, somehow something crept past the walls he'd erected in his heart. The music, the prayers, and even the sermon were a soothing balm to his soul. Maybe he was turning a corner.

He propped a hip on one corner of his desk and stared out the window. *I don't want to do this.* He sat there for another moment.

*You're a better man than that. You need to apologize. It's time.*

Brandon sighed. He knew when God was talking to him. He used to listen for God's voice regularly, but had gotten out of the habit. Yes, it was time.

He punched the numbers into his phone and as it began ringing, his heart pounded.

"This is Morgan Anderson," her voice said pleasantly.

"Ah—hello, Morgan. This is Brandon St. Clair."

There was a beat of silence. "Yes?" Her voice had turned brittle.

"Well, um, hi. I thought I would return your call. I've been really busy."

"I'm sure you have." Silence yawned between them.

Brandon squirmed. "I, um—well, yeah. I—look. We got off on the wrong foot at Landon and Kelsea's. I—I was just—" He stopped, unable to get the words out.

"Yes?" she prompted.

*Man, she's not making this easy.*

His conscience pricked at him. *You think you deserve to get off easy?*

Brandon stood, walked over to the windows, and planted his feet in a wide stance. "I behaved badly, Morgan. There's no excuse, but I was overworked, and tired, and I—it was a very rough year." He swallowed. "Please, would you accept my apology? It would—it would mean a lot to me."

There was silence on the other end of the line for a few seconds, and Brandon held his breath. Finally, she spoke. "I—yes, I suppose. And I said some things that I shouldn't have, too. I'm sorry."

He let out a heavy breath. "Wow, I, uh, I feel so much better." *I probably shouldn't have said that.*

To his surprise, she laughed softly. "Me, too."

They chatted for a few moments—mostly about their common

niece and nephew and then April and Shelbie—haltingly at first, and then more comfortably.

"So, hey—would you like to see the house?" Brandon heard himself ask. "I'm not asking for your professional opinion or anything. Just come. The girls would love to see you. We're going to grill burgers on Sunday afternoon. About four?"

She didn't say anything. And Brandon had no idea why he had extended the invitation. He swallowed. "Morgan?"

"Sure, yes, that would be fine. Can I bring anything?"

"Oh, no. It will be very informal. Just, um, bring yourself. And there'll be someone special there who I want you to meet."

"Sounds good, Brandon. Well, thank you. Oh—could you text me the address?"

"Will do. See you Sunday, Morgan."

"See you then."

# 17

MORGAN LOOKED AT the clock again. Had it moved since she'd looked at it last? She checked her phone. Time was crawling by, but it was moving. She couldn't leave yet, or she would arrive way early and appear too anxious.

She checked herself in the mirror again. Should she wear the green top instead? No, she'd already changed twice. *You look fine.*

Morgan grabbed an eyebrow pencil and held her breath as she made one more adjustment. *Why are you so concerned about looking perfect?* she scolded herself. *This isn't a date. You're going to see the girls...and Brandon's just being nice. We're practically family. He hasn't done one thing to indicate that he's interested in you.*

And what if he was? Morgan didn't have the answer to that. Other than the fact that he was outrageously handsome, and seemed to be a good parent, he hadn't demonstrated any redeeming qualities to make Morgan think that he was worthy of her attention.

She puttered around in her kitchen until it was time to leave. She knew the area where the address was. A couple of years ago, she'd gone to a home not too far from it for a private art showing. Her phone gave clear directions and she made good time.

Morgan turned left onto Evergreen Place. It should be on the right…she passed one palatial home after another. *Wow.* This was some neighborhood. There it was, 48. She pulled into the wide, custom brick driveway and parked behind Brandon's SUV, which now had Illinois plates. A compact car with Wisconsin plates sat next to it. Morgan shook her head to herself. If the cars were in the driveway, what was in the four-car garage?

The house was enormous, all brick and glass. The yard looked new and fresh, and was clearly professionally landscaped, as were all the homes in the neighborhood. She wondered if Brandon had a gardener. This new job of his must be really something.

She rang the doorbell and waited. When the door opened, Morgan was shocked to see a beautiful, petite woman in jeans and a pink v-neck top. Her wavy blond hair was caught up with a glittering clip, and reached halfway to her waist. She had sparkling dark brown eyes and dimples. "Hi, I'm Sara St. Clair," she said. "You must be Morgan. Welcome!"

Morgan's heart dropped. This must be the "someone special" that Brandon had wanted her to meet. *He was married!* Maybe that's why he had moved to Chicago. Kelsea hadn't said anything about that. She glanced at the woman's—correction, *young* woman's left hand, but it was wrapped around the door in such a way that Morgan couldn't see whether or not she wore a ring.

"Yes—yes, I'm Morgan, nice to meet you," she said. Goodness, but this was awkward. Sara had to be a decade younger than Brandon! His first wife had only been gone a little over a year, and he'd been so devastated just a few months ago. Apparently, he'd gotten past that and moved on.

Morgan knew she couldn't turn and run away, so she stepped into the house. This was a terrible idea. She would make some excuse and get out as quickly as she could.

She took in the two-story entryway and tried not to gawk. It was easily bigger than her entire living room. Sunlight streamed in the multiple windows, throwing rainbows off the gorgeous crystal chandelier hanging overhead. A curved staircase graced the room.

"Miss Morgy!" April and Shelbie cried as they ran up behind Sara. Both of them came right to Morgan and held their arms out, and she leaned down to hug them.

"It's wonderful to see you, girls!" Morgan said.

Shelbie hopped up and down. "You hafta see my room!" she exclaimed. "It's purple!"

Morgan laughed. "I could have guessed that." She turned to April. "What color is your room?"

April smiled shyly. "It's pink and green, like a garden."

"Ooh, I'll bet it's pretty," Morgan said.

"Go ahead, girls, take Morgan upstairs." Sara looked at her. "I'll go check with Brandon and see how the burgers are coming." She glided away.

Morgan set her purse down, and April and Shelbie each took a hand. She spent the next ten minutes with them looking at their pretty bedrooms and meeting their dolls and stuffed animals. When they were finished, they walked down the hall. Shelbie skipped ahead of Morgan and April. "Wanna see Daddy's room?" Shelbie asked.

"Girls?" Brandon's voice floated up from below. "Come on downstairs."

*Just in time.* They reached the top of the stairs, and as Brandon looked up, his face broke into a smile. He wore cargo shorts, sandals, and a close-fitting navy t-shirt. He looked tanned and fit, and completely at ease. "Hi, Morgan. I see you got the tour."

Morgan's heart fluttered in her chest. *Wow, he's more handsome than ever now that he's relaxed and in his own home and...married.* She immediately felt like she had been doused with cold water.

She managed a smile as she followed the girls down the stairs. "I just saw their rooms." The girls ran ahead, and into what Morgan assumed was the kitchen. She stopped on the bottom stair, which put her even with Brandon. Morgan tucked a wayward strand of hair behind her ear and looked around. Anything to keep her eyes off him. "This is a beautiful home."

"Thanks. It's sure different than anywhere else I've lived." He lifted a shoulder. "I'm beginning to wonder if it's too big. And it's farther from the city than I'd like."

"I live in the city," she said. "I wish I could go to the country."

Brandon made a face. "Not me. I'm a city boy, through and through." He looked at her and smiled. "I'm glad you came. You look great." *He had the most beautiful eyes.*

Morgan felt her face heating up. "Oh, um, thanks." She could hardly breathe in his presence, and becoming infatuated with a married man broke all kinds of rules for her. She scooted around him and stepped off the stair. He turned to her, and she looked away again. "Listen, I'm so sorry, but I'm not going to be able to stay. Something unexpected came up." *That was certainly the truth.*

Brandon's face fell, and Morgan felt terrible. But she had to get out of here. She picked up her purse.

"Morgan, are you sure? The burgers are ready and the girls are so excited—"

Her stomach clenched. *April and Shelbie.* Morgan felt terrible for disappointing them, but she knew she couldn't get through a meal with Brandon and Sara. Morgan reached for the door handle. "Please tell them I'm sorry, and that I promise to come another time and make it up to them." She glanced around to avoid meeting his eyes. "Your home is beautiful. I'll text you some names of some decorators you can contact. Goodbye, Brandon." She slipped out the door as quickly as she dared, made a dash for her car, and drove away without a backward glance.

# 18

BRANDON STOOD IN the foyer with his hands on his hips. He scratched his head. *What was that all about?* Morgan was here one moment, and gone the next. He had a feeling he was missing something.

Sara came in. "Dinner's almost ready." She looked around. "Where's Morgan? Using the bathroom?"

Brandon shook his head slowly. "No...she left." Her scent still lingered and he was filled with all kinds of conflicting emotions.

"Left? Why?"

"I have no idea. She all of a sudden said that something came up, and she had to go. Something happened, I'm sure of it." He tilted his head at Sara. "Did you say something to her?"

"What, me? No! I just introduced myself and the girls came in and took her up to show her their rooms." She tilted her head back at him. "Maybe *you* said something to her?"

He replayed their very short conversation in his mind, and was more perplexed than ever. "No, I didn't."

Shelbie skipped into the room. "Miss Morgy!" She stopped and looked around. "Where's Miss Morgy?"

"She had to leave, sweetie," Brandon said. He looked at Sara.

"Why she leave?" Shelbie wailed.

Brandon ushered his small daughter toward the kitchen. "Let's eat," he said. He looked over his shoulder at his sister. "I'll figure this out later."

The food was delicious, but Brandon hardly tasted it. The girls were cranky, and he snapped at them once and had to apologize.

"We've had a busy weekend," Sara said. "Girls, let's get upstairs for baths." She looked at Brandon. "Do you want to go with them, or clean this up?"

"I'll do this," he said. He was still distracted, disturbed by Morgan's quick, unexplained exit. He texted Landon. *Hey, has Morgan texted Kelsea tonight?*

His brother answered quickly. *I don't know. Why?*

Brandon didn't feel like explaining. *Never mind. It doesn't matter.*

*What's up, bro?*

*It doesn't matter. Thanks. Gotta go.*

Brandon got the leftovers into the fridge and the dishwasher loaded. He looked at his calendar and began preparing his mind for the work week. Then he set some reminders on his schedule for tomorrow and went upstairs to read to the girls and tuck them into bed. Sara said goodnight and went downstairs.

After he said prayers with the girls and turned off the lights, he went into his bedroom to make sure his clothes were ready for morning. Sara had helped him choose a new comforter and linens, and the room didn't have the devastating effect on him that it once had.

He continued to think about Morgan as he put his laundry away. It occurred to him that he was very disappointed that she hadn't stayed, and he didn't know what to make of that. He thought about how pretty she looked, in white cropped pants and royal blue sandals that matched her top, and a long, flowing scarf in shades of blue, yellow, and green. Her long, golden hair had been piled casually on top of her head with pieces of it hanging down to frame her face. Her gorgeous green eyes were perfectly made up in a way that somehow made them stand out. They were absolutely mesmerizing.

Brandon sat down on the edge of the bed. *I think I'm attracted to her.* The thought both thrilled and scared him. He hadn't given any woman a second glance in the almost year and a half that he'd been a widower.

He headed downstairs and had just stepped off the bottom stair when his phone pinged. It was Landon.

*Sara introduced herself to Morgan as Sara St. Clair.*

*So what?* Brandon thought. He responded, *It's her name. How else would she introduce herself?*

*She never said she was your sister. Think about it, man. Put yourself in Morgan's shoes.*

"Oh, no..." Brandon finally understood. He sat down on the bottom stair. *I got it, thanks,* he typed, and signed off. He sat there for a long time, deep in thought, and finally, a slow smile spread across his face.

# 19

MORGAN GATHERED UP her things to get ready to leave work. It had been a long day, a long week already, and it was only Wednesday. She and Joyce Sheldon had exchanged a few e-mails. Morgan had more questions than ever, and was starting to think that fostering was the way to go. She had asked Joyce to send her the necessary paperwork to prepare her application, but hadn't heard anything back yet.

Maybe she would get out of town this weekend, go to the country and paint. Morgan's good friends, Luke and Miranda, lived on a large farm west of Chicago. There was a secluded, rustic cabin on their property overlooking a beautiful pond, and Morgan had an open invitation anytime she wanted to come. *Yes, I'll go,* she decided. She needed to clear her head of Brandon St. Clair and decide if she was ready to move forward and bring a child into her life.

The first thing Morgan had done when she arrived home from Brandon's house on Sunday evening was to delete the picture of him from her computer. Then she immediately texted her sister. Morgan didn't want to admit that she'd run away from Brandon's house, so she skipped that part. *I met Brandon's wife* was all she had said. Of course, Kelsea called her right away, and they sorted the whole thing out. Morgan tried to be upbeat and laugh it off, but she was absolutely mortified at her misassumption. In the three years that she'd known her brother-in-law, she had only heard him refer to his younger sister as *Peanut*. Morgan begged Kelsea not to tell Landon, but by then he had heard his wife's end of the conversation and knew something was going on, so of course they had to share the whole story with him.

Morgan knew it would eventually get back to Brandon, and she could never look him in the eye again. Or Sara.

Morgan didn't fall asleep for a long time that night. She thought about retrieving the deleted photo and decided to leave it be. The thing that haunted her the most was that she seemed to be attracted to Brandon St. Clair, and that terrified her. Morgan didn't have a lot of experience with men. She didn't date in high school because she was so busy taking AP classes and designing sets for the drama club, and spending all her nights and weekends in art galleries and at art shows. College was more of the same, with a few occasional dates. Getting her PhD before she turned thirty left little time for romance or anything else, and she'd never really met a guy that challenged her intellectually or who interested her.

Until Patrick. But she wasn't going to think about him.

Maybe, just maybe, Brandon was a little interested too, and that's why he had invited her to his house. And then she completely blew it. But maybe he was just being nice, and wasn't even interested. Morgan had no idea how these male/female games worked.

Brandon had almost completely filled her thoughts since Sunday night. And then, as if she had the power to conjure him up just by thinking about him, he appeared in the doorway of her office, holding a large bouquet of calla lilies.

Morgan was standing at the round meeting table in her office, sorting through some papers, and almost dropped the pile of folders that she was holding. Heaven help her, he was unbelievably handsome in a navy suit, crisp white shirt, and a blue patterned tie. Her entire body went cold, then hot, and her knees turned to jelly. Morgan felt her face flaming. She could hardly make eye contact with him.

"Hi," he said with a smile.

*This cannot be happening.* A thousand thoughts collided inside Morgan's mind. First, of course, was that he'd talked with Kelsea and Landon. Otherwise, how did he know that her favorite flowers in the whole world were calla lilies? She wished the floor would swallow her up.

"Hi," she tried to say back, but hardly any sound came out.

He stepped into her office and tipped his head toward the door. "Mind if I close this?"

Morgan shook her head. He shut the door and suddenly, the room felt half its normal size.

Brandon walked over to her. "Let's sit down," he said, gently taking her elbow. She must have looked on the verge of fainting. Morgan sank into one of the chairs at the round table. He laid the flowers down and pulled up a chair next to her.

She felt like she could burst into tears at any moment. She swallowed. "Brandon, I'm so embarrassed—"

"Shh," he whispered. "You don't have anything to be embarrassed about, or to be sorry for." His amber gaze held hers for a moment. "Are you seeing anyone right now?"

*Surely he can't mean...* "Am I seeing anyone?" she heard herself say. No way was she going to answer him for fear of making another misassumption.

"What I meant to say was, are you dating anyone?"

"Am I dating anyone?"

He nodded.

She shook her head.

"Would you go out with me?"

Morgan thought she must be hearing things. "Would I go out with you?"

Brandon glanced around. "Is there an echo in here?" he said with a smile. "Yes. I want to take you out, on a date."

"On a date?"

He laughed, and Morgan almost melted into a puddle at his handsomeness. She wanted to pinch herself. She had to be dreaming. "I don't understand."

Brandon scratched his chin. "When I invited you over last Sunday, I wasn't thinking anything. I guess I just figured that it would be an extra goodwill gesture to apologize for how badly I acted toward you when we first met."

He took a breath, reached out, and wrapped his hand around hers. Morgan swore a jolt of electricity shot clear down to her toes. "But when you left, I was so disappointed, and that surprised me. I did a lot of thinking that night, and realized that I was attracted to you, and that I was looking forward to getting to know you better."

Morgan's heart began to pound. She looked down at Brandon's long, smooth fingers holding hers, and she gazed into his eyes again. *His incredible golden amber eyes.* They took on a twinkle. "And then, when I found out why you had left so suddenly, I realized that if you weren't interested in me, you wouldn't care whether or not I was married." His smile got bigger. "Am I right?"

Something in Morgan's heart burst, and she felt liquid joy running through her veins. She couldn't believe that Brandon St. Clair was sitting here, holding her hand and telling her that he was attracted to her and wanted to date her.

It gave her confidence to not hold back. She nodded. "Yes. You were right."

He let out a breath. "Oh, good," he said, and they both laughed.

"Sara doesn't look anything like me," he explained. "She's blond like Landon, but he and I look alike. Our older sister Reagan has dark hair like mine, but she looks like Sara." He grinned. "Does that make sense?"

Morgan nodded. "Yeah, it does. Kelsea and I don't really look alike. She resembles our mom, and I look like our dad." She felt a surge of boldness. "I can't believe this is happening," she said. She felt like her smile might split her face open.

"Me, too," Brandon said. His eyes sparkled. He let go of her hand and picked up the bouquet and held it out.

"I love calla lilies, thank you." She slid him a mischievous look. "How did you know that they're my favorites?"

"Kelsea may have told me."

"I figured," Morgan replied with a giggle. She couldn't remember the last time she had giggled.

Brandon leaned forward and rested his arms on the table. "Let's figure this out together. I'm close to Landon, and you're close to Kelsea. What's your comfort level with what we each tell them?"

Morgan thought for a moment. "I think I'd like to keep things to ourselves until we figure out things out a little more," she said.

"That's exactly what I was thinking. For now, it will be our secret." He smiled, and Morgan's stomach did a flip. He took her hand again. "I've talked with them, and the misunderstanding about Sara will stay with the four of us, and we'll never mention it again. Do you understand what I'm saying?"

Morgan let out a breath of relief. "Yes. Thank you, Brandon."

"Sara will never know, unless you choose to tell her. Okay?"

She nodded. He stood and helped Morgan to her feet. "I think I owe you a dinner."

Morgan laughed. "I'm the one who ran out. I owe *you* a dinner."

His eyebrows lifted. "Are you free tonight?"

"I could be persuaded."

"In that case..." He leaned down and brushed his lips across hers. Morgan thought she might faint. "Do you need some more persuading?" he whispered. His eyes sparkled.

Morgan held her breath. *I'll never get another chance like this.* Then she nodded, and everything went into slow motion. As he came closer, his amber eyes darkened a shade, and once Morgan closed her own eyes, her other senses took over. The feel of his soft, firm lips on hers, and the solidness of his shoulders as she ran her hands up and over them. His unique, masculine scent. The sound of her sigh as his arms pulled her close, and of his soft answering moan. The taste of his mouth intermingled with hers.

When they finally came apart, he just held her, for which she was grateful. She was definitely experiencing sensory overload.

If Brandon St. Clair kissed her a million more times—and Morgan sincerely hoped that would be the case—she would still remember *this* kiss for the rest of her life.

# 20

*GO BIG OR go home.* That was his and Landon's mantra in everything they attempted. The St. Clair brothers had always set big goals in their professional and personal lives, and it was the reason Brandon had been able to so boldly state his intentions to Morgan tonight. And, for heaven's sake, to kiss her before the date even began. He'd never done anything like that before. But he couldn't keep his eyes off her rosy lips, and almost before he realized what he was doing, he was kissing her.

That second kiss was really something. Brandon was overwhelmed by her feminine softness, and the way she fit in his arms. Almost before he could wonder if he was moving too quickly, he realized that she was as eager a participant as he. They were both breathless when they came apart.

Once Brandon had figured out that he was attracted to Morgan and that she certainly must feel the same way, he set his course for full-steam ahead. Darla was the only woman he had ever dated, and they had met when they were seventeen. Brandon had no patience for dating games, or any knowledge of how they worked.

He and Morgan were sitting in his SUV now. She wore a long, flowing skirt with a swirling pattern in vibrant blues, greens, and purples, and a blue gauzy blouse. The total effect brought out the green in her eyes, and Brandon could hardly keep from staring at her.

"You're the one who knows this city," he said. "Where should we eat?"

"Gosh, there are so many good restaurants," Morgan replied. "What are you in the mood for?"

Brandon's mind went to a place that it had no business going on a first date. He dragged his gaze from her and shifted in his seat. "I'll eat just about anything." He looked out the window. "It's a beautiful fall evening. Maybe somewhere with a patio?"

"Oh, my gosh!" Morgan exclaimed, causing him to jump. "Autumn Evening!" When Brandon didn't say anything, she smiled. "It's a restaurant, and it has a patio. It's perfect."

They got there in under twenty minutes, and it *was* perfect. It might have been the most perfect evening in Brandon's life, or at least in a very long time. After they were seated on the patio and the server brought glasses of water, Brandon studied the menu and was surprised when he heard Morgan say, "What looks good to you?"

*You,* he instantly thought. He felt his face flush, and took a long drink of his water. He couldn't remember anything that he'd just read. "I—wow," he gulped. "To tell you the truth, my stomach is so jittery, I don't think I can eat much."

Morgan laughed and gave him a dazzling smile. "Me, too." She tucked a strand of hair behind her ear in what seemed like a nervous gesture. Brandon wanted to grab her hand and kiss it.

"Would you want to split an entrée?" he asked, and she nodded and looked relieved. They ended up each ordering a salad and sharing an order of fettucine Alfredo, and later, a piece of raspberry cheesecake.

He wanted to know everything about her. She'd grown up in Kankakee, Illinois with her mom, dad, and of course, her older sister. Their dad died of a heart attack when Morgan was ten and Kelsea was twelve. Brandon held her hand as she talked about that period in her life, and how art filled the deep fissures of her soul and helped set the course for her life's work.

"I know you think art therapy is silly," she said.

Brandon held up a hand. "Don't hold me responsible for anything I said the weekend we met," he said. "Although, I really don't understand it." He smiled. "But I'm willing to try."

"How's April doing?" Morgan asked.

Brandon let out a deep breath and shook his head. "Some things are better since Pea—Sara—is here with us and keeps the girls on a schedule, but April still wakes up crying during the night, and sometimes she disappears during the day and we find her curled up on her bed."

"I'm sorry," Morgan said softly. "I was older when I lost my dad, and it took me a long time to work through it. Something like that changes you forever."

Brandon nodded. "I would give *anything* in the world for my girls to not have to go through this," he said softly. He felt his eyes tearing up and was surprised when he felt Morgan's soft, smooth hand on his. She didn't say anything, but he felt immensely comforted by her touch.

They had coffee with their dessert, and stayed long after everyone else had left, holding hands almost the entire time. He couldn't keep his eyes off her long, graceful fingers. Brandon felt like they were in a private, romantic universe of their own, with hundreds of twinkling lights on the fence and in the trees around them, and the cool, calm breeze playing with Morgan's luxurious, sun-streaked hair. He itched to run his fingers through it.

Their server finally appeared, an apologetic look on his face. "We're getting ready to close," he said. Brandon signed the check with a generous tip, and they left.

He laced his fingers with Morgan's and they walked slowly to the car. When they got there, he turned and laid his hands on her shoulders. "This was a perfect evening," he whispered. "Thank you for going out with me."

"Thank you for asking," she said, and lifted her face to his. Brandon explored her lips and savored the tastes of raspberry and coffee. Then he looked into her gorgeous green eyes and rubbed his hands up and down her arms. "I—it's so amazing to hold you," he said. "You're so tall, and so close." He swallowed. "Darla was really short." Then he realized what he was saying, and his breath caught. "Morgan, I'm so sorry—"

She shook her head and raised one graceful hand to touch the side of his face. "Don't be, Bran. It's okay. She was part of you."

"I—wow." Brandon pulled her a little closer and smiled. "Bran? I like that. No one has ever called me that."

Morgan smiled. "It fits."

"Where's your car?" he asked. Brandon wished he could take her home.

"I took the El to work. There's a station a block away."

*Perfect.* Brandon tilted his head at her and smiled. "You are *crazy* if you think I'm going to let you take the El home." He unlocked the passenger door and helped her in.

It was about a twenty-minute drive to her condo, and felt like two. They found so many things to laugh and talk about. Brandon felt like a teenager when he walked Morgan to her doorstep and took her in his arms.

"Can you come for dinner Friday night?" he said. "The girls will be so excited."

"I'd love to. What about Sara?"

"You mean, should we tell her?" Brandon chuckled. "Not yet, unless you want to hear about it on CNN. She can't keep a secret."

Morgan's laughter was like music to him.

"We'll sneak off for kisses," he said huskily.

"Then I'll definitely come. Text me when you get home?" Morgan asked.

"I live way out in the 'burbs," he said. "It'll take me a while. Will you still be up?"

Her eyes sparkled at him under the porch light. "I don't think I'll be able to fall asleep anytime soon."

He laughed and touched his forehead to hers. "I understand. Completely." Then he kissed her, slow and sweet, holding himself to one kiss. "Goodnight, Morgan." He waited until she'd gotten inside and locked the door.

Brandon replayed every moment of their date on the way home, and couldn't stop smiling. Forty minutes later, he pulled into his garage and sent her a text. *Made it home. Sweet dreams.*

*They sure will be* ☺, she replied.

# 21

"DR. ANDERSON?"

Morgan snapped back to the present. She'd been staring at her phone screen, which now held the picture of Brandon with Isaac that she'd been able to recover from her computer last night. She'd looked at it at least a thousand times today.

One of her most promising master's students, Lexi Montgomery, stood in her office doorway. "Oh, I'm sorry—hi, Lexi," she said. "Come on in."

She spent the next fifteen minutes with Lexi, who laid out her plans for a very promising research project. Another student came after that, and then Morgan got through all her e-mails and answered them. Before she knew it, her office hours were over.

She felt like she'd been in a dream since last night. *Was it just last night?* Morgan looked at the time. It'd been less than twenty-four hours. She touched her fingers to her lips. *That kiss.* Not the first one—although she'd felt that one clear down to her toes—but the second one, in her office. Morgan felt that one in every part of her body. She'd never been kissed like that before. And she couldn't believe that she'd kissed him back.

And his subsequent kisses were just as powerful.

Morgan had never experienced a man like Brandon St. Clair.

He was so bold and confident and commanding. He was really interested in *her?* Quiet, boring, studious Morgan Ashley Anderson?

Her phone pinged an alarm, and she realized it was time for the weekly department faculty meeting. Morgan gathered her things and locked her door behind her.

Her cell rang. "Dr. Anderson," she said as she walked down the hallway.

"Dr. St. Clair," came the suave reply.

Morgan thought she felt her feet come off the floor. "Hi," she said, and grimaced inwardly. Why couldn't she think of something more interesting to say?

"Hi," he answered. Then he laughed. "Now I'm the one echoing *you.*" Morgan joined his laughter. "How's your day going?"

"Great. It's going great," Morgan replied. "What about you?"

"My day is—fantastic," he said. "I can't stop thinking about last night, and I can't stop thinking about how good it feels to hold you."

Morgan stopped dead in her tracks. No man had ever said anything so romantic to her. She had no idea how to reply.

"I'm sorry," Brandon said. "Too much, too soon?"

"What? No, not at all, Bran. I—" she looked around to make sure she was alone. "I had such a great time last night."

"Oh no, I sense a *but* coming," he said softly.

Morgan took another deep breath. "Not at all. What I was going to say was—that I can't stop thinking about you, too, and—" *You can do this.* "I can't wait to kiss you again."

"Wow." He let out a low whistle, and Morgan giggled. Her face felt hot. "You just made my day," he said. His voice had gone a little husky, and Morgan suppressed a shiver.

"You made mine, too, just by calling." She was almost to the conference room. "I'm sorry, I have to go. Faculty meeting. Bleh."

"Sounds like our staff meetings. I'll let you go. I'll call you tonight."

"You'd better," she said with a smile. *Where are these bold words coming from?*

"Bye, Morgan."

"Bye, Bran." Morgan slipped her phone in her pocket and entered the room.

The department chair, Dr. Juanita Ross, looked up. She had been Morgan's mentor all through her master's and doctoral work, and knew her well. "Hi, Morgan," she said. She stared at Morgan for a moment.

"Um—hi, Juanita." Morgan quickly found a seat.

Juanita gave her a quizzical look. "You look—different. Is something going on?"

*Breathe.* Morgan felt a couple of other colleagues sizing her up.

"You look happy, like really, really happy," Juanita said.

Morgan flipped her hair over her shoulder. "Oh—yes, I'm happy. Um—Lexi Montgomery just came up with a really amazing idea for a research project." She resisted the urge to laugh hysterically. Morgan uncapped her water bottle and took a gulp.

"That's great," Juanita said. She didn't look entirely convinced. She looked around the table. "Well, let's get started."

# 22

THE HOURS BETWEEN Wednesday night and Friday crawled. Brandon couldn't wait to see Morgan, but he knew he had to act casual and pretend that she was nothing more than a family friend coming over for dinner.

He got home from work and decided to take a shower. When he walked into the kitchen, Sara and the girls were there. "Chicken is ready to go on the grill," she said. He picked up the plate and gathered the other supplies he'd need.

"Whoa," Sara said, and gave an exaggerated wheeze. Brandon stopped. "What did you do, bathe in aftershave?" She raised her eyebrows and smiled.

*Oh no.* He rolled his eyes. "So I shaved. You're such a drama queen." He hurried out the door.

Brandon forced himself to stay by the grill and let Sara and the girls get the door when Morgan arrived. When April and Shelbie led her out onto the deck, his heart began a crazy dance. She wore a beautiful flowered dress with a full skirt that floated around her legs. It was casual, yet elegant.

"Hi, Morgan," he managed to say calmly. "Glad you came."

"Hi, Brandon, thanks," she said.

*Is her heart beating as hard as mine is?*

The girls wanted to show her the yard and all their outside toys. April showed great delight in pointing out the fall flowers that the landscaper had planted. The girls monopolized her attention and that was fine with Brandon. He didn't know if he could have a conversation with her and keep his wits about him.

They sat down to eat, and Sara and Morgan chatted easily. Sara was a very talented vocalist and had been majoring in music.

"I made a new friend today," Shelbie announced. Sara had begun taking the girls to a nearby park.

"Oh, who's that?" Brandon asked.

"His name is AJ. I like the name AJ. I want our little brother's name to be AJ."

"Me, too," said April.

*Oh, no.* Brandon forced himself not to cringe. Why wouldn't the girls drop this obsession about having a little brother? "Who can eat ten peas first? Ready, set, go!" Fortunately, the game distracted the girls. When Brandon chanced a glance at Morgan, she was looking down at her plate, and her cheeks were definitely tinged a little pink.

Morgan scooted her chair back. "Could someone point me to the restroom?"

Brandon popped up. "I'll show you where it is." He opened the French doors and ushered her through. Once they were through the kitchen, he grinned and took her hand. His heart was hammering. He led her into the half bath off the large entry foyer, turned on the light, and closed the door. In about a second, she was in his arms. "I've missed you so much, babe," he murmured.

She gazed up at him with a gorgeous smile. "Babe? I like that. No one has ever called me babe."

He locked his arms behind her waist. "I've never called anyone that. It fits." He bent his head to kiss her, and they spent a few more moments smiling and whispering about absolutely nothing. It was enough for Brandon just to hold her. "I should get back. Wait a few minutes and then come back out."

Morgan nodded and giggled. "Sneaking away to a bathroom. This is so romantic."

Brandon laughed. "I couldn't wait one more minute to kiss you." He put his hands on her shoulders. "Could I come to your place for a while tonight, later? I'll tell Sara I have to go check on something at the Center."

Morgan's emerald eyes sparkled. "I'd like that. Do you remember how to get there?"

Brandon nodded, then hesitated. "Could you do me a favor?" he asked. She nodded. "Even though I'll see you in a little while, *please* call or text me when you're safe at home. I just—I just need to know."

She reached out and squeezed his hand, and Brandon knew that she understood. "I will, I promise."

Brandon touched his lips to hers. "Save me some kisses," he murmured.

"I will."

Brandon willed his heart to beat normally and hurried back to the patio, slowing his steps as he arrived. Sara looked at him quizzically. "That took a while."

He sat and took another helping of potato salad. "I heard a noise outside."

"Maybe it was the neighbor's cat," Sara mused.

"It was. That's what it was. The neighbor's cat."

She tilted her head at him. "None of our neighbors have a cat, Brandon."

Brandon ignored her and turned his attention to his daughters. "Tell me about going to the library today, girls."

# 23

MORGAN KICKED OFF her shoes and laid her purse and keys on the hall table. She turned on some lights and cast a critical eye around her condo. What would Brandon think of it? It was so much smaller than his expansive home.

Morgan was a tidy person and there really wasn't any clutter, but she straightened up some things and checked her coffee pods. She knew Brandon drank coffee and she hoped there would be something there he liked.

Then she ran up to her bedroom, spritzed on her favorite light scent, and swiped on some lip gloss. Morgan stared at herself in the reflection. What was that business about Brandon's girls wanting a little brother? She faintly recalled something about it from last spring at Kelsea and Landon's house.

Morgan sat down on the edge of her bed. What was she going to do? Should she say something to him about her infertility issues? Her head and her heart were at war. *No, it's definitely too soon.*

The doorbell rang, and she scurried back downstairs and drew in a shaky breath before opening the door, willing the butterflies in her stomach to stop fluttering.

He completely filled the doorframe. "Hi," he said. Brandon's smile reached from ear to ear, and his handsomeness nearly caused her to melt.

"Hi, come in," Morgan said shyly. All of a sudden, she felt—well, she didn't know what she was feeling. They'd been together in her office and a restaurant, and in his car in the parking lot—all public places—and then at his home tonight with Sara and the girls in close proximity. But now they were completely alone.

Morgan was both excited and terrified. She wasn't sure what he expected. She closed the door and turned to face him.

He reached out and took her hand. "What's the matter, Morgan?"

"What's the matter?" she echoed.

Brandon took her other hand and smiled. "When you're nervous, you repeat whatever I say. And it's *adorable*."

She couldn't help but laugh, and he joined her. "Come here." Brandon wrapped his arms around her, and tucked her head into the space between his shoulder and neck. They stood there like that for several moments, his hand stroking her hair. "I just want to spend some time with you and get to know you better," he said softly.

"Sounds perfect," Morgan replied. She let out a breath. "Would you like some coffee?"

He smiled. "I'd love some," and followed her into the kitchen. Morgan learned his favorite flavor of coffee, and decided that as soon as he left, she'd go online and order a case of it.

When they went back into the living room, Morgan realized that she'd left her laptop open on the coffee table. *Oh, no.*

"Nice screensaver," Brandon commented with a sparkling smile that rivaled the one in the photo.

Morgan set the tray down and wondered how to explain it to him, but he didn't give her the chance. Instead, he pulled her into his arms. "I'm extremely flattered," he whispered, and then captured her lips in a delicious kiss.

They sat down on the couch, and both of them sipped their

coffee. "I didn't take that picture of you," Morgan said. "It showed up on my phone after I got home from St. Louis. Do you remember who took it?"

Brandon frowned. "I don't. There were so many phone cameras around all weekend." He pulled his phone out and held it up. Morgan was surprised to see the background was a picture of her with April and Shelbie in Landon and Kelsea's backyard. She remembered they had been looking at a caterpillar. "You took that?" she asked.

He shook his head. "Nope. I found it on my phone after I got home." He fixed her with a long gaze. "I couldn't bring myself to delete it."

Morgan laughed. "I'm extremely flattered," she said softly, and boldly leaned in and kissed him.

"Somebody must have been trying to do some matchmaking that weekend," Brandon said with a grin. Then he asked her about her work, and Morgan lost herself talking about her research interests and her patients. She could tell by his questions that he was sincerely interested.

Suddenly, his watch beeped, and Morgan hoped that he wasn't going to leave. She was surprised when he took her mug from her and set both of them down on the table, then wrapped both arms around her. She looked at him. "What's going on?"

"Kissing break," he said.

She laughed. "You set your watch for a kissing break?"

"Yep. Sixty seconds of kissing, then twenty minutes of talking, then sixty more seconds of kissing." His eyes sparkled and Morgan felt herself drowning in them.

"Oh, Bran," she said, trying not to laugh. "That is so adorable. And so precise."

He leaned in. "No talking during kissing time, babe," he whispered, and pressed his lips to hers.

When his alarm went off again, she sighed. "That went too fast."

He drew back and picked up his mug. "I know, but I also know my limits," he said, and then he winked. That almost undid Morgan. So she asked him to tell her about his new job, and was fascinated by it. She thought of all kinds of questions to ask him.

The time sped by and they went through several cycles of talking and kissing breaks. Then Brandon's watch made a different kind of beep. He sighed. "That means it's time for me to go." Morgan looked at the clock and was shocked to realize that he'd been there for three and a half hours.

She walked him to the door, and they wrapped their arms around one another. "Thank you for coming over," she said. "I had such a wonderful time."

"Me, too," he said. "Can I see you again this weekend?"

Her heart tripped. "Yes! Of course. What did you have in mind?"

"Have you ever been to an NBA game?"

She shook her head.

"How about tomorrow night?"

"I'd love it," Morgan said with a smile.

He smiled back. "Good. The Bulls are in town. I'll come by for you around 6:30. I should be able to get away for a while on Sunday afternoon. We'll figure out something to do."

"Why don't I plan it, since you planned tomorrow night?"

"It's a deal." He kissed her, and Morgan thought this may have been the best night of her life.

Brandon opened the door and stepped out. "Goodnight, babe," he whispered.

"Goodnight, Bran. Text me when you get home?"

"I sure will."

# 24

IT WAS WEDNESDAY morning, exactly a week after their first date, and Brandon hadn't seen Morgan since Sunday afternoon. Three dates in three days had made it the best weekend he could remember in a long time. It was a good thing they were having dinner tonight, because he didn't think he could go another day without seeing her.

He pulled on his suit jacket, walked into the kitchen, and poured coffee into his travel mug for the commute into work.

Sara was slumped at the kitchen table in her fluffy robe, and had a serious case of bedhead. She glared at him. "What is up with you and this whistling all of a sudden?"

Brandon stopped. He didn't realize he'd been whistling. "You're such a grump in the morning, Peanut."

"That's because I should be sleeping for another four hours," she yawned. April and Shelbie skipped into the room. They were still in their pajamas. "How do they have so much energy at this time of day?" Sara muttered to no one in particular.

Brandon set his things down and opened his arms. "Come give me hugs, girls." He squatted down and his daughters covered him with hugs and kisses.

"Do you have a meeting tonight, Daddy?" April asked.

"Yes, but it won't be late, I promise. I'll be home in plenty of time for stories and bedtime." He and Morgan had decided that on the nights they could get together, to do an early dinner. Brandon was thankful that her schedule had that kind of flexibility.

Brandon said goodbye to Sara and the girls and climbed into his SUV. He set his phone in its holder on the dash and hit speed dial as he pulled out of the driveway. "Morning, babe," he said when Morgan answered.

"Morning, Bran." They fell into easy conversation. She told him everything she had planned for the day. "Where do you want to have dinner?" she asked.

"Well, it's our one-week anniversary, so it should be special," he replied.

"One week? Wow, you're right," Morgan said. She sounded surprised.

"It feels like a lot longer, doesn't it?" Brandon said.

"Yes, it does."

"I'm enjoying every minute of it," he said.

"Me, too." He could hear the smile in her voice.

"How about Peppito's?"

"Perfect. I haven't been there in a while. See you at five? I'll meet you there. I'll be coming straight from a session."

"You're riding the El today, right?" he asked.

"Yes, why?"

"Because that means I can take you home and get a proper goodnight kiss."

"Count on it," Morgan responded. He could tell she was still smiling.

They said goodbye and Brandon turned his attention to the road. He hadn't even realized he was stuck in traffic. He drummed his fingers on the steering wheel and thought about the last week. *I can't believe it's only been a week.* It was amazing, being with Morgan. Sometimes a spear of guilt would prick him. Was it too soon? Darla had been gone for almost a year and a half. Brandon had been sure that he would never, ever be interested in being with anyone else. And then it just happened.

*Am I in love with Morgan?* Brandon honestly couldn't answer that. It was way too soon. All he knew was that it felt so good to not be alone, to have someone to fill all the lost and lonely places of his soul. He wanted to join life again, to do all the things he used to enjoy. He wasn't sure how Morgan had liked the Bulls game. She'd spent most of the night with her hands over her ears.

Sunday afternoon, she'd taken him to some art gallery. Brandon was bored out of his mind, but enjoyed the opportunity to hold her hand and watch her lovely features come to life as she explained all kinds of things about the artwork to him.

Brandon arrived at the restaurant first, and waited for Morgan in the lobby. Every time the door opened, his gaze flew to it, and when she finally walked in, he felt his chest swell at her loveliness.

Her hair fell past her shoulders in soft waves, and she was dressed in teal-blue in her typical graceful, flowing style. Then it hit him. This was one of the biggest differences between Morgan and Darla—Morgan was so feminine. Dar was pretty, but clothes, hair, and makeup had never been her priority. She pulled her hair back in a ponytail and pretty much wore scrubs or jeans and a t-shirt 24/7. Once a year she might put on a dress and some makeup for a special occasion. It had never bothered Brandon because that was her style and he loved her, but now with Morgan, the contrast was striking.

Brandon wanted so badly to sweep Morgan into his arms and kiss her senseless, but settled for a quick peck. "Hi, babe," he murmured.

The hostess ushered them to their table, handed them menus, and left. Brandon let out a sigh.

"What's wrong, Bran?" she asked.

He reached for her hand and leaned in close. "Nothing, except that I want to go somewhere and be alone with you and kiss you until neither of us can breathe."

Her face turned pink and she squeezed his hand. "It's probably a good thing that we're in public," she said. "But I'll hold you to that." She smiled and her gaze rested on his lips.

He inhaled sharply, then raised her hand and kissed it. "Not fair," he said with a smile.

She responded with a musical laugh. Brandon's heart skittered in his chest.

They ordered their food and he asked her about her day. Brandon thought they would never get through the meal, but when they got in the car, he looked at the clock and realized that they'd only been in the restaurant for an hour. That gave him plenty of time to get Morgan home and say goodnight to her before he needed to leave for home.

As soon as they got through her front door, he pulled her into his arms and made good on his promise. When they finally came up for air, he buried his face in her hair and breathed her in. "Mmm...tonight was...wonderful."

Morgan tipped her head back and gazed up at him, and ran her fingertip along his bottom lip. "Better than the art gallery?"

"What? I enjoyed that, too." He grinned at her.

"Liar," she whispered with a smile.

He laughed. Then something occurred to him. "What about the game Saturday night?" He locked his hands behind her waist.

Morgan looked surprised. "Oh, I liked it," she said a little too brightly.

Brandon brushed a kiss on her lips. "Liar," he said. He moved in for a longer, deeper kiss.

When he turned his attention to her neck, Morgan ran her fingers up and through his hair. "Just being with you is enough for me," she whispered. "It doesn't matter where we are or what we're doing."

Brandon's lips found hers again. "Me, too." His watch alarm beeped, and he loosened his hold on her. "I wish I didn't have to go." He touched his forehead to hers.

Morgan put her finger over his lips and shook her head. "April and Shelbie are your priority right now. I wouldn't have it any other way." She cradled his face in her hands and whispered, "you're such a good dad, Bran," and he felt like he could fly.

"I'll call you after the girls are asleep."

"I'll be waiting," she said.

The next week and a half flew by. He ended up making two quick, unscheduled trips, and was up to his neck in work at the Center. She was busy, too, and they managed a few quick lunches and stolen kisses.

One evening when they were at Morgan's condo, they had just finished their takeout meal when a steady, gentle rain began to fall. Morgan grabbed an umbrella and begged Brandon to go for a walk. At first, he protested. Walking was a means by which to get from point A to point B. He and Darla had certainly never done anything like that. Almost from the day they'd met, they were immersed in studying or work, and later, caring for two babies and juggling two high-powered, stressful careers.

But as he and Morgan strolled in the early evening twilight, Brandon began to relax and focus on the sights, sounds, and smells of autumn around them. The rain began to come down a little harder, and he felt like they were in a world of their own under the umbrella. He thoroughly enjoyed holding Morgan close and stopping for an occasional kiss. It was a completely wonderful, romantic experience.

The weekend of Halloween, Sara wanted to go to a movie with some friends, so Brandon invited Morgan over. The cover story was that she was coming to measure some walls. Sara had gotten fairy princess costumes for the girls, and he took them to a few nearby houses while Morgan stayed at the house and passed out candy.

The girls were so excited that "Miss Morgy" was there, and between that and the candy he'd let them eat, it was hard to get them to sleep. But finally, once he was sure they were down for the night, he led Morgan to the family room couch and took her into his arms. She was right; just being together was enough.

Brandon had told Sara to text him when she was on her way home, so he was confident that they'd have enough time for Morgan to get away before Sara arrived.

"What are you doing Sunday?" he said. "We could do something during the afternoon."

Morgan nibbled on her lower lip and looked a little sheepish. "Well, Sunday is my birthday."

"Babe! Really?" Then it occurred to Brandon that they'd never gotten around to little details like that. "What would you like to do? I'll take you out." The Bears were in town that weekend and were the hottest ticket in town. Brandon had a standing invitation for the owner's box. Wouldn't that bowl Morgan over if he took her there? It wouldn't be as fast-paced and noisy as the basketball game. He started to open his mouth, and then her face lit up.

"There's a symphonic wind concert at U of I. I know the conductor and I'm sure we could get tickets. They're doing Vivaldi's *Four Seasons*, one of my favorites."

Brandon had no idea what any of that meant, and he thought it sounded like a horrible way to spend an afternoon, but it was her birthday, so she should be able to choose. He smiled at her. "It's a date," he said.

"So, when is *your* birthday?"

He sighed. "Christmas Eve."

"Really? Poor Bran," she said, sounding sincere.

"Yeah, I always felt gypped growing up. But now it's not so bad, really. It's more or less a holiday, so everyone's around." He gazed into her eyes. "Maybe we can get together on my birthday this year." That was a pretty bold move, to suggest that they might spend Christmas together, but he wanted to see her reaction.

She smiled and rubbed her hands over his shoulders. "Maybe we can," she said a little flirtatiously. "I think we'd have to tell our families that we're dating," she said.

"Yeah," he agreed. "What are you doing for Thanksgiving?"

"I'm not sure. What about you?"

"I think we're all going to my parents' house this year. If Landon and Kelsea and the twins come, I'm sure you and your mom would be welcome."

"That'd be fun," Morgan said. "Will your older sister come from Florida?"

Brandon shook his head. "I doubt it. Reagan's a workaholic. She's not exactly the black sheep of the family, but she's not as close as the rest of us are." He shrugged. "If she comes, it will be last minute, and she'll just blow in like a hurricane."

Morgan laughed. "What does she do?"

"She's an assistant editor at the *Miami Herald*." Brandon's phone pinged, and he read the text. "Darn, Sara's on her way." He leaned in for a kiss. "You didn't get any of the walls measured."

She trailed a fingertip along his jawline. "Guess I'll have to come back sometime."

"Guess you will."

# 25

MORGAN CHECKED HERSELF once more in the full-length mirror. She'd splurged and bought a new outfit: a midnight blue scoop-neck top with three-quarter-length sleeves and a long, flowing skirt with a handkerchief hem and swirls of blue and silver throughout. Morgan loved how the skirt sparkled when she moved. Silver sandals and jewelry were the perfect complement. She enjoyed looking her best for Bran.

Morgan opened the door to his knock, and sucked in a breath. He looked like he'd stepped straight out of *GQ* in gray slacks, a navy blazer, and open-necked blue checked shirt.

"Happy birthday, babe," he said, sweeping her into his arms for a luscious kiss. "You look amazing."

"Thank you," she said breathlessly. "So do you." He smelled and felt wonderful. His aftershave or cologne had a heady, woodsy scent that Morgan was growing *very* fond of.

Bran pulled her close and kissed her again and again, as if he had all the time in the world. His lips trailed along her cheek to her neck. Morgan sighed. She felt incredibly beautiful and desired in a way that she had never experienced before.

He worked his way back to her mouth. "When does this *One Year* thing begin?" he said between kisses.

Morgan giggled. "It's *Four Seasons,* silly."

Brandon's eyes danced as he looked at her. "Which is—"

"One year," they said in unison.

Morgan laughed and picked up her purse. "Come on," she said. Brandon helped her into her jacket and they went out the door.

They arrived at the concert hall and found their seats about ten minutes before the concert began. Morgan saw some people that she knew, and was thrilled to introduce Brandon as her boyfriend. This day couldn't get any better. She opened her program and began to peruse it, and Brandon did the same.

"Now see, this is what I don't get," he said, pointing to something. "Tell me what that says."

Morgan wasn't sure what he was getting at. "Cello?"

"But what does c-e-l-l spell?"

She giggled. "Cell."

"Right," he said. "Like red and white blood cells. So why isn't c-e-l-l-o pronounced *sello?*"

Morgan laughed. "Bran, you're so cute."

The lights dimmed and the concert got underway. Brandon held her hand, and Morgan was so excited and proud to be here with him. This was the best birthday ever.

Well into the first half of the concert, the music reached a crescendo and Morgan was distracted by a movement out of the corner of her eye. A pregnant young woman sitting a few seats down in the row in front of them flinched. She and the man next to her laid their hands on her rounded belly and giggled and grinned at one another.

Morgan felt the breath leave her, and her eyes filled with tears. She would never feel a baby move inside her. She would never share that moment with the man she loved. Morgan reached for Bran's hand and was horrified to see that he was *asleep!* She nudged him and he startled awake. "Oh, sorry," he muttered. He rubbed his fingers over his mouth and sat up straighter, stifling a yawn.

Morgan turned away from him and wiped her eyes.

They went to the lobby during the break. "You need some caffeine," she said.

"I'm really sorry, Morgan. I had a long week." He did look tired, and Morgan tried not to be irritated with him. But really, falling asleep during a concert was terrible etiquette. And she was still out of sorts over the pregnant woman.

They returned to their seats for the second half, and when it had been underway only about five minutes, Brandon's pager started to buzz. He quickly turned it off and whispered to Morgan, "I'm sorry. Something must be up. Let me go make a phone call." He stood and crept along the row until he got to the aisle.

The couple next to Morgan looked at her disapprovingly. "He's a doctor," she whispered. Their sour expressions relaxed a bit.

Morgan had silenced her phone at the beginning of the concert, but she took it out in case Bran texted her. Sure enough, he did. *Babe, I'm so sorry. A patient developed complications and I've got to go in. I'll text you if I can wrap it up quickly and hopefully we can still do dinner.*

Morgan sighed. So much for the best birthday ever. *I understand, Bran,* she texted back. She tried to tamper her disappointment by reminding herself that this was life with a doctor.

When the concert concluded, she still hadn't heard from him, so Morgan took an Uber home. She changed into comfortable clothes, turned on the fireplace, and made a grilled cheese sandwich for dinner. She thought about what it would be like to have a child to celebrate her next birthday with, and decided then and there to call Joyce Sheldon the next day and get the process started.

She was feeling much better when Bran called just before nine o'clock. "Babe, I am so, so sorry," he said.

"Did you have to do surgery?"

"Yeah. We had to open a guy back up and do some repair work. He did too much, too soon. I just got out. Morgan, I promise I'll make it up to you. I had a gift for you and everything."

"Bran, it's okay. This wasn't your fault. But I'm not sure you were enjoying the concert that much, anyway." She tried to laugh to take the sting out of her comment.

"It was good, just not what I'm used to," he said. "Someday I'll take you to my kind of concert." He laughed.

"What? Some heavy metal thing?" she said teasingly.

"No, but you'll probably want to bring earplugs," he countered. They both laughed.

"I need to clean up and get home," Brandon said. "I mean it, Morgan, I'll make it up to you for tonight. Sweet dreams."

# 26

BRANDON STARTED THE car and turned out onto Michigan Avenue. He yawned. What a day. Not at all what he had hoped for. He really did feel badly about how Morgan's birthday turned out. Darla, of course, always understood when these things happened, but he wasn't sure Morgan would.

He needed some bro time, and speed-dialed Landon.

"Hey, bro," Landon answered.

"This a good time?"

"Yeah. I'm feeding my son a bottle. Let me put you on speaker. What are you doing?"

"Just finished a surgery, on my way home."

"On a Sunday night? Must not have been planned."

"You can say that again." Brandon gave his brother a quick summary of the surgery, and told him the name of the patient, who was a well-known athlete. He knew Landon would keep the information confidential.

Landon whistled. "Man, you sure travel in some high-class circles these days."

"I know. It's still hard to believe sometimes. Anyway, there's something I need to pick your brain about." He and Morgan had made a pact not to talk with Landon and Kelsea about their relationship, but he wasn't going to reveal anything. He just needed his brother's advice.

"I'm all ears," Landon said.

"Well, I've—hmm. Okay. I've started seeing someone."

"You don't say." His brother's voice didn't hold any censure.

"Yeah. I wasn't planning it. I didn't think I'd ever be interested in anyone again, but it just happened."

"What's her name?" Brandon heard the smile in his brother's voice.

Brandon smiled. "Nice try, bro. Not giving out any info right now."

Landon laughed. "Okay."

"It's only a couple of weeks in. Anyway, the thing is, we're not at all alike. I mean—like not at all. She doesn't follow sports *at all*." Brandon knew his brother would understand the significance of this more than anyone else. "But we find things to talk about. I could talk with her forever. And she's beautiful, inside and out."

"And she's a great kisser," Landon added.

"And she's a great kisser," Brandon repeated. He sighed. "Man, is she ever." He thought about how gorgeous Morgan looked this afternoon and the potent kisses they'd shared. He wished they could have skipped the boring concert.

"Sounds like you're hooked."

"Yeah, I think I am. But it's so weird. I try not to compare her to Dar, but it's hard. We loved all the same things. I just haven't found any common ground yet with—"

Landon jumped right in. "With who? Say that again? I think you were breaking up there for a moment," he teased.

"Nice try!" The two brothers chuckled. "Oh, I'm fine," Brandon said. "I just, I don't know, I just wanted to share it with you."

"I'm glad you did," Landon said. "Give it some time, and it'll either work out, or it won't."

"Gee, bro, that's brilliant. Let me write that down," Brandon said drily.

The two brothers laughed. "I'm really glad you've decided to rejoin life," Landon said.

"You don't think it's too soon?"

"No, I don't. Do you really see yourself raising April and Shelbie by yourself, and then being all alone in twenty years when they leave home?"

"I haven't really thought that far," Brandon admitted. "Until very recently, I've been focused on getting through one day at a time." He sighed. "But I know I don't want to spend the rest of my life alone. It's just been hard to admit that. You know, it feels a little like I'm being unfaithful to Darla's memory." He swallowed around the lump in his throat.

"What would Dar tell you to do?" Landon asked.

Brandon snorted softly. "She'd kick my butt and tell me to grab life by the horns and make it count."

"Exactly. It's all part of the healing process," Landon said quietly. "Just take it one step at a time. And I'll be praying for you."

They went on to talk about the twins and other things, and Landon told him that he and his family were definitely going to Wisconsin for Thanksgiving.

"Great, the girls and Peanut and I will be there, too."

"You won't believe how much the babies have grown," Landon said.

"I'll bet! Well, thanks for being there for me. I'll see you in a few weeks."

"Hey, bro, did you and Morgan ever get together?"

Brandon almost drove off the road. "What?"

"You know, did Morgan ever get back to look at your house for artwork and all that stuff?"

His heartrate returned to normal. "Oh—yeah. She's coming to measure walls. Sometime. I'm not sure when." Brandon hoped he had his story straight.

"Oh, that's good," Landon said. "Well, talk to you soon. Love ya, man"

"Love ya, man." Brandon disconnected. *Whew. That was close.*

# 27

MORGAN HELD OUT until Tuesday night, and then called her sister.

"Can you talk for a little while?" she asked.

"Morgy, are you okay?" Kelsea was the protective, older sister and was always afraid that something was drastically wrong.

"I'm fine, I just need some sister time."

"Okay. Let me do a couple of things and get Landon on baby watch and I'll call you right back."

"Don't tell him anything," Morgan said.

"What do you mean? I just need to make sure he'll look after the twins. I'll call you right back." Kelsea disconnected without another word.

Morgan let out a sigh. Maybe this wasn't such a good idea. Then she scolded herself. *Keep it vague. She won't figure anything out unless you reveal too much.* She sat down at her kitchen table and drummed her fingers until the phone rang.

"Hi," she said.

"Morgy, are you sure you're okay? What's going on?"

"Kels, I'm *fine,*" Morgan said with emphasis. "I'm just—well, I wanted to tell you that I—I'm sort of dating someone."

She heard her sister gasp. "That's wonderful! What's his name?"

Morgan rolled her eyes. "Oh no. This is still very new and I'm not going to jinx it."

"Are you back with Patrick?"

"What? No!" Now that Brandon was in her life, Morgan couldn't figure out what she had ever seen in Patrick.

"Where did you meet him? What does he do?" Kelsea bubbled.

*Not on your life, sister.* "It doesn't matter, Kels," Morgan said firmly. She was bound and determined not to leave any bread crumbs for her sister to follow.

"What does he look like? Morgy! Is he *TDH?*"

Morgan laughed joyously. She could go down this road. "Oh, Kels, he's *so* TDH!" Kelsea laughed with her. "And he's just— he's *completely* different from Patrick. He makes me feel things that I've never felt before." Her voice had gotten quieter.

"Is he a good kisser?"

"Mmm, the best. I've—I've *never* been kissed like this."

"Sounds like you're in love, Morgy."

"What?" Morgan's heart began to trip. "No, I'm not—it's, I've only known him for a very short time."

Kelsea gave a dry laugh. "True love doesn't know what a clock or a calendar is, Morgy. Take it from the expert."

Morgan had to give her sister that one. Landon and Kelsea had met under very unusual circumstances and were legally married just eight days later, but they didn't know it. Then they went their separate ways and were reunited three weeks later, got engaged, and stayed married. It was one of the most unusual love stories ever.

"I know. But this is so different, Kelsea. Every minute of my life is filled with him. When I'm with him, it's incredible, and when I'm not with him, I can hardly breathe. We never run out of things to talk about, but we're so different."

"You and Patrick were too much alike, Morgan."

"I know that now. But this guy—Kels, he knows *nothing* about the arts. He went with me to a symphonic wind concert for my birthday and fell asleep before the intermission!"

Kelsea laughed. "I'd fall asleep at one of those concerts, too. What's he into? Wait—let me guess. Sports?"

*Revealing that won't be a bread crumb. Half the men in Chicago are TDH and into sports.* "Yes, big time. But it's not just that. He's really outgoing, and loves noise and crowds, and you know me, how much I like my calm, quiet life."

"Maybe you need to come out of your shell a little," Kelsea said.

"Maybe I do." Morgan sighed. "And I don't know whether or when I should tell him about my infertility."

"I know, it's hard. Morgan, I know that's what ended things with Patrick, but his reaction was proof that he wasn't worth it. He wasn't the guy for you. And you'll know when it's the right time to tell *this* guy, and if he's the right one, it won't matter to him. He'll love you no matter what."

Morgan felt close to tears. "You're probably right. Anyway, I just had to tell someone."

"I'm glad it was me, Morgy," Kelsea said warmly.

"Well, who else would I tell?" Morgan said with a laugh. "You can't tell Landon," she begged.

"Why not?"

Morgan couldn't think of an answer she could tell her sister. "Well, it's still so new. Just don't say anything until I know if this is going to take."

"Not trying to be pushy," Kelsea ventured, "but what does this do to your plan to foster or adopt?"

Morgan sighed. "I'm not sure. That's another thing I'm confused about. I've been playing phone tag with a woman who's the one to help me get all the paperwork going. So that's stalled, and I guess I just need to pray about it."

"I'll keep praying, too," Kelsea assured her.

Morgan changed the subject. "What are you guys doing for Thanksgiving?" Of course, she already had a good idea.

"We're going to Landon's parents in Wisconsin. I think Brandon and his girls and Sara are coming, too."

"Well, if Mom doesn't go to Uncle Steve's, I should go home to be with her." The prospect of spending the holiday weekend in Kankakee filled Morgan with dread.

"You and Mom should come to Wisconsin!" Kelsea exclaimed as if she had just discovered the secret to the fountain of youth. "Unless you can't stand the thought of being around *Dr. Moron,*" she said with a chuckle.

Morgan nearly burst into hysterical laughter. She would have to come clean with Bran about that. "I suppose I can put up with him in order to see my niece and nephew." She hoped she sounded convincing. "Are you sure your in-laws won't mind?"

"I'm sure they'd love to have you. They have a huge house with room for everyone. I'll set it up."

Morgan smiled. *Was it really going to be that easy?* "Um, I guess," she said, trying to act like it wasn't the best idea ever.

"I want to see you, Morgy," Kelsea said. "You won't believe how big the babies have gotten."

That was something Morgan could get excited for. "Okay, then. You'll talk to Mom?"

"I'll talk to Mom. I'll see you in a few weeks!"

"Thanks for the sister talk, Sissy. Love you."

"Always. Love you back. Oh, Morgan! Did you ever get together with Brandon?"

Morgan almost dropped the phone. "Huh? What?" she stammered.

"You know. Did you ever get back over to his house to look at some ideas for artwork?"

Morgan smiled to herself. Oh, she'd gotten back to Brandon's house, but they always found something else to do rather than measure walls and talk about decorating. "Ah—yeah. I went back once and did some measuring. Gotta go, Kels. See you soon!"

# 28

BRANDON HAD BEEN trying to think of a way to make it up to Morgan for blowing it on her birthday, and the perfect opportunity may have just been handed to him.

Steve Lambetti was standing in the door of his office and had just invited him to fly with the Blackhawks to a game in Toronto on Sunday.

"Can I bring a date?" he asked.

"Sure," Lambetti replied.

"It's a turnaround trip, right?" Brandon was getting an idea of how these things worked.

"Yeah, we'll get home late, but we'll get to sleep in our own beds. We'll fly out of Midway Sunday morning. I'll text you the gate number and departure time. Don't forget your passport."

"Thanks, Steve."

He immediately texted Morgan. *Do you have a passport, babe?* If she didn't, that would nix his whole plan. She didn't reply right away, and he looked at his watch. It was Thursday, which meant she was in a session. Two hours later, his phone rang when he was on the way home.

"Okay, you've got my attention," she said, with no preamble.

He laughed. "So, do you have a passport? And are you okay with flying?"

"Yes to both," she replied. He could tell she was about to explode with curiosity.

"Well, then, are you free on Sunday?"

"Bran! What in the world do you have planned? I can't go jetting off halfway across the world on Sunday. I have classes to teach on Monday."

"Who said anything about going halfway across the world?" he said coyly.

"Well, now you *really* have me flummoxed," she said.

"Flummoxed? Who uses that word?" he teased.

"Okay, then. Bewildered. Perplexed. So curious, I'm about to pass out!"

Brandon laughed again. "You're adorable, babe. This is to make up for messing up your birthday. I promise I'll have you home by midnight."

Her sigh rippled into his ear. "If you were here, I'll bet I could kiss you into telling me where we're going."

His heart skipped a beat. "I'm sure you could. So, what do you say?"

"Bran, this is crazy. I don't do crazy things. Are you sure I'll be back by Monday? I have a really full day."

Brandon thought about the trips he'd taken over the past two months on the various private jets and chartered planes. No airport security, no lines, no delayed or canceled flights. "I promise, you'll be back by Monday."

"What should I wear?"

"Well, it's November, so wear whatever you would wear in Chicago in November."

"So, no tropics," Morgan said. "We must be heading north."

"I didn't say that," Brandon replied. "You're a sneaky one, Dr. Anderson."

Her laugh sounded like wind chimes. "I'll see you Sunday."

"No, you'll see me tomorrow night. You're coming for dinner and to measure the walls or something, remember?"

"Oh, yes. I thought—did I measure the walls already?"

"You sound flummoxed, babe."

She giggled again. "Oh, no, I didn't. So yes, I'll come to dinner tomorrow night and measure some walls."

"I just pulled in the garage. See you tomorrow night."

"Bye, Bran."

# 29

MORGAN COULDN'T BELIEVE it. They were flying to Canada on a chartered plane with the Chicago Blackhawks! That *was* crazy, and as she'd told Bran on the phone the other night, she didn't do crazy.

But hadn't her sister said just the other night on the phone that Morgan needed to come out of her shell?

Morgan loved sitting with Bran, holding his hand, and when he introduced her to various coaches and players as his girlfriend. She could tell he was popular with everyone. They gave him fist bumps and high fives and called him "Doc."

The game was the noisiest event Morgan had ever experienced, even louder than the basketball game. "Canadians really love their hockey," Bran shouted into her ear at one point. It was almost impossible to carry on a conversation. But the Blackhawks won, so the home fans weren't as noisy at the end.

After the game, Bran said they may as well sit and relax. They weren't going anywhere until the players had showered and dressed. There were two players' wives along for the trip, and Morgan chatted with them for a little while. They told her that more wives and children traveled with the team when it was an overnight trip, but since this was just a quick day trip, most had stayed home.

When they finally left the arena and trooped out to the chartered bus, they were surprised to see that it was snowing, and had been for some time. Morgan wondered nervously if the weather might delay their flight. But when they got to the airport they were ushered right onto the plane, and her fears abated.

They got settled in their seats and buckled in. Brandon squeezed Morgan's hand. "Thank you for coming with me. I hope this made up for your birthday."

"It was wonderful, Bran, thank you," Morgan said.

She looked out the window where the snow swirled around them. "I wonder why we aren't going yet?"

"Hmm, I don't know," Brandon replied. "Maybe they're going to deice us."

"I hope we don't get home too late. My day tomorrow is insane, packed from beginning to end." Morgan yawned and laid her head on his shoulder.

The most important reason for Morgan to be back in Chicago tomorrow was for an early morning meeting with Joyce Sheldon to begin the process of becoming a foster parent. They had finally connected and just got their calendars to sync. Morgan was fortunate that Joyce had worked her in, but now she wasn't even sure if this was the right time to move forward, given her new relationship with Bran, and she still hadn't said anything to him about it, and didn't know if she should. She was torn because being with him and the girls made her want a family of her own even more, but it didn't feel like the right time to bring it up with him. She didn't want him to think that she was dating him in order to get a ready-made family.

The pilot's voice came on over the intercom. "Good evening, folks. An update from the cockpit. This storm moved in more quickly than they anticipated, but they think we can get out. We're next for deicing and then we should be cleared for takeoff. We'll keep you updated."

"See? We'll be fine," Brandon said, and squeezed Morgan's hand. After a few minutes, he looked over her shoulder out the window and they watched the deicing process together. Then the plane backed out of the gate and rolled across the tarmac and stopped.

And sat. And sat some more. Morgan began to grow restless.

The pilot came on again. "Sorry, folks. We need to go back to be deiced again, and then they're going to try to get us out."

"I don't like this, Bran," Morgan whispered.

He pulled her close. "We'll be fine, babe," he murmured. They sat and cuddled while the process was repeated, and then the plane rolled out again.

Twenty minutes later, Morgan felt the plane turn around and head back toward the terminal. She could tell by looking out the window that it was almost whiteout conditions.

"Well, folks, you can probably tell that we're headed back to the gate," the pilot said. They've closed the airport, so we'll deplane and try again in the morning." A wave of grunts rolled through the cabin.

Morgan's eyes widened. "Bran! We're not going home? I have to be home tonight!"

Brandon tried to quiet her. "Babe, I'm so sorry."

"I can't believe I did this. I never should have come."

"Morgan, I'm sorry, I didn't think about a weather delay."

"This is terrible!" She pulled away from him and wrung her hands. "I just need a moment to think."

Brandon didn't reply. Most of the players had gone to sleep, and now woke up and shuffled off the plane. When they got back in the terminal, a man that Bran said was the front office rep gathered everyone around. He'd just gotten off his phone. "Sorry for the inconvenience, everyone. I've just been talking with the airport authority folks, and they're following this system closely and think they'll be able to get planes back in the air by six a.m., so we want to keep everyone here and board by five or five-thirty. This will be our gate. Since we don't go through TSA, you need to stay in this wing of the terminal. There's not much open, but they've opened up a coffee shop down that way on the left, and we'll run a tab." He pointed back over everyone's heads.

There were grumbles all around and one of the players called out, "Can they open a bar and you run a tab there, Bill?"

Everyone laughed. "Sorry, no," Bill said. "You know the rules, guys."

The group began to disperse and Brandon turned to Morgan. "I'm so sorry, Morgan." He took her hand. "It's a two-hour flight, so we'll come close to making it home by morning."

"But I'll be all stinky and rumpled in these clothes," she complained. "By the time I get home, take a shower, and get to my—where I need to be, it will be too late."

"Morgan, I'm sorry. What can I do—"

She waved him off. "I need to get on the phone," she said, and walked away from him. She knew there was no way he could have foreseen this, and she was angrier at herself for taking off on a lark than she was at him.

It took her about fifteen minutes to make all the arrangements. She'd left a voicemail for Joyce, canceling their meeting and apologizing profusely. Morgan hated canceling appointments. She was always afraid that it left an impression that she wasn't organized and reliable. She feared that Joyce would think she wasn't responsible enough to care for a child.

"I have my morning covered," she said to Brandon. "It wasn't easy. And those international minutes are going to make my phone bill skyrocket." He held out his arms to her, and she came to him. "No more crazy outings with you," she scolded.

He rubbed noses with her. "I'll pay your phone bill. Can I kiss my way back into your good graces?" he murmured, running his lips up under her ear and around to her neck.

Morgan squirmed away from him and stilled his hands. "We're in public, Bran," she said with a twinkle in her eye.

He wrapped his arm around her and began to walk. "Then let me buy you a cup of coffee."

# 30

MORGAN OPENED HER eyes and stretched. The first thought that popped into her mind was *it's Friday*. The second one caused a delicious quiver to start in her stomach and spread outward. *I'll see him tonight*.

The Canada debacle didn't turn out as badly as Morgan had first anticipated. They got off just before six o'clock and the pilots pushed them along to make good time. Bran ordered an Uber for her and it was waiting when they landed in Chicago. Since they didn't have to deal with customs or baggage claim, that saved some time. Morgan got home, showered, changed, and was on campus by nine o'clock.

The best part about the whole trip was sitting up all night with Bran in the airport, first in the little coffee shop, and then in a quiet corner of the terminal with the snowstorm raging all around them. She apologized for being so upset, and they held hands and talked about everything under the sun. Morgan felt like they were in their own little romantic cocoon. Everyone around them was asleep or not paying them the least bit of attention, and they got some really nice kissing breaks in.

Then, on the plane, Morgan slept in his arms, and he treated her to a spectacular wake-up kiss as the sun came up outside the window.

He filled her thoughts constantly, and when they weren't together, when their schedules allowed, they were either on the phone or texting back and forth. The last week and a half had flown by, mostly due to Morgan being tied up with an art show. But Brandon had also been away on a trip and she had only seen him once this week, for lunch on Wednesday. They were both busy yesterday and couldn't get their schedules to mesh. He'd invited her to the house for dinner again tonight—this time under the guise of coming to look at the rooms and walls and begin figuring what kinds of art and other decorative items would go best, now that she had measured them. She couldn't wait to see him—and the girls and Sara—tonight.

But then, the thought that was never far from her mind settled around her like a dark cloud and dampened her enthusiasm. Was it time to tell him about her infertility issues? Morgan nibbled on her thumbnail. It was a horrible conundrum. They'd only been together for a little over a month, but it felt like forever. There was never a place in the conversation to insert, "oh, by the way, I can't have children," and bringing up something so personal and with such obvious implications for a long-term commitment was a huge risk.

One she hadn't taken with Patrick, and it cost her dearly.

She'd met Patrick Carrington in the fall four years ago in the library at UIC—University of Illinois, Chicago—when she'd gone to pick up some books for a research project. She was staring at a wonderful Monet, and he'd stopped and they began to chat about it. That led to coffee. Over the next month they had lunch, dinner, or coffee at least once a week, went to a symphonic concert, and an art show. And lots of walks. Patrick loved to walk along the shoreline of Lake Michigan.

He was an Assistant Professor of English Literature at UIC. He was tall—though not as tall as Brandon—and slim with sandy blond hair and bright blue eyes. He was quiet and thoughtful, and by the end of their first month together, he'd held her hand several times, but hadn't kissed Morgan even once.

When the city got its first snow on a Sunday afternoon, he called and invited her on a walk. It was a soft, gentle snowfall with big, fat flakes and an uncharacteristic absence of Chicago's notorious wind. And then, Patrick had kissed her for the first time, and Morgan thought she might really be falling for him.

They continued walking, and soon passed a family—a mom, dad, and two small children, a boy and a girl, all holding hands. The children were catching snowflakes on their tongues and squealing, and the parents were laughing with them. Patrick turned to Morgan and said, "They look so happy, don't they? Maybe that will be us one day."

Morgan stopped and began to weep, and Patrick frowned at her. "Morgan, what's wrong?"

In halting sentences, she explained to him about her medical condition and the likelihood that she would never bear children. Morgan hoped that he would take her in his arms and assure her that it was okay, and that they would work through it together. She was in no way prepared for what he said next.

"Oh, dear. I—I certainly didn't expect that." He glared at her. "Didn't you think that was something important enough to share with me right up front? I feel like you've been dishonest with me, Morgan. Are there other things you're holding back?"

Suffice to say, the conversation went downhill from there. When Patrick began talking about how important it was to his parents that he carry on the Carrington bloodline, Morgan knew that their budding relationship had withered and died.

That was the last day she saw or heard from him, and she hadn't sought out or encouraged anyone since.

Morgan sighed. There was a definite spark with Brandon that had never been present with Patrick, who had been too much like Morgan—quiet and deliberate. His kiss was nice. Brandon's kisses set her on fire. From the moment his lips touched hers, she wanted more.

What was she going to do? Tell him now, or later? Morgan

knew deep down that there was too much to lose if she made the wrong choice.

She was still conflicted about whether to tell Bran about her desire to bring a child into her life. But the more Morgan worked with the arts program in Chicago, the more she fell in love with the children. She'd felt terrible about having to cancel her appointment with Joyce, and hadn't heard back from her yet about rescheduling. Was this God's way of closing the door? Morgan wasn't sure if she should try to make contact again, or wait for Joyce to make the next move. She hoped the woman wasn't mad and had decided to give up on Morgan.

She got up and checked her phone, then sat up and reached for her devotional book. For years, Morgan had started her day with a dose of God's Word. It was the perfect way to fill up for the day ahead. She asked Him for wisdom about how to handle both of her dilemmas.

When Morgan came out of the shower, she found a missed call and a text from Brandon, and as she read it, her heart sank. *Gotta fly to LA to do a surgery, dinner will have to wait until later in the weekend. I'm so sorry. I'll call you when I know more. I can't wait to see you. Saving up all of my kisses ☺*

Morgan sighed and ran her fingers over the word *kisses*. This man was almost too good to be true. But maybe this was her answer. It would buy her some time to make a decision about what to tell him, and when.

She got through her busy day and grabbed her phone every time it made a noise. It was after four o'clock and she had just arrived home when he finally called. "Babe, I'm so sorry I had to cancel our plans, and that it took me so long to call. Surgery took longer than expected, and now I've been asked to consult on another case up in San Francisco. I probably won't get home until sometime on Sunday."

Morgan could already see the long, lonely weekend stretching out in front of her. "It's okay, Bran," she said. "I'll let you make it up to me." It still surprised her how the bold, flirtatious words came to her so easily these days.

"I absolutely will," he whispered. "And in less than a week, we'll have five whole days together for Thanksgiving. I can't wait." No one knew that Morgan was driving up with them. They were going to concoct a story about her car having issues at the last minute so that she would have to catch a ride to Wisconsin with Brandon, Sara, and the girls.

And no one had any inkling about the bombshell that Brandon and Morgan were going to drop on everyone once they got there.

Morgan's stomach did flips. "I can't wait to see the look on Kelsea's face when we tell everyone about us."

Brandon laughed. "And Landon's."

"And Sara's," they said in unison, and then they laughed together.

"I hope April and Shelbie will approve," Morgan said softly.

"Morgan, they'll be so excited, you know they will," Brandon said. "Oh, here comes a nurse looking for me. I have to go."

"She'd better not be beautiful," Morgan warned him.

"She's sixty with buck teeth and warts all over her face," Brandon said teasingly. Morgan laughed. "I'll text or call you when I can, babe. Have a good weekend."

"You, too. See you soon."

Morgan set her phone down and smiled to herself. What to do with all this time now? Maybe she would just go to Luke and Miranda's cabin for the weekend and paint. She looked at the clock. Even if she hurried to pack, she'd hit the heavy weekend outbound traffic. She went into her bedroom and stood in front of her dresser. "I'll go in the morning," she said to her reflection. It was perfect. She'd have two full days there to paint, recharge her batteries, and sort out her feelings about Brandon and their possible future.

Morgan went to bed early and hit the road early the next morning. She unpacked her things and was painting by nine o'clock. She turned her phone off (the service was spotty anyway) and immersed herself in the work—which wasn't really work to her, but soothing therapy. She'd texted Miranda and they were out of town at her in-laws' for the weekend, so Morgan was completely alone, which was fine with her. Solitude was different from loneliness, and Morgan loved her solitude.

When she took a break for lunch, she turned her phone back on and saw that there was a missed call from Brandon. She walked around the perimeter of the cabin, hoping to get service, but no luck. For some reason it was worse than usual. She began to text him but figured with no service, why bother?

Morgan packed a few supplies and decided to take a walk. It was a gorgeous late fall day and she was inspired by the muted colors and autumn scents. The temperature was perfect and the breeze was gentle. Morgan felt herself unwinding.

She hiked through the woods and found a beautiful spot next to a little creek, and set up her things. Before dusk settled, she packed everything up and headed back to the cabin and had a simple supper of some crackers, cheese, and grapes. She checked her phone again but there was no service.

After a while, Morgan built a fire, then went outside and sat on the porch to watch the sun set, and then the stars came out. Millions—no, billions—of stars glittered down on her. Morgan sighed deeply. This was what she loved about the country. It fed her soul. She loved the rich cultural aspects of living in the city, but sometimes, it sucked the life out of her. She sat there, deep in thought, and wondered if she could find a happy medium. The problem was, her work was in the city, and she didn't know if she wanted to take on the tiresome commute.

She sat there for another hour, and her thoughts wandered to Brandon. What if things progressed between them to a permanent relationship? Morgan couldn't imagine living in his million-dollar home. Even with some of the ideas she had about how to decorate it, the new, contemporary style didn't fit her at all. The wealthy suburb in which it sat wasn't at all Morgan's cup of tea, either. Brandon was beginning to express doubts about it, too, but he said he was a "city boy" and if he decided to make a move, it would be that way.

"This is something else I need to pray about, right, Lord?" Morgan said to the heavens. She decided to go inside, fix a cup of cocoa, and paint some more. She did some of her best work late into the night.

She saw her phone on the counter and checked it once again. Now she had service, and Morgan was stunned to see *fifteen* missed calls from Brandon, seven voice messages, and twelve texts! What in the world? Had something happened to him, or the girls? Morgan's heart went into overdrive.

# 31

BRANDON WAS BESIDE himself. *Where was Morgan? Why wasn't she picking up?* He didn't have a key to her condo, and he'd been banging on the door for twenty minutes. He walked back out to his SUV and texted her again. *Babe, where are you? Call me, Morgan. Please, please call me.*

Brandon was beginning to feel like he was getting right with God again, but this was testing his faith. His heart felt like it was about to bang out of his chest. *If anything happens to her, I don't know how I could*—his phone rang and he grabbed it.

"Oh, Morgan! Thank God. Where are you?" he shouted.

"I'm at a friend's farm. Bran, I'm so sorry, the service out here is terrible. Are you okay? Are the girls okay?"

"Yes, yes. I just—" Brandon gulped in air. "I'm sitting outside your condo. I ended up not having to go to San Francisco, so I flew back to surprise you. But I—I just couldn't imagine why you weren't here. And then when you didn't pick up, I was afraid—" His throat closed.

"Oh, Bran. I'm so sorry."

"Morgan, I'm coming to you. Text me the address." The words spilled out in a rush.

"Bran, it'll take you almost ninety minutes. Why don't I meet you—"

"No!" he shouted. "Morgan, don't go—don't go *anywhere*. Don't move—babe, *please*, stay right there. I'll come to you."

She sounded worried. "Bran, are you sure you're okay to drive?"

"I'm fine. I'm already on my way. Text me the address, quick, in case you lose service again."

"Okay, I'm hanging up now and I'll text you." She followed through on that promise, and then called him back. "Did you get my text?"

"Yes," he said, and they talked for a while longer. He felt better, and Morgan began asking him questions about the surgery. He figured she was trying to keep him focused and calm. But after about twenty minutes, the call dropped, and he couldn't get through to her again.

# 32

ONCE SHE LOST service, Morgan spent the next hour putting her painting supplies away and trying in vain to get service on her phone, and finally took a blanket out on the porch and wrapped up in it to wait for Brandon. The stars kept her company and she talked to God, too.

When she saw headlights coming up the gravel drive, she ran to the SUV. Brandon cut the engine, tumbled out, and swept her into his arms.

"Morgan, oh babe," he murmured. She heard him take a deep breath, and choke back a sob. He held her so tightly, she could hardly breathe. Then he was kissing her desperately, and she could feel tears on his cheeks. He whispered her name over and over and stood there, just holding her and rocking back and forth. "I can't do this, I can't do this," he sobbed.

"Can't do what, Bran?" She stepped back and cupped his wet cheeks in her hands. His handsome face was ravaged with pain.

"I can't—I—if anything ever happened to you—" He all but fell on her, sobbing. "I couldn't go through that again. I couldn't."

Morgan's heart broke for him. "Let's go sit on the porch swing," she said quietly, and led him there and pulled the blanket around them. He wrapped her in his arms and they sat there for a long time, not saying anything, just rocking. Then she felt his lips on her hair.

Brandon drew back and stared at her. Starlight shone down on them like diamond dust, and filtered light from inside the cabin spilled across his features. As she looked into his eyes, Morgan's heart melted, and at that moment she knew what he was going to say, and exactly how she was going to respond.

He spoke so softly, Morgan could hardly hear him. "I was going to say that I can't love you, Morgan. But it's too late. I'm already so in love with you." He leaned in and touched his lips to hers. "So in love with you," he whispered.

"Oh, Bran," she said softly, cradling his face in her hands. "I love you with all my heart." And their next kiss was like nothing Morgan had ever known, and tears of joy bubbled up and ran down her cheeks. Brandon's kisses were so sweet and beautiful, and then Morgan's joy turned to fear, and she began to sob.

"Sweetheart, Morgan, what's wrong?" Brandon looked at her, his eyes dark with worry.

"I—oh, Bran, I have to tell you something," she sobbed, covering her face with her hands. *I waited too long.* "Something I should have told you right away, but it's—I—" Morgan didn't know how she was going to tell him.

He swallowed, and she could see the panic in his eyes. "Are you married? Are you sick? Are—"

Morgan gasped. She grabbed his hands and squeezed. "No, no! Oh, Bran, no. I'm so sorry—I'm not handling this right—"

He tenderly touched her face. "Please, just tell me. Whatever it is, we'll get through it together, Morgan. I love you so much. Whatever's wrong, it doesn't matter."

Morgan took a deep, shaky breath, and then her story came out, haltingly at first, and then in a river of tears and rushing words.

"Shh, shh," Brandon whispered. "It's okay, babe. It doesn't matter. I mean it, I mean it." He held her tighter. "It wasn't something you needed to tell me until it felt like the right time to *you.*"

"I—it's just not something you bring up on a first date, or a second date. But then—Bran, now you're *stuck* with this—and your girls want a little brother. I won't hold you—"

He cut her words off with a deep, passionate kiss. "Oh, Bran," she whispered.

He gazed at her. "Morgan, if things keep going, and we get to that place, we'll already have a family."

"I know, but—"

He shook his head. "No buts. How do you feel about the girls?"

Morgan spoke without even thinking "Oh, Bran. I love them like they were my own—" She stopped and felt her jaw drop.

He tilted his head at her. "See? And there are all kinds of ways to grow a family." He kissed her and touched his forehead to hers. "God works these things out."

She nodded. *Should I tell him about my hope to foster or adopt?* No, this wasn't the time. She'd already hit him with enough big news. The breeze kicked up and she shivered. "Would you like to go inside?"

He nodded, and followed her in. Morgan realized that she'd never fixed her cocoa, and asked Bran if he'd like that, or coffee. She felt badly that she didn't have his favorite kind at the cabin, but she hadn't expected him to be there.

"Cocoa sounds good," he said.

She fixed their mugs and joined him on the couch in front of the fire. When they'd finished, Bran pulled her close, and she curled up with her head on his chest, listening to the steady sound of his heartbeat. Morgan thought she could stay here just like this for the next fifty years.

After a while she looked up at him. "Tell me about Darla," she whispered.

"You sure?"

Morgan nodded.

He was silent for a few moments. "Well, I met her in Chemistry our junior year of high school. We were assigned as lab partners. She was a little thing—only about five foot one, and she always struggled with her weight a bit." He shrugged. "I told her it didn't matter." He fingered Morgan's hair. "Her hair was about the same color as yours, and she wore it long most of the time, pulled back in a ponytail. She was pretty low maintenance." He smiled. "Your hair is thick. Hers wasn't."

"Did she always want to be a doctor?" Morgan asked.

Brandon nodded. "Yep. A lot of med students don't choose their specialties until they're done with rotations, but she always knew she wanted to be a neurosurgeon." He shook his head. "She was one of the best. We went to college and then med school together. She was—I tell you, what she lacked in size, she made up for in determination." He smiled. "She was from Dallas. Her family moved north when she was thirteen, and she had a personality as big and bold as Texas. I would go to watch her surgeries whenever I could. She ran her OR like a drill sergeant, but everyone loved and respected her. She was really something. So outgoing and full of life. Not afraid of anything."

Morgan smiled. "Sounds like Shelbie."

Brandon nodded. "Yes, Shelbie is very much like her mother." He pressed his forehead against Morgan's and took her hand. "She'll never know her," he whispered. "She'll never remember."

Morgan put her arms around him. "I'm sorry," she murmured. They sat like that for a while and then Brandon cleared his throat.

"I want to tell you about that night," he said softly.

"Only if you're sure," Morgan said. She felt him nod.

Brandon took a deep breath. "We had a shortage of orthopedic surgeons at the hospital, and I had been working long hours for about three months. Then they hired another guy, and it started to ease up a little bit. I finally got a night off, and we were at home with the girls." He swallowed. "Dar needed a few things from the store and I offered to go, but she said since I'd missed so many nights at home, why didn't I do the girls' baths and story time and put them to bed." His eyes grew moist. "I—ah, she blew me a kiss, said 'love y'all,' like she always did, and I said the same thing back, and she went out the door and—and that was it."

Morgan squeezed his hands.

"We each had an SUV," he said, "but we still had this little Triumph convertible that had been our first car in college. After April came along, we couldn't all fit in it, so it mostly sat in the garage, but we had such great memories and couldn't bear to part with it."

Brandon stared off into the distance. "It was a beautiful early June evening, and Dar decided to take it. She loved to fly along in it with the top down." He shrugged and shook his head sadly. "There was a wide, downhill curve a couple of miles from our house. She took it too fast and lost control. She was wearing a seat belt but the car flipped and she—she died instantly." He closed his eyes.

"It happened on her way there, just a few minutes after she'd left, I wasn't even expecting her back yet when the doorbell rang." He swallowed. "When I saw the two policemen standing on my front porch, I knew." Tears ran down his cheeks. "My first call was to Landon. He caught the last flight out of St. Louis that night. Stayed with me for over a week. I couldn't have gotten through it without him."

Morgan got up and brought him a handful of tissues.

He blotted at his eyes. "It's taken me a long time to come to grips with the fact that it was just one of those things, that it wasn't my fault."

She took his hand. "Of course it wasn't your fault, Bran."

"I know. But when something like this happens, we want someone or something to blame. They checked out the car thoroughly to see if it was a mechanical issue. I had hung my hopes on that, but there wasn't a thing wrong with it."

Brandon drew Morgan into his arms, and they talked long into the night, about faith and family and relationships and all sorts of things. She'd never felt so close to another human being in all her life.

The next thing Morgan knew, it was morning, and Bran was kissing her awake.

# 33

BRANDON BURIED HIS *face in her neck. She was so warm and soft, and her hair was like silk and smelled like something heady and floral, not her normal shampoo. This was the absolute best way to start the day. His mouth moved across her cheek to her soft, full lips, and he sighed and pulled her closer.*

"Oh, Bran," she whispered.

Brandon froze. His heart leapt into his throat. *Morgan.* They'd fallen asleep on the couch. He sat up and scooted away from her.

"Bran, what's wrong?"

"Nothing, I—I'll be right back." He jumped up and made a beeline for the bathroom.

Brandon closed the door behind him and leaned against the sink. His heart still pounded. He put the toilet seat cover down and sat with his head in his hands. *Dear God.* How could this have happened? It didn't take a genius to figure out that after all the emotions of last night, that he'd—that he must have been dreaming of Darla. But how could he—*I love Morgan,* he told himself. *I do. I know I do.*

*Does she know? How will I ever fix this? If she doesn't know, should I tell her? I don't want to keep secrets from her.* The thoughts pinged around his head like it was a pinball machine.

Finally, he stood and splashed water on his face and rinsed out his mouth. Brandon took a deep breath. *Help me, God,* he prayed as he reached for the door handle.

The aroma of freshly brewed coffee assaulted him. Morgan was standing at the sink with a mug, staring out the window. She turned and looked at him, and there wasn't a doubt in Brandon's mind.

She knew.

Brandon took careful, quiet steps toward the kitchen. He saw another mug sitting on the counter, but coffee was the last thing on his mind right now. He continued walking toward Morgan until he was just a few feet away from her. He felt like he was approaching a skittish animal who might bolt at any second.

She set her mug down on the counter and folded her hands in front of her.

"I'm so sorry, Morgan," he whispered. He waited for her to scream at him, or tell him to leave. But what she did next completely shocked him.

She held out her hand, and he took it. "It's—it's okay, Bran," she whispered. A tear escaped and rolled down her cheek.

"Oh, babe," he whispered, and broke into tears himself. She was so beautiful, so forgiving, and Brandon felt like the most horrible man on earth for causing her this pain.

They moved at the same time and were in each other's arms. They stood there for a long time, just holding one another. Then he took her by the hand and led her back to the couch and pulled her close.

"I meant what I said last night, Morgan. I love you. I don't know how—"

She put a finger to his lips. "She was your wife for almost fifteen years," Morgan said. "She's been in your life for half of it. She's the mother of your children." Brandon saw her swallow. "She will always be a part of you." She gave him a sad little smile. "I just have to learn to accept it. And I will." She let out a slow stream of air. "I'll be okay."

Brandon tried to think how he would feel if the tables were

turned, and his gratitude for Morgan's love and understanding took a herculean leap. He brushed a lock of hair off her face. "Telling you everything last night was emotional for me," he said. "It was really the first time that I'd talked about it to anyone, other than Landon. And I told you some things I've never told him." He blew out a breath. "I guess my subconscious took over." He felt his eyes filling once again. "Morgan, I would never, ever intentionally do or say anything to hurt you."

Her hand rested gently on his cheek. "I know," she whispered. "Maybe you need more time. We've moved awfully fast."

Brandon frowned. "What? No, Morgan. I know that I love you."

"And I love you, Bran. But maybe your heart isn't fully healed yet."

He didn't know what to say to that. "Are you saying—" he could hardly bear to speak the words. "Do you want to take a step back? Take a break?"

"Not really. But maybe we should put the brakes on a bit to let your heart catch up. We can see how things go at Thanksgiving," she said. "Maybe we should wait to tell our families. Let's pray about it and see what God says."

Brandon was ready to turn this over to God. "I think that's a fantastic idea." He took her hands. "Are we okay?" he whispered.

Morgan nodded. She looked tired, but he didn't think she was holding anything back.

He stood, and lifted her to her feet. "I need to get home," he said. "Can I bring my travel mug in for a fill-up?"

"Sure."

Brandon came back into the cabin and she filled the mug and handed it to him. He set it on the counter and opened his arms. He wanted to give her the choice.

She came right to him, and Brandon's heart lightened a bit. He held her and drew in a deep breath to memorize her essence. "I love you, Morgan," he whispered.

"I love you, too, Bran. Text me when you get home."

Brandon nodded.

# 34

AFTER BRANDON LEFT, Morgan sat by the fire and cried and had a long talk with God. She felt inadequate, and like she would never fill the space in Bran's heart that Darla once had. She didn't know how to be a mother, and could never give Bran a son, or the girls a brother or even a sister.

She spent some time in prayer, and opened her Bible. Her devotional for that day was eerily timely. It talked about how God's plans are better than our plans, and how desperately He wishes the very best for all of His children. Morgan also realized that with a surrendered heart, her hopes and dreams would change to be the ones that God wanted all along for her, instead of the other way around. Morgan couldn't pray enough prayers to change God's plan for her to something she concocted on her own, if it wasn't His best for her.

Morgan left for home a little after noon, filled with peace. She lifted her prayers to God and asked Him to heal Bran's heart, to show him His plan, and to lead both of them on whatever path He had for them.

She began counting the moments until she'd see Bran again, and have five whole days with him and their families in Wisconsin.

# 35

"COME ON, GIRLS! You don't have to take every doll you own to Grandma and Grandpa's," Brandon called up the staircase. He looked at his watch. "Mor—Miss Morgy is going to be here any minute. Let's get a move on!" Since Morgan lived in the city, it made more sense for her to drive here and leave her car, since it was on the way. Brandon wanted to get on the road. It was a three-hour drive with no traffic, which certainly wasn't going to be the case the night before Thanksgiving.

Sara's voice came from just behind him. "I'm glad Morgan caught us before we left." She stepped around him and started up the stairs. "I'll get the girls. My bag's in the kitchen, ready to go."

Brandon ran a hand through his hair. *That's right. The Morgan's-having-car-trouble story.* They had talked a little on the phone and texted, but he hadn't seen her since he'd left the cabin on Sunday morning. With it being a short work week, both of them were extremely busy. He missed her terribly, but her suggestion to take their burden to the Lord in prayer had been a good one. Brandon didn't feel like he'd gotten an answer yet, but he felt like he was back on even footing with God again.

He rolled his eyes when he saw Sara's "bag." It was the size of a small vehicle, and even before he grabbed the handle, he knew it weighed as much. As he was wrestling it into the back of the SUV, he saw headlights, and Morgan pulled into the driveway. He'd left the right-side garage door up, and motioned her to pull in next to Sara's car.

Brandon trotted into the garage and opened Morgan's door. He glanced toward the door to the house and leaned in for a quick kiss. "Hey, babe," he whispered with a grin.

"Bran! Where are Sara and the girls?" Morgan was grinning, too.

"Inside. We're fine." He helped her out of the car. "I don't know how I'm going to spend three hours in a car with you and pretend that you're nothing more than Landon's sister-in-law." He grabbed her bag—which was more reasonably sized than Sara's—out of the trunk and rolled it to the SUV.

Just then, Sara and the girls came bursting out of the house. "Remember, your car was making a noise," he whispered to Morgan.

"Miss Morgy!" April and Shelbie squealed, and ran to her. Brandon's heart swelled as he watched Morgan hug them. Then he was busy with all the totes and bags that Sara pressed into his hands.

"What's all this stuff?"

"Things the girls and I need," his sister replied. "Hi, Morgan. Oh, your boots are so cute."

"Hi, Sara. Thanks."

"I hope your car trouble isn't anything serious."

"Umm, no, it's just making a rattle, but I didn't want to chance it."

"Well, I'm glad you can ride with us," Sara said. "Makes more sense anyway."

Brandon shook his head and moved things around in the back. "We're not going to Europe for a month, Peanut," he muttered. "You need to be more sensible, like Morgan."

"Whatever," she retorted. She and Morgan helped get the girls buckled in, and Morgan moved to climb in the back seat.

"You sit up front, Morgan," Sara said.

"Oh—you don't have to do that." Morgan glanced at Brandon.

"I want to. I'll probably fall asleep anyway." She clambered into the back seat and sat between her nieces.

"Well, let's get this show on the road," Brandon said. He and Morgan got in, and after a few more adjustments, they were off.

"Ah, I noticed the skis on top of the car," Morgan said. "Who's going skiing?"

"All of us, on Friday," Brandon said. "It's a family tradition."

"It's a blast," Sara called out. "Do you ski, Morgan?"

She shook her head. "No, I've never been. I guess I've just never wanted to."

Brandon wanted to take her hand and promise to help her learn, but instead he said, "We've gotten Kelsea on skis. It's easier than you think."

Morgan laughed. "I'd love to see that. I'm sure she won't go this year with the babies."

"St. Clairs are on skis before they can walk," Brandon said, and slid a smile her way.

"Darn right," Sara chimed in.

Morgan shook her head. "Well, I've brought plenty to do, so I can just stay at the house out of the way on Friday."

Brandon decided not to push it. He turned the radio on to get the traffic report and turned his attention to the road. Morgan chatted easily with the girls and Sara, and he was content to listen to them. Morgan fit so well into his life. He found himself anxious to come clean with their families about their relationship, but didn't want to run ahead of God. He was really looking forward to the long weekend and hoped that he and Morgan could sneak off for some time alone, but with all the people there, it wouldn't be easy.

Once they cleared the suburbs, the trip went by quickly, and when they were about an hour from his parents' house, the back seat went completely quiet. Brandon looked in his mirror. "Are they asleep?" he said softly to Morgan.

She turned around and looked. "Yes," she nodded. Brandon put his arm on the console between them and turned his hand, palm up. He looked at Morgan. *It's your choice, babe.* She smiled and laced her fingers with his. He squeezed her hand, and she squeezed back.

*This is going to be the best Thanksgiving ever.*

# 36

MORGAN WAS SO happy to be at Brandon's parents' home. As soon as they'd arrived, she'd slipped into the role of being simply Kelsea's sister. It was both exciting and a little scary to think that someday, she might be a true member of the St. Clair family, instead of a shirt-tail relative.

The house was a rambling, multi-level abode. Sara happily shared her room with Morgan, and Kelsea and Landon and the babies were camped out in the family room on the lower level. Brandon and the girls were in his and Landon's old room, and Morgan and Kelsea's mom, Beth, was in the room that had belonged to Reagan St. Clair many years ago.

It was tortuous to be there with Brandon and act as if he was just her sister's brother-in-law and someone whom she didn't know all that well. Morgan busied herself talking with Kelsea and helping with the babies—who had changed so much since last May. They had little personalities now. Morgan was amused that Rose was the spunkier of the two, and little Isaac was sweetly calm. The two sisters agreed that they had to make a way to get together more often.

Morgan also loved watching her mom interact with her grandchildren. Beth Anderson had waited a long time to be a grandma, and loved every minute of it. Morgan could just imagine her joy if she inherited two more instant granddaughters someday.

It was a busy day getting dinner ready, and Morgan was happy to help. Janice St. Clair had already communicated through Kelsea that she would love for Morgan to decorate the place cards, and had gathered all the supplies for that. Morgan had a great time doing it, and let April and Shelbie help.

Finally, all the food was ready and it was time to sit down at the large dining room table. Janice and Beth had set the cards out, and Brandon was directly across from Morgan. Everyone held hands, and Jim gave a beautiful blessing. Then they began passing the dishes and chattering.

"Honey, where's the hot mustard?" Jim called to his wife from his end of the table.

"Dad, you and your hot mustard!" Sara exclaimed. She rolled her eyes at Morgan. "He slathers it on everything."

Janice jumped up. "Oh, let me grab that right now." She scurried away and was back in seconds. She set the jar down in front of Jim, and he reached up and gave her lips a peck.

Shelbie was sitting next to her grandpa. "Why do you always kiss Grandma?" she asked. Everyone around the table laughed.

He grabbed his granddaughter's little hand. "Because I love her!"

"Ohhhhhh," Shelbie said, drawing the lone syllable out. "Then Daddy must love Miss Morgy!" She took a bite of her roll and didn't notice that everyone else had stopped eating.

Morgan's heart began to pound, and her gaze flew to Brandon.

His amber eyes sparkled at her and then he smiled. "Well, babe, I think God just answered our prayer." Out of the corner of her eye, Morgan saw her mother's jaw drop, and Kelsea and Landon exchanged a triumphant look. Brandon laid down his napkin, stood, and walked around the table to her. Morgan rose and he took her hands.

Brandon looked at their family members, every one of whom was grinning from ear to ear. "Morgan and I have been together for over a month. We're still working through some things, but Shelbie's right." Then he stared into Morgan's eyes. "I'm very much in love with Morgan."

Morgan was oblivious to everything and everyone else in the room except this amazing man. Her smile felt a mile wide. "And I love Brandon with all my heart." And then he framed her face with his hands and kissed her, and everyone began to clap and cheer.

"I knew it!" Kelsea exclaimed. Her face was filled with joy.

"You did not!" Morgan exclaimed. She and Brandon wrapped their arms around one another, and she looked up at him. "Bran, I didn't tell."

Sara pointed at Kelsea. "You only knew because I knew first, and told you," she said in a sing-song voice.

"You did not!" Brandon rolled his eyes. "We kept it a secret."

"Well, obviously not from Shelbie!" Landon interjected. Laughter raced around the room. Brandon kissed the top of Morgan's head and returned to his seat.

Sara set down her utensils. "If that's the best you two can keep a secret, you're in trouble." She tented her hands in front of her and looked around the table, no doubt to garner everyone's attention. Sara loved to entertain a crowd. "Whenever Morgan comes over, she finds an excuse to leave the room." She flicked a hand at her brother. "Then *he* leaves, and in a little while, *she* comes back—with swollen lips—and then *he* comes back—smelling like her perfume!"

Everyone laughed uproariously—even April and Shelbie, who didn't understand a thing. Morgan thought she and Brandon laughed the hardest.

"I saw you holding hands in the car last night," Sara added smugly.

Brandon looked at Morgan and shook his head. "She was

faking being asleep," he said. "I should have known. She did that all the time when she was little."

"And," Sara said, "what about that rattle in your car, Morgan?"

Morgan felt her face heating up, and bit back a hysterical giggle. Brandon looked at his sister. "You think you're so smart, Peanut," he said with a grin.

"Bro, Kelsea and I knew," Landon said. "You started calling me with woman questions at the same time Morgan started calling Kelsea with guy questions."

Morgan and Brandon looked at each other, wide-eyed.

"Neither of you gave anything away about who you were dating," Kelsea said, "but we figured it out." She grinned at Morgan.

"And your stories didn't sync up exactly," Landon added with a twinkle in his eye.

Morgan and Brandon just stared at one another, smiling.

"Did all this begin last Mothers' Day at Kelsea and Landon's?" Beth asked.

Morgan and Brandon answered in unison. "Definitely not!" They burst out laughing, and everyone joined in.

"Sounds like there's a story there," Landon said.

When the laughter died down, Jim raised his glass. "To Brandon and Morgan, and whatever the Lord has in store for them."

"To Brandon and Morgan," everyone echoed, and clinked glasses. Brandon leaned across the table, touched his glass to Morgan's, and winked.

"I love you," he mouthed.

*This is the best Thanksgiving ever.*

# 37

AFTER DINNER, LANDON, Kelsea, Brandon, and Morgan offered to do all the clean-up since their moms had prepared most of the meal. Janice and Beth were happy to join Jim in the family room with all the children. Brandon couldn't wait to finish the chore so he could get Morgan out of there. Their kiss in the dining room in front of their families had been very circumspect. He had gone several days without a real kiss, and couldn't wait to get her alone.

He thought he was being helpful, but all he was really doing was trailing around after Morgan. She was working at the sink when Brandon came in with the rest of the glasses. He deposited them on the counter, wrapped his arms around her waist, and whispered in her ear. She giggled.

"Oh honestly, you two, get out of here," Kelsea said good-naturedly. "Landon and I will finish."

"You sure?" Brandon asked. He grabbed a towel and handed it to Morgan so she could dry her hands.

"Yes, we're sure," Landon said. "It's like being around two teenagers." He wiggled his eyebrows. "And if you leave, I can get a few moments alone with my wife."

Brandon didn't waste any time. He grabbed Morgan's hand and pulled her into the family room, where a Disney movie played on the large TV screen. "April and Shelbie, Miss Morgy and I are going for a walk. Be good until we get back," Brandon instructed.

"Bye, Daddy. Bye, Miss Morgy," April said. She was sitting in an overstuffed chair holding Isaac, supervised by Grandpa.

Shelbie stood and put her hands on her little hips. "Are you gonna kiss Miss Morgy again, Daddy?" she asked.

All the adults hooted with laughter. "You bet I am!" Brandon answered with a grin, and the laughter got even louder. He helped Morgan on with her coat, and ushered her out the door.

Holding hands, they walked down the long driveway and turned left when they got out to the road. After they had reached a more secluded spot, Brandon stopped under a tree and pulled her into his arms.

And kissed her with all the love in his heart.

He rested his forehead against hers. "I love you so much, Morgan."

"I love you more, Bran."

"Impossible!" He squeezed her until she squealed. Then he got serious. "Morgan, I've spent a lot of time with God since last weekend, and He's given me peace. And obviously, He answered our prayer tonight. A part of me will always love Darla, but I'm head over heels in love with you now, and ready to move forward."

"As long as I'm your present and future, that's all I need," Morgan whispered.

They kissed again, then walked, arm in arm. It was a cold, clear night. The stars were out and there was a three-quarter moon. As they ambled along with the moonlight washing over them, Brandon had never felt so content and at peace.

"So, you called Kelsea for advice?" He smiled at Morgan so she'd know that he wasn't upset.

"And you called Landon?" she countered with a lilt in her voice.

"I didn't give him any clues," Brandon said. "What did you tell her?"

"Just that you were TDH and into sports."

He eyed her warily. "What's TDH?"

Morgan stopped and looped her hands around his neck. "Tall, dark, and handsome," she whispered, and pulled his head down for a kiss.

After a few moments, they resumed their walk.

"Are you ready for tomorrow?" he asked.

Morgan looked at him. "Don't tell me you're one of those people who goes to the mall at midnight to be the first in line when the stores open." She shook her head. "It sounds like something you would totally be into. Crowds and chaos."

He grimaced. "You know I'm not a shopper." They both laughed. "No, remember? We're all going skiing."

Morgan stopped walking. "Oh, I'd forgotten about that."

He leaned over and nuzzled her neck. "I'm going to teach you to ski."

"Bran, really, I—it won't work. I tried to ice skate once and it was a disaster. I have weak ankles."

He sighed. "Babe, skiing is completely different from ice skating."

Morgan twisted her hands in front of her. "I'm just such a klutz, Bran. I don't want to embarrass you in front of your family. Really, I'd rather stay at the house. I brought things to work on."

"Like what?"

"Knitting. And I have papers to grade."

Brandon couldn't believe what he was hearing. "*Knitting?* My grandma knits. That's for old ladies."

Morgan stopped walking. "It is not! I'm making scarves and hats and mittens for the girls for Christmas. A friend of mine spins and dyes her own yarn. They'll be one of a kind." She looked a little hurt, and Brandon felt badly for what he had said.

He pulled her into his arms and kissed her forehead. "I'm sorry. I shouldn't have said that. But especially now that you're my girlfriend, everyone will expect you to come skiing. You can't let life pass you by while you sit at the house painting or knitting or grading papers." He pulled her close and she let out a soft sigh. "For me?" he whispered, and kissed her in a way he knew that she loved.

When they came apart, she looked at him dreamily. "That's not fair, Bran, and you know it." He could tell she was teasing. "Okay, for you, I'll try."

# 38

"I TOLD YOU I couldn't ski!"

Morgan bit down on her lip to keep from screaming. Bran squatted next to her. He removed his gloves and ran his fingers expertly over her ankle, which was already beginning to swell.

"I don't think it's broken," he said. "But it's a bad sprain." He turned his head in Landon's direction. "We need to pack snow around it to try to minimize the swelling."

Morgan clamped her mouth shut. She was so embarrassed. Even April and Shelbie were naturals on skis. She was so cold, and now they were packing snow around her lower leg, ankle, and foot. Kelsea took her scarf off and handed it to Brandon, and he wrapped it around the snow pack. Then he stood.

Landon motioned to Kelsea. "We'll get you up, Morgan." In one swift movement, they did that, and Bran scooped her up in his arms and walked across the slope to a far-off spot where Jim had brought Brandon's SUV as close as he could get it. Morgan buried her face in his neck and cried.

Kelsea ran to catch up with them. "I'm coming, too, Morgy." She opened the back door and Jim and Brandon got her situated in the back seat.

Morgan grabbed the collar of Brandon's coat. "Are we going home?" she said through her tears.

"No, I want to get an x-ray to be sure," he said. He leaned in and kissed her cheek. "I'm sorry, Morgan. I'm really sorry."

She nodded but didn't say anything.

"I'll be with you every minute," Brandon said. He ran around to the other side and got in, and tenderly put her injured foot in his lap. Kelsea and Jim got into the front seat, and Jim drove them to the hospital. It felt like an eternity to get there, but the trip only took about twenty minutes.

From the moment they got in the ER, Dr. St. Clair took charge. If Morgan hadn't been so miserable, she would have been impressed and swooning over his commanding presence. Once they got some pain medication into her, she began to relax. Bran kept his promise and never left her side.

The x-ray showed a bad sprain, just as he had predicted, and Morgan's foot was tightly bound. An hour later, they left with more pain meds, bandages, and a pair of crutches. Bran got her settled in the back seat with her foot propped up on some wadded-up blankets. Then he went around and slipped in next to her and took her in his arms.

As his father drove them home, Bran held her close and whispered in her ear, "Babe, I'm so, so sorry. I shouldn't have pushed you to do something you didn't want to do."

"I don't know how I'm going to get through the end of the semester," she said softly through her tears. "I have so much going on. I'm not even going to be able to get around. Those crutches will be a nightmare with the snow and ice we already have on the ground. And I won't be able to drive. And my bedroom and bath are on the second floor." Her pain-filled mind was swimming with unsettling thoughts.

"We'll figure it out together, Morgan, I promise," Brandon said, stroking her hair.

When they got back to the St. Clair's house, everyone was

waiting for them. Brandon carried Morgan in and took her straight upstairs to Sara's room. "Sara, can you sleep with the girls tonight?" he asked his sister. Morgan looked at him with surprise. He laid her down on the bed. "I'll make a bed on the floor."

"Bran, you can't sleep on the floor," Morgan said.

"I'm not leaving you," he said. He looked at Beth and Janice who had come into the room with everything the hospital had sent home. "Mom, could you get some more pillows and blankets?"

"Of course," Janice said and hurried away.

"Morgan, would you like some tea, or cocoa?" her mother asked. "Something to eat?"

Morgan nodded. "They gave me some crackers at the hospital, and they said the pain medication might make me nauseous on an empty stomach."

Janice came back into the room, her arms laden. "How about some soup?" she asked.

"That sounds good," Morgan nodded.

Brandon squeezed her hand. "Mom makes the best vegetable barley soup and homemade bread," he said. "It's part of our Friday-after-Thanksgiving tradition." He and Beth took the pillows and blankets and got Morgan situated.

"I'll go help Janice," Beth said. She planted a kiss on Morgan's head.

"Thanks so much, Mom," Morgan said.

Brandon sat down gingerly next to her and took her hand. "I love you, Morgan. I'll stay with you every moment." He kissed her tenderly, and Morgan's heart melted.

She touched the side of his face. "I'm so lucky to have you," she whispered.

Kelsea appeared at the door. April and Shelbie were each holding one of her hands. "Are you up for some company, Miss Morgy? The girls are a little worried about you."

Bran scooted away from her a little. "Of course," Morgan said, holding out her hands. "Come on in, girls."

"Just be careful not to bump Miss Morgy's leg," Brandon said.

April and Shelbie stood by the side of the bed and took her hands. "I'm sorry you got hurt, Miss Morgy," April said.

"Does it hurt bad?" Shelbie asked.

Morgan didn't want to scare them. "It hurts a little, but I took some medicine and it feels better." The girls stayed for another few minutes and then went with Kelsea, promising to make some pictures for Morgan to help her feel better.

"They're so precious," Morgan murmured after they had left.

Bran's amber eyes were tender. "They already love you," he whispered.

After that, her mother came in with a tray with soup and bread. Morgan didn't think she was hungry, but finished every bite, and then fell asleep with Bran holding her hand.

They drove back to Chicago Sunday morning, and by that time Morgan was feeling much better. When they got to Bran's house, there was a large box waiting for them. Somehow, he had come up with a little battery-powered scooter on which she could rest the knee of her injured leg and motor along. She thought it was ingenious, and was relieved that it would make it possible to get around campus.

Bran carried her into the house and laid her gently on the couch, and Sara brought some pillows and an ice pack for her ankle. Bran knelt by her side and took her hand. "We want you to stay here and let us take care of you."

"We have it all figured out," Sara said. "You can stay in my apartment and I'll sleep upstairs. There are like twelve empty bedrooms up there," she quipped, and Morgan smiled. Sara held out her hand. "Give me your condo keys, and text me everything you need."

"I still can't drive," Morgan said. "I guess I can take the Metra to work from here."

Brandon shook his head. "No way. Sara and I will take you to campus and your sessions and pick you up."

Morgan couldn't believe it. She shook her head in disbelief.

"Give up, Morgan, you're outnumbered," Sara said with a smile. Morgan got her keys out of her purse and handed them to Sara.

"I'll take the girls with me, if that's okay," she said. Brandon looked at Morgan and she nodded. "They'll love helping, and it will give you two some time alone." Sara wiggled her eyebrows and left with a wave.

"She's really something," Morgan said. "She's terrific."

"Yeah, she is," Brandon said, and leaned in to kiss her. "Isn't this better than going home?" He kissed her again. "We'll practically be living together." Another, longer kiss.

Morgan giggled. "With three chaperones," she said. But she was so relieved to have someone taking care of her. It felt like family. Maybe, just maybe...

"I love you, Morgan," Bran whispered.

# 39

THEY FELL INTO an easy routine over the next week. Brandon loved seeing Morgan at the start and end of each day, and he could tell that the girls loved it, too. She completely fit in with them, and he was becoming more and more convinced that they had a solid chance at a future together.

The night before she went home, after the girls had gone to bed, Morgan asked if they could talk. They sat down by the fire and Brandon thought that he could spend every night for the rest of his life like this.

"There's something I need to tell you," she said. "I don't know exactly how to say it."

Brandon tried to think of anything he'd done wrong, or said, that could cause Morgan to look so serious. He took her hand. "You can talk to me about anything, Morgan, you know that."

To his relief, she smiled at him. "I know, but I don't want you to get the wrong idea."

"You let me be the judge of that," he said, and squeezed her hand.

And then she started talking about her infertility issues and her deep desire to foster or adopt one or more children. Morgan's beautiful features came to life when she talked about some of the children in the arts program who had captured her heart, and how she wanted to give them a loving and safe environment. "I know we haven't talked specifically about our future, and I'm not trying to force that conversation," she said. "But this is so important to me, and I just thought I should tell you how I felt."

He raised her hand to his lips and kissed it. "I'm glad you shared it with me," he said. "We already agreed that there are lots of ways to grow a family, and I'm completely in agreement with you." They sat by the fire for a long time and talked about their childhoods, growing up, and what Morgan's family felt like after her father died. Brandon was more in love with her than ever.

Morgan went back to her condo the next Sunday night. She told Brandon that she needed to get through the last two weeks of her semester without distractions, and kissed him goodbye and whispered in his ear that she loved the way he distracted her.


Brandon was busy at work, too, and suddenly, it was December 23. They had Christmas with Sara before she drove home to Wisconsin for two weeks. Morgan had given her a silk scarf that she had painted herself, and Sara gave Morgan a beautiful pair of earrings. Brandon was grateful that there was a strong bond between them.

Then it was his birthday, Christmas Eve, and they packed up April and Shelbie and drove to Beth's house in Kankakee. It was cold but clear and sunny, and it felt entirely natural to be in the car with his girls in the backseat and Morgan by his side, holding his hand.

"Are we going to Unca Landon and Aunt Kelsea's house?" Shelbie called out.

"No, remember, we're going to Grandma Beth's house," Brandon answered. He squeezed Morgan's hand. They had agreed at Thanksgiving that the girls could call her that since she was their little cousins' grandma.

"Yay!" the girls shouted.

"I love Grandma Beth!" Shelbie said.

"She's fun," April added.

Kelsea and Landon and the twins were already there when they arrived mid-afternoon. They'd gotten several inches of fresh snow overnight, and there was a festive air in the house. He and Morgan had shipped a box to Beth full of gifts for April and Shelbie from "Santa," and Brandon looked forward to wrapping those with Morgan tonight after the girls had gone to bed.

After they got all their gifts and suitcases inside, the girls went with Grandma Beth to read a story to the twins and get them down for a nap. Brandon joined Morgan, Landon, and Kelsea in the family room.

Brandon loved seeing the home where Morgan had grown up. He was instantly drawn to the wall where hers and Kelsea's growing-up pictures were displayed. "Weren't you the cutest little girl?" he teased. He stopped at a photo of the family taken out on the front steps of the house. It was obvious that Morgan looked like her dad.

She came and stood next to him. "This is the last picture of the four of us," Morgan said softly.

Brandon put his arms around her and held her. "What was his name?"

"Andrew. He went by Andy. He was the best dad, so much fun."

Brandon kept looking at the pictures. "Oh, this is a great one!" he burst out laughing, and Morgan giggled.

Kelsea piped up. "I don't even have to ask which one you're laughing at. My eighth grade graduation." In the picture, Kelsea was dressed in black pants and a top, her arms crossed in front of her and one hip jutted out in a defiant pose. Her long, dark hair hung limply on each side of her face, and she scowled at the camera. It looked like she was wearing scruffy, black tennis shoes. Morgan stood next to her in total contrast. Her golden hair was curled and pulled back with a headband, and she wore a pale blue dress with a flowered scarf, and white sandals with a matching purse. She stood proud and tall and smiled for the camera as if she were on Hollywood's red carpet.

"You had a flair for fashion even back then, babe," Brandon said, giving her a squeeze.

"I was so mad that Mom refused to let me wear jeans," Kelsea said. "I was supposed to change out of those tennis shoes, too, but I think she was too worn out over the battle to push it."

Landon grinned at his wife and took her hand. "I can't wait until Rose Elizabeth gets to be that age. What goes around comes around." They all laughed.

Just then, April and Shelbie burst into the room. "Grandma Beth said we could build a snowman!" Shelbie shouted.

"Shh!" April scolded. "You'll wake the babies."

"Grandma Beth said we could build a snowman!" Shelbie repeated in a stage whisper.

Beth followed them, holding two pairs of snow pants. "They got these out of their suitcase. I said they had to ask you, Brandon."

He smiled. "It's fine with me." He looked at Morgan. "Do you mind if I go outside with them?"

She shook her head. "Not at all."

"Actually, I'd love to go with them," Beth said. "You stay in here where it's warm and relax."

"If you're sure," Brandon said.

"I'm sure," Beth said with a smile. "Oh, girls," she said to Kelsea and Morgan, "could you finish putting the lasagna together, and make up the salad?"

"Sure thing, Mom," the sisters answered in unison. Beth followed April and Shelbie out of the room.

"Mmm, sounds good," Brandon said.

"It's our traditional Christmas Eve meal," Morgan said. "We'll have turkey with all the trimmings tomorrow."

Kelsea looked at Morgan. "Mom couldn't wait for the girls to get here. I think she was more excited about them coming than you."

Morgan laughed. "I know she's happy to have little ones in the house for Christmas. It makes it more fun for everyone." She stood. "Come on, Sissy, let's get to it." They went into the kitchen and the two brothers sat and chatted for a while about inconsequential things.

Brandon got up and went into the dining room to look out the front window and check on the girls, and Landon followed him. April and Shelbie's faces were flushed with joy, so different from last year's Christmas that had been drenched with grief. He felt his brother's gaze on him. "I'm really glad we're here," Brandon murmured.

Landon smiled. "I can't believe how much your life has changed just since last May when you visited us in St. Louis."

Brandon raised an eyebrow. "Yeah, the new job was a game-changer." But he knew what Landon was really getting at, and let out a breath. "I'm ready to move on, and I want to spend the rest of my life with her."

"You giving her a ring tomorrow?" Landon asked.

"No," Brandon replied, "I'm thinking Valentine's Day."

"That's great, man," Landon said, and reached out to squeeze his brother's shoulder. "I'm really happy for you."

Brandon hesitated. He didn't want to betray Morgan's confidence if Landon didn't already know about her infertility issues, but he wanted Landon to know. He lowered his voice. "She—we probably won't be able to have children of our own," he said, "but we've talked about how great we think fostering and adopting are. We're completely in sync about that."

Landon nodded. One glance between the brothers told Brandon everything. "I can't wait to see what God has in store for you," Landon said.

"Me, too," Brandon said with a grin.

Kelsea called from the kitchen, "you guys want some Christmas cider?" Brandon correctly guessed that this was the source of the enticing aromas of cinnamon and clove. When he and Landon got into the kitchen, he pulled Morgan around a corner where they could have a moment of privacy.

"I just had a conversation with Landon," he whispered, "and, well, I mentioned your infertility issues, just in a general way. It just sort of came up. I hope I wasn't breaking confidence."

"Bran, it's okay," she answered. "He knows. It all began back when he and Kelsea met and were married."

"I would never—"

She silenced him with a finger to his lips. "Bran, I know." She smiled. "Let's go get some cider."

They went back into the kitchen, and Brandon sat on one of the bar stools at the counter. Morgan came and perched against his knee, and their arms automatically went around one another.

Landon set down mugs of cider for them, and Kelsea began putting the food they'd prepared for dinner into the fridge. "You want some help, Sissy?" Morgan asked.

"Don't worry, I've got it." She raised an eyebrow. "It doesn't look like you and Dr. Moron could bear to be more than an inch apart from each other, anyway."

Brandon felt Morgan blanch, and make a sound in her throat.

"Oh, whoopsie!" Kelsea said, and she and Morgan began to laugh.

Morgan covered her mouth as a hysterical giggle escaped. She laid a hand on Brandon's shoulder. "Bran, I'm so sorry. That's what I called you in my head the weekend we met at Kelsea and Landon's!"

He threw back his head and laughed, and heard Landon's laughter join his. He pulled Morgan close. "I *was* a moron that weekend."

"I'll bet you've been called worse at the hospital, bro," Landon said with a grin.

"I *know* I have," Brandon said. He planted a kiss near Morgan's ear. "I love you, babe," he whispered.

The family went to church together for the five o'clock Christmas Eve service, and Brandon's heart was full. April and Shelbie wore their pretty new Christmas dresses from Grandma and Grandpa St. Clair. Then they all came back to the house for the delicious Italian dinner, after which Beth and Morgan brought out a birthday cake and ice cream. Everyone sang and Brandon blew out the candles. He already knew what he was going to wish for, and looked right at Morgan when he did it. Her gorgeous green eyes sparkled at him in the candlelight.

Then he opened his gifts. The St. Clair family had always recognized Brandon's birthday apart from Christmas, and made sure that the celebration was memorable. Brandon was filled with gratitude and touched by everyone's generosity. There were gifts from Landon and Kelsea, Beth, and the girls. April and Shelbie were excited and proud of the paperweights they had made him, and he promised to put them on his desk at work. Brandon loved the small framed silhouette portraits of them that Sara had arranged.

"Here's one more," Morgan said. She held up a long tube wrapped in white tissue paper and tied with a pink ribbon on one end and a purple one on the other.

"Open it, Daddy! Open it!" the girls squealed.

Brandon extended his arms and held the tube lengthwise in front of him. "I think I need some help. Each of you can untie a ribbon."

"I get the purple one!" Shelbie said, hopping up and down. They did as he instructed, and helped him get the paper off, then he carefully pulled out a large sheet of paper and unrolled it.

"What is it, Daddy?" Shelbie clapped her little hands.

"It's us!" April exclaimed.

"Oh, Morgan," Brandon breathed. It was an incredible pencil drawing of the girls in an outdoor setting. It looked a little like their backyard. In the picture, April sat cross-legged on the grass, picking petals off a flower, looking serene and thoughtful. Shelbie was trying to catch a butterfly that was just out of her reach, her little face filled with joy and wonder. It was a black-and-white sketch, except for the flower, which was pink, and the butterfly, which was shades of purple.

Brandon didn't have the first clue how Morgan had captured the essence of his daughters so perfectly. He would treasure this gift forever. He felt a lump in his throat. "This is so beautiful, babe, thank you."

"You're welcome," Morgan replied. "I'll have it framed when we get home."

Brandon passed the picture for Kelsea, Landon, and Beth to look at. "Wow, that's amazing," Landon said. "I have no artistic talent whatsoever."

"Morgan, you outdid yourself on this one," Beth said, her face beaming with pride.

"This is one of your best, Morgy," Kelsea agreed. "Would you do a sketch of Rose and Isaac?"

Brandon exchanged a glance with Morgan. "Why don't you wait until tomorrow, Kelsea?" he said.

Kelsea clapped her hands. "Ooh, I can't wait!" she exclaimed.

Brandon held out his arm to Morgan. "Come here," he said. "Thank you," he whispered when she got close enough, and then he kissed her.

"Happy Birthday, Bran," she whispered back.

"Daddy, you *always* kiss Miss Morgy!" Shelbie exclaimed.

"Yes, I sure do," Brandon said. His heart was so full. *Best birthday ever.*

# 40

MORGAN HAD SPENT many Christmases in this house, but none compared to this one. She looked around the chaos that reigned in her mother's family room, and her heart felt steeped in joy. The house was filled with laughter and love. Christmas wrapping paper and ribbons were everywhere, despite her mother's attempt to gather them up after each gift had been opened. The babies weren't walking yet, but they were scooting around and putting everything in their mouths. April and Shelbie were excited about everything and were great little helpers. Everyone loved their homemade Christmas gifts from Morgan, and she was relieved that the sweater she made for Bran fit him perfectly. It was the best Christmas Morgan could remember.

She sat on the floor with her back against the couch. Bran sat next to her.

"Here's the last one," he said, handing her a slim, flat box about eight inches square. Morgan had been holding her breath, wondering if he might give her an engagement ring. The prospect both thrilled and scared her.

"Should I try to guess what it is?" Morgan said, giving the box a shake. It was very light, and didn't make any noise.

"Betcha can't," he replied with a lazy smile.

She unwrapped the box to reveal a thick cream linen envelope lined in gold foil, and was more intrigued than ever. When she opened it, her heart leapt into her throat. "You're—you can't be serious," she said. "Bran!"

"What is it?" Kelsea asked.

"Tickets to an exhibit at the Palomino Gallery in New York in February," Morgan said. Her heart beat erratically.

"I'm guessing that's some kind of artist," Landon said.

"Only the most incredible post-impressionist artist of the twentieth century!" Morgan exclaimed. "Bran, how did you—I can't believe—"

He laughed. "Well, full disclosure—I had help from Juanita Ross." He looked at the others. "Morgan's colleague," he clarified. "I asked her about getting you a painting or taking you to an art event, and she told me this artist, Angelina Palomino, was one of your favorites, and the name rang a bell."

"Jacko Palomino, the Bears' linebacker," Landon interjected.

"Bingo," Brandon nodded. "Angelina is his sister. One phone call, and I had these tickets."

Morgan cupped his chin in her hand and kissed him. "Bran, this is an amazing gift. Thank you so much."

He put his arm around her. "There's two tickets. Okay if I tag along?"

A romantic weekend in New York with him? That was a big step. Morgan couldn't believe it. "Of course," she whispered.

He kissed her cheek. "Merry Christmas, Morgan."

"Merry Christmas, Bran."


It was Christmas night. All the kids were in bed. Landon and Kelsea had gone for a walk, Beth was somewhere else in the house, and Morgan and Brandon were cuddling on the couch in the living room.

He and the girls were driving to his parents' in Wisconsin

tomorrow afternoon to have Christmas with them, and Morgan would take the train back to Chicago in a couple of days. Bran was planning to arrive home on December 30.

"Let's talk about New Year's Eve," he said.

Morgan had been thinking about it. She hoped for a quiet, romantic night alone. Sara would still be in Wisconsin and Morgan knew Brandon wouldn't want to leave the girls. She thought they could stay in, make homemade pizzas, then do a craft or play games with the girls and put them down early. "All right," Morgan replied. "What do you usually like to do?"

"Well, I usually like going out on New Year's Eve, but last year I didn't do anything," Brandon shrugged. "I stayed home with the girls and was in bed by ten." Then he perked up. "But the Center is renting out the Allegra for the night. I have to be there, and I want you to go with me so I can show you off to everyone." He kissed Morgan on the sensitive spot on her neck.

She squirmed away from him. "Bran, I, um, wow. The Allegra." She knew it was one of Chicago's trendiest nightclubs, even though she'd never set foot in it. "I don't think I even have anything fancy enough to wear."

"Me, either. But I'm renting a tux. You could probably rent a dress. Giselle told me she's doing that."

Morgan liked his assistant. "Is it going to be a big event?"

He nodded. "They're expecting about six hundred people, a lot of managers and coaches and players and their wives and girlfriends. It's one of those seen-and-be-seen things. I have to be there."

"What about the girls?"

He shrugged. "I'll hire a sitter. Sara gave me a couple of names."

Morgan frowned and twisted her hands in her lap. "Bran, I just—I'm not comfortable in big crowds. Especially celebrities and people like that. I'd feel so out of place."

He ruffled a hand through his hair. "Well, that's the circle I travel in now. They're really just people, like anyone else." He pulled her closer. "You'll be on my arm all night. I'll never leave your side." He lowered his voice to a whisper. "Morgan, I can't go there alone. I need you there with me." He put his hands on either side of her face and kissed her once, twice, then slid his arms around her and deepened the kiss.

Morgan kissed him back and all her doubts vanished for a few moments. She told herself this wasn't a good idea, but couldn't resist him. "Are you trying to kiss me into saying yes?" she said as his lips trailed along her jawline and neck.

He laughed softly. "Maybe. Is it working?"

Morgan sighed. "Yes."

# 41

BRANDON RANG THE doorbell and waited for Morgan to answer. When she did, he wasn't prepared for what he saw.

She was utterly gorgeous. He whistled long and low. "Oh, wow, babe." He stepped in and closed the door. She wore a beautiful deep purple gown, high, silver pumps, and matching jewelry.

Brandon took her in his arms and slowly danced her around in a small circle. "You'll be the most beautiful woman there," he whispered. In her tall heels, she was closer than usual, and he took advantage with a long, slow kiss.

"Renting this dress was a great idea. I'll have to remember to thank Giselle. It really wasn't that expensive." She fingered his bow tie. "You look amazing, Bran," she said. She wore the silver bracelet he'd given her for her birthday.

"Your hair is beautiful." It was gathered into a knot at the nape of her neck. Brandon reached out and gently turned her so he could touch a golden curl.

"It's a chignon," she said. "Thank you."

He kissed her again. "Thank you for coming with me," he whispered when they came apart. "I love you."

"I love you, too."

In the car, he told her about all the people he thought would be there. She hadn't heard of most of them, even the biggest names. Sometimes, she would gaze at him with a deer-in-the-headlights look, and he would squeeze her hand. "Morgan, I'll be by your side the whole time. It'll be fine."

When they stepped into the club, Brandon laced his fingers with Morgan's, and she held on tight. They were immediately swept into the crowded, noisy, jubilant crowd. Brandon began making the rounds, trading back slaps with the men and bowing over the women's hands. He proudly introduced Morgan to everyone, and was so happy to have her there with him.

They spent the next hour moving through the room. Brandon felt as comfortable here as he did in the surgical theater. He loved the electricity in the room and enjoyed talking with people. He even met a few superstar athletes that he didn't know, yet. This evening was going to pay dividends for his career.

At one point when the crowd was packed tight, a woman with bright red hair wearing a short, skintight sequined copper dress slid by them. She gave a little finger wave and smiled up at Brandon. "Good evening, Dr. St. Clair," she cooed, and moved on.

"Who was that?" Morgan whispered.

He frowned. "I'm not sure. She might work in the Cubs' front office."

A waiter approached them with a tray. "Champagne?" he asked.

"Ah—no, thanks," Brandon replied. "Can we get some water?"

The waiter indicated a station with a silver carafe. Brandon led Morgan there and got each them a glass. "Do you want to go to the buffet now?"

She nodded. They filled their plates and found two seats at a round table. When they were finished, Brandon stood and held out his hand. "I need to make the rounds again." He pulled her close and kissed her temple. "You're doing great, babe."

# 42

MORGAN CLOSED THE bathroom stall door and let out a sigh. She didn't need to use the facilities, but she sat anyway. She just couldn't stand it one more minute. She had to get away.

Morgan rubbed her temples. The absence of noise should have been calming, but it wasn't. She was so out of her element. The constant movement, the press and heat of the crowd, the flashing lights, the loud music with its bone-rattling bass, all of it unnerved her. She felt like her smile was plastered on her face, and thought everyone else looked that way, too. None of it felt sincere. It was obvious to Morgan that the women were trying to outdo each other. She wished she had been brave enough to stay home and let Brandon come without her.

She heard the click of heels on the tile floor. "I just need to fix my makeup," a female voice said. "Brandon St. Clair is the hottest man *ever* in a tux! Did you see his mousy girlfriend?" Morgan peeked through the crack between the side of the stall. It was the redhead in the shimmering copper dress. She stood at the sink next to another woman.

"I heard she's an artist or something," the second woman said.

"Ugh," said Miss Copper. "Why would he want to be with someone like that? I heard that he's really into extreme sports and all kinds of exciting things. I can think of one extreme sport I'd like to do with him," she purred. There was no mistaking her meaning. Morgan cringed.

"Well, he looks pretty happy with her. If he's seriously involved with someone, give it up, Sheba," the second woman said.

Miss Copper put on a heavy coat of bright red lipstick and pouted at herself in the mirror. "Hey, they're all fair game until they're married. You know my motto. Whatever Sheba wants, Sheba gets. And Sheba wants that rich, sexy doctor. Come on, let's go. I am ready to par-tay!" Morgan waited until she'd heard the doors close and their footsteps had faded away.

She stepped out of the stall and looked at the woman in the mirror. Compared to most of the women out there, Morgan looked and felt like a wet dishrag. She shook her head slowly. *Why would he want to be with you?*

Morgan looked at her phone. It was only a little after ten. She couldn't believe they'd only been here two hours. It felt like two days. She steeled herself and returned to the party. It felt louder than when she'd left just ten minutes ago, but with the way the alcohol was flowing, she shouldn't have been surprised.

It took her almost another ten minutes to locate Brandon, chatting up a noisy group, and she leaned against him with relief. He slid his arm around her. "You okay?" he murmured into her ear.

She took a deep breath and shook her head. He looked into her eyes with surprise. "Are you sick, Morgan?"

"I just—the noise and everything, it's too much," she said. He looked like he didn't know what to say.

"I can—I'll just call an Uber and go home," she said.

"What? No, absolutely not, Morgan," he said sharply.

She almost burst into tears. "I need to go, Bran. I'm sorry."

He nodded. "All right." He looked around and took her hand. "I just have to say goodnight to a couple of folks."

Twenty minutes later, they finally left. Neither one of them said much in the car. When they pulled up in front of her condo, she turned to him. "I'm sorry, Bran."

"It's okay." He opened his arms. "Come here." He held her and kissed her forehead. "Can I come in?" She nodded.

Morgan was so happy to be back in her quiet, serene home. She laid her purse and keys on the hall table and turned to Brandon. Before she could apologize again, he kissed her tenderly. Then he took her hand and led her to the couch.

"I don't know what came over me," Brandon said, and he squeezed her hand. "I'd rather be here with you, Morgan. Honestly, I would. But I love crowds and excitement and noise. It invigorates me." He kissed her again. "Do you want me to turn the fireplace on?" She nodded.

He did that, then removed his jacket and sat. Morgan curled up next to him and laid her head on his chest. "I get my energy from the quiet," she said. "I know that doesn't make sense, but it does, to me." They sat and talked for over an hour and took kissing breaks, and then Brandon stood and raised her to her feet.

"It's almost midnight," he whispered, and they watched the last minutes of the year tick away on the clock over her mantel. At exactly midnight, he kissed her with a depth of passion yet unknown to Morgan, and all her doubts melted away.

"I love you, Dr. Morgan Anderson," Brandon said as he smiled into her eyes. "And I hope that we're together just like this at midnight on New Year's Eve for many, many years to come."

# 43

THE NEXT TWO weeks flew by. Morgan was busy preparing for the next semester, which would begin the third week of January. Brandon had one scheduled trip and two unscheduled ones, and she had hardly seen him. It looked like they were both free this Saturday, and she hoped they could spend some time with the girls, and then some time together, just the two of them.

He called her Friday night. "Hey babe, I'm on the plane coming home from Seattle."

Morgan's heart took wing. "When will you be home?" she asked.

"Not until about one in the morning."

"Can we get together this weekend? I miss you."

"Absolutely. That's one reason I was calling. How would you like to go skydiving tomorrow?"

Morgan was horrified. "Skydiving?"

"Yeah, one of the Cubs players has a timeshare plane, and is taking a group skydiving tomorrow. He invited me to come and bring a guest."

"Oh, Bran, I can't. I could never do that."

She heard him sigh. "Morgan, you're going to miss out on life if you don't try new things."

That got her hackles up. She'd tried skiing, and look how that turned out. "Brandon, I try new things all the time, and my life is just fine. I just don't happen to want to jump out of an airplane. And isn't that a pretty dangerous thing for a father with young children to be doing?"

He sighed again. "It's probably safer than driving on the Kennedy during rush hour. Dar and I used to do fun things all the time, even after the girls were born."

Morgan felt a sting as if he had slapped her. "Well, I'm not Dar!" she exclaimed.

"Sweetheart, that's not the point," he said. Neither of them said anything for a moment. "Morgan, I don't want to pass up this chance. There will be people there I need to meet. Will you come with me, or not?"

"No, Bran, I won't," she said firmly. Then she softened her voice. "But can we do something with the girls Saturday night?"

He sounded resigned. "Yeah, I'll call you when I get home tomorrow afternoon."

"I'll plan everything for tomorrow night. You won't have to do a thing." She paused. "I love you, Bran."

"I love you, too," he said, and disconnected.

# 44

WHEN THEY'D FINISHED the skydive and gotten back to the airport, Brandon had a text from Morgan. He looked at the time. *Perfect.* She was already at his house. She'd gone over early so Sara could spend the rest of the day and evening with friends. *On my way, I love you,* he texted her back.

When he got home and went through the kitchen door, Morgan was standing at the stove and the girls were at the counter doing something with tissue paper and scissors and glue and a bunch of other little messy things.

"Hi, Daddy!" they screamed. He kissed each of them on the head.

"We're making stained glass," Shelbie said.

"Those are awesome," he said. Then he went to Morgan and kissed her. "Mmm, what do you taste like?"

She pointed at the pot on the stove. "Homemade spaghetti sauce," she said. "I'm trying," she said with a laugh. Morgan held out the spoon to him, and he tasted it.

"Yum, it's good," he said. He kissed her again. "But you taste better."

She put the spoon down and ran her hands over his shoulders. "Thank you."

He put his hands on her waist and smiled at her. "I like coming home and seeing you and the girls here in the kitchen."

Morgan swallowed and nodded.

"Hey," he said. "Let me go up and change, and then I'll be back and we'll have pasgetti, right, girls?"

"Right, Daddy!" they said with glee.

He kissed Morgan's cheek. "And I'll tell you all about my day. It was incredible!"

Brandon took a quick shower, changed, and went back downstairs. Morgan was putting the finishing touches on dinner, and the girls were setting the table. He helped Morgan get the food, then they sat and held hands and he prayed for the meal.

Brandon loved this. It felt like a real home. It felt like family. He was hungry and eagerly took his first bite. And chewed. And chewed some more.

"Is it okay, Bran?" Morgan asked. She nibbled on her lip in a way that signaled to him that she was nervous.

"It's delicious! That's why I'm not talking, I'm too busy enjoying it."

"It's sooooooo good! I love pasgetti!" Shelbie exclaimed.

April nodded. "Me, too. I've never had crunchy pasgetti."

Morgan's face fell and she looked like was going to cry. She laid down her fork. "I didn't cook the noodles long enough."

Brandon leaned over and kissed her on the cheek. "You'll get it next time. The sauce is amazing, babe. And it's not about the food. It's about being here, sharing a meal together." *As a family,* he almost added.

She squeezed his hand and gave him a tremulous smile, and Brandon felt like the sun had come out. After Thanksgiving, his birthday, and Christmas, he thought that it was time to have a serious talk about their future. He was thinking about proposing during their trip to New York next month.

"Who wants to hear about Daddy jumping out of an airplane?" he said.

"Me, me, me!" Shelbie squealed.

April's eyes got wide and she looked at Morgan. "I would be so scared!"

"Me, too!" Morgan replied.

So Brandon told them about the whole day and how exhilarating and fun it was, and what it felt like and looked like floating down from the sky. At one point he made a reference to his jumping buddy, Sheba.

"Who's Sheba, Daddy?" Shelbie said.

"She's one of the ladies who works for the Cubs," Brandon said. "She came by herself and so did I, so they put us together."

He noticed after that, Morgan got very quiet, but he didn't think anything of it. They finished dinner and Brandon tidied up the kitchen while Morgan helped the girls finish up their projects and clean everything up.

After they got the girls ready for bed, read books and said prayers with them, he and Morgan went back downstairs. The fireplace was going in the family room, and Brandon busied himself putting some soft music on. When he turned around, he was shocked to see Morgan standing there in her coat.

"Babe, what are you doing?"

"I'm going home, Bran. It was a long week, and I'm tired."

"I thought—I thought we would have some quiet time together. Just you and me. The way you like."

She sighed and looked away from him. "No, I need to go."

He went right to her and put his hands on her arms. "Morgan, what's wrong?"

Her eyes filled with tears, but she didn't say anything.

Brandon wrapped his arms around her and rubbed his hands over her back. "Come on, babe," he murmured. "Come sit with me and tell me what's wrong, and we'll figure it out together."

She let out a sigh and stood limply while he removed her coat, and he took her hand and led her to the couch. Brandon knew enough not to say anything, to let her talk first. He wrapped one arm around her and they sat there for several minutes with the soft music swirling around them.

Finally, she spoke. "Bran, I think it's time for us to talk about our future."

It was like she knew exactly what she was thinking! He took her hand and kissed it. "I was thinking the same thing."

"I'm not sure that this is going to work," she said.

Brandon's heart stopped. "Morgan, what do you mean? I thought—I love you! And you love me. What doesn't work?"

She swiped at her eyes, and Brandon quickly got up and grabbed some tissues from the kitchen counter. He sat next to her again and pressed them into her hand.

Her gorgeous green eyes were shiny with tears, and filled with pain. "We're so different," she said.

"Well, opposites attract," he said.

"But a couple needs to have a certain amount of things in common for it to work."

"I thought we did," he said quietly.

"Think about it, Bran. At our very core, we're totally different people. You're extroverted, I'm introverted. You're a city boy. I yearn for the country. You look at a picture of a river and think about white water rafting. I look at it and think about painting it." She paused. "The term *concert* means something entirely different to each of us."

Brandon took her hand in his. "We share a common faith," he pointed out. "We share the same core values. We both value family." He saved his strongest argument for last. "We both love the girls."

She nodded, and tears rolled down her cheeks again. "I do love the girls, so much. And I love you, Bran. But—" She let out a slow breath. "I'm just a wet blanket to you. I'm not any of the things to you that Darla was. She was a gourmet cook. I can't even make spaghetti. Look at what happened when you tried to take me skiing. I can't stand sports and crowds and noise. You need someone who will jump out of planes with you. That's not me."

Her voice caught. "You need someone like—Sheba."

Brandon was horrified. "Sheba?" he said in disbelief. "Where did that come from? Morgan, just because—"

Her voice shook. "I overheard her at the New Year's Eve party. She's had her eye on you for a long time, and she means to have you."

"Well, she's not going to get me!" Brandon shouted. He shook his head in frustration. "Morgan, how could you think that I would give a woman like her a second look?"

Morgan closed her eyes, and began to shake. Tears rolled down her cheeks. "Bran, you need—someone—who—" She could hardly get the words out. "Who can—give you a son—the—the brother the girls—want." April and Shelbie had made another mention during dinner about wanting a baby brother, and Bran had shut them down.

Brandon scooted closer to her. "Morgan, we talked about that, and it doesn't matter. *I love you.*" He lowered his voice to an impassioned whisper and said it again.

She blotted her eyes with a tissue and sighed. "I don't doubt your love for me, Bran," she said sadly, "but I wonder if it's really enough. I feel so inadequate most of the time because I'm always saying no to things that you want to do, or getting hurt. You travel in circles that are completely foreign to me. And when we do things that I like to do, you're bored and you fall asleep or you're trying to get service on your cell, or—"

"Morgan, I'm so sorry. Let me—"

Morgan slipped out of his arms and stood. "I need to go."

Brandon stood and put his arms around her. The food from dinner swirled in his stomach, and he felt the first stages of panic. "Morgan, I—" His voice cracked. He swallowed. "I can't lose you, babe, I can't."

Tears ran down her cheeks. "I—I just need some time to think, Bran. Please, just give me some space."

She leaned up and kissed his cheek, and then she was gone.

# 45

OVER THE NEXT four days, Brandon could hardly function. It was like losing Darla all over again. He couldn't eat, couldn't sleep, and couldn't concentrate on anything. Fortunately, he only had one surgery scheduled, and he was able to assign it to another doctor. He knew enough to not trust himself to be at the head of an operating table in this state.

Even though it almost killed him, he honored Morgan's request for some space, and didn't call or text her. By Wednesday night, he felt like he'd been wandering in the desert for weeks with no water. Morgan fed his soul, and he felt like he was drying up.

After he got the girls to bed, Brandon went to his room and spent a long time trying to compose a text, but couldn't find the right words. Finally, he typed *I miss you. Could I come by your office tomorrow after work for a few minutes?* He stared at it, and hit send.

He jumped up and busied himself getting his things ready for morning so he wouldn't go crazy. She might already be asleep. She could have turned her phone off. He conjured up every excuse he could think of for why she might not answer him.

When his phoned pinged with an incoming text, he leaped across the room to get it. He read the one-word response.

*Yes.*

*Yes!* That one solitary word gave him hope. He felt like he'd gotten his life back. Brandon fell back on his bed, his heart thundering. *Thank you, God!* He drew in great gulps of air. He lay there for a few moments and then got up and opened his top dresser drawer. He reached for the black velvet box, and opened it. The solitaire diamond winked at him, and he reached out and touched it. He was planning to propose to Morgan on their upcoming trip to New York, but desperate times called for desperate measures.

Brandon closed the box, walked into the closet, and put it into his jacket pocket. Then he went online to make another purchase. He wanted everything to be perfect for tomorrow night.

# 46

MORGAN LOOKED AT the e-mail one more time to make sure she wasn't dreaming. She was sure she'd read it a hundred times since it landed in her inbox a half hour ago.

She leaned back in her chair and covered her mouth with her hands so she wouldn't scream or giggle or laugh out loud. Morgan looked at the time. Brandon would be here any minute, and she couldn't wait to share her good news with him.

Morgan had missed him so much since Saturday night. She'd hardly eaten or slept. She knew now that she had completely over-reacted about Sheba, and couldn't imagine her life without him. Of course they were different. She and Patrick had been too much alike. Brandon was—well, he was her perfect complement. Morgan knew he adored her. *I love him so much, God. We'll make it work.*

She heard a noise at the door, and her heart burst with love when she saw him standing there, tall and handsome and holding a bouquet of calla lilies.

By the time he'd closed the door behind him, she was in his arms. "Bran!" Tears rolled down her cheeks.

"Morgan, I love you so much," he said, his voice cracking. And then his soft, warm lips were on hers.

"I love you, Brandon. I'm so sorry," she said over and over. She couldn't get enough of his kisses, and it seemed that he couldn't, either.

Finally, they had to come up for air. He touched his forehead to hers. "This is where it all began," he said. "Right here in your office. You, me, and these." He held up the bouquet.

Morgan thought that was the sweetest thing she had ever heard. She smiled at him. "Where did you find calla lilies in Chicago in January?"

He locked his arms around her. "I didn't. I had to order them online and have them delivered, overnight." He pulled her closer.

*This man is so amazing.* "Oh, Bran," she sighed. "You make me feel so special."

"You *are* special," he said. "And I have some other special things planned for tonight, starting with dinner at Autumn Evening—but not on the patio."

She smiled. "That sounds perfect. But I have some amazing news to share with you first!" She took his hand and led him to a chair, and before she could sit down in the one next to him, he pulled her onto his lap. Morgan giggled and looped her arms around his neck. She was so happy, she could hardly get the words out. "I got an unexpected e-mail this afternoon. Do you remember what NCAT is?"

He nodded. "The National Consortium for Art Therapy."

"Very good, doctor," she said with a grin. "You're looking at the NCAT Art Therapist of the Year!"

Brandon's eyes lit up. "Morgan, that's fantastic!"

"I can't believe it, Bran. People usually don't get that award until they've been in the field for a really long time. I went back and looked, and I'm by far the youngest recipient. I just can't believe it!"

Morgan wondered if he'd lost as much sleep over the past few days as she had. His gorgeous eyes looked as tired as Morgan's felt, but they sparkled at her now. "I am so, so proud of you, babe," he whispered.

She smoothed one hand over his lapel. "And that's not all." She took a breath. "I was also the recipient of NCAT's annual research grant. I made a proposal for something that I'd like to discuss with you."

"With me?"

She nodded. "I, um—well, I did an informal research study a few years ago about using art therapy with high school athletes who had been injured, and I submitted this proposal hoping to pilot it with professional athletes, and hopefully publish it." She searched his eyes, anxious for his reaction.

"Wow. I've—I've never thought of that," Brandon said. "You know, six months ago I would have thought that was crazy, but you, Dr. Anderson—" he gave her a quick peck on the lips. "You are so amazing, and so smart, and so beautiful, and right now, you could talk me into doing *anything* for you." He wiggled his eyebrows and swooped in for another kiss that was definitely not a quick peck.

Morgan laid her head on his shoulder. "No one has ever received the research grant *and* the award in the same year. I'm the first."

"I'm so proud of you," Brandon said, and kissed her temple.

She straightened up. "Will you be my date for the award ceremony?"

"You bet," he said, grinning at her. "Name the day and time, and I'll be there in my tux."

Morgan almost swooned, thinking of him in a tux. She ran her fingers through his hair. "It's always here in Chicago," she said, "so we don't have to travel. Sunday evening, February first."

A shadow crossed his features. "Morgan, tell me you didn't just say Sunday the first."

"Yes, that's what I said. It's on Sunday the first. Weekend after next."

Brandon closed his eyes. "Morgan, it can't be. That's Super Bowl Sunday."

"What?"

"Sweetheart, it's the *Super Bowl*. And the Bears are playing in the Super Bowl this year. I have to be there. I was going to invite you to come with me."

"I know about the Super Bowl," she said, fiddling with the knot of his tie. Since Morgan had been dating Brandon, she'd been proud of how she'd kept up with Chicago's pro sport teams. "Is the game at Soldier Field? You could go there for a while, and then meet me at the award ceremony. It's at the Chesterfield."

Brandon looked at her somberly. "Babe, the game is in San Diego." His eyes were filled with pain.

Morgan felt her world starting to crumble. *No!* "San Diego?" she croaked.

"Morgan, I'm so sorry."

"You can't get out of it?"

He shook his head. "Even if I could—Morgan, it's the *Super Bowl*."

She crossed her arms. "It's a game, Bran," she said hotly. "I'm getting two very prestigious awards that I've worked very hard for." He didn't say anything. "This is important to me."

He squeezed his eyes shut and opened them again. "And I'm so proud of you, Morgan, but I can't—I can't be there, babe. I'm so sorry." He tightened his hold on her.

Morgan pushed away from him, stood, and walked around to her desk. She couldn't remember when she'd ever been so angry. "A few minutes ago, I was amazing, and smart, and beautiful, and you would do *anything* for me." She stood behind her chair.

Brandon stood. "Morgan," he pleaded, "If it were any other night, I would be there. But I *cannot* get out of this." He rammed a hand through his hair. "I promise, I will make it up to you." He thought about the ring in his pocket and looked at her for a few silent seconds. "Can we just—are you—well, can we go to dinner now?"

Morgan wanted to scream. "I'm not going anywhere with you, Brandon," she said in a low voice. "You need to leave."

"Morgan—"

"Leave now." Her voice was stronger now. His mouth dropped open. "I mean it."

He walked to the door, paused, and looked at her with tortured eyes. "Morgan—I love you."

"You've made your choice. Goodbye, Brandon."

# 47

WHEN BRANDON PULLED his SUV into the garage, he couldn't even remember driving home from Morgan's office. He was in a complete stupor. Fortunately, the girls had a dance lesson tonight, so they and Sara wouldn't be home for at least another hour. He couldn't face anyone tonight.

Brandon shuffled into the kitchen and just stood there. He was haunted by the memories of Morgan being there with the girls the other night when he came in. All his hopes and dreams of making a life with her had turned to ashes. Brandon didn't know how he was going to fix this. *It's impossible. I can't be in two places at once.*

He got a drink of water and went upstairs, got out of his suit and threw it across a chair, and got into bed. *Not feeling well, going to bed early,* he texted his sister. *Hug and kiss the girls goodnight for me.*

He lay there for hours, numb, but unable to sleep. When his phone pinged with an incoming text, he was shocked to see that it was 10:30. He hadn't heard Sara and the girls come in.

It was Landon. *If my wife knew I was talking with the enemy, I'd be sleeping in the garage tonight. Are you ok?*

Brandon sat up and put his head in his hands. After a few moments, he texted back. *No.*

*I'm here if you need me, bro. Now or later.*

Brandon heaved a huge sigh. He sat there silently for several minutes. *Who schedules anything on Super Bowl Sunday?* he finally texted.

*I'm sorry,* Landon texted back.

*I can't talk about this now.*

*It's okay. Praying for you.*

*Thanks.*

Brandon got back under the covers and lay there staring at nothing in the darkness. The next thing he knew, his alarm was going off. He didn't think he'd been asleep for long. He moved like an automaton through his morning routine. When he walked into the kitchen, Sara and the girls were there.

"You feeling better?" Sara asked.

"No, but I have to go into work," he responded quietly.

April and Shelbie seemed to know that something was wrong. They got up and came to him, tugging on his pant legs. Brandon's heart gave a painful squeeze. His girls meant everything to him. They would always be there for him.

He gathered them up in his arms. Soon, they'd be too big for him to lift both of them up at once. He buried his face in their sweet, little-girl-scented hair.

"I love you, Daddy," April said, and gave him a peck on the cheek.

"Why you sad, Daddy?" Shelbie frowned at him.

He tickled them and they began to squeal and laugh. He set them down and kissed both their cheeks. "I'm not sad! Who could ever be sad around the two best girls in the whole world?"

They skipped back to resume their breakfast. Sara eyed Brandon warily. "Are you okay, Brandon?" she said softly.

"I'm fine. I have a boatload of work to do today. I'm headed to San Diego on Monday." He poured coffee into his travel mug and headed for the door. "See you tonight," he said, and walked out the door.

# 48

MORGAN UNLOCKED HER office door and wrinkled her nose. She'd had patients and field visits the end of last week, and hadn't been back to her office since the night Brandon left. Her eye went immediately to the trash can, where she could see the wilted calla lilies sticking out. She set her things down, grabbed the can, and marched down the hall with it until she found a larger trash receptacle, and dumped everything in.

When she got back to her office, she poured some oil in her diffuser and turned it on. Then she played the messages on her answering machine while she got things out of her bag and got organized.

The first two messages weren't important, but Morgan stopped when she heard the next one. "Morgan, it's Joyce Sheldon. I'm so sorry I've been out of touch since you left your message several weeks ago. My mother died and I've been in Ohio dealing with that and getting my dad settled in a new place." Morgan's heart went out to the woman. "Anyway, I'm back in Chicago now and trying to get caught up, but I should have some time to meet with you later this week if you're still interested in fostering. All the best to you in the new year. Bye."

Morgan sighed and sat down. With the holidays and all the

ups and downs with her and Bran, she hadn't thought at all about her hope to become a foster parent. Maybe this was her answer, if she and Bran were over. But right now she didn't have the emotional energy to think about something as important as taking on the responsibility for a child. She had to give herself time to heal first. Maybe she would call Joyce and see what she thought.

The next message began to play, and there was silence. Morgan looked up from what she was doing, and her heart slammed in her chest when Brandon's voice came on. "Morgan, I'm just getting on the plane for San Diego. I love you, babe, more than I ever thought I could love anyone. We'll talk when I get back—"

Just hearing his voice was torture. Morgan didn't want to hear another word. She punched her finger to stop the message replay, and hit *delete.* If only there were a delete button to erase him out of her head and her heart.

Of course he'd called her office phone. She hadn't taken any of his calls since the other night, nor answered any of his texts. It was over. Morgan couldn't take any more of the roller-coaster emotions of this romance, and Brandon had clearly shown where his priorities lay, it didn't matter how many times he told her he loved her, or how amazing his kisses were.

*Stop thinking about him.*

Her phone pinged with a text, and Morgan just stared at it, afraid to touch it. But she couldn't ignore it. She had students and patients who depended on her.

She took a deep breath and checked it. The text was from Kelsea. *How are you, Morgy? I'm worried about you.*

Morgan sighed and tucked a strand of hair behind her ear. *I'm swamped with work. I'm fine.* She tossed the phone back on her desk and sank into her chair. Tears filled her eyes. Morgan's future stretched before her, bleak and lonely. She would only be able to spend holidays with her sister and her family if none of Landon's family was around.

Of course she had called her sister right after Bran had left her office the other night, and poured the whole story out and cried and cried. Kelsea agreed that it was an impossible situation and that if Bran really loved Morgan, he wouldn't think twice about where to be. That he was even considering going to San Diego was bad enough in Kelsea's mind.

Morgan wondered how things were in the St. Louis St. Clair household.

She opened her computer and began sorting through her e-mails. She straightened her spine and took a deep breath. *You're Dr. Morgan Anderson, NCAT Art Therapist of the Year and recipient of the annual research grant. You are so blessed to have a fulfilling career and friends who respect and care for you, and a mom and a sister who love you.*

Her eye wandered to a hand-drawn picture in a frame on her desk, a Christmas gift from April. Four figures were holding hands. They were labeled, Daddy, Miss Morgy, April, and Shelbie. *My family,* the title read.

Morgan put her head in her hands and burst into tears.

# 49

BRANDON PULLED HIS hotel room door closed and walked down the hall. Another long night of tossing and turning had passed. He had big, dark circles under his eyes and knew he looked awful. Someone had made a comment about it yesterday and he'd made up a story about being under the weather.

He'd been in San Diego since last Monday, trying to lose himself in the revelry of the most celebrated week in sports. He ran himself ragged from sunup to sundown, missing nothing. Desperately trying to fill the gaping hole in his heart with noise and people.

It wasn't working.

And now it was Sunday morning. Game day. He rode the elevator down and headed for the breakfast buffet, even though the thought of food held no interest for him. Brandon saw a knot of people gathered around someone. The familiar sight of TV cameras and microphones told the story. Something was happening, and the media was there to get it on tape.

It was Kyle Jordanski, one of the Bears' back-up quarterbacks. Brandon had gotten to know him a little bit earlier in the week and thought he was a stand-up guy. They'd made plans to get together when they returned to Chicago. Brandon walked up to the edge of the crowd to listen.

"Well, like I said, they've gotten her stabilized, and the baby is safe for now, but I'm headed home to be with them," Kyle said.

"When did her labor start?" a reporter asked.

"Sandi called me last night around ten, and her dad came to stay with our daughter while Sandi's mom went to the hospital with her. They admitted her and are trying to stop the labor." He smiled. "They want my son to cook for another two weeks at least." A titter went around the group.

Another reporter pushed a microphone closer. "Kyle, how does it feel to be giving up a chance to play in the Super Bowl? Hasn't that been your dream since you were a boy? And the Bears have been waiting for this day for years."

"Was it a hard choice to make?" someone else called out.

"Well, of course I've been looking forward to it, too, but this is my wife, my son, my family. The choice was easy," he said. "I made the choice the day that I took vows for better or for worse. Even before that, really, when I chose to love Sandi. Other than my salvation, she's the most precious gift that God has given me, her and our children."

Jordanski flashed his trademark smile that the fans loved, and Brandon heard the cameras clicking all around him, recording the moment for history. "This is a game," Kyle continued. "My life is waiting for me back in Chicago." He waved. "I appreciate your prayers for Sandi and the baby. Thanks, guys."

The reporters shouted more questions, and Kyle moved away with his agent, Tom Kirby. Other Bears security personnel formed a phalanx around the two men and they began to walk away. Suddenly, Brandon had the strongest urge to talk to Kyle.

"Kyle!" He shouted. Jordanski turned and his eyes lit up with recognition. Brandon caught up to him.

"Hey, Brandon," Kyle said as the security detail took a step back. He extended his hand for a shake.

"I'm sorry to hear about your wife and baby. They're in my prayers."

"Thanks, I appreciate that. I really do want to get together when things settle down."

"Kyle, they're holding the plane for us," Tom Kirby said. "We need to go."

Jordanski nodded at Brandon. "Take care, doc."

"Thanks, Kyle. You, too." Brandon stood rooted to the spot, watching the cluster of men as they moved down the hallway, getting smaller and smaller until they turned the corner and disappeared.

Jordanski's words echoed in Brandon's head. *This is a game.* The same exact words that Morgan had used. *My life is waiting for me back in Chicago.*

Brandon's life flashed before his eyes. He hung his head. *And I'm 2,000 miles away.*

# 50

MORGAN SHOULD BE enjoying herself. She was surrounded by people she'd known for years, ever since she began college. The art therapy community was like family to her. She'd seen people tonight that she hadn't seen in a very long time, and it felt like they'd never been apart. Everyone was heaping love and praise on her. They respected her as a person and as an artist and art therapist, and it should have filled her with indescribable joy. This should have been one of the happiest nights of her life.

Instead, she felt dead, empty, and hopeless. If a million people had been here to celebrate this night with her, it wouldn't have mattered without the one person who mattered most to her in the world.

Morgan still couldn't think of him without her stomach going into painful spasms. She looked down at her plate. She'd eaten hardly anything even though the food at the Chesterfield was some of the best in all of Chicago.

She had invited her mother to the awards banquet, but Beth had come down with the flu yesterday. Morgan felt horribly guilty that her first response when her mother called was relief. Beth knew that her daughter and Brandon weren't seeing one another anymore, but they hadn't talked about it much, and Morgan didn't think she could take an evening of her mom's tender pity.

Her mother would also notice that Morgan's clothes were hanging on her. When she had put on her favorite go-to "little black dress" tonight, she'd had to put several pins in it.

"Morgan?" She felt a hand squeeze her shoulder. It was her colleague, Juanita Ross. "You're a million miles away."

"Sorry, Juanita." Morgan tried to dredge up a smile.

Juanita squeezed her hand. "Are you okay?"

"I'm fine."

"They want to begin in a few minutes. Do you want to visit the powder room first?"

Morgan stood and collected her purse. "Um, yeah, sure." When she returned to the meeting room, people were milling around visiting, and Juanita waved at her from the stage. Morgan joined her and Dr. Ed Faraday, the current president of NCAT. Ed indicated where Morgan should sit, and she took her seat next to Juanita. Two other NCAT board members were seated on the stage as well.

Dr. Faraday stepped to the podium and quieted the crowd. He gave the usual greeting, the acknowledgement of the fine meal provided by the catering staff at the Chesterfield, and then launched into his speech. Morgan pasted a smile on her face and nodded in all the right places. She rose when they presented her with the award and then the plaque for the research grant, and accepted congratulations from her colleagues on stage. She smiled for the photographer and stepped to the podium, and concentrated on forming cohesive sentences to express her deep appreciation to everyone there.

And then she sank back into her seat to thunderous applause, and wished that she could just go home and cry her heart out. Morgan knew that people expected her to stay around and socialize, but she knew a back exit, and planned to escape the minute this was over.

Morgan didn't think anything of it when a stagehand hurried to Dr. Faraday and pressed a note into his hand. He opened it and read it. "Folks, if you would take your seats, please" he said to the crowd, "someone else has asked to say a few words tonight in Dr. Anderson's honor."

Morgan couldn't imagine who it could be. And then, she looked past Dr. Faraday and she saw him.

*Bran.*

# 51

BRANDON TOOK A deep breath, straightened his lapels, and walked out onto the stage. He saw Morgan's look of utter shock, and hoped she wouldn't faint. He wanted more than anything to gather her into his arms and never let go, but he had to fix things first.

Brandon stepped to the podium. "Um, hi. I'm Dr.—" he swallowed, and it occurred to him that he didn't want to use his title here and be mistaken for the wrong kind of doctor. *How ironic.* "I'm Brandon," he corrected himself. "Brandon St. Clair." He scanned the crowd. About a third of the attendees were men. "I'm just curious—could I ask—has anyone heard the score of the game?" His phone had died in the cab on the way in from the airport.

Nervous male laughter rippled through the room. "Ten-seven, Bears at the half," a man called out.

"JoJo caught a pass with eight seconds left and ran it in for the TD," another man shouted. There were a few claps and whistles. Brandon smiled to himself. JoJo Collins' knee had healed beautifully.

Brandon nodded. "Are any of you men here instead of at a Super Bowl Party, to be with the woman you love?"

He saw nods and smiles, heard some more claps and whistles.

"Well, that's why I'm here, too," Brandon said. He turned around and looked at Morgan, his beautiful Morgan. He turned back to the audience. "I—well, I've been in San Diego this week. Because of my work, I've had the privilege of traveling with the Bears and experiencing Super Bowl week out there."

Brandon could tell that he had the audience's rapt attention, especially that of the men. He rubbed his chin. "So, I had a reserved seat in one of the boxes at the stadium, but I was miserable. I'm in love with Dr. Morgan Anderson, and I knew I needed to be here, so I left San Diego and flew home in time to see her receive these fantastic awards."

After Kyle Jordanski left, Brandon had run after him and begged him to hold the plane while he dashed upstairs to his room and packed his things.

He turned and looked at Morgan, who was fighting tears. "I am so proud of you, babe."

Brandon felt his face heat up as the room exploded with applause and whistles. As it faded away, a booming male voice called out, "Man, you must *really* love her!" The crowd laughed.

Brandon nodded. "Yes, I do," he said confidently. "I love her more than anything in this entire world." He turned and looked at Morgan again, and tears were streaming down her cheeks. He held out his hand and she rose gracefully and came to him.

He stepped away from the podium and took both her hands. "I resigned my position," he said softly. He'd taken care of that with one phone call from the plane to the Center's board chairman.

Her teary eyes went wide. "You resigned your position?"

"Is there an echo in here?" Brandon resisted the urge to laugh but instead, squeezed her hands, and she squeezed back. "Yes, and it was the right decision." He smiled at her sheepishly. "You're now dating an unemployed doctor." He swallowed. "If you'll have me back."

"Hey!" the man with the booming voice called out. "Somebody turn the overhead mikes on. We want to hear this!"

The crowd burst into laughter and applause, and Brandon grinned at Morgan and let out a breath.

"Anything you want to say to me, you say to them." She dipped her chin at the audience. "These are my friends."

"Fair enough," Brandon said with a nod. It didn't matter to him. If there were a million people in the room, it wouldn't matter. He had eyes only for Morgan.

Brandon waited for the audience to quiet down. He knew he had one chance to get this right. He gazed into her beautiful emerald eyes. "You know mine and my brother's mantra is *go big or go home,*" he said boldly. He heard his voice coming across the PA system, and it gave him strength. "That's what my life came down to today. I could either *go big*—keep the high-powered job, hang out with professional athletes, fly all over the country and go to the World Series and the Super Bowl." He paused. "Or I could *go home.* I couldn't have it both ways."

"I came home, Morgan. Home to you."

Brandon stepped a little closer to her. "When I lost—my wife, for days and weeks and months, it felt like my heart wasn't even beating." He took her lovely, graceful hand, the one that created such inspired, beautiful works of art, and placed it over his thundering heart. "Do you feel that, Morgan? That's because of you."

He heard a collective gasp and a swell of murmurs from the crowd as April and Shelbie walked out on stage, holding hands and wearing their red and white Christmas dresses. They looked like two little fair-haired angels. From the wings, Sara gave Brandon a teary smile and a thumbs-up. He'd called her from the plane, and she'd followed his instructions to the letter. A wave of love washed over Brandon for his sister.

Morgan was crying now, and covered her mouth with both hands.

Brandon rubbed her arms. "I brought reinforcements," he said with a smile. The audience laughed.

He felt a tug on his sleeve. "You hafta get down on your knees, Daddy!" Shelbie ordered.

The crowd roared, and Brandon grinned. "I was just getting to that part." He pulled the black velvet box out of his pocket, opened it, and dropped to one knee. "Dr. Morgan Ashley Anderson, I will always come home to you. You keep my heart beating, you complete our family circle. I love you so much, Morgan, and I will love you forever." He looked at the girls, and hoped Sara had coached them well.

"Will you please be our mommy?" April and Shelbie said in unison.

"And will you be my wife?"

# 52

MORGAN KNEW SHE would never answer two more important questions in her life. Her heart blossomed with love for this family that God had brought to her. But which question to answer first?

She knew what God expected. Her heart would always belong to her husband above all else.

Morgan could hardly speak for the emotion that clogged her throat, so she nodded vigorously. "Yes, Bran, yes," was all she managed to choke out. She saw him slip a ring on her finger, but she didn't even look at it. She reached for him and his strong arms came around her.

Morgan felt a sense of peace wash over her, and never wanted to let him go. But then she felt tapping on her hip, and looked down. There was Shelbie, smiling up at her, and sweet April. She bent down and gathered them in her arms. *My girls.* They were everything she had prayed for. Morgan would never need another child—biological or adopted—to be fulfilled as a mother.

"Of course I'll be your mommy, April and Shelbie. I love you so much."

She picked up Shelbie, and Bran picked up April, and they formed a little circle. Bran leaned over and touched his lips to hers. *All my dreams are coming true.*

Morgan could hardly believe it when the audience cheered.

She'd forgotten they were even there. As she looked out over her friends and colleagues, they rose to their feet.

Bran took her hand, and they faced the crowd. The girls were smiling and waving at all the people. After a couple of moments, the noise died down.

"Daddy, and Miss Mommy," Shelbie said in loud, clear voice that echoed through the loud speakers, "are we going to get a baby brother now?"

# EPILOGUE

*THREE MONTHS LATER, MOTHER'S DAY*

BRANDON MADE ONE last check in the mirror and walked over to the large window overlooking the backyard. In less than hour, he would marry Morgan at the five-acre country property that they had bought together, surrounded by their families and a few close friends. He and the girls had moved in, after selling their too-large and too-pretentious suburban home. The movers brought Morgan's things two days ago, and she was looking forward to setting up housekeeping.

It was the perfect place for them—a rambling, custom-made cedar and stone home overlooking a beautiful pond. Best of all, it was secluded but only ten minutes away from shopping and restaurants, and close to the depot where they could catch the train into Chicago. Brandon was beginning to appreciate the serenity of country life. It would be a great place for their daughters to grow up. As long as Morgan was by his side, he would be happy anywhere.

They were finding ways to compromise. Cross-country skiing was one of them. And last weekend, they'd gone boating on Lake Michigan with some friends and really enjoyed that.

Brandon wanted to start saving for a speedboat. Morgan dreamed of a pontoon boat.

After resigning as Medical Director at the center, Brandon wasn't unemployed for long. They hired him back to build and oversee something that was part of his long-range plan, a sports medicine and orthopedic center for high school and college athletes. He got to name his terms: days only with the occasional emergency surgery and very little travel. The most important thing to Brandon was being available to his wife and family.

He was so proud of Morgan, and knew that she could do anything she set her mind to. He listened patiently as she agonized over how she would juggle her career with her important new roles as wife and mother. After a lot of discussion with him, and prayer, Morgan decided to resign from her art therapy practice, at least until April and Shelbie were in school. The other two therapists in the group were very understanding and gave her an open invitation to come back anytime in the future. Then she had a heartfelt talk with Juanita Ross and they worked out a perfect teaching schedule where Morgan would only have to go into campus two days a week.

There was a fabulous glass-enclosed four-season room on the south side of their home with its own entrance, and she planned to turn that into a studio and do art lessons there, and continue her research. Morgan wanted to get used to being a mom, and then they would pray about becoming foster parents or adopting to grow their family, and let God lead. Both Brandon and Morgan were passionately committed to the idea.

He looked around the master bedroom at the brand-new furniture he and his bride had chosen together, and Morgan's beautiful artwork and other handcrafted accessories that graced the room. Tonight, it would become their oasis. His parents and Grandma Beth were taking the girls with Landon and Kelsea and their family to a nearby hotel with a water park for two nights, and then he and Morgan would pick up April and Shelbie on Wednesday and drive to Indianapolis for a three-day family vacation. The big draw there was the famed children's museum. Then they planned to drive north to Wisconsin where the girls would stay with Brandon's parents, and he and Morgan would enjoy a few more days alone before coming back home to begin their new life as a family.

Brandon's heart was full to overflowing. He closed his eyes and whispered, "You would like her, Dar. She'll be a wonderful mother to your girls." He was amazed at how Morgan thought of little ways to keep Darla's memory alive. She was confident in Brandon's love now, and her tender nurturing had helped April blossom into her sweet, content former self. Brandon couldn't believe it when he recently overheard April talking to one of her little friends. "I had a first mommy who I'll see again in heaven someday, and now I have a second mommy, and I love her very, very much."

Brandon breathed a prayer to God, full of gratitude and thankfulness.

The door opened behind him, and his brother walked in, holding his cell phone. He was dressed in a black tux identical to Brandon's, and his face was serious.

Landon closed the door. "Bro, you need to sit down," he said. "We need to talk."


Morgan thought her heart was going to burst with joy. *Today is my first Mother's Day, and my wedding day.* April and Shelbie had woken her up this morning, dropping the "Miss" and calling her *Mommy* for the very first time. They covered her with hugs and kisses and gave her homemade cards. She loved them so much.

Brandon had stood in the doorway with a cup of coffee, smiling and watching her with the girls. As Morgan stared at him, she knew exactly what he was thinking. Tomorrow and all the mornings thereafter for the rest of their lives, she would wake up next to him.

Now, she and her sister were waiting for the ceremony to begin. She stared at the glittering diamond on her left hand. In just a few moments, a beautiful wedding band would rest next to it. "You look stunning, Morgy," Kelsea said. "Your dress is simply amazing."

Morgan loved her wedding dress. It was classic, a simple but elegant creation of satin, lace, and pearls with a vintage flair. When she first saw it—even before she tried it on—she knew she would wear this dress when she married Brandon.

Kelsea dabbed at her eyes. "I hope this waterproof mascara is the real deal, because I know I'm going to cry buckets and I'll look like a raccoon."

"Me, too," Morgan said with a smile. "At least you have an excuse." Kelsea was almost three months pregnant with another set of twins, and could cry at the drop of a hat. Morgan sighed. "But I'm so happy, I know I'll cry nonstop."

There was a knock at the door, and Landon called out. "Can I come in?"

"Yes," Kelsea called back.

He stepped in and stopped. "Hi. Ah, Morgan—I know you didn't want Brandon to see you before the wedding, but we need to come in. It's important."

Morgan's stomach gave a lurch. "Is something wrong?"

To her immense relief, Landon smiled. "No, something is very, very right." He held out his hand to Kelsea. "Come out here with me, sweetheart, and we'll give them a moment." Kelsea and Landon left, and Brandon walked in.

*My TDH for life,* she thought as her heart fluttered. She never got tired of seeing Bran in a tux. Today, he looked especially rugged and handsome. He closed the door and turned to look at her. His gaze swept from the tips of her toes to the top of her head, where her mother had fashioned an elegant French twist, topped off by flower-covered comb and a flowing veil.

He took a step forward. "Oh, babe," he said, and she could see that his eyes were moist. "You are so, so gorgeous."

In the next moment, she was in his arms, and she whispered between kisses, "so are you. I love you so much, Bran."

"I love you, Morgan." He held her close for another moment, then stepped back. Without breaking eye contact with her, he called out, "you can come in now."

Landon and Kelsea came back into the room, and the four of them stood in a little circle. Landon let out a breath. "Okay. Here's what's happening. A little while ago, I got a phone call from a guy that I went to law school with. We've kept in touch, but I haven't talked with him in a couple of years. He specializes in private adoptions. A fifteen-year-old girl gave birth yesterday, and changed her mind about keeping the baby. Her parents support that decision. She's signed away her rights, and so has the baby's father. It will be a closed adoption.

"Ben—my friend—said that he hadn't thought about me in a long time, but suddenly this morning, after all this happened, he felt a strong urge to call me." Landon looked at Brandon and Morgan. "The baby is full-term and healthy. He's yours if you want him."

"Him?" Morgan croaked. She felt her legs start to buckle, and Brandon's arm came around her waist to steady her.

Landon nodded. "You can pick him up on Wednesday—" Morgan was stunned to see her brother-in-law's eyes well up as he struggled for composure. "In Indianapolis."

Morgan gasped, and her hands flew to her mouth. The room went still, and she heard her heart pounding in her ears. She looked up at Brandon, and tears ran down his cheeks. "Oh, Bran!" she cried, and threw her arms around him. He buried his face in her neck and they both cried.

"This is—the answer—to the girls' prayers," she stammered. She touched his damp cheeks. "We're doing this, right?"

He looked at her somberly. "Only if you're okay with it, if you're ready for it."

There was no doubt in Morgan's mind. *God has given me more than I could ask or think.* "Oh my goodness, yes!" she exclaimed, and Brandon put his arms around her and kissed her.

She accepted a handful of tissues from Kelsea, who was crying tears of joy. Morgan looked at Landon. "Doesn't it cost a lot for a private adoption?"

She saw the two brothers exchange a look. "It's taken care of, Morgan," he said quietly, and his eyes shone. "Happy wedding."

"I can't believe this. I can't believe it, thank you, Landon," she said, and gave him a heartfelt hug. Then she fell into her sister's arms. "I'm having a baby on Wednesday!" she squealed.

"Oh, Morgy! Look at how God has answered all of your prayers!" Kelsea wept. The sisters clung to one another, rocking back and forth.

Landon smiled. "If you two can stop crying, I think we need to get this wedding underway. Everyone is here, if you're ready."

Morgan blotted her eyes and looked between the two men. "Did Reagan make it?" They had mailed their older sister an invitation, but didn't receive a response. Phone calls and texts had gone unanswered.

Landon and Brandon exchanged a glance, and Brandon shook his head. "I didn't really expect her to come, but I was hoping she would."

Landon reached for the doorknob.

"Oh, hold on!" Kelsea waved her hands and looked at Brandon and then to Morgan. "I have a card for you from Rose and Ike. Rosie asked me to give it to you just before the ceremony." She rifled through her bag and drew out an envelope, and handed it to Morgan.

Brandon came over to her and they opened it and held the card together. "You read it," she said. Morgan didn't think her voice would hold up.

Brandon's voice was clear and strong. *"Congratulations on your marriage, Morgan and Brandon! I knew last Mother's Day weekend that you were meant to be together. Isn't the Lord wonderful? He has answered your prayers beyond all that you could ask or think! We hope you will never doubt His faithfulness ever again. Give your beautiful daughters a hug from us, and tell them to—"* Brandon's eyes grew wide, and his voice wavered. *"Tell them to take good care of their little brother! Come to St. Jardin on us sometime! We are turning our honeymoon resort into a family resort! Much love, Rosie and Ike."*

Morgan's mouth fell open, as did the others, and all four of them stared at one another for a long moment.

Brandon turned the envelope over. "It's—it's postmarked a week ago," he said in disbelief.

Morgan couldn't believe it. "How—how did she—?" A chill raced down her spine. She and Bran stared at one another.

He held up his hand. "There's more. *"P.S. Did you ever meet the lawyer who contacted you about coming to Chicago, Brandon? That's Ike's oldest nephew, David. He's such a nice young man."*

Brandon's jaw dropped. "David Goldman—he's the one who first called me about the job." He shook his head and looked at Morgan, then to his brother and Kelsea. "Do you mean to tell me that little lady with the pink Converse and pink hair—?" his words dropped off.

Kelsea laughed uproariously. "That Rosie! I do believe she's God's angel, doing His work on this earth!" She and Landon wrapped their arms around one another, and Morgan felt Brandon's arms come around her.

He kissed her forehead and whispered in her ear. "Are you ready to marry me, Miss Morgy? I mean, Dr. Anderson?" His amber eyes danced. "Mrs. St. Clair? Dr. Mrs. St. Clair? Dr. Anderson-St. Clair?" She'd told Bran that she wanted to take his name, but he'd left the decision completely up to her about what to be called professionally, and she was still thinking about it.

Morgan couldn't wait to be his wife and the mother of his daughters and his son. She pulled him close and whispered in his ear. "You can just call me babe."

ERIN
STEVENSON

St. Clair
Family
No. 3

Bait
and
Switch

# PROLOGUE

**DANE**

DANE CORSICA PUT the car in park, turned the engine off, and stuck the key in the pocket of his leather jacket. Then he tipped his head back, closed his eyes, and got into character.

Thirty seconds later, he exited the vehicle and strode confidently into the waterfront seafood restaurant. He knew exactly where he was going, and passed the check-in station where about a dozen people were waiting to be seated. No one gave him a second look. Dane walked through the restaurant to a door in the back that led to a private dining room.

He slipped through it and took in the scene. Ten people, all of whom he expected. Except for one.

*Oh no, what is she doing here?* Dane's eyes bored into hers, and she stared back, never blinking.

"All right, now that pretty boy is here, we can get started," grumbled the man at the head of the table.

*I'll deal with you later,* Dane telegraphed to the woman.

*Bring it, Corsica,* she telegraphed back.

1

**REAGAN**

REAGAN ST. CLAIR slipped into a chair on the back row and adjusted her designer sunglasses on the bridge of her nose. Good. No one noticed her late arrival.

She smoothed the full skirt of her flowered halter sundress over her knees. The dress, high wedge sandals, and the luxurious blond curls flowing from under her oversized couture summer hat were so far from her usual look that surely, no one would recognize her.

Reagan's right leg began to tremble. She clasped her hands tightly together and pressed them against her knee, willing the shaking to stop.

*I hate weddings.*

The image of Paul in bed with her best friend still had the power to sear Reagan's memory, even ten years later. His and Reagan's wedding was just a month away, and everything had to be canceled, despite his pleading and begging for exoneration.

Reagan could forgive, but not for infidelity.

Her gaze drifted over the small bridal party gathered in front of a rose-covered arch and rested on her brother Landon, standing as best man for their younger brother, Brandon. The St. Clair men cut fine figures in their tuxedos. Standing at six foot four, they could pass for twins even though they were almost a year apart in age. Their features were nearly identical, the only difference being that Landon was blond and Brandon's hair was dark brown.

There looked to be less than a hundred people gathered for the small, intimate Sunday afternoon wedding. From the back, Reagan recognized a few older relatives that she hadn't seen in years. She supposed the others in attendance were from the bride's family, or some of her and Brandon's colleagues.

"Join hands, please," the minister said. Brandon turned to face his bride, Morgan, and the look of pure love and joy on her brother's face nearly broke through Reagan's façade. If anyone deserved happiness, it was Brandon. His first wife of over a decade, Darla, had been tragically killed in an automobile accident two years ago. Reagan hadn't met Brandon's bride yet, and hoped she didn't have to today.

Two little blond girls in pink and lavender flowered dresses stood with them. They had to be Brandon's daughters, April and Shelbie. Reagan had seen them only once, at their mother's funeral. She recalled the maelstrom of emotions she felt when meeting them for the first time: incredible sadness for their loss, an unexpected overwhelming connection with them upon the realization that they were her flesh and blood, and a complete lack of knowledge of how to interact with such small children.

The early afternoon sun beat down on the garden wedding, and Reagan was happy for her ridiculous hat. She craned her neck to get a better view. Morgan was similar in coloring to Darla, but tall and slender. Morgan and Brandon had met exactly a year ago on Mother's Day at a family event, yet another one Reagan had missed.

She would have missed this family event, too, if she didn't need a place to hide. After this current mess with her job was over, Reagan was going to do some serious soul searching and figure out how to reconnect with her family.

Her leg began to tremble again, and before she could reach for it, a man slipped into the seat next to her. He wrapped his hand around hers and squeezed.

*Dane.* Her unlikely comrade-in-arms, given their respective careers. Always there for her. Reagan let out a breath and squeezed back.

"Breathe, Reagan," he whispered in her ear. "We'll get through this."

## 2

**DANE**

DANE CORSICA SLIPPED a casual arm around Reagan's bare, tanned shoulder and took the opportunity to glance behind them. He did a sweep one way and then the other. An outdoor wedding was a logistical nightmare from a security vantage point. Too many ways in and out. But Dane was convinced they hadn't been followed.

He smiled to himself as one of Reagan's blond curls brushed against his fingers. Who knew she could be so gorgeous? Dane had known her for four years and had never seen her in a dress, or any makeup save a dash of lip gloss. The absence of Reagan St. Clair's signature long, dark brunette braid was the most dramatic change of all.

It was a good disguise, one that might save her life.

Dane resisted the urge to yawn. They'd been on the run for almost seventy-two hours, and needed to get completely underground. Dane didn't know who he could trust.

But Reagan did.

When she'd pitched her idea for them to come to the Chicago area for this family wedding, Dane was completely against it. Despite that Reagan was distant from her family, she insisted that she still wanted to be part of this day and see her brother get married. And since they had to get out of Florida and go *somewhere*, why not go to Illinois?

He'd finally relented, and told her it would work for the short term. But then, he would have to find a better solution, a deep, off-grid place to keep both of them safe while he unraveled this mess. The problem was, he couldn't go to any of his usual sources. Reagan insisted that her brother, Landon, could find something for them.

Dane had never seen Reagan so certain, so resolute, and he was out of options. So here they were, mere feet away from someone Dane had never met, but whom he would have to trust to keep both himself and Reagan alive and safe.

It went against everything the DEA had taught Dane, but he trusted Reagan, and Reagan trusted her brother. That would have to be good enough for now.

"I now pronounce you man and wife," the minister announced. He smiled at the groom. "Brandon, you may kiss your bride." Dane came out of agent mode just long enough to witness the bridal couple's loving embrace. He looked away.

"Ladies and gentlemen, I'm proud to introduce, for the first time, Dr. Brandon and Dr. Morgan St. Clair!" *That's right, Reagan said he's an MD and she has a PhD.* The audience broke into applause.

Dane tightened his arm around Reagan. "You ready?" He felt her nod. "It's up to you now."

## 3

**REAGAN**

REAGAN KNEW SHE would have just a split second to catch Landon's attention. *Please, God, let him remember.* Then she winced inwardly. It was highly unlikely that the Almighty would listen to her. They hadn't been on good terms in years.

Reagan had placed herself on the aisle so that she would have the best chance of making eye contact with her brother. She watched her nieces skip by, hand-in-hand. Then came their father and new mother, their faces bursting with joy. Brandon didn't even look her way. If Reagan had been holding up a flashing neon sign announcing her presence, she doubted he would have noticed.

*Here we go.* Next came Landon with the matron of honor, his dark-haired wife, Kelsea, who was also Morgan's sister. That's how Brandon and Morgan had met. Reagan lifted a hand to touch the brim of her hat, and the movement caught her brother's eye.

The instant his eyes connected with hers, Reagan moved her hand an inch and tugged on her right earlobe.

*Score.* Landon's amber eyes widened for a split second, but he didn't break stride, and he and Kelsea were gone.

Reagan casually turned to Dane. "He saw me," she murmured.

"Good job," he whispered. He looked around. "Let's get out

of here before any of the other guests start coming by." That was fine with Reagan. She didn't want to chance seeing her parents or her sister. Not until this case was closed and she was safe again.

They rose, and Dane took her hand, pulling her behind a row of tall bushes. "There's an unlocked shed about fifty yards to the south," he said. "Down a slight slope and around behind some trees. You're sure your brother will know to follow us there?"

Reagan nodded. "Positive. He'll be watching me. Our old signal meant *trouble, meet me right away.*" It was from long ago when she and her brothers had fancied themselves amateur detectives in their Wisconsin hometown, but Dane didn't need to know that.

"Well, if anyone else notices us slipping away, they'll just think I want to be alone with the most beautiful woman here." Dane winked at her.

"In your dreams, Corsica," Reagan smirked. In all the years that she and Dane had worked together, he'd never crossed the line, probably because Reagan had never given him any encouragement. He was handsome, to be sure, and the best agent—DEA, FBI, or otherwise—that Reagan had ever worked with. But he was also nine years younger than her (he thought it was only seven since Reagan had fudged about her age), and that was too much. It just didn't feel right to her. Sometimes when she made a pop culture reference from her era, Dane would look at her blankly.

Despite that, he was incredibly mature for his age, and one of the best friends Reagan had ever had. But sometimes, when you tried to make it something more, the friendship didn't survive. And Reagan needed all the friends she could get.

The reception was set up on the deck behind Brandon and Morgan's cedar home on a rolling country property west of Chicago. It was a beautiful setting. From their vantage point behind the bushes, Reagan watched the crowd making its way up to the deck. She thought she recognized a couple of her cousins. Then her heart gave a lurch as she saw her parents, each holding the hand of a small girl and boy. Those must be Landon and Kelsea's twins. She swallowed. *More next-generation St. Clairs.* She felt a familiar twinge of regret that she would probably never give her parents grandchildren. Then followed the ever-present justification that given her time-consuming career and discomfort around children, it was probably for the best.

"Dear heaven, who is *that?*" Dane hissed into her ear. Reagan followed his eye to a petite young woman in a flowered sundress, with thick, honey-blond hair that cascaded halfway down her back. She had sparkling brown eyes, dimples, and a thousand-watt smile. As she greeted someone, her melodious laugh floated to them on the breeze.

"That's my sister, Sara." Sara looked even more grown-up than she had just a few months ago at Christmas.

"She's a little taller than you, but other than that, she could be your twin," Dane murmured. His eyes were riveted on Sara. "Your *much* younger twin," he added.

Reagan bumped her shoulder against his arm. "Gee, thanks," she drawled. But he was right. It hadn't occurred to her, but she and Sara looked very much alike except for their hair color. Now that Reagan was disguised as a blonde, the resemblance was a bit eerie. "She's, um, fifteen years younger than me."

Dane frowned at her. "Really?" *Oops. He's probably trying to do the math.*

Reagan nodded. "She was mom and dad's surprise. The boys were twelve and thirteen when Sara was born. They've always called her *Peanut.*"

Dane and Reagan began to stroll toward a line of trees, and the ground got a little more uneven. Dane put his hand around Reagan's waist to steady her. "I don't want you to fall off those shoes," he said drily.

Reagan resisted the urge to laugh. "Thanks. These sure aren't my Birkenstocks," she retorted. She picked her way gingerly around a tree root.

She saw the wooden shed in the distance, and in another twenty seconds or so, they reached it. Dane pulled the door open and ushered her in, then pulled the door almost closed, leaving a sliver of an opening.

Reagan's eyes adjusted to the dark, and she took off her sunglasses and her hat, and set them on a short stack of wooden crates. Dust motes danced in the sunlight streaming in from a west-facing window. The shed contained a riding lawn mower, wheelbarrow, and the usual yard implements. "This isn't so bad."

"Well, I should be able to scope out a good hiding place," Dane said with a smile. He didn't say anything, and seemed to be perusing her. "I don't think I've ever seen you in a dress."

Reagan let out a breath and fingered her skirt. "Yeah, it's been a while." She thought for a moment. "Maybe the South Florida Press Awards banquet, three years ago?"

"Yeah, I wasn't there," Dane said with a laugh. "You look completely different without your braid."

"Don't I know it?" Reagan said. Without it, she felt like she was missing a friend.

There was a soft tap at the door, and Dane sprang in front of her, his hand moving quickly inside his jacket. He turned his head and put a finger to his lips.

"Reagan?" came the whisper through the crack in the door. Dane nodded.

"Yes, come in," she said softly. Dane took a step to the side. The door opened, and Landon entered. He reached for Reagan, and she saw Dane pull the door closed behind him.

"Oh my gosh, Reagan." Landon's arms came around her, strong and secure. Reagan felt rare tears coming to her eyes. "What are you doing here? You haven't been answering any of our texts or calls, so I figured you were chasing a story." He pulled back and looked at her. "What's with the hair?" He fingered a curl and smiled. "You look like Peanut."

"I know," Reagan replied. She couldn't go soft now. Dane materialized at her side, and Reagan cleared her throat. "Landon, this is Dane Corsica." The two men shook hands. "Dane's DEA."

Landon didn't blink. He looked at Dane. "You armed?"

Dane pulled one side of his jacket back to reveal his holster.

Landon nodded, and looked back to Reagan. "What's going on?"

Reagan exchanged a glance with Dane. She pulled a dollar bill out of her purse and held it out to her brother. "I want to hire you as my attorney."

Landon tilted his head at her. He pocketed the bill and looked between her and Dane, his features serious. "Okay, anything you tell me is now protected by attorney-client privilege."

Reagan let out a breath. "Well, the short story is that I work with the DEA sometimes on news stories, and Dane and I trade favors." Landon's eyes darkened a shade.

"Not those kind of favors," Dane muttered. Reagan's face burned.

"Reporters and agents have mutually beneficial relationships," she explained.

Landon rolled his eyes. "Yeah, that sounds a lot better, sis. Go on," he prodded.

Reagan was aware of Dane standing next to her. Why was she flustered? "So anyway, Dane has been working a case undercover, and I got an anonymous tip and went in undercover to investigate on my own, and we ended up at a meeting together, in Miami. It's a drug case connected to Cuba."

Landon frowned. "Sounds like just another day in South Florida." Dane smirked.

"Right," Reagan said. "So anyway, Dane and I ended up at this meeting, and neither of us knew the other one was going to be there. We left separately, and arranged to meet up at one of our normal drop spots where we leave information for each other. But one of us was followed, and we were shot at."

"What?" Landon asked sharply. "Were you hit?"

Dane shook his head. "We managed to get away, but we don't know which one of us was followed, or by whom. Reagan—"

Landon put his hand up. "Hold it." He turned his palm up.

"Oh, got it," Dane said, and produced a dollar bill. Landon slid it in his pocket. "Go on."

Dane nodded. "We've shared our information, but it doesn't sync up, and we need more time to figure it out. This story has the potential to be really big. I snuck home and got a few things that I needed to go underground, and planned to finish making the arrangements the next day. But Friday morning, it was all over the news in Miami that the two of us were being sought for questioning about this drug case. I think somebody turned on us."

Reagan picked up the thread. "We needed to get out of Florida, and I really wanted to come to Brandon's wedding, so I convinced Dane to come here."

Dane put his hands on his hips. "I have a private network that I use in situations like this, to find safe houses or get cash or weapons to me, but obviously I can't trust anyone." He paused. "I'm not willing to chance it. So we're completely on our own."

Landon palmed the back of his neck and looked at his sister. He let out a breath. "You always had to be Nancy Drew," he muttered. A smile tugged at the corner of his lips.

Reagan rolled her eyes and tried not to laugh. "He and Brandon were the Hardy Boys," she said to Dane, "but they grew up to be a lawyer and a doctor instead."

Landon looked at his sister with pride. "And you grew up to be the best investigative reporter to ever work for the *Miami Herald*."

Reagan frowned. "Well, I'm an Assistant Editor now, but you know reporting is in my blood. Anyway, I was trying to wrap this up so I could come to Chicago, but I wasn't sure I could, so that's why I wasn't answering any of your texts or calls. When Dane and I realized we needed to get out of Florida, I insisted that we come here. To *you*," she added.

"Landon, can you find somewhere we can hide?"

# 4

## DANE

DANE SAT DOWN next to Reagan on the bed. They were in a spare bedroom in the basement of Brandon and Morgan's home. Landon had snuck them a plate of food, two pieces of wedding cake, and some punch.

"Is it spiked?" Reagan asked hopefully. Landon shook his head.

He was gone now, and Dane and Reagan were alone. She removed her hat and shoes, and sat on the bed rubbing her feet.

"How do women stand these?" she groaned. "Shoe designers must be in cahoots with podiatrists and chiropractors."

Dane pushed her hands aside. "You're about to be treated to the Dane Corsica magic fingers foot massage," he announced, wiggling his fingers.

Reagan yawned. "If I wasn't so tired, I'd argue with you." She lay down on her back and smoothed out her skirt. "All right, Corsica. Work your magic."

Dane stood and removed his suit jacket, unbuttoned his sleeves and pushed them up, then resumed his spot next to her and started rubbing. He didn't know a thing about how to give a foot massage, but he wasn't about to let her know that.

"I like Landon," he said. "I can see now why you wanted to

come to him for help. The attorney-client privilege thing was a good idea." Dane could tell that Landon was still a little wary of him, but that was a good sign, too. After they'd told Landon everything, he said he needed to get back to the reception, and also needed a few moments to think about next steps.

So Dane and Reagan stayed in the shed and fifteen minutes later, Landon returned and gave them instructions to go through an unlocked walkout basement door and then to the bedroom and wait for him there.

Dane rubbed Reagan's feet for a little while longer and they chatted.

"Should I start calling you *Nancy?*" He couldn't resist teasing her.

"We were such dorks," she said with a laugh. "The three of us were convinced we were helping to keep the streets safe for the citizens of Baraboo, Wisconsin."

Dane laughed. "Baraboo? You're making that up."

"It's real. Check the map."

"Is it anywhere near Green Bay?"

"Nope. It's closer to the Dells." She smiled. "That's one redeeming quality about you, Corsica." He and Reagan shared a deep devotion to the Packers.

They fell silent for several minutes. "Do you think he'll be able to find us a place to hide?" Dane asked. He was already trying to figure out his next move if Landon St. Clair didn't come through.

Reagan didn't reply. She had dozed off. *Maybe I have the magic touch after all.*

It was going to be interesting, going completely off-grid with Reagan. Dane took the opportunity to stare at her heart-shaped face. She really was lovely with makeup and wearing a blond wig and a dress. This Reagan was very different from the real Reagan. That Reagan wore jeans or cargo shorts year-round, plain t-shirts, flip-flops or Birkenstocks, little to no makeup, and of course, her dark brunette braid.

The real Reagan St. Clair moved comfortably in the still-male-dominated world of newspapers, was amazingly tech-savvy, and one of the smartest women Dane had ever met. She was small and spare, but Dane had seen her go toe-to-toe with men twice her size, and reduce them to rubble.

She could also drink most of them under the table, and he'd seen her use that to her advantage.

Dane looked at his watch and yawned.

A knock sounded at the door. Reagan sat up and Dane's hand automatically went to the grip of his weapon. "It's me," Landon's voice came. He poked his head in. "I have Kelsea, Brandon, and Morgan with me," he said.

Dane and Reagan looked at one another for a couple of seconds.

"That's the deal," Landon said. "You can trust them. Everyone else has left."

"Mom and Dad and Sara?" Reagan asked. "And all the children?"

"Yes," Landon said.

Dane nodded, and Reagan followed his lead. She started to run a hand through her hair as though to tidy it, then realized the futility of it and stopped. "Okay," she said.

"But we meet here. We stay in this room," Dane said. Even though they were surrounded by people that Reagan trusted, Dane was still vigilant. He had reconnoitered the basement, and knew two ways to get out.

Landon opened the door, and in came the two women, still in their wedding finery, and Brandon in his tux, minus the jacket, who immediately went to Reagan and scooped her up in his arms. "You came," he whispered. "Thank you."

Dane saw that Reagan was fighting for composure, unusual for her. He stood and extended his hand. "Dane Corsica," he said. "Congratulations." He shook Brandon's hand and nodded to his new wife.

Morgan stepped forward and enveloped Reagan in a hug. "Thank you for coming. It means so much to Bran."

"Welcome to the family," Reagan said politely.

Kelsea St. Clair followed suit. "I'm so happy to see you again, Reagan," she said. Dane knew Reagan well enough and wondered why her brothers hadn't told their wives that she wasn't really a hugger.

There was a moment of awkward silence, and Dane and Reagan sat on the bed again. Brandon St. Clair lowered himself onto the only chair in the room and pulled his bride down to sit on his knee. Landon moved a small ottoman over for his wife. "Kelsea's expecting again," he said proudly.

Reagan didn't say anything. "Congratulations," Dane offered.

"It's another set of twins," Kelsea said. She rolled her eyes in her husband's direction. "He walks in the house, and I get pregnant with twins."

Everyone laughed, and it broke the tension.

"Is that how it works?" Brandon said with amusement. He looked at Landon. "Bro, I think you and I need to have a talk. There's a better way to achieve that." Everyone laughed again, and Dane decided right then and there that he really liked Reagan's brothers.

When the silence settled in, Landon took the lead. "I've given them a very broad sketch of your situation," he said to Dane and Reagan. He looked at the three newcomers. "Do you have any questions?"

Morgan St. Clair gestured to Dane's holster. "Is that loaded?"

"Yes, it is. Believe me, Mrs. St. Clair, we're all safer with it loaded than not."

She blushed and looked at her husband, then back to Dane. "I love being called Mrs. St. Clair, but you can call me Morgan."

Brandon gave his wife a squeeze, and his expression was so full of love and adoration that Dane had to look away.

The newly-married groom looked at his sister. "Landon said you were being Nancy Drew again," he said with a wink.

Reagan rolled her eyes. "Why did I come here?" she muttered.

"Seriously, Reagan, what were you doing?" Brandon asked.

Dane wanted to take charge, and stood, assuming "agent" stance, shoulders back, feet firmly planted, thumbs hooked on his belt loops. Still, Landon towered over him by a few inches. "Reagan and I were both working undercover on a case. One of us was followed, and we were shot at. Now the authorities are looking for us." He looked somberly at Brandon and the women. "This has the potential to be really big, but I don't want to share any of the details beyond what Reagan has told her attorney." He glanced at Landon.

"So, what are you going to do now?" Brandon asked.

"Reagan's safety is my only concern," Dane said. "I have this weapon and another one with me, and several thousand dollars in cash. I bought a car with cash, but I want to get rid of it soon. That's how we got here. I have other assets stashed in places around Florida that I would normally go to, but law enforcement is looking for both of us down there. We had to flee."

He looked at Reagan, and her normally proud and confident posture had vanished. Her arms were wrapped around her middle and she appeared smaller than she was. Dane lowered himself down next to her, and she immediately sat taller. He looked at Landon. "I won't leave her. I can't trust any of my usual resources. We need a place to stay, completely off grid." He turned to Brandon and Morgan. "Don't worry, we're not asking to stay here," he said. "It's not secure enough."

Dane thought that Brandon looked a little relieved. Morgan certainly did.

Kelsea St. Clair looked at her husband. "What about—" She flipped her gaze to Dane and Reagan. "Would you consider going out of the country?"

Landon nodded. "I was thinking the same thing," he murmured.

Dane rammed a hand through his hair. "I would, but I don't

have an alias for her, no passport or documents. That's the one thing I didn't get to before the bottom dropped out," he said. "And I only have one set of documents for myself." It had all happened too fast. He looked at Landon. "Where were you thinking?"

"St. Jardin."

Dane nodded. "Interesting." He knew of the picturesque island country, but had never been there. "Do you know someone there?"

Landon and Kelsea exchanged an amused look. "We sure do," Landon said. "Our close family friends own a honeymoon resort on St. Jardin. That's where Kelsea and I met."

It took a moment for those words to sink in. *Isn't everyone at a honeymoon resort already married?* But Dane had to let that go for now. "It sounds great, but without a passport, I can't get Reagan there." He racked his brain. "It's too big a risk for me to use any of my regular contacts to get documents made."

The six of them sat silent for several moments, deep in thought.

"Peanut!" Brandon exclaimed. Everyone looked at him quizzically.

"Oh, I get it," Landon said. He looked at Reagan. "We use Sara's passport for you." His eyebrows lifted. "It might work."

"Other than the fact that posing as someone else and using their passport is probably a federal offense," Kelsea commented.

Landon's face betrayed no emotion. "There are loopholes."

"What about the age difference?" Dane asked. He was still figuring that out. Either Sara St. Clair was younger than she looked, or Reagan was lying about her age.

"Hey!" Reagan said with a frown.

Dane looked at her. "I'm not trying to be funny. It's a legitimate concern," he said apologetically.

"Maybe if you were questioned about it, you could say that 'Sara' has been ill," Brandon suggested.

No one said anything. Dane stood and crossed his arms in front of him. "What about your friends who own the resort? Can we leave them out of the loop on this? I really want to contain this to the people in this room."

Landon stroked his chin. "Rose and Ike Goldman. They're an older couple," he said. He looked at Kelsea. "I know they can be trusted, but yes, I think it's best to not share the details with them. You want to blend in and be treated like all the other couples there." Everyone nodded.

"Their honeymoon package runs from Sunday to the next Saturday." Landon looked between his sister and Dane. "Can you two pose as a newlywed couple for the next week?"

Dane's eyes met Reagan's. Her expression didn't change one iota. The classic Reagan St. Clair poker face. "Yes," they said in unison.

Landon nodded. "You'll be missing the first day, and you don't have a reservation, so I'll have to call the Goldmans and set that up."

"You could tell them that you have friends whose honeymoon plans—uh," Dane stopped, trying to think of his next words.

Kelsea St. Clair's brown eyes lit up. "Whose honeymoon plans fell through. They discovered at the last minute that it was a scam."

Landon and Dane nodded. "That works," Landon said. "So you'll be Sara and—whatever your alias is, a newlywed couple. That way, her passport can still say St. Clair."

"Ike and Rose haven't met Sara, have they?" Morgan asked.

"No," Landon said. He looked at Reagan. "Just make sure the Goldmans never see your passport. Rosie is sharp. She knows how young Sara is and would see through the 'illness' story in a heartbeat. Always use your married name—your *fake* married name." He turned to Dane. "What's your alias?"

"Trey Armstrong," Dane replied.

Landon nodded. "That works."

The group sat in silence for another moment. "I'm waiting for someone to poke another hole in this," Dane said.

The silence continued.

"Duh," Brandon said. "How do we get Peanut to give up her passport?" He looked to his brother. "We can't bring her into this. She can't keep a secret."

"I'll handle her," Landon said. No one else said anything.

"She isn't planning any international travel for the next few months?" Dane asked.

"No, she's nannying for us," Brandon said. "At least she has been, but now that we're married, Sara's going to go back to Wisconsin to Mom and Dad's." He looked at his bride. "But, we're—" he squeezed her hand and grinned. "We're adopting a baby boy. We're picking him up on Wednesday in Indianapolis."

Dane immediately slid a glance at Reagan, and her façade cracked ever so slightly. "Oh— congratulations," she sputtered. She quickly regained her composure. "That would be a great excuse to get Sara to stay a little longer, wouldn't it?" she asked.

Landon looked at his brother and new sister-in-law. "If you guys would do that, I'd feel better having the real Sara under our control, so to speak. At least to know her movements."

Morgan nodded. "I'd welcome the help, actually. She's terrific with the girls."

"Good, that's settled," Landon said. "And just so we're clear, we're not bringing Mom and Dad into this in any way, until absolutely necessary. Hopefully after everything is wrapped up and Reagan is safe and there's no story to tell." He looked at his sister.

"That's more than fine by me," Reagan said.

"When can we leave for St. Jardin?" Dane asked. "I want to get out of Chicago. Someone's going to figure out quickly that Reagan has family here, and come sniffing around."

"Are we in any danger?" Morgan St. Clair asked.

"Not so long as you claim that you haven't seen Reagan recently." Dane sighed. "I wish I could order a protection detail for all of you, but my hands are tied."

Landon appeared to be calculating. "I think we can fly you out tomorrow night. I'll get you a hotel room tonight with cash, and tomorrow we can get you both outfitted to go on a tropical honeymoon."

"I volunteer to shop," Kelsea St. Clair said brightly. Her husband, Morgan, and Brandon laughed.

Landon looked around the group. "Anything else?" His gaze rested on Dane.

"I'll need you to pick up some things for me, too. Electronics and such," Dane said.

"I can do that." He eyed the group one more time. "All right, that's a wrap," Landon said. Everyone stood. "Sis, I know you may not be into praying these days, but I want to pray right now." Dane could tell it wasn't a request.

He saw Reagan swallow. Landon held a hand out to Reagan, and to Kelsea on his other side. Reagan grasped Dane's hand, and Dane found himself holding Morgan's hand. The circle closed, and they bowed their heads while Landon prayed for Dane and Reagan's safety, God's blessing on their plan, and Brandon and Morgan's new marriage and family.

Dane hadn't been part of anything like this for a long time. He pushed those memories aside. Despite his discomfort, peace settled over him like a warm blanket. Yes, this was strange, indeed.

# 5

## SARA

SARA ST. CLAIR closed her eyes and breathed in the scent of roses and gardenias. She'd caught the bridal bouquet that her new sister-in-law, Morgan, had thrown. It wasn't even a contest. You would have thought Morgan had eyes in the back of her head, her aim was so true.

Sara gently laid the bouquet on the dresser and sat on the bed. It had been a beautiful wedding and a nearly perfect day with family. The only thing that made it less than perfect was that their older sister, Reagan, hadn't shown. Because of their age difference, Sara and Reagan weren't really close, but why would her sister not show up for Brandon's wedding? She hadn't even returned phone calls or texts. Sara knew that Brandon had held out hope that Reagan would swoop in at the last minute. Sara tamped down a frisson of irritation. No doubt her sister was tied up with some big news story. With Reagan, work always came first.

Now, Brandon and Morgan were sequestered at their home for two blissful days alone. The rest of the family was camped out at a Chicago area hotel with an indoor water park. Jim and Janice St. Clair, Landon, Kelsea, and hers and Morgan's mom, Beth, were armed and ready to pamper and spoil all the grandkids. Sara was there, too, but her parents had gotten a separate room for her and told her to relax. She'd been taking care of April and Shelbie for almost a year and although she adored them, it would be nice to have down time.

What to do with an entire evening to herself? She'd stuffed herself with the delicious food at the reception, so she wasn't hungry. Maybe she'd go to a movie. But first things first, to get out of this dress.

As soon as Sara had changed into jeans and a comfortable top, there was a knock at the door. She smiled to herself. *I wonder if Grandma and Grandpa need reinforcements already.*

She opened it and saw that it was Landon.

He frowned. "That was quick. Did you look through the peephole? I didn't hear the chain disengage. Did you even have it on?"

Sara rolled her eyes as he brushed past her into the room. The door closed behind him. "No, and no. Who else besides the family would knock at my door?"

He turned to face her, hands on hips. "You're too trusting, Peanut."

"Landon! I am not a baby," she countered. "I spent most of the last year completely in charge of your nieces. Brandon trusted me. I'm almost twenty-two years old. I'm an adult." She planted her hands on her hips, mirroring his pose. "If it was midnight, the chain would have been on, and I would have looked. It's five thirty."

He squeezed the bridge of his nose with one hand, and dropped the other one to his side. "I know, Pea—Sara, I'm sorry," he murmured. Landon let out a gusty sigh. Sara was surprised to see genuine contrition in his amber eyes.

"Look, can we sit? I need to talk with you about something."

"All of a sudden, you're all serious," Sara said, eyeing him warily.

Landon lowered himself into one of the chairs, and Sara sat

down across from him on the bed. "Yes, I have a serious, adult-sized problem that I need your help with," he said. "And right now, you're the key to solving it, but the thing is, I'm not going to be able to explain much. You're going to want answers, but you'll just have to trust me."

Sara was intrigued, but didn't say anything for a few seconds. She couldn't imagine her oldest brother having a problem that only she could solve. "Okay," she responded quietly.

"I need to borrow your passport." Landon said the words evenly, and his gaze was steady.

"My—my passport?" Sara was thoroughly confused. Her passport had exactly one stamp in it, from her history class trip to England her senior year of high school. And it had sat in her desk drawer ever since. Why would her brother want her passport?

"Yes." He continued to look at her steadily.

"I—wow. That's an unusual request," Sara said, fishing for a little more information.

"It is." He wasn't biting.

She twisted her lips as her mind whirred. "It must be important."

"It is."

Sara let out a sigh of frustration. "Could you just tell me—"

Landon interrupted her. "The only thing I can tell you is that it might save someone's life."

Sara lifted her eyebrows. "Oh." She was silent for a moment. "How long do you need it?"

He lifted one shoulder. "Not sure. A week or two at most." He paused. "Are you planning to leave the country?"

"Well, no." The passport was just sitting in her desk drawer collecting dust. Sara knew her brother wouldn't ask this of her unless it was really important, and it sounded as if it was.

"All right, then." Landon leaned forward, elbows on knees. "I need it as quick as you can get it. Best case scenario, you leave right now, drive home, and bring it back tonight."

*Goodness.* "Tonight?" Sara watched in amazement as he

reached in his pocket and produced a set of car keys. She gasped with delight. "You're letting me take your new car?" Kelsea and the twins had flown to Chicago earlier in the week and rented a vehicle. Landon drove his own up from St. Louis on Friday.

Landon grinned and lifted the keys up high before Sara could grab them. "It's mine, but the firm leases it." Landon was a partner at St. Louis' most prestigious law firm, originally Jacoby & Jamison. They rebranded themselves as JJS when they named Landon a partner several years ago and had since grown into a widely respected and revered legal powerhouse.

Sara popped up and lunged for the keys, and Landon stood. She got her hands around them, but he held on. "I mean it, Peanut, set the cruise control. No speeding. No food in the car. You can have a drink, but it has to have a lid."

Sara rolled her eyes. "When did you turn into Dad?" she muttered. He released the keys into her hand.

"What were you planning to do tonight?" he asked.

"Nothing, really. Maybe go to a movie."

"Do you have friends from college who live around here?"

Sara considered that. "Yeah, not real close friends, but a few other people. Why?"

Landon stretched and let out a yawn. "That'll be our story. I don't want Mom and Dad to know about this. If it comes up, you met up with some friends to hang out."

Sara busied herself transferring things from her small clutch that she carried to the wedding back into her regular purse. "Whatever, that works."

"And no calls or texts to anyone about going home tonight, or about this—at all."

Sara began to open her mouth. "Not even Caitlyn," Landon said quickly.

*Not even her best friend?* She stopped and looked at him. "This feels like a cover-up, big brother. This—whatever you're doing—it's legal, right?"

Landon gave her a stern look. "You know I can't break the law," he said. Then he relaxed his expression. "But I can twist and bend it a bit. You let me worry about that. Just go home, grab the passport, and get back here. Text me when you're on your way back."

Sara nodded, and headed for the door. Landon was right behind her. He reached down to give her a hug. "Thanks for doing this, Sara. I know you're all grown up, but you'll always be our Peanut."

*SUNDAY EVENING*

**REAGAN**

DANE AND REAGAN'S flight left O'Hare almost an hour late and bumped all the way to Atlanta. After a short layover, the flight to St. Jardin was much smoother, for which Reagan was thankful. Shortly after takeoff, she pretended to fall asleep. Reagan needed some time to think. She was uncharacteristically rattled by her disguise, the fake marriage, and being with her family, even though she'd only made contact with her brothers.

It was wonderful to see both Landon and Brandon so happy and in love with their wives and children. Soon, they would have seven children between them! She wasn't at all jealous, but it magnified Reagan's failures and shortcomings in her own mind. She knew her parents were disappointed that she hadn't gone the marriage and family route. Reagan had no doubt that her younger sister would choose that path, even though Sara was "dabbling" in college and trying to figure what she wanted out of life. She was still so young.

After Paul's betrayal before their wedding, Reagan had thrown herself into her job to drown out the pain. Before she knew it, work completely filled her life. She loved what she did, and she was good at it, so it was just easier to take on more in order to build a higher, thicker wall around herself. She'd gone out with a handful of men over the years, but had a two-date rule. Only once had she thought about extending it to three, but decided in the end to stay true to herself.

And just like that, a decade had gone by and Reagan was, by her own devices, alone.

Reagan felt Dane shift in the seat next to her, and snuck a peek at him. He was either asleep, or pretending to be, too. He had to be exhausted. They'd spent almost twenty-four hours in the motel room that Landon got for them. Reagan had spent most of that time sleeping and Dane had spent most of it awake—making plans and dispatching Landon to purchase burner phones, a secure laptop, and all kinds of other equipment that Dane needed to conduct untraceable research on their case. Kelsea had gone shopping for all the personal items that Trey and Sara Armstrong would need for their honeymoon trip.

Reagan was now Sara Cecily Armstrong, even though "her" passport, of course, still had her last name listed as St. Clair. She glanced at Dane, who was beginning to stir. His papers listed him as Trey Michael Armstrong, from Traverse City, Michigan, which worked since the real Sara had been a student at the University of Michigan for two years. They'd made up a vague cover story about meeting there.

Dane touched her hand. *Make that Trey.* Reagan swallowed.

He spoke in hushed tones. "You like your rings?" His finger moved over Reagan's wedding band and rested on the beautiful solitaire diamond.

"Well—I guess," Reagan stammered. "But I told you I didn't need the engagement ring. A plain band would have been fine." She stared at the gold band adorning Dane's finger. It looked so out of place.

"I know it would have been fine with *you,*" he said, lowering his voice to a whisper, "but I was thinking about what Sara would want. You know—Sara with the blond curls and the dresses and make-up." Reagan didn't say anything, and Dane smiled. "That Sara would want a big, beautiful diamond, and since I'm expensing it and will be reimbursed for it in the long run, that's what I got—or rather, what Kelsea got."

Reagan smiled to herself recalling Kelsea's delight at being sent ring shopping. "You're right," she murmured, then sighed. It was beginning to annoy her, not being in her own skin. Not to mention that it was exhausting trying to act soft and feminine, two traits that most definitely did not describe her. But as Dane said when they set this up, the best disguise would be one that was as far from her real self as possible.

"Do you think you'll ever get married, for real?" Reagan asked.

Dane didn't say anything for several seconds. "I don't know," he finally said. "You?"

"I came close once," Reagan said.

"How close?"

"A month." She shrugged. "He cheated on me. I guess I'm glad I found out before the wedding."

Dane shook his head. "Don't settle. Hold out for the best. The best of the best." He looked at her intently. "You deserve it, Reagan."

"Thanks," she said. "So do you."

"I enjoyed meeting your family," he said. "They're pretty religious." Reagan could tell it was just an observation; his voice held no censure.

"Yeah, they are," she said. "Just one more way that I'm different from them."

"You're not religious?"

"Not really. I was, you know, raised in the church and everything. Our family was there whenever the doors were open. But when I started getting interested in journalism my junior year of high school, it opened my eyes to all kinds of different world views. I started making new friends that didn't go to my church, and discovering new ways of thinking. It was so liberating."

Dane's eyes twinkled. "How liberating?"

Reagan slid him a smile. "No comment." She wanted to get the spotlight off of herself. "What about you? Do you go to church?"

Dane appeared to squirm. "Well—I was raised in a Christian family, too. But I kind of stopped going a few years ago, just got busy with work and—just other things."

"Well, you're in a high-pressure, high-stakes career," Reagan whispered, "and you're really good at what you do." Dane didn't reply, and that was typical of him. He didn't see how extraordinary an agent he was.

The plane started its final descent, and Reagan straightened in her seat. How long would they be stuck on this island, under the pretense of being married? Landon had told them that the usual stay at the resort was about a week. What would they do after that if they still needed to stay underground?

She felt the landing gear come down, and looked out the window. It was night, and millions of stars glittered in the expanse above. Below, Reagan only saw darkness, and assumed that they were still over the water.

The plane touched down and bumped once before settling into its smooth coast down the runway. Reagan closed her eyes, pressed her spine into the seat back, and resisted the urge to extend her right leg and foot as if pressing on a brake pedal. She had flown all over the world on every kind of conveyance imaginable, and loved every aspect of flying except the landing. That probably stemmed from an incident on a transatlantic flight landing in Germany about seven years ago. It had been raining and for some unexplained reason that was never determined, the jet skidded off the runway. Luckily, there were no injuries, but it was still a very scary incident, one that Reagan hoped never to repeat. Her heartbeat sped up now, just remembering it.

She flinched and her eyes flew open when she felt Dane's arm come around her. "Relax, sweetheart," he murmured into her ear. "You can't jump every time I touch you if we're supposed to be married." His hand kneaded her arm.

"Dane—"

"Shh. Trey," he corrected her.

She swallowed. "Trey," she repeated. She lowered her voice to a whisper. "We need to set some ground rules about that."

One side of his lip twitched. "Don't worry, I promise your virtue will remain intact," he whispered. His chocolate brown eyes sparkled.

"Just never mind about my virtue," Reagan whispered back. The jet was almost to the gate. "We'll talk about this later." She busied herself with her carry-on.

Dane removed his arm. "I look forward to it," he drawled with a dimpled smile.

## DANE

DANE FOLLOWED HIS "wife" out of the terminal. Even though it was late night, the curb was filled with vehicles. Some of them even looked operational. He and Reagan had both traveled extensively in other countries and knew that sometimes, you had to take what was available, and pray that it got you to your destination in one piece. "What do you think?" he murmured.

Suddenly, someone grabbed him from behind, and Dane instinctively reached for his weapon. Which, of course, was back in Illinois with Reagan's brother.

He whipped his head around and let out a breath. There stood a slip of a girl with shining dark eyes and black hair pulled into a ponytail, holding a hand-lettered piece of cardboard that said *OOBER*.

"Hi! I am Monique! But you can call me Moni!" Her smile was nearly as wide as the island. "I drive. I take you anywhere you want to go," she said in a sing-song voice.

Dane resisted the urge to laugh. Moni looked like she was about fourteen. "Hold on a minute." He looked at Reagan in the hope she would take charge.

Reagan eyed the girl and smiled. "You have a valid driver's license, Moni?"

Moni's head bobbed up and down. "Yes, I have driver's license. My Uncle Louie gave it to me."

Dane couldn't hold the laughter in this time. "How old are you, Moni?"

"I am seventeen," she said. Dane and Reagan exchanged a skeptical look. She held up her hand. "I never have accident, I swear. I will take good care of you and your lady." She reached out for Dane's roller bag. "I will drive slow and get you there safe."

Dane looked at Reagan. She lifted a shoulder. "Let's live a little, Trey," she murmured with a smile and a wink.

Dane held on to his bag. "I've got this, Moni. Just take us to the car."

Impossible though it seemed, her smile grew bigger. "You will be happy. I will keep you safe." She practically skipped along the sidewalk in front of them. They passed car after car, most of them dark, non-descript four-door sedans. Then Moni stopped, and extended her arms wide. "Ta-da!" she sang out.

"Oh, this is—your car?" Dane asked. She stood proudly in front of a rusted Gremlin that may have been lime green at one time.

"Yes, this is Sadie-belle!" Monique exclaimed. "My Uncle Louie gave her to me!"

Dane could tell that Reagan was having as much trouble holding it in as he was. He cleared his throat. "Uncle Louie is a generous guy."

"He won her in poker game!" Moni opened the trunk, which amounted to unhooking something that looked like an elastic hair tie wound between two hooks soldered to the trunk lid and bumper. "Sadie-belle is good car." After considerable pushing, pulling, and squeezing, they got the bulk of their luggage into the trunk and got the door mostly closed and secured with the hair tie. Dane and the rest of the bags ended up shoehorned into the backseat, with Reagan in the front passenger seat.

"Where to?" Moni asked, her ever-present smile dancing.

"Ah, the St. Jardin Honeymoon Resort, on Paradise Cove," Dane said.

Moni's dark eyes grew large. "Ah, Rosie and Ike! Ooh, la-la!" She exclaimed. "You newlyweds! I drive fast. I know you want to get there fast!" She popped the clutch and attempted to peel out from the curb, but Sadie-belle wasn't made to peel out. They came to a bone-jarring stop.

Dane felt his teeth rattle. "Moni, it's okay. We don't need to get there fast." *We just need to get there alive.*

A chorus of horns blared behind them. Moni leaned out her window. "Cool your jets, boys!" she shouted.

Dane covered his face with one hand and took a deep breath. *Maybe we should have taken our chances and stayed in Florida.*


The trip could have been filled with drama, but once they got out of the airport, Sadie-belle ran smoothly (for the most part) and Moni kept her original promise to drive safely (for the most part). She chattered throughout the entire thirty-minute trip about the island of her birth and her large, interconnected family, which of course included Uncle Louie, who ran a popular bar.

When they arrived at the resort and Dane peeled himself out of the backseat, he could hardly stand straight. Reagan noticed him rubbing his back, and busied herself getting everything out of the trunk while Dane pulled out his wallet. "How much?" he asked Moni.

She lowered her eyes and quoted a price that seemed ridiculously low to Dane. "Is that in euros or dollars?" he asked. "Never mind." He gave her twice what he thought she had asked for.

Her eyes grew wide as saucers, and she pumped Dane's hand. "Thank you, sir! You need anything while you are in St. Jardin, you go to the Bahama Llama Boogie Shack and ask for Louie."

She poked a thumb at her chest. "Uncle Louie always know where to find me! Moni help you with *anything!*" She backed away, smiling and waving. "Thank you, sir! Thank you ma'am! You have good honeymoon! Ooh la la!"

As Sadie-belle lurched away, Dane felt a wave of exhaustion wash over him. All he could think of was getting a full night's sleep. Thanks to Landon, he had all the equipment he needed to dig into this case and get it solved. Then he and Reagan could get back to Miami and resume their lives.

Dane held the door open for Reagan and followed her into the deserted lobby. His gaze rested on the blond curls that hung halfway down her back, and the full, although rumpled, skirt of her blue and white sundress that swirled around her legs as she walked. He swallowed. *Our lives in Miami may look a whole lot different after this week.*

They stepped up to the desk and were greeted by a short blonde whose pink nametag read *Molli.*

"You must be Mr. and Mrs. Armstrong," she said with a friendly smile. "Welcome to St. Jardin! I hope you had a good trip."

"Yes, we are, and we did," Dane said. "Thank you." They quickly got through the check-in process, and were informed by Molli that breakfast would open on the patio at seven o'clock the next morning, and that the owners were looking forward to meeting them.

She handed them two key cards. "I'm sorry we don't have any bellhops on duty to help you with your luggage." Dane and Reagan assured her they would be fine.

As soon as they found their room and the door closed behind them, Reagan dumped her bags on the floor and turned to Dane. "Okay. Time for ground rules."

Dane held a finger to his lips, and took out a special piece of equipment about the size of a deck of cards. Reagan crossed her arms in front of her and waited impatiently until he had swept the room for listening devices. "All clear," he said.

"Ground rules."

Dane fought the urge to cringe. "Can we do this tomorrow? I'm exhausted. I just want to go to bed."

"Wrong choice of words, Corsica."

He rolled his eyes. "I meant *sleep*."

Reagan studied the king-sized bed, decked out in shades of pink. It had an abundance of pillows, which she grabbed and arranged in a wall down the middle of the bed.

"Really, Reagan?" He wasn't in the mood for one of her lectures.

"You'd prefer to sleep in the bathtub?"

He reached his arm out and snared one of the pillows. "At least give me one for my head."

She sighed. "Fine." She removed a pillow from the pile. "Don't take it personally, Dane. I share hotel rooms and beds with all kinds of colleagues when I'm on assignment. This is standard operating procedure."

"I guess I can—"

Reagan cut him off. "Rule number two: be fully dressed at all times, and anyone needing to change clothes does it in the bathroom. With the door closed."

"That sounds like two rules," Dane said. "So if we both need to change, we both go into the bathroom?" He couldn't resist adding a roguish smile. Engaging in this lighthearted banter was giving him a burst of energy.

She rolled her eyes. "You know what I mean."

"What's rule number three?"

"Rule number three is—stop it!"

"Stop what?" Dane asked innocently.

"Stop—looking so, you know—cute and silly." She look completely flustered.

"I can't help it if I'm cute, Reagan. It's my cross to bear." He rubbed his hands together. "Reagan St. Clair, rattled. The guys won't believe it."

"*The guys* will never hear about this," she countered.

"True." Still, it was fun to tease her. And she'd never believe him if he told her the reason why he had no designs on her.

Dane unzipped his suitcase, found his toilet kit, and headed for the bathroom. "In about thirty seconds, I'm going to be asleep on *my* side of the bed," he said firmly. "You can tell me rule number three tomorrow."

*TUESDAY MORNING*

**SARA**

SARA OPENED HER eyes and looked at the digital clock on the hotel nightstand. It was just after eight o'clock. Her parents had told her to relax and sleep in, but Sara still felt that she had to get up and get going. She still couldn't get used to it. *I don't have to be anywhere today. No classes, no job, no April and Shelbie to look after.*

Sara's quick trip home on Sunday night went off without a hitch, and she arrived back just after midnight and delivered her passport into Landon's waiting hands. He said he would cover for her Monday morning if she wanted to sleep in. Sara spent the rest of the day with the family, and especially enjoyed getting acquainted and playing with her youngest niece, Rose, and her little nephew, Isaac. Landon and Kelsea seemed to be busy with something and really weren't around much until late afternoon. After the little ones went to bed, the adults ordered pizza and played dominoes. It was a very relaxing day.

Sara flopped onto her side and pulled the light cotton blanket up. *Nothing to do today but figure out what to do with the rest of my life.*

When she had left college after her second year, dissatisfied with her major, the chance to take a break and nanny for Brandon's girls was an answer to prayer. All of her friends thought she was crazy to take on that kind of responsibility, and always asked how she could stand being with two preschoolers day in and day out.

But the fact was, Sara loved it. She had gotten the girls involved in all kinds of activities and made it a point to get to know their little friends and their nannies or au pairs, and in a few cases, their mothers. Sometimes, she offered to watch the other children, and had a blast playing with them and coming up with all kinds of fun things for them to do. It honestly didn't bother her to have charge of half a dozen little ones all at once.

Now, she was actually entertaining the idea of going back to school for an early childhood degree. Education was a big deal in her family, and Sara was expected to complete college, and she wanted to, even though she hadn't landed on the right major yet. But in the meantime, she needed to decide whether to go back to Chicago with Brandon and his growing family. Immediately after the wedding on Sunday, when he and Morgan had made the joyous announcement to the family about the baby, they begged her to come back and help with April and Shelbie for another few weeks or months while they got settled. Sara didn't know what she was going to do in the fall, so she might as well go back to Chicago. She would need to make a decision pretty soon about school. It wasn't as if she could show up on the first day of classes.

Just as she was going into the bathroom, her phone rang. It was her best friend, Caitlyn. They'd met the first day of choir freshman year, been inseparable throughout high school, then gone to the University of Michigan together to major in vocal performance. The difference was, Caitlyn knew exactly what she wanted to do and was now just a year away from obtaining her degree.

"Hi, Boo," Sara said into the phone. She set it on speaker and laid it on the counter.

"Hey, Boo," Caitlyn answered back. They had called each other this for so long that neither of them could remember how or why it began.

"How was the wedding?"

"Oh, it was gorgeous, perfect. I'm so happy for Brandon and Morgan. And guess what? They're adopting a baby boy this week—he just fell into their laps. It was one of those God things." She explained more of the details.

"Did you catch the bouquet?" Caitlyn asked.

Sara snorted. "Yes. *That* was a waste. I'm not even seeing anyone."

"You never know," Caitlyn said. "So, when will you be home?"

"Tomorrow. I know you were hoping we could spend the summer together at home, but I'm probably headed back to Chicago next week to help out with the girls while they get settled with the baby. I don't know how long I'll be there."

"Boo! You can't!" Caitlyn wailed.

"I'm sorry," Sara said. "I'll miss being with you, too."

"That's not it," Caitlyn explained. "You're not going to believe what I have to tell you."

"What?" Sara said. She got her toothbrush out, rolled paste onto it, and started brushing her teeth.

"I just got a phone call from one of the Disney producers down in Florida," Caitlyn said. Last summer she'd gotten a job singing at Disney World. Sara had auditioned and been accepted too, but gave it up to help Brandon's family. "They had a last-minute cancellation and need a soprano. I turned it down—you know, because I'm taking summer school so I can graduate next spring. But I told him you might be available, and he pulled your audition tape and wants to talk to you!" Caitlyn let out a squeal.

Sara dropped her toothbrush into the sink and did a quick

rinse. "You're kidding me!" She looked at her astonished reflection in the mirror, then turned and went back into the bedroom. Her mind was swirling with the implications of this door opening. Was this God's way of pointing her in a direction? The second chance to sing with Disney was huge. But what about Brandon and Morgan and their family?

Sara sat down on the bed. "Oh, wow. I have no idea what to do." She pulled her thick blond waves into a ponytail.

"You're going to call Lance Petrie back right now!" Caitlyn exclaimed. "He's waiting to hear from you. I'll text you his number. You *have* to do this, Boo, you'll never get another chance."

Sara's heart skittered. "I know. Okay, I need to think about this. But I'll call him. Thanks." She disconnected and within seconds, got Caitlyn's text with the phone number. She stared at it, and thought about Brandon and his family. Sara had already come to his aid once. Why did they still need help? Most families got along fine when a new baby joined the family, unless the mother needed extra time to recover from the birth, which certainly wasn't the case now.

"I'm doing this for me," Sara whispered. "God can still close this door if this isn't the path He wants for me." She said a quick prayer, and made the call. Her heart pounded as the phone began to ring.

"Lance Petrie," came the deep voice.

"Oh, hi—hello, Mr. Petrie," Sara said, willing herself to calm down. "This is Sara St. Clair, calling from Wisconsin. You—"

"Sara, yes. Hello! It's great to hear from you. Please, call me Lance."

"Okay, um, Lance. Well, I hear you have an opening for a soprano."

"No, we have an opening for *you,* Sara. I was in another part of the organization last year, and didn't hear your tape until now. You're fantastic. Why didn't you sing with us last year?"

Sara's heart began to beat erratically. *Wow.* "I—I had a family situation come up. I was needed—well, I was just needed." She didn't want to get into a bunch of details.

Lance spoke quickly but sincerely. "I admire that. But I hope the family can get along without you this year. When can you be in Orlando?"

*This was moving fast!* Sara's mind raced. She would need to get a hold of Brandon, and talk with her parents. She took a deep breath. "When do you need me?"

"Day after tomorrow? We're already in rehearsals. We'll make your flight arrangements. We'll e-mail you a list of everything you need to bring. Oh—you have a passport, right?"

Sara's heart plummeted. "Um, well, yes, sure, but won't I just be in Orlando?"

"Nope," Lance said. "This show is going to do some Caribbean island hopping from the get-go, so you'll need your passport. I need to run, Sara. My assistant will e-mail everything to you, you'll need to sign and fax or e-mail the contract back to us, and if you have any questions, just ask her. I'll probably meet you in a couple of days. I'm so happy you're going to be with us this year!"

"Thanks, Lance," Sara managed to say. Her mind was reeling. No way was she letting this opportunity slip through her fingers. *How am I going to get my passport back?* She had no idea what Landon planned to do with it, just that he'd have it back to her in a couple of weeks.

But now, she'd been handed the opportunity of a lifetime, and Sara didn't have a couple of weeks.

She got up and paced back and forth, then called Landon's cell, which went straight to voicemail. Maybe he and his family were sleeping in, although with twin toddlers, she doubted it. Sara nibbled at her thumbnail. She hated to bother Brandon on his honeymoon, but she needed answers and something told her that he would know what was going on. Her brothers were super close and had no secrets. Sara was going to have to let Brandon know that she wasn't coming back to Chicago, but wasn't ready to do that yet, until she could solve this passport issue.

He picked up on the third ring. "Hey, Peanut." He sounded completely relaxed, which made Sara feel guilty for letting him down.

"Hey," she said. "How are the newlyweds?"

"Very happy," Brandon said. Sara loved hearing the deep contentment in his voice. "So what's up?"

"Right," Sara said. "Well, I was wondering if you knew anything about why Landon asked to borrow my passport."

Brandon didn't respond for a moment. "What did he tell you?"

"He didn't tell me anything. Just said it was a personal issue and to trust him."

"And you trust him, right? So you gave it to him."

"How do you know I gave it to him?"

"I don't. I was asking if you did." Brandon said, but Sara knew she had caught him.

"You weren't asking, you were *telling* me that you knew I gave it."

"Peanut, you're splitting hairs. Why are you asking about this now?"

"I just started thinking that it was a really strange request, and wanted to know." She waited a few seconds. "You know something, don't you, Brandon?" Sara was confident she could squeeze the information out of him. She'd had years of practice, and she knew her brothers. There was a reason why Landon was the attorney in the family, and Brandon wasn't.

"Look, I—" Brandon let out a breath. "Landon is the one who made the request. He should be the one to share the details, if he wants to."

"I tried to call him, but his phone was off." Sara didn't admit she could just walk down the hall and ask him in person, but she'd have to concoct a way to get him alone. "Come on, Brandon, you owe me." She inserted levity into her voice so he'd know that she wasn't upset with him. "I put my life on hold for you."

He laughed. "Oh, you're going to keep bringing that up forever, aren't you?"

"If necessary," she said with a smile. "Come on. I don't need *all* the details. Just tell me a general idea. I'm intrigued." The fastest way to get information out of Brandon was to pretend that it wasn't important.

He sighed loudly. "Okay. It was for Reagan."

"Reagan?" Sara couldn't imagine. *Landon said my passport could save someone's life! Was he talking about our sister?*

"She got herself in some hot water working on a story and needed a place to hide. Landon sent her to the honeymoon resort on St. Jardin to hide out for a little while. She disguised herself as a blonde, and since she looks like you—well, do I need to spell it out?"

*What? Where and when did they see Reagan?* Sara sat down on her bed in disbelief. Reagan had traveled to St. Jardin on Sara's passport? Was that even legal? It had to be, if Landon had arranged it. "Are you kidding me, Brandon? When did you see Reagan?"

She heard her brother gulp. "Sara—it's not important."

"It's important to me! You haven't been out of Chicago in over a week. Was she here, in Chicago?"

Brandon didn't say anything, and Sara decided to wait him out. Finally, he spoke. "We saw her, just after the wedding. She was there."

Sara gasped. "Where? I didn't see her."

"They came late and sat in the back row, and left right away, and didn't stay for the reception."

"I can't believe this. Did the whole family see her, except for me?"

"No, not Mom and Dad. Just Landon, Kelsea, Morgan, and me."

It all made sense now, Landon's request for the passport. "So you guys just left me out. I'm so tired of being treated like a child!" Tears pricked at her eyes.

"Pea—Sara, I'm sorry. We just didn't—it all happened very quickly, and Landon thought this was the best way to handle it."

Sara couldn't wait to get off the phone and give it to Landon with both barrels. But then she changed her mind. *They left me out of their plan, so I won't include them in mine. I'll figure out a way to get my passport back on my own.*

But she couldn't let anything on. She took a breath and sighed. "I overreacted, I'm sorry."

"It's okay, Peanut."

Sara rolled her eyes to herself. *Things will never change.* "Well, I have to go. Hug Morgan for me."

"If I have to," Brandon said dramatically.

Sara disconnected and tossed her phone down, then flopped back on her bed and rubbed her forehead. *What am I going to do?* She lay there for several minutes until a plan begin to form in her mind. *Can I really do this? YES, I can. I'm almost twenty-two years old, I'm an adult. If I drag my brothers into this, they'll put up all kinds of roadblocks. I'll always be "Peanut" to them, but I'm a grown woman and can make my own decisions.*

She ticked through the points in her plan just to make sure she'd covered all the bases. Sara had driven her own car down from Wisconsin, so that wasn't a problem. She'd spend a little time with the family today and tell them about the last-minute invitation to work with Disney—leaving out the part about needing a passport. Then she'd drive home, pack for the summer, and implement the rest of her plan. And she would call Brandon.

Sara sat up and grabbed her phone. There was the text from Lance Petrie's assistant, Dawn. She punched in the phone number. "Hello, Dawn? This is Sara St. Clair. Could you please make an adjustment to my flight to Florida? I need to fly into Miami tomorrow, first thing. I'll get myself up to Orlando the day after. Thanks for your help."

## 9

**REAGAN**

REAGAN LOOKED AT herself in the full-length mirror and tugged at her white shorts. They were shorter and tighter than she was used to. She had paired them with a bright orange sleeveless shirt made out of some soft, flimsy material that had a ruffle along the v-neck. She hated the ruffle, but all of the other clothing items in her suitcase had something just as objectionable.

The bathroom door opened, and Dane came out, looking rested and chic and casual in Bermuda shorts, a form-fitting blue t-shirt, and topsiders.

He gave a low whistle, and Reagan wished the ground could swallow her up. "Look at you, Mrs. Armstrong," he said, showing his even, white teeth.

Reagan slipped her feet into flat, comfortable sandals. Dane—"

"Trey," he corrected her. "Come on, get with the program, Sara," he said in a teasing voice. He stepped closer, and Reagan caught a whiff of his aftershave.

She rolled her eyes. "This shirt is awful." She began to unbutton it. "I'm going to change." Then she noticed Dane's raised eyebrows and felt herself flush. Her hands stilled.

"You almost broke rule number two!" Dane exclaimed with mock horror. "I was going to tell you not to change, but on second thought, go right ahead." He grinned at her.

"Whatever!" Reagan was flustered. "At least you're wearing clothes that match your normal style." She quickly did up the buttons. "I haven't worn a ruffle since I was—like, five."

"You look great. Come on, we're already late for breakfast."

"Let me check my hair one more time." Reagan's hair was now dyed blond, thanks to a connection Morgan had sent to the hotel before they left Chicago, an elite hairstylist with some kind of special, fast-acting hair dye. Dane had decided that with the abundance of water activities on the island, it would be safer than a wig. Reagan stepped in front of the mirror and made an adjustment. "I wish I could have just slapped it in a braid," she muttered.

Dane laughed. "I'll bet you do. Come on, let's go. I'm hungry."

"You're always hungry," Reagan grumbled. She leaned closer to the mirror. "I think I put on too much mascara." She let out a frustrated sigh. "I barely know how to do all this stuff. Kelsea gave me a crash course."

"She's a nice gal," Dane commented. "Both of your sisters-in-law seem great."

"They are. My brothers chose well." Reagan wished she could get to know them better, but felt completely inadequate when she thought about how they had it all—fabulous husbands, motherhood, and their respective careers. Kelsea owned a thriving pet sitting business, which she ran from home with a crew of teenaged employees, and Morgan was an artist and college professor.

"All right, I'm ready," Reagan said. Dane held the door for her. As soon as it closed and locked behind them, Reagan gasped. "Oh no, I forgot my key card!"

Dane slipped his hand in his pocket and flipped a key card out. It quickly disappeared again. "Good thing I'm here to take care of you."

"Oh, that'll be the day, Cor—" Reagan was startled as Dane swooped in and kissed her on the cheek, near her mouth.

"You can't call me *Corsica* out here," he whispered in her ear. "And loosen up." He put his arm around her waist, and started walking. "Good morning," he said pleasantly to a couple who was approaching from the other direction.

Reagan pasted a smile on her face and nodded at the couple. This was going to be a long week. As soon as they were past, she turned to Dane. "You just broke rule number three! No kissing."

"It was only on the cheek," he whispered. He took her hand. "*Sara,* we can't be convincing to anyone if you act like the ice queen."

"I am not an ice queen! And you're *not* here to take care of me." Nothing got her hackles up more than a man telling her that she needed to be taken care of.

Dane looked at her in frustration. "All right, simmer down." He turned to face her, gently squeezed her arms, and looked around. "You have my word, I won't break any of your rules." His voice got even quieter, and his eyes were serious. "We're good friends, and I don't have any intention of altering that." He was silent for a beat. "Understand?"

Reagan nodded. "I just don't feel like myself. I feel completely out of control."

"You're not *out* of control, but you're not *in* control, and you're not used to that." He raised his eyebrows at her. "Am I right?"

Reagan literally felt a weight come off her shoulders. "Wow, yes, you're right." Dane took hold of both of her hands.

"I need to be in control now," he said. He looked around and lowered his voice. "I know you don't like that, but we're still on an assignment."

Reagan let out a breath and nodded. "Okay," she said reluctantly. Dane let go of her hands and offered his arm, and they walked in silence.

They arrived at a beautiful patio behind the main lodge, overlooking the turquoise sea. The breakfast buffet was loaded with all kinds of delicious-looking food. "Landon and Kelsea warned me about this," Reagan whispered to Dane. "I'm sure gonna want to run every day, or I won't be able to fit into anything by the end of the week." She stopped with a spoonful of cheesy hash browns mid-air. "Hey, maybe that's a thought."

Dane laughed. "Did you bring your running shoes?"

"Oh, shoot! No. Maybe I could buy some in town. Kelsea told me they have shopping expeditions."

They walked to a table in a far corner with their plates and sat down. Dane made sure to sit facing the patio, and lowered his voice. "I'm not sure we should leave the resort. And we're not flush with cash right now, either."

Reagan frowned. "Landon offered to loan you some money."

Dane cut into his waffles and took a hearty bite. "I know," he said as he chewed. "But I already had to accept a loan from him for some of the equipment. And this isn't a vacation, remember that. Please," he added with a smile.

Reagan nodded, and popped a red, ripe strawberry into her mouth. It was probably the best one she'd ever tasted in her life. She reached for another one.

A woman's voice cut into her thoughts. "Hi! We're Drew and Cassi Carson, from Pierre, South Dakota. May we sit with you?"

Dane and Reagan exchanged a glance. "Sure," Dane nodded with a smile. Reagan forced a smile, too.

The Carsons sat. "Where are you from?" Cassi chirped, her strawberry-blond curls danced. Her fair-haired husband smiled and nodded at them.

"We're Trey and Sara Armstrong, from Michigan. Nice to meet you," Dane responded politely.

"Hello," Reagan murmured.

"Your hair is beautiful," Cassi gushed to Reagan. "Is it natural?"

"Honey!" Drew Carson shook his head and looked at Dane and Reagan apologetically. "Sometimes, she has no filter."

"I'm just being friendly," Cassi said with a smile. Apparently, her husband's apology didn't faze her. "Have you ever been to the Caribbean? This is our first time." She seemed to have quickly lost interest in Reagan's hair.

"No, we've never been here," Reagan said.

"We just got married last weekend." Cassi rubbed her husband's shoulder. "This is so exciting. Did you just get married, too?"

"A couple of weeks ago," Dane said. "On the—" It looked to Reagan like he was trying to figure out the date.

"On the second," she said, coming to his rescue. "May second."

"Yes, that's right, May second," Dane said.

"You'd better remember your anniversary, Trey. Get it tattooed somewhere to remind you," Drew Carson said, which elicited a laugh from everyone. Reagan didn't recall seeing any tattoos on Dane and wouldn't, unless he broke rule number two, or maybe if they went swimming.

"Good morning!" Reagan looked up to see a spry, white-haired couple approaching. From Landon and Kelsea's description, she knew it had to be Rose and Ike Goldman. She had shared about them with Dane, so he was prepared, too.

"You must be the Armstrongs," Rose said. She was pink from head to toe, from her pink-tinged bouffant hair to her pink Converse, her trademark. Her pink rhinestone cat-glasses glittered in the morning sun.

Dane stood to shake their hands. "Yes, I'm Trey, and this is my wife, Sara," he said, touching Reagan's shoulder. She greeted the Goldmans and kept her head down. Landon and Kelsea had cautioned her about getting too close to Rose. The woman had never met Reagan or her sister, but she'd seen family pictures. Even though they were a few years old, Kelsea said if anyone were to make the fantastical leap from young Sara to present-day Reagan as a blonde, it would be Rose.

"We're so glad you could salvage your honeymoon," Rose said.

"Oh no! What happened?" Cassi Carson's blue eyes filled with concern.

"There was a mix-up with our other plans, and they fell through," Dane said. He looked at Rose and Ike. "We really appreciate you letting us come a day late."

"That's no problem, son," Ike said, patting him on the arm. He exchanged a look with his wife. "We're especially happy to help friends of Landon and Kelsea St. Clair." Reagan buried her nose in her cup of yogurt.

"And we want all of our couples to get the best start to their marriages!" Rose said.

Cassi giggled and laid her head on Drew's shoulder. "I can't imagine being anywhere better than this!" she exclaimed. She looked at Reagan. "Just wait until you see the sunset tonight!"

To Reagan's relief, Rose and Ike moved on to the next table after a kind offer to come find them if they needed anything. She dug into her breakfast again, and Dane did the same, while Cassi chattered and Drew mostly listened and nodded.

The Carsons finally left with a promise from Cassi to find them at lunch and sit together again, and Reagan let out a breath. "That's the worst part about being at one of these places, when someone like that gloms into you and wants to hang out all the time."

"Yeah, and no room service here," Dane said, "so we have to come out of the room for meals. Man, that was good," he said, rubbing his stomach. "Landon warned me."

"Do you want to go for a walk?" Reagan asked.

Dane frowned. "No, sorry, we need to get back to the room." He lowered his voice to a whisper. "Remember, we're not on vacation." He stood and held out a hand to Reagan. "And no one will question us if we just stay there." He wiggled his eyebrows and Reagan felt her face heating up.

When they got back to their room, Dane locked the door behind them and retrieved his laptop and other equipment from his suitcase that was inside the closet. Reagan swept the room for bugs and gave him a thumbs-up.

They sat down together at the table. Dane rubbed his hands together. "Okay," he said, "Let's get started. I feel ready to tackle this after a good night's sleep."

Reagan folded her hands in front of her. "Squeak is the key to this. I feel it in my bones."

*Squeak* was the nickname used by just about everyone in Florida for their popular governor, who had been a high-profile state politician for over three decades. Dane threw his head back and let out a gust of air. He and Reagan had had this discussion in the car on their way to Chicago. "Reagan, you can't solve cases by feeling something in your bones."

"Are you telling me you never trust your instincts?"

"Yes, but I never let them lead me. You have to let the *facts* lead you." Reagan started to interrupt him, but he had a head of steam going. "Fact: our squeaky-clean governor has been in public life for over thirty years without one blemish on his record. You've met him. He's the cleanest guy—well, he's the cleanest guy I've ever seen. A public servant, completely upright, terrific family, not one whiff of any trouble with any of them."

She nodded. "Yes, I've met him on several occasions, and you're right. He's the epitome of clean. But people can change, Dane. You've seen how the lure of drug money can tempt the cleanest of them."

"Where's your proof? You saw the governor talking with Doug Navarro at a public gathering." This is what had brought Reagan to the meeting back in Miami.

She tilted her head at him. "Dane, it wasn't a smile and a handshake at a public event. I took a shortcut behind the stage to get to someone on the other side, and the two of them had their heads together in a secluded spot behind the stage. Navarro is one of the drug cartels' dirtiest operatives. Can you think of one reason that our governor would be anywhere around him?"

Dane shook his head. "Reagan, take a step back—"

His tone sounded placating, and that made her mad. Reagan raised her voice over his. "You know how the governor prides himself on being completely transparent and above-board. Every pie that Navarro has his fingers in is questionable at best. He has dozens of lowlifes to do his dirty work, and insulates himself. That's why you, the FBI, and even the Miami cops have never been able to hang anything on him. There's *nothing* good about Navarro. There's no reason for Squeak to be in his presence, let alone having a serious discussion with him."

"I know, I know, you told me," Dane muttered. "Okay, let's review *my* case from the top. Navarro has been making a lot of trips back and forth to Cuba since some of the trade restrictions between the Cuban government and the US are starting to lift. He's representing a conglomerate of businessmen, and it looks like just another cocaine smuggling operation to the DEA. There's a pattern to those, but over the past couple of months, that pattern has changed, but we don't know why. That's why I was sent in undercover. And then you showed up at the meeting and everything fell apart." Dane rubbed his eyes.

Reagan crossed her arms in front of her chest. "You act like it's my fault that everything fell apart."

"That's not what I meant. I was just stating the sequence of events. You showed up at the meeting. Everything fell apart."

"And we still don't know what any of this has to do with our governor," Reagan said.

Dane corrected her. "We still don't know IF any of this has to do with our governor. Reagan, it just doesn't make any sense."

Reagan crossed her arms in front of her. "He's the key to this, I'm sure of it."

# 10

**DANE**

DANE WAS GLAD they weren't required to dress for dinner. To him, *dressing up* meant wearing shoes instead of sandals. He was a Florida native and enjoyed the casual culture. Dane wore a suit when he had to, but felt much more comfortable in the clothes he now wore: a blue and white striped button-down shirt, untucked and open at the neck, khaki shorts, and his topsiders.

*What was taking Reagan so long?* Dane rapped on the bathroom door. "Can we go? I'm getting hungry."

"Do you have a tapeworm or something, Corsica?" Reagan snapped. "I'll be out in a minute."

He squeezed the bridge of his nose. *Gosh, she sure is prickly today.* Dane thought back to his and Reagan's earlier conversation. He didn't want to reveal that he'd known the governor personally most of his life, having been a long-time friend of Dane's dad. Reagan had some good points, but Dane couldn't reconcile them with what he knew of the man.

Reagan marched out of the bathroom, looking lovely in a peach and yellow sundress and matching sandals. Her hair was

426

piled on top of her head and parts of it sort of stuck out, but it was pretty, and he told her so.

She grunted. "I can't stand this long hair in the heat. If I can't put it in a braid, this messy bun thing is the next best thing. Kelsea showed me how to do it."

Dane resisted the urge to sigh. *All I did was give her a compliment.* "You could put it in a braid if you want," Dane said. "It's blond. It's not going to give you away."

Reagan shook her head. "I don't think I should. Having it *not* in a braid helps me to stay in character."

They arrived at the main dining room and stood in line with other couples. When they got to the front, they were told that each couple would dine alone tonight, and to choose one of the small, round tables. Dane took Reagan's hand and led her to one in the farthest corner, and pulled out her chair.

She looked as if she might protest, then clamped her lips together. "Thank you," she murmured as she sat. Dane took his seat with his back to the wall.

"Good girl," Dane whispered. "See, it's not so hard."

A server came and offered them drink choices. They both ordered the non-alcoholic fruit punch.

Dane waited until the server was out of earshot. "You could have had a drink."

She shrugged. "I know, but I would have felt funny drinking if you weren't. And I know you don't."

Dane was surprised she'd noticed. "You do? When did you figure that out?"

She laughed. "I've known you for four years. So I figured it out about three years, eleven and a half months ago."

Dane frowned. "We haven't spent that much time together outside of work."

"Call it my reporter's nose." The server delivered their drinks and left. Reagan took a sip. "Oh, this is really good. I don't even miss the alcohol."

Dane smiled. "I have a question for you. Landon and Kelsea met here, at this honeymoon resort, but if they weren't married, why were they here?"

"That's a funny story," she replied. "They were both supposed to marry other people on New Year's Day. Kelsea's fiancé backed out a few days before, and Landon—well, he was literally left standing at the altar."

"Ouch."

"In front of five hundred people. It was awful."

"I'll bet," Dane said.

"Both of them had made a reservation here for their honeymoons, and they both decided to come alone. So Rose pretty much threw them together."

Dane laughed. "She's something else."

"And then, on the last night, all the couples had to take part in this historic island ritual, some kind of symbolic marriage ceremony—but it wasn't legally binding—and a couple of weeks after they got home, Landon and Kelsea found out that they really were married."

Dane's eyes opened wide in amazement. The server set salads down in front of them. "There's more to the story," Reagan said. "It's much better coming from them. You'll have to ask them to tell you about it sometime," Reagan said.

An uneasy feeling settled over Dane. "Do you think we'll have to do that symbolic marriage ceremony?"

Reagan's fork stopped in mid-air. "Gosh, I don't know. I didn't even think about it. We'll have to figure out a way to get out of it." She shrugged. "I can come down with a migraine or something."

Dane nodded and took another bite of his salad. There was no way that he was going through any kind of a marriage ceremony. *No way.* If Reagan's "headache" didn't do the trick, Dane would think up something else to get them out of it, even if he had to shoot himself in the foot.

Then he remembered, his weapon was back in the states with his other possessions that Landon now had.

"That was amazing," Reagan said. "I may never eat again. Until breakfast!" she added with a laugh.

"I agree," Dane said. He stood and helped her to her feet. "Come on, let's get back to the room." He lowered his voice. "And hit the computer again."

Reagan came to a standstill and looked around. They were completely alone. "We've been cooped up in that room all day. We're at one of the most beautiful beaches I've ever seen, *from a window*. Can't we take a walk? Just this once?"

Her pleading eyes were hard to resist. "I guess a short walk wouldn't hurt," he said softly.

They walked outside through the gardens to a path leading down to the shore. There were about a hundred couples at the resort and although not all of them were outside, it seemed that Dane and Reagan couldn't go more than a few steps without encountering someone kissing or embracing or at least holding hands.

Before they got to the water, they removed their shoes and left them by a rock pile. They stood at the water's edge for a while, content to let the waves lap at their feet. Then they began to walk.

There was about thirty minutes of daylight left, and it promised to be a beautiful sunset.

Dane drew in a deep breath and opened all of his senses to his surroundings. The ocean was myriad shades of blue and teal. Where it met the horizon was a deep sapphire giving way to peach, pink, and purple. The rhythmic crash of the waves soothed him, and his skin came to life as the sea breeze washed over him. He could smell the salt and taste its tang. Under different circumstances, he would enjoy this tropical paradise, especially if he were here with the right person. He stole a glance at Reagan, and waited for some kind of physical reaction to kick in, for his heart to accelerate, or his face to break into a grin, or to be overtaken by an irresistible urge to sweep her into his arms.

But none of those things happened. And if they had, he wouldn't have acted on them.

Dane's burner phone vibrated in his pocket. Besides Landon, there was only one person who had this number. Dane looked at the screen, and his heart sped up. *I hope this doesn't mean trouble at home.*

# 11

**REAGAN**

"I NEED TO take this in private," Dane said. They had gone far enough that no one else was nearby. "Hold on," he said into the phone. Then he turned and walked away.

Dane had a burner phone for Landon to keep in touch with them, and he'd given one to Reagan too, just in case they got separated. She didn't know if Dane had given his burner number to anyone else. If it was Landon, she was sure Dane wouldn't leave her out of the conversation. Dane kept his back to her for several minutes, then began pacing back and forth, while still talking. His face was somber.

Reagan studied his profile and felt a little regretful for the times she'd snapped at him today. They'd been together in close proximity for five days now. That was something Reagan wasn't used to, and she supposed Dane wasn't, either.

He disconnected the call, and Reagan thought he would walk back her way, but instead he put his hands in his pockets and stared out over the ocean. The muted oranges, pinks, and purples had given way to a blaze of color, but Reagan sensed that he wasn't even seeing it. She sat down on the sand.

Ten minutes passed. It was almost dark, and he still hadn't

moved. Reagan finally approached him. "Is everything okay? Was that Landon?"

She got the feeling that he'd forgotten about her. "No, it wasn't him." Dane said, and took off walking. Reagan trailed after him. By the time they got back to where they'd left their shoes, it was almost too dark to find them.

Dane didn't say a word the whole time, and once they got into the building where Reagan could see his face, it was expressionless. He swiped the key card in their door and held it open for her to go through.

He locked the door behind them and went to his suitcase in the closet where he hid the bug tracker. After he'd swept the room, he sat down on the edge of the bed. He folded his hands over his knees and didn't say anything for a moment.

"I need to tell you something," Dane said.

He didn't say anything, and Reagan steeled herself.

He took a breath. "I have a son."

That was the last thing Reagan expected him to say. For once, she was at a loss for words. "I—I had no idea, Dane." Her heart began to race. "That phone call—is he okay?"

For the first time since he'd gotten the phone call, Reagan felt like he saw her. His features softened. "Yes, he's fine. Thanks." Dane let out a breath. "I—I'm sorry I didn't tell you about this earlier."

"It's okay," Reagan said. "It's not like we're really married or even dating. Your personal life isn't my business." She sat beside him, leaving some space between them.

He ran a hand through his hair and sighed. "So. I—uh, yeah. His—well, his mother and I met about six years ago in Miami. She—we, had a very brief fling and then she found out she was pregnant." He hung his head and wiped his hand across his mouth. "And we got married. We haven't lived together since he was a couple of months old. We—it just didn't work. But I help support him, and we, well, we sort of co-parent him."

"I'm sorry, Dane. I didn't know you were divorced."

He twisted the wedding band around on his finger. "Well, we never did get divorced. She—she wanted the protection of marriage, and even though I was pretty certain we'd never reconcile, I wanted my son's parents to be married." He winced and shook his head. "I'm sure that doesn't make any sense."

*Protection of marriage? That's an odd phrase,* Reagan thought. "It doesn't have to make sense to me," she said. They sat in silence for a few moments.

"What's his name?" Reagan asked softly.

Dane smiled. "Danny. He's five." His features softened. "He's my whole world. I'm crazy about him."

Reagan smiled back. "That's wonderful, Dane. I'm glad you're in his life."

Dane stood and began to pace, and rammed his hands through his hair. "Well, I'm about to be a much bigger part of his life. His mother is dead. That's what that phone call was about."

Reagan felt her jaw drop, and her heart sped up. "Dane, that's awful. I'm so sorry." So technically, he was a widower now. It was hard for Reagan to wrap her head around that.

Dane rubbed a hand across one eye. "Reagan—she, she overdosed. My—Danny's mother was, um, Blayze."

Reagan frowned. "Blaze?"

"With a *y*. Blayze, you know—the—"

Reagan gasped. "*Blayze?* The supermodel?" Dane nodded. Her jaw dropped again. "You were married to *Blayze*?"

Dane looked at her somberly. "I know it's hard to believe. Her real name was Sally Ann. I've actually had Danny for more of his life than she has, and completely for most of the last year. She was starting to get into the party circuit again, and I refused to let her be anywhere around him when she was messing with that stuff." Reagan's mind was still reeling at his revelation.

He sat again next to her and put his head in his hands. "She tried, especially at first, but she was never cut out to be a mother.

Her life growing up was such a mess, she didn't have any role models or anything normal to reference." He sighed. "I tried so hard to convince her to get help. Money wasn't an issue and she could have paid for the best rehab program anywhere in the world, ten times over. But in the end, she just didn't want it."

Reagan hesitated, then laid her hand on his back. "I'm so sorry, Dane. I'm sorry for Danny," she clarified. "No little boy should have to go through losing his mom, no matter what the circumstance." A feeling of great sadness washed over her. "Was he with her—?" She let the question trail off.

Dane straightened up a little and shook his head. Reagan's hand fell away. "No, fortunately, no. He's been with my brother since I left Florida with you. He and Landon are the only ones who have the number for my burner phone."

"Where does your brother live?"

"Miami. He's a—don't laugh. He's a pastor."

Reagan burst out laughing, then covered her mouth. "I'm sorry."

He smirked and shook his head. "I know. Anyway, he's a big part of Danny's life, too, so that's good. Very stable."

"Is Danny with your brother and his family now?"

"Shane doesn't have a family."

"Shane? Your brother's name is *Shane*?" Reagan fell back on the bed and broke into peals of laughter. "They named you Shane and Dane. I hope *your* parents never meet *my* parents!" She took a breath and sat up. Dane was just sitting there with a goofy grin on his face, shaking his head.

"Yeah, I thought about that when I met Landon and Brandon," he said. He rolled his eyes. "Our parents would probably become best friends." They sat in silence, each wrapped in their own thoughts.

Dane put his head in his hands and made a frustrated noise. "I can't believe—she—I, I'm really not feeling grief right now. Shouldn't I be overwhelmed with grief? But the woman I loved ceased to exist a long time ago. I think I'm—I think I'm angry. Yes, I'm angry. Does that make me a terrible person?" Reagan thought these were rhetorical questions, and he just needed to process his feelings.

Dane stood and began to pace back and forth. "Did she even think about—about what this would do to her *son*?" He looked devastated. "He won't even—he won't even remember her," he said, his voice nearly a whisper.

"I'm so sorry," Reagan murmured. She wished there was something she could do or say.

Dane blinked rapidly. "I need to—I'm going for a walk."

Reagan understood that he needed some time alone. "I'll see you in the morning, then."

Without another word, he left.

## 12

## DANE

DANE HARDLY SLEPT that night. A long walk on the beach usually calmed him, but his emotions were still stirred up. He lay in bed for a long time thinking about Sally Ann and their brief, tempestuous marriage. At first, they'd both wanted to make it work. Dane was deeply in love with her—or at least the Sally Ann side that she showed to him. The Blayze side was disturbing and dark, and Dane wanted nothing to do with her. Unfortunately, that side fought a hard battle and ultimately won possession of Sally Ann's soul.

Dane had always held out hope that she would leave the toxic world of high fashion, turn back into Sally Ann, and make a family with him and Danny. As the years wore on, he finally accepted that it wasn't going to happen, but he never took steps to end the marriage, and neither did she. Now, he wasn't bound to her, even legally. *I'm a widower.* Dane always associated that word with older men. He couldn't wrap his head around the fact that he was now free to seek another relationship and even remarry someday.

In her business, Blayze liked being able to play the "husband card" when it suited her. If Dane was being honest with himself, he'd played the marriage card on occasion, too, if a woman showed interest. Honestly, he'd been burned and had a full enough life juggling his career with fatherhood. Danny was his priority, and he was going to be very careful about bringing a woman into his life.

He and Reagan were at breakfast, sitting by themselves in the corner. They'd purposely come late hoping to avoid the Carsons, and it almost worked. The perky couple was just leaving as Dane and Reagan sat down, and came over to say hello. They managed to keep the conversation short, and breathed a sigh of relief when the couple left.

"So, could I ask—where you met Blayze?" Reagan asked.

Dane lifted an eyebrow and took another forkful of his delicious omelet. "I never took you for a Blayze fan."

Reagan rolled her eyes. "I'm not—you know I'm not into all that fashion stuff. But—really, um, *Trey*, we're talking an *international* star here, not just any run-of-the-mill celebrity."

"Well, it's not really a very interesting story. I went to a club, she was there, and we left together." His face flushed.

"Did you recognize her?"

"No. She wore a disguise. She couldn't go out in public as herself."

Reagan nodded. Blayze had auburn hair and electric blue eyes. "That makes sense. So, what did she look like that night?"

Dane hemmed and hawed for a moment. "She—she was, she wore a wig with long, blond hair," he finally said. "And brown contacts."

"Ah," Reagan commented.

"What's that mean?"

"You have a type. You're attracted to brown-eyed blondes."

"If you say so," he smirked. "Her real name was Sally Ann Fogg. She was from Kentucky."

"So, how exactly did you meet her?"

437

Dane squirmed in his seat. "The same way everyone meets at a club."

Reagan shrugged. "I don't go to clubs."

"Well, I don't, either," he said. He scooted his chair back. "I'm going back for seconds. You want anything?"

Reagan gaped at him. "Are you having a growth spurt?"

"Is that a crack about my age?" Dane playfully cuffed her on the shoulder as he went past.

When he returned to the table, he dug into his food. Reagan was done with hers, and sipped at her coffee. "I still can't believe you and your brother have rhyming names."

"Yeah, that's pretty crazy."

"So, what will you name your next son?" Reagan teased. Her face immediately fell. "I'm so sorry! That was insensitive of me."

Dane smiled. "You're fine, Sara." He took a drink of his coffee. "Nothing that rhymes with *Danny,* that's for sure!" They both laughed. Then he grew thoughtful. "I didn't choose a responsible mother for my son the first time around, but if I get another chance, I'll be much more careful." His eyes locked with hers.

Reagan looked at him warily. "I sure hope you're not asking me to volunteer for the job!"

Dane almost spit out his coffee. "No," he said with a chuckle. "Definitely not."

Reagan let out an exaggerated sigh of relief. "Good. Glad we're in agreement on that," she said with a grin.

Dane's phone vibrated in his pocket. "It's Shane," he whispered to Reagan. "Shane, what's up? Is everything okay?"

His brother's voice reassured him. "Danny's fine. Absolutely fine, I promise. But you told me to call if anything looked fishy."

"What's going on?" Dane exchanged a worried look with Reagan.

"Someone must have leaked that he's here with me. I have reporters calling, and some of them are starting to gather outside. It's not paparazzi-level, but it might get there."

Dane ran a hand through his hair. "You haven't said anything to a reporter, right?" He instantly regretted the words. "Shane— I'm sorry, I didn't mean that."

His brother's soothing voice came down the line. "No worries. I haven't said a word, and I've stopped answering the phone for now. We're fine here, we'll hunker down. I just wanted to let you know."

Dane felt panic rising in his chest. *What have I done? My son just lost his mother, and I*—"Shane, I need to see him."

"Aren't you out of the country?"

Dane's mind spun. "Yes. Hold on. Give me a moment." He closed his eyes and weighed all the implications of bringing Danny to St. Jardin. "I want you to bring him here. It won't be a long plane ride, and it will be completely safe. I can't use a credit card right now, but if you buy the tickets and get him here, I'll pay you back—"

"Dane, I'll handle it. For starters, tell me what country you're in," he said drily.

"St. Jardin."

"Really? I've always wondered if it's as beautiful as people say. I'll let you know when I find a flight."

Dane thought about the taxi choices at the airport, and didn't want his son subjected to any of that. "Rent a car when you get here," he said. "I'll text you the address where I'm staying." No way was he going to explain that it was a honeymoon resort, or anything about Reagan. There'd be time for all of that later. Dane let out a deep breath. "Shane, thanks so much." He was fortunate to have a brother who would drop everything to do this for him.

"You know I'll do whatever it takes to keep Danny safe."

"Be sure you're not followed when you leave." Dane felt helpless. He couldn't call on any of his usual sources to help his brother get out of the country undetected.

"You're not the only one with good contacts. We'll be fine."

Dane had an idea what Shane meant by that, and felt mildly relieved. He disconnected and let out a breath.

"They're coming here?" Reagan asked.

Dane nodded. "I can't—he's my son. I have to keep him safe. The paparazzi are starting to sniff around. They've made the connection between Danny and his mother and traced him to Shane."

Reagan put her hand on his and squeezed. He was surprised how much comfort he found in that simple gesture. "Of course he should be here with you. It's private, and it's safe." She laid down her napkin. "Are you done? We can take some coffee back to the room and dig into our case again."

Dane sighed inwardly. He and Reagan would probably end up arguing over "their case" and not get anywhere. Honestly, he felt like he'd make more headway on his own.

They decided to detour back through the main lodge to stop at the coffee station. Rose was there in the lobby and called over to them. She wore a long, flowing tie-dye muumuu in shades of pink, and her Converse. "Yoo hoo, Sara! Did you get signed up for the spa day?" She handed Reagan a pamphlet.

Dane resisted the urge to laugh out loud. *Reagan, at a spa day?*

"No, I didn't," she replied. She opened the pamphlet and perused it. Dane was shocked at the next words that came out of her mouth. "I've never done anything like this. It sounds fun." She looped her arm through Dane's. "But I'm not sure I could spend a whole day away from my husband."

Maybe this was a blessing in disguise. "You should go, honey. Really, it's okay." The endearment felt awkward rolling off his lips, and he hoped he didn't sound too eager to be rid of her.

Reagan looked surprised. "You're sure?"

"Yes, I'm sure. But of course I'll miss you," he added. Dane patted her arm and began to step away, and felt Rose's blue-eyed gaze on him.

"Whatever will you do with yourself all day, Trey?"

"Ah—well, I brought a great book to read. Maybe I'll go lay

on the beach and—read it." Why did he feel like she could see right through him? He leaned down and planted a kiss on the top of Reagan's head. "Have fun. I'll see you later this afternoon. Love you," he added. *I hope I sound like a devoted husband.* He smiled and waved at the ladies and left.

Dane got back to the room, locked the door, and swept it for bugs. He got all of his equipment set up and settled in. Then he realized he'd forgotten his coffee. He yawned. *Oh well, I'll take a break later.*

He stared at the computer screen for a long time. *Maybe I've been going at this from the wrong angle.* He went through all his notes on Navarro again. Then he decided to get a hold of one of his confidential informants to see if he'd heard anything. It would be risky, but Dane was willing to take that chance.

Dane went to a completely dark web site, navigated through a bunch of back doors while covering his tracks, and finally got where he wanted to be. He pulled up Buzzy's handle and was relieved to see that he was online. Dane typed: *Need more on N's recent activities. 6.* It was heavily encrypted and Buzzy would need to use their sixth encryption series to unravel it.

Dane leaned back and stretched his arms above his head while he waited for a response. He thought about what his and Danny's future would look like without his mother. Sally Ann didn't have any family, so Dane wouldn't have to worry about that. He knew his parents and brother would continue to be the support network he needed to help raise Danny. Dane sighed. He really needed to start going back to church. Danny went with Shane sometimes and loved it.

His thoughts were interrupted by a reply from Buzzy. Dane went to work right away and was stunned when he decoded it. *Look into Phil Diamond,* it said. *That's all I can give you.*

Phil Diamond? Dane searched his memory. *Isn't that the guy who runs Diamond Pharmaceuticals?* They were based in Florida. Not one of the biggest pharma companies, but they held their own, and they had a good reputation. After a few clicks, Dane had some very up-to-date information. Since the trade embargo with Cuba had been relaxed, Diamond had been sending teams of scientists there to share research and equipment. Nothing wrong with that. How could Diamond be connected to Doug Navarro?

But then one sentence in an interview quoting Phil Diamond piqued Dane's interest. *"Cuba's state-run health care system has access to some promising anti-cancer drugs that aren't yet available in the US. We hope to collaborate with Cuban scientists to make those available to us for clinical trials and pave the way for FDA approval."* The article had been published by the *Miami Herald* about a month ago. The reporter who conducted the interview was Reagan St. Clair.

## 13

**SARA**

SARA FLEW OUT of Chicago early Wednesday morning. Her dad drove her to the airport and she felt terribly guilty for deceiving him, even if it was just a little white lie. *Going to Miami instead of Orlando is just a teeny little lie, right?*

Her direct flight landed in Miami just before noon. She had a long layover that would give her plenty of time to get everything done. The first unknown factor in her plan was whether Reagan had changed the code on her apartment door. Sara had stayed there for two nights last year during spring break, and for a week between Christmas and New Year's just a few months back. She and Reagan got some sister time while their parents stayed at a hotel. Fortunately, the code was the same. She was relieved to not have to ask the building manager to let her in.

The biggest hurdle to overcome was to find Reagan's passport. Sara didn't even know if it was at the apartment, but she was betting on the fact that since Reagan was in disguise, she had left Florida without it. If it wasn't there, Sara's last resort would be to call Landon, come clean, and demand that he get her passport back from Reagan and overnight it to Orlando. Because Sara was *not* going to miss this chance to sing with Disney.

443

Sara was uncomfortable at the prospect of rifling through her sister's things, but decided to ask for forgiveness later instead of permission now. To her great relief, it was in the second desk drawer she opened, in plain sight.

Sara adjusted the baseball cap on her head. She had bought a brunette wig and fashioned it into a long braid after securing her own hair under an elastic nylon cap. The baseball cap gave her an added layer of security. She walked through the apartment house lobby, pulling two large roller bags behind her, complete with her sister's luggage tags. Sara's ID was tucked away in one of her suitcases, she now had Reagan's passport in her purse, and was outfitted in some of her clothes, right down to her Birkenstocks. She tossed in an extra set of Reagan's jeans and a t-shirt just in case.

She avoided eye contact with the doorman, who smiled and held the door for her. "Did you call an Uber, Ms. St. Clair?" He asked, gesturing to a black SUV.

*First test passed with flying colors!* "Yes, thank you," Sara said quietly, averting her face. The less said, the better. He helped load her suitcases in, and she climbed into the backseat.

She would spend only one night in St. Jardin. As soon as her flight landed, Sara would go to the resort, switch passports with Reagan, and get a hotel for the night. She had an early morning flight and would be in Orlando by noon tomorrow to begin her adventure.

Best of all, her brothers would be none the wiser. Sara would call Landon tomorrow, or maybe she'd just let Reagan take care of it. If Reagan was posing as a newlywed bride, Sara wondered who her groom was. Probably some guy from work. All her sister ever did was work. Sara didn't think she'd even gone on a date in over a year.

Sara was really proud of herself for planning this without any help. She'd been meticulous about the details. The only thing she hadn't been able to do is add a dozen years to her face, but she didn't think that was a problem. *Being an adult isn't so hard after all,* she thought happily. She spent the rest of the ride dreaming about singing with the Disney show. This could be her big break.

Sara checked her bags through and got in line at security. *Now for the next test,* Sara told herself. *The one that really counts.* Getting past Reagan's doorman was one thing, airport security was entirely another. She flashed her passport when asked, and was waved on. *Whew.*

Now Sara could finally relax. She had plenty of time. She had thought about wandering around Miami before coming to the airport, but decided to play it safe. There was no worse feeling than running to catch a flight, and there was no room for error now. She got a late lunch and bought a magazine at one of the airport shops.

Sara sat and thumbed through the magazine for a while. She decided to use the restroom before her flight. She hated the microscopic bathrooms on planes. She glanced at the time. It would need to be quick. They would be boarding her flight in a little while.

When she came out of the ladies' room, she turned right and then realized she was going the wrong way, so she quickly made a u-turn.

And slammed right into someone. A tall, masculine someone.

"Oh! I'm sorry," she sputtered as she retreated and regained her footing.

The tall, dark-haired man looked startled for a second, and then he looked deeply into her eyes. Everything around Sara went into slow motion and then telescoped down to the two of them, no one and nothing else.

And for several seconds, time stood still.

He reached out and gently touched her arm. "Are you okay?" he asked with a look of concern.

Sara's face burned. "I'm fine, thanks."

She left as quickly as she dared, found a quiet corner, and

hunched down in her seat. Reagan was a somewhat recognizable figure in Miami, and the last thing Sara needed was to call attention to herself. Her mind wandered back to the man she'd bumped into. He sure was handsome, but much too old for Sara. *What am I thinking? I'm about to embark on a new adventure. I don't have time for romance.*

A couple of times, Sara felt like someone was watching her, but figured she had an overactive imagination. Finally, her flight was called. She walked across the tarmac and boarded the staircase of the small, twin engine aircraft. Landon and Kelsea had been to St. Jardin multiple times and said they always flew into the island's airport on regular jets, but Sara didn't have the luxury of time, and took the first flight she could get.

It looked like the plane had about thirty seats. Sara was in the last row on the left, across from the handsome man and a little red-haired boy. That must be his son. She didn't recall seeing him when she bumped into the man, but then again, she was focused only on his dark good looks, his kind, sparkling eyes, and his gentle touch on her arm. Sara's face burned with embarrassment. She averted her gaze and slid into the window seat and buckled in.

The flight attendant came through the cabin to make one final check before takeoff. "This seat is empty," she said, tapping the seat next to Sara. That was fine with her. She was tired and planned to sleep for the ninety-minute flight, so she was happy that she would have the armrest to herself.

Sara watched Miami disappear as the plane climbed higher in the sky. Within seconds, they were completely over the water. She continued staring out at the ocean until she felt a movement next to her. It was the little boy from across the aisle.

"Hi! I'm Danny," he said with a gap-toothed grin.

"Hi, I'm—" Sara paused. "I'm Sara." It wouldn't matter which name she shared with a little boy.

"Wanna see my Legos?" He pulled out a little carrying case especially made for them from of his backpack.

Sara looked past him and met those warm brown eyes and engaging smile. "Is it okay?" he called over. "If he's bothering you, please tell me."

There was no wedding ring on his left hand.

Sara took a breath. "He's fine," she said with an answering smile.

"Send him back when you're tired of him," the man said. Sara was happy to give Danny's dad a break.

Sara smiled and helped Danny fasten his seat belt. Over the next half hour, he was so engaging that Sara forgot she was tired. He told her all about his Legos and then moved on to talk about his other favorite toys, his friends at daycare, his neighbor's dog, Dexter, and how excited he was to start kindergarten soon. He was just adorable and seemed to have the attention span of a gnat. He reminded Sara a little of her niece, Shelbie.

They played a little card game and then he pulled out a coloring book and some markers, and invited Sara to color a picture with him. When they finished, Danny put everything away and pulled out an iPad, slapped the headphones on, and started to watch a cartoon. The flight attendant brought sparkling water for Sara and apple juice for Danny.

As soon as the plane began its descent, Danny's dad motioned to him to come back over, and Sara helped him pack up his things. "I enjoyed meeting you, Danny."

"Bye, Miss Sara. Thank you for playing with me."

For a moment, Sara wondered if Danny's dad used him as a way to meet women, and half expected Danny to ask for her e-mail or phone number. But he simply darted back to his seat and let his dad fasten his seat belt.

"Thanks, Miss Sara," the man echoed. He really did have the most beautiful smile, but it appeared this was a chance encounter, nothing more.

Sara stared out the window as they got closer and closer to the ground—at least she hoped the pilots could see some land, because they were still over complete darkness, which she assumed was water. Before she knew it, they were racing down the runway, and slowed to a stop.

Now, her real work would begin. Sara rehearsed her speech to Reagan and hoped her sister wouldn't be angry with her for following her to St. Jardin. Maybe she would let Sara sleep in her room at the resort so Sara wouldn't have to spend money on a hotel room.

*You've got this. You're an adult. And by this time tomorrow, you'll turn the page on a brand new chapter.*

# 14

**SHANE**

SHANE COLLECTED HIS and Danny's luggage off the carousel and got in line at the rental car counter. St. Jardin's airport was small, and it was only a few steps from one area to the other. "Stay right with me, buddy," he said to Danny, who was singing to himself and looking around.

Shane saw "Miss Sara" still standing near the carousel, and couldn't stop thinking about her. When the beautiful little brunette collided with him in the airport, he was fairly certain he recognized the *Herald* reporter, Reagan St. Clair. Shane had never met her in person, but he had a general sense of what she looked like and had seen her a couple of times from afar at crowded events. When you saw that dark braid, plaid shirt, and Birkenstocks, there was no mistaking who it was.

So many thoughts had collided in Shane's mind during those few seconds. First, how lovely she was, how beautiful her sparkling brown eyes were, and that up close, she was much younger than he expected. Then, he immediately wondered if she had arranged their "chance" meeting to get close to Danny, but then he answered his own question in the next breath—a top-tier

449

investigative reporter like Reagan St. Clair would never be chasing a story about Blayze, no matter how compelling, and she couldn't have gotten through to the secure area without a boarding pass, anyway. There were no photographers around her, and if he'd suspected in the very least that she was up to something, he'd have whisked his nephew out of there in a heartbeat. On the plane, she was sweet as could be, and Shane didn't have any qualms about Danny sitting with her.

In all his years ministering to the people on the streets of Miami, Shane had met people from all walks and stations of life, from the downtrodden and broken to some of South Florida's most successful and famous athletes, politicians, and business moguls who came to volunteer at his church and associated ministries—some of them for a photo op and some out of a sincere wish to give back. Shane had the spiritual gift of discernment, and had good instincts concerning people. Still, he couldn't figure Reagan out.

Why was she calling herself *Sara*? Something wasn't adding up, even how sweet she seemed to be. Reagan St. Clair had the reputation for being a real no-nonsense scrapper. Maybe she was on a big story and was playing a part. And maybe when he got back to Miami he'd look her up and find out what this business was all about. *Just to make contact as an interested member of the community,* he told himself.

He watched Reagan wrestle a large suitcase off the carousel, roll it back a few feet, and then pull it behind her. She must be waiting for more of her luggage. Shane's heart tripped. *Hey, we could offer her a lift.* Just then, a tall, muscular man in jeans and a black t-shirt stepped next to her, put his arm around her shoulder, and leaned in close to talk to her.

So, she'd come to St. Jardin to meet a man. Shane felt a surprising spear of disappointment. *She's too young for you, anyway.*

"May I help you, sir?" The young woman at the rental car

counter was speaking to him. Shane handed over the required documents and glanced down at his nephew.

*Where was Danny?* Shane's heart began a crazy dance. He whirled around and saw Danny crouched down behind Reagan's large suitcase, as if he were hiding. "Danny!" he called. The little boy looked up and skipped back over to his uncle. Reagan and the man hadn't even known he was there.

Shane squatted down and hugged Danny as his heart returned to its regular rhythm. "You have to stay right by me," he said. "Don't do that again."

Danny hung his head. "I was gonna hide and then say *surprise* to Miss Sara. And say goodbye to her again."

*Poor little fellow. He's had enough loss lately. It won't hurt to take a moment to tell her goodbye.* Shane signed the rental agreement and took the car keys. "Okay, now we can—" he turned and looked at where Reagan had been standing, but she and the man were gone. A whole new wave of travelers flooded the baggage claim area. Well, that was that. "Come on, buddy, we're going to go see Daddy now."

"Oh goody! Yay, yay, yay!" Danny cheered, skipping ahead of Shane. It appeared that he was able to forget about "Miss Sara" very quickly.

It was too bad that Shane couldn't do the same.

## 15

**SARA**

SARA LET OUT a breath. She was home free. After arriving in St. Jardin, she filled out the paper immigration and custom form and cleared immigration. She didn't have anything to declare, and now she was waiting for her second suitcase to appear on the carousel when she heard a man's voice next to her. "Welcome to St. Jardin, Ms. St. Clair," he said softly.

*Why did someone here know her name? Did he mean Reagan?* Sara swallowed and glanced up at the man. His expression didn't look welcoming at all. Her heart began to pound. *How would he know that Reagan was coming here?* Sara was confused. No one at all should have known that either she *or* Reagan were coming here.

Suddenly, she felt the man's arm come around her, and something hard pressed into her side. Icy fear snaked through her veins. "Give me your phone," he whispered, and Sara handed it over. An announcement came over the PA, and he spoke a little louder into her ear. "You'll be coming with me. Mr. Rogers can't wait to see you."

452

Sara's heart began to beat wildly. *What was going on?* "Who is Mr. Rogers?" she asked sharply, and winced as the discomfort in her side turned to pain. Tears sprang to her eyes.

"Which suitcase is yours?" the man hissed into her ear.

"Th-th-the blue one," she stammered, gesturing to the carousel.

"We'll get it together," he said. He lowered his voice. "My associates are stationed at every door, so don't try anything." His tone convinced Sara that he meant business. Her gaze darted to two doors that she could see, and a non-descript, muscular man stood at each. *Dear heaven, what is going on with my sister?*

Sara wondered if Danny and his dad were still around. Maybe she could signal to them somehow. She looked around as dozens of people spilled into the baggage claim area. At least one other flight must have just arrived.

"Don't even think about it," the man said in a clipped voice, and Sara's fleeting hope evaporated. The man grabbed one suitcase and motioned to Sara to get the other. He latched on to her arm in a vise grip and propelled her out a door, where a black SUV was waiting. "Let's go."

*Lord, help me.*

# 16

**DANE**

DANE HURRIED REAGAN through dinner so they could go for a quick walk on the beach. He was anxious to grill her in private about her interview with Phil Diamond.

"The seaweed wrap was amazing," she gushed as they exited the main building and headed for the beach. "I'm definitely finding a place in Miami to do that again when I get home." Dane resisted the urge to roll his eyes. Reagan hadn't stopped talking about the spa day since she finished up, just a few moments before meeting him for dinner.

He took her hand to hurry her along and looked around to ensure that they were alone. "Reagan, I need to talk with you before Shane and Danny get here. I made some progress on the case." He quickly caught her up. "I asked one of my CIs for something more on Navarro, and he told me to look into Phil Diamond."

Reagan frowned. "From Diamond Pharmaceuticals? I just interviewed him."

Dane nodded. "I know. I read the article."

"Diamond's legit. Why would he and Navarro be connected?"

454

Reagan removed an elastic hair tie from her wrist and caught her blond hair up in a ponytail as the wind whipped it around her.

"I don't know, but it's definitely interesting. Here's one scenario: what if Navarro is trying to get his hands on some of the anti-cancer drugs from Cuba to conduct illegal trials in the US? That would totally be his MO and explain why he's working with a group of businessmen. Conduct the trials, find out which drug or drugs has the best results, and then buy it cheap before it goes on the market, and make a killing. Or better yet, send a group of mercenaries into Cuba to take over the lab where it's manufactured."

Reagan stopped walking. "But how is the governor connected?'

Dane's head was beginning to pound. He still refused to believe that a man he'd known and admired his whole life could be involved with this. He felt his phone vibrate, and picked up.

"We're just leaving the airport," Shane said. "What room are you in?" Dane gave him the address to his "hotel," but couldn't bring himself to reveal that it was a honeymoon resort.

"Two-twelve," Dane said. "Shane—I need to explain, I'm here undercover—"

"No time," his brother interrupted. "My phone's almost dead. See you soon." He disconnected.

Dane let out a huge sigh. No telling what Shane's reaction would be. He turned back toward the resort and pulled Reagan with him. "They're on their way in from the airport. I need to make sure I put everything away." He'd come back to the lobby to meet Shane and Danny. That way he could explain Reagan to Shane before they met.

When they got back to the room, Reagan disappeared into the bathroom and a few minutes later, he heard the shower running. *What was she doing?*

Dane finished putting his notes away, then walked over to the closed door. "Reagan, why are you in the shower? They'll be here soon. I'm going down to the lobby to wait for them."

"Hold on! I'll be right there. I want to go with you. I have to let the conditioner set for another two minutes."

Dane buried his head in his hands and groaned. Since when had Reagan become so—so *fussy* about all these girl things? He bet that she'd never used conditioner once in her life before this week. He walked out onto the balcony and stared out over the ocean. Then he came back in, walked to the fridge, took out a bottle of water, and gulped half of it down. "Reagan, I'm going downstairs," he said.

A knock came at the door, and Dane groaned again. *That can't be them. Either they were halfway here when Shane called, or they made good time.* He set his water bottle down. As soon as he put his hand on the knob, the bathroom door opened, and out walked Reagan in a short terry-cloth robe, her head wrapped in a towel.

"Oh good, maybe they're here."

*And you're half dressed.* Dane thought. This wasn't going to go well. Because Shane was a pastor, he took pains to avoid any situation that could be misinterpreted. And if there was *any* situation that fit the bill, this was it. Dane turned the knob and sent a quick, desperate prayer heavenward. He hadn't really talked to God in a while, but the urge to do so came instinctively.

As soon as he opened the door, Danny let out a squeal and Dane squatted down. "Daddy!" Danny launched himself into Dane's arms

Dane closed his eyes and wrapped his arms around his little son, breathing in his unique little-boy essence. He rose to his feet, bringing Danny up with him. "Uh, hi," he said to his brother, who was staring at Reagan, who was staring at Dane.

Dane could see the wheels spinning in his brother's head as he took in the room, the bed, Reagan, and the wedding band on Dane's left hand that rested on Danny's head.

"You're married? *Since yesterday?*" Shane asked, his expression incredulous.

"Ah—no. Shane, this is Reagan St. Clair." He figured his

brother, being from Miami, would at least know who she was, and might be impressed to meet a local quasi-celebrity.

"Reagan St. Clair?!" Shane exclaimed. He put his hands on his hips. "Dane, whoever this is, she's an impostor!"

"An imposter?" Dane and Reagan exclaimed in unison.

Reagan glared at Shane. "You have no idea what you're talking about!"

"Well, I'm from Miami, and I know what Reagan St. Clair looks like. And she was on my flight—our flight," he said, with a nod toward Danny. "But she was calling herself Sara. Trying to be incognito, I guess."

"I liked Miss Sara," Danny said. "She played games with me and we colored a picture."

Dane set his son down and quickly moved to Reagan, who looked like she might faint. Her face had gone white. "Dane," she said, reaching for him. He grasped her around the waist and guided her to the loveseat.

"We'll figure it out," he said softly. Dane put his hand on Reagan's shoulder and looked at his brother. "This really is Reagan St. Clair. She's been working a case with me, and we had to go underground, which is why we're here."

Shane glowered at Reagan. "Do you know how old he is?" he shoved his thumb at Dane.

"You've got to be kidding!" Reagan shouted. "We're *not* married!"

"Great, so he's just your boy toy?" Shane said with a look of disgust.

Reagan glared at him. "You are *so* out of line! This is none of your business—"

A whistle cut the air. Dane cocked his head at Danny, who was looking out the sliding-glass door through his cupped hands, oblivious to the adults' conversation. "We'll talk about this later." He tried to put his thoughts in order. "Shane, tell me about the woman on the plane. It's important," he implored.

Shane ran a hand through his dark hair. "She looked like Reagan St. Clair, she had a long, dark brown braid, and wore a baseball cap, jeans, a plaid shirt, and sandals." He looked at Reagan. "I've seen you a couple of times on local TV and once at a Dolphins game, but I've never met you." His eyes narrowed. "Now that I look at you, I'm sure she was quite a bit younger."

"Yeah, I get that part. I left my AARP card at home," Reagan snapped. She looked at Dane. "Sara must have been wearing a wig." She removed the towel from her head. Her damp blond hair tumbled past her shoulders.

"Reagan is in disguise," Dane explained. "She dyed her hair blond and we brought her here under her sister, Sara's, passport, without her knowledge."

Shane frowned. "Is that even legal?"

Dane continued. "Reagan's—our attorney arranged it. Sara is a blonde—and yes, she's quite a bit younger than Reagan."

"Does Sara live in Miami?" Shane asked.

"No, she's from up north," Dane said.

Shane looked at Reagan. "Why would she disguise herself as you and come to St. Jardin?"

Reagan put her head in her hands and then looked up at Dane. "She must have found out that I had her passport," she said. "Brandon probably blabbed." Then her eyes widened. "She knows my door code. I bet she went to my apartment, got my passport, disguised herself, and flew here as me. But *why?* We need to get a hold of Landon."

"Wait," Dane said. He looked at Shane. "Did you see Sara leave the airport? Did she say where she was going? Did you see her get a taxi, or rent a car?"

Shane's eyes grew wide. "She—oh, wow. No, she didn't tell us why she was coming here. I didn't really talk with her. The seat next to hers was empty, and Danny sat there for most of the flight." He looked at Reagan apologetically. "I was going to offer her a ride, but she left the St. Jardin airport with a man. Who's Brandon? Who's Landon?"

"A man?" Reagan exclaimed. She jumped to her feet. "She doesn't know anybody here! Dane, what are we going to do?"

Dane felt a tug on his pant leg. "Daddy, I'm hungry."

Dane squatted down so he was eye-to-eye with his son. "Oh, buddy, I'm sorry," he said. He looked at Reagan. "We don't have anything to eat here, do we?" She shook her head.

Reagan started pulling clothes out of a drawer. "I'm going to look for her."

Dane quickly stood and went to her. "You'll be playing into their hands," he said. He held her arms. "Reagan, you have to stay here. Let me handle this." They stared at one another for a few charged seconds, and then she deflated like a balloon.

"All right."

Dane grabbed his burner phone and took Danny by the hand. He spoke rapidly to the two adults. "I'm almost out of international minutes on this. I underestimated how many I'd need. I'm going to the front desk to use their phone to call Landon collect. I'll find Rose and Ike and ask them to get Danny some food." He hoped his unspoken message conveyed that he would trust no one else with his son. He turned to Shane. "I need you to text me a description of the guy that Sara left with, and any other details that you can remember from the moment you met her—anything she said, anything she did."

Dane thought of something else. "You're sure you and Danny weren't followed?"

Shane looked at him evenly. "I told you, I have resources, too."

*Of course he did.* But Dane didn't need to know the particulars. Finding Sara St. Clair was his priority now. He took a breath. "Reagan, promise me you'll stay here, for now. Don't even leave the room until I can figure some things out. He moved close to her. "*And get dressed,*" he hissed.

Reagan crossed her arms in front of her. "Is *he* going with you?" She glared at Shane.

"No, he's going to stay here to make sure you do." He looked at Shane, who looked as unhappy about the situation as Reagan did. "Try not to kill each other before I get back."

# 17

## REAGAN

AS SOON AS the door closed behind Dane and Danny, Reagan made sure it was locked. Then she grabbed her clothes and marched into the bathroom without a word to the man standing in the middle of the room.

The nerve of him! Looking down his nose at her and jumping to all kinds of conclusions about her and Dane. Reagan's blood boiled as she tugged the brush through her damp hair. She laughed mirthlessly to her reflection in the mirror. He was a pastor! *That figures.* Reagan had met more holier-than-thou types than she could count, and had no use for them.

Reagan quickly dressed and spent the next ten minutes applying her makeup. She was starting to like how it made her feel, although she wished she knew how to do things with it so that she would look prettier and younger. Not that she cared one whit about Shane Corsica's insulting comment about her age.

When Reagan came back to the room, he was standing by the sliding glass door that he must have opened, staring out at the darkness. The pleasant tropical breeze drifted into the room.

461

"Just for the record, I don't have any designs on your brother," she said crisply. "I've known him for four years. We work together sometimes and he's a friend, end of story."

Shane shoved his hands in his pockets. "I overreacted, and I'm sorry," he said. "My little brother is all grown up, but you can tell I'm pretty protective of him." His brown eyes, so much like Dane's, held genuine contrition.

Reagan sat down in one of the chairs. "You asked who Landon and Brandon are. They're my brothers."

Shane's eyes grew wide, and he threw back his head and laughed. "Oh, no! That's unbelievable. I've never met any other brothers with rhyming names. I thought my parents were the only ones with a sense of humor."

*He sure is handsome when he smiles.* Reagan couldn't help smiling herself.

Shane sat down in the other chair. "So, there are four of you?"

"Yes, I'm the oldest, then Landon and Brandon. The three of us were born within four years. And then Sara was my parents' surprise, when we were in our teens. Do you and Dane have other siblings?" She couldn't recall him ever speaking of anyone other than an older brother.

"No, I'm eleven years older than Dane. My mom had three miscarriages between us."

"That's too bad," Reagan replied. Suddenly, she felt uncomfortable, and jumped up. "Would you like some water?" she said as she walked over to the fridge.

"Sure, thanks." She handled him a bottle and uncapped hers and drank deeply. "I wish Dane would get back. I can't imagine who my sister is out there with." She began to pace. "It should be me. They probably thought it *was* me."

"Well, you know Dane's one of the best minds out there. He'll figure this out," Shane said with confidence.

Reagan stopped mid-pace. "I have to look for her. I can't just sit here. Dane's *not* going to keep me on the sidelines," spat angrily. She turned abruptly, went to the desk, and began to gather the things she'd need. Suddenly, she felt a gentle touch on her arm.

"Hey," Shane said softly. Reagan stiffened, ready to do battle with him like she always did with Dane. But when she looked up, she didn't see challenge in his eyes. She only saw compassion.

"I can't imagine what I'd feel like if my brother was out there, helpless." He gave her a small smile and one eyebrow lifted. "Except that Dane wouldn't be helpless, because, you know, he's Dane." Shane looked at her apologetically. "I'm not doing a very good job at this." He seemed to study her more deeply. "You strike me as someone who thinks logically and has a great capacity to solve problems with just the right combination of thinking strategically and trusting your instincts."

Because of hers and Dane's disagreement earlier in the day, Reagan said the first thing that came to mind. "You don't think trusting your instincts is a bad thing?"

Shane shook his head. "No. In many cases, I think it's God-given. I think it can lead you to right conclusions. But if your emotions are deeply involved, they can compromise logical thinking and hijack the ability to interpret your gut instincts clearly."

Reagan couldn't believe how plainly he made his point without coming across as judgmental. "And I'm too emotionally involved in this," she murmured.

He nodded and gave her a gentle smile.

The frustration in her body dissipated, but was replaced by raw fear. "I just—if anything happens to her—" Reagan didn't cry often, and couldn't help the tears that came spilling out. "It's my fault. It's all my fault." She felt Shane's arms come around her. There was nothing inappropriate about his embrace. It was just one human being offering another solace, and Reagan felt immensely comforted.

"Shh," he whispered, and rubbed circles on her back. Then he began to pray in a conversational, soothing way. He prayed for God's protection over Sara and for Dane to have wisdom about what steps to take to find her. He prayed for Reagan to trust Dane's professional training and for her heart to be comforted so that she could be empowered to help bring about her sister's rescue.

When he whispered *Amen*, Reagan actually felt the burden lift from her shoulders. She'd never experienced anything like it. Shane took a step back and Reagan looked into his deep brown eyes. For a long moment, neither of them spoke. Finally, Reagan swallowed. "Thank you, Shane," she said.

"You're welcome."

Reagan excused herself to get a tissue. When she came back into the room, Shane had sat again.

Reagan was fascinated by him. "So, you're a pastor?"

He turned and looked at her. "Yeah. Yeah, I am."

"What church do you work for?"

Shane didn't say anything for several seconds. He leaned forward, elbows on his knees. "I run the Miracle Center."

*The Miracle Center?* Reagan plopped down into the chair. She couldn't believe it. The Miracle Center wasn't just a church. It was a gigantic organization that provided all kinds of services to the needy in Miami: transition housing for the homeless and recent parolees from prison, plus a prison ministry. A meal program that fed thousands. A rehab center. Job training and placement. A huge clothing and food distribution warehouse along with a department store that rivaled Walmart and Target. Free medical and dental services. After-school and tutoring programs for children and teens. A fleet of coffee shops. A sports program for teens. The list went on and on. Reagan had heard recently that they were making plans to open a small hospital. The Miracle Center had made a real difference in thousands of lives. It was legendary in Miami, and other cities had tried to replicate it, but only with marginal success. Miami's flagship organization outshone them all. It wasn't a church, but a ministry, and it had a mega-church with thousands of members at its center.

Reagan knew that one man had started the Miracle Center

more than a dozen years ago and was at the helm of it all, but didn't know anything about him. And it would seem that he was sitting right here a few feet away from her.

"Wow—you're—" she couldn't even speak.

Shane grinned again. *That smile.* "Yep, that's me." He finished his water and tossed the empty bottle toward the trash can. It landed perfectly in the center.

"Do you really—do you really sleep only two or three hours a night, every night?" Reagan remembered reading that once.

Shane laughed. "Yes, that's true."

Reagan's face burned. *Of all the things to think of to ask him!* "I'm sorry, that was a silly thing to say." She giggled. *What is wrong with me? I never giggle.*

"If you'd like a tour sometime, I'd be happy to do that," he said.

*I really shouldn't.* "I'd like that," she heard herself say.

# 18

**DANE**

DANE PUT HIS key card in the door and braced himself. He had no idea what he would find in the room. Shane, tied to a chair perhaps, with a washcloth stuffed in his mouth? But they were just sitting there, talking. Knowing Shane, he had probably kept Reagan busy to take her mind off Sara.

Reagan shot out of her chair. "What did you find out?" Dane noticed that her eyes were a little red.

"Not much. Sara got a phone call yesterday from Disney, an invitation to tour with them this summer. She told the family that they were flying her to Orlando today to begin rehearsals. She left this morning."

"That's right," Reagan said. "She was going to do that last year but went to help Brandon with our nieces instead."

"She didn't say anything about going to Miami first. Landon didn't know anything about it." Dane reached for his laptop and opened it. "I'm going to see if I can trace her flight plan." He tapped on some keys and then grunted. "Yeah, she flew to Miami under her own name, and then she flew here using your passport, Reagan." He tapped some more keys and frowned. "She's booked from St. Jardin to Orlando tomorrow morning under her own

466

name, so she must have been planning to come here to get her passport back. She must need it for the Disney gig."

Shane frowned. "You mean anyone can look up someone else's travel plans in a few seconds?"

Dane cocked an eyebrow at his brother. "I can."

"Oh," Shane responded. He drew the lone syllable out. "Where's Danny, by the way?"

"With the resort owners. I told them I would explain everything later. They were happy to spoil him and get him some food."

Shane stood and smiled. "Do you think they could spoil me and get me some food? Or does this place have a restaurant? I didn't get dinner, either."

"Oh, Shane, I'm sorry. Yes, I'm sure they could." Dane asked him to bring Danny back when they were both finished eating.

He locked the door behind his brother and turned to face Reagan. "I'm going out. I've got to get the airport security tapes so I can see who Sara left with. I know you want to be out there looking for your sister, but—"

"I'm fine staying here, for now. I know you'll put me to work when you're ready."

*Who is this woman, and what has she done with Reagan?* Dane sputtered, trying to think of something to say. He couldn't read Reagan's expression. It was some kind of cross between confidence and contentment.

"Go on. Get moving, Corsica," she said, giving him a push. He didn't have time to figure this out now. He grabbed jeans and a different shirt and headed for the bathroom to change. "Hey, wait a minute," Reagan said as he passed by her. "How are you going to get the tapes? You don't have any official jurisdiction here."

Dane grinned. "Remember? Someone told us to call on her if we needed *anything* while we're in St. Jardin. I'm going to see Louie at the Bahama Llama Boogie Shack, and find Moni."

# 19

## SARA

*I'VE NEVER BEEN so scared in my life.* Two men were in the front, and the big man who escorted Sara got into the back seat with her. As soon as the doors of the black SUV closed, it roared away from the curb. Her stomach roiled. "Buckle up," he ordered. Sara put on her seat belt with shaking hands.

The man leaned over into her personal space, and her heart began to pound. He slipped a blindfold over her eyes and secured it. Sara held her breath. To her relief, the baseball cap held her wig securely in place.

"If you behave yourself, I won't need to use these," the man growled. Sara heard a clinking sound that might have been handcuffs.

As they drove, Sara tried to put her thoughts in order. *I'm on my own in a foreign country. No one knows I'm here. Do they even have an embassy here?* She swallowed back tears. She would do anything right now to just be *Peanut* and have her family hovering over her.

*Think, Sara. You're the only one who can help yourself out of this mess.* She tried to remember specific things about the man who had approached her in the airport. He was tall and big, muscular, with dark hair, and dark skin or a tan. Was he Jardinian? Sara had no idea what a St. Jardin islander would look like. She wasn't even sure how he was dressed. It had all happened so fast.

Sara felt so disoriented with the blindfold. She tried to listen for external noises that could give her a clue to where they might be going, but the vehicle was well-insulated and all she could hear was muffled sounds.

It felt like they were on a twisting road. Their speed varied greatly and Sara had no idea how far they'd gone. Finally, they made a left turn and about fifteen seconds after that, a right, but that didn't mean anything to Sara, either. She was disoriented and didn't know if they'd traveled for a half hour or ten minutes.

The car made another left turn and slowed to a stop. After about ten seconds, Sara thought she heard some kind of electronic gate opening, and the vehicle began to move again, but very slowly. They traveled for at least another minute, by Sara's estimation. Were they on a small road, or a driveway?

The car came to a stop, and she felt the man lean into her space. His breath was warm on her cheek, and she held her breath. "We're here. Just so you know, we're completely isolated. If you try to scream or make a ruckus, there's no one around to hear you." Sara shivered as she felt him come closer. "And if you misbehave, I have a gag and handcuffs that I can use. You understand?" Sara nodded. She heard his door open and close. A few seconds later, her door opened and the man grabbed her arm and pulled her from the vehicle.

"Come on, walk with me," he ordered. It felt like they were on concrete. The first thing Sara heard was the ocean. The breeze was saturated and she could smell the salt in the air. Beyond that, she couldn't distinguish anything.

She thought they walked around the front of the vehicle. Then, she heard a door open. "Step up," the man said from in front of her. She followed him through the door and then he turned right.

They might be in a hallway now. She strained to hear any sounds, but it was perfectly silent. After several seconds, the floor changed to carpet. They made two left turns, a right, another left, and then the man stopped.

"We're going into an elevator," he said quietly. The doors closed behind them with a soft *whoosh* and she could feel them ascending. Sara could tell that they were in a well-appointed car as opposed to a freight elevator. For some reason, that gave her comfort.

The doors opened quickly, and that told Sara that they weren't in a high-rise building. Would there even be skyscrapers on the island? It was still deathly quiet, and smelled like new paint. She followed the man down a thickly carpeted hallway, and then he stopped and she heard a door unlock. He guided Sara into the room and she heard the door close and lock. The man told her to sit. It felt like she was in a soft, luxurious upholstered chair. She heard the man moving around the room, and then he returned to her and removed the blindfold.

Sara blinked as her eyes adjusted to the soft light. She was shocked to realize that they were in what looked to be an opulent hotel room. The sight of the lavishly decorated king-sized bed filled her with panic, and her heart began hammering. The man pulled up a smaller chair and sat close to her, their knees almost touching. She memorized as much about him as she could: his battered tennis shoes, jeans, his plain black t-shirt. His black hair, glittering dark eyes and beard, the earrings in both ears. She could tell he had a lot of tattoos, but couldn't discern any detail.

"You'll stay here until Mr. Rogers arrives later tonight, Ms. St. Clair," he said. His English was heavily accented, but understandable. "He wants you to be comfortable, but you won't be permitted to contact anyone." He stared her down. "If you decide to cause any trouble, you'll face the consequences." He tipped his head at handcuffs, blindfold, and a gag that were laying on the table next to them.

Sara almost opened her mouth to ask who *Mr. Rogers* was again, and then it occurred to her that if they thought she was Reagan, that maybe Reagan was supposed to know him. No doubt it would be to her advantage for them to keep thinking that she was her sister. If Reagan were here, she wouldn't be scared out of her wits. *What would Reagan do and say?*

"I look forward to meeting with him," Sara said evenly. She kept her gaze steady on the man. Her mouth was so dry. "Could I get some water, please?"

The man got up, went over to a kitchenette, and opened a small fridge. When he came back, he held the bottle out, and then Sara saw a pistol in his other hand. "Just in case you thought of throwing the water in my face or something," he said. He tipped his head toward the door. "There are two more men outside the door, and they're armed, too," he said.

Sara sighed inwardly and uncapped the bottle. It appeared she was going to have to see this through.

"May I have my suitcases?" she asked. She already knew what the answer would probably be.

The man didn't blink, didn't move a muscle. "No."

Sara desperately hoped that the man or his associates wouldn't go through her luggage, although she held out little hope. Her driver's license and credit card bearing her real identity were tucked away in a pocket, and she knew they'd be found.

And if these people discovered who she really was, what would happen?

**20**

**DANE**

DANE CALLED FOR a taxi from his burner phone and told them to pick him up at the entrance to the resort, out on the main road. He didn't want the Goldmans or anyone else to see him leaving.

Fortunately, the taxi looked reliable and the driver looked older than sixteen. "Bahama Llama Boogie Shack," he said as he climbed in.

The man grinned. "You play poker with Louie?"

"Ah, no," Dane replied.

When the taxi pulled up to the restaurant, Dane looked at the building and thought there must be some mistake. But the neon sign and the life-sized llama statue bedecked in tropical flowers assured him he was at the right place. He went through the door and looked around the colorful two-story structure. He pegged Louie right away. He was the biggest, most exuberant guy there, clearly in charge.

"Welcome, amigo!" he exclaimed as he walked behind the bar. "What can I get for you?"

"Nothing right now, thanks," Dane said. "Are you Louie?"

The man grinned. "I sure am. And I know I can find something for you to drink that you will like!"

Dane smiled back. "Well, maybe later. I'm in a bit of a hurry right now. I'm actually looking for your niece, Moni. She told me—"

"Ah! You are her American friend! She told me all about you! Moni!" he shouted toward the back. The saloon doors opened and Moni swept out.

Her already happy face lit up. "Oh, sir, hello! So good to see you again!" She grabbed both of Dane's hands with hers. "You did meet Uncle Louie?"

"Yes, I did." Dane smiled at Louie. He touched Moni on the arm and lowered his voice. "You said to find you if I needed anything while I was here. Can we talk in private?"

"Of course, sir!" she replied in a stage whisper. She wiped her hands on a towel and set it down. "Come outside in back."

Dane followed her through the bar, down a hallway, and out the back door. As soon as the door closed, they found themselves in the quiet, tropical night air. "What can I do for you, sir?"

Dane smiled. "First of all, Moni, just call me Trey." Better to use his alias.

"Okay, sir Trey!"

*That was even worse.* "I need your help." Moni nodded enthusiastically. "I need to find someone, an American. It's very important. She left the airport a little while ago with a man, out one of the doors from the baggage claim area." Dane swallowed and lowered his voice. "I need to see the security tapes at the airport. Do you understand what I'm asking, Moni?"

"You want to steal the tapes?"

Dane closed his eyes. "No, no, not steal them. I just need to borrow them. Could you or Uncle Louie take me to see someone at the airport? Do either of you know anyone who works there who I could talk to?"

"Yes! I will make phone call! You wait here!" Before Dane knew what had hit him, she had slipped back inside the bar.

*Oh Lord, what am I doing?* Dane looked up and dragged his hands over his face. Then he began to pace.

A few minutes later, he heard a chugging noise coming from his left, and here came Moni and Sadie-belle. "Let's go, sir Trey!" Moni exclaimed. Dane got in and they took off in a cloud of exhaust. "I will take you to airport! We're going to see my brother, Gustav!" Dane decided not to ask how someone in Moni's Jardinian family ended up with the name *Gustav.*

It was a quick trip to the airport, and Moni chattered happily all the way. Dane's mind was on a hundred other details, and he had a hard time keeping up with her. As soon as they pulled up to the curb at the arrivals area, a tall youth with shoulder-length dark blond hair and gray eyes slid into the back seat, and Moni took off.

"This is Gustav!" she said. Dane and Gustav nodded to one another. Dane thought he might be a little older than Moni, but he sure didn't see any family resemblance.

"You have a phone?" Gustav asked Dane, and Dane nodded. Gustav passed a device a little bigger than a phone to Dane. "Here is tapes from baggage claim for last two hours. If you find what you are looking for, you can transfer it to your phone. Then I have to take this back."

"We will ride around while you look!" Moni said.

"That's great, thanks," Dane said, and began surveying the tapes. With the information Shane had given him, it was easy to pinpoint the time frame. His heart went into overdrive as he saw Reagan—make that *Sara*—on the screen. Her disguise was unbelievably accurate. He saw her get her first suitcase off the carousel, and the man quickly joined her. Then Dane saw his little son come and crouch behind the suitcase for about twenty seconds, then he rejoined his Uncle Shane at the rental car counter. Soon, they left and more people began pouring into the area. The man and Sara got her other suitcase, and then, Dane lost them in the crowd.

After about fifteen seconds, he spied them again, and the man was holding tightly to Sara's arm and guiding her along. It looked like she was searching for someone—probably Shane and Danny. Unfortunately, the man seemed to know where all the security cameras were, and kept his face averted. Dane didn't find one good, clear shot of him.

As soon as he and Sara got outside, a black SUV slid up to the curb. In a matter of seconds, they loaded the luggage and Sara in, and were off. Dane looked at the SUV from every angle and was stunned to see that there were no license plates of any kind on it. "What the—" he murmured to himself.

"You find what you looking for?" Gustav said from over his shoulder.

"Yes, and no," Dane said, frustration starting to build. "This vehicle has no license plates." He saw Moni and Gustav exchange a look. "Does that mean anything to you?" Dane tried in vain to locate any other identifying marks on the vehicle. Even the make and model were missing.

"Ah—there is an underground syndicate that operates on the island," Gustav said. "All I know is they have power and the police are in their pocket. It is probably them."

Dane finished uploading the footage to his phone as they approached the airport again, and returned the device to Gustav. Moni stopped at the curb outside the departure area, and Gustav quickly unfolded himself from the back seat. "Thanks, Gustav," Dane said as he leaned out the window to shake his hand.

"You're welcome. Anything for my sister's friend." The young man smiled and waved as he went back into the airport.

Dane shook his head. "That was amazing, Moni," he said. "I'm very fortunate that your brother works in airport security. That was very helpful."

"Oh, Gustav no work in security," she said brightly. "He airport janitor."

# 21

**REAGAN**

REAGAN OPENED THE door to Shane and Danny. "Did you get something to eat?"

"Yes, they took good care of us," Shane replied. "The food was excellent."

"I had grilled cheese!" Danny said happily. "That's my favorite." He sat down on the bed and began bouncing up and down, singing the theme song from a kids' TV show about being a nice neighbor. He was a cute little guy and Reagan wondered if she could get to the point of feeling comfortable around him.

Reagan smiled at Shane. "The food here is outstanding," she said. "I didn't bring my running shoes, and I'm afraid I'll be a whale by the time we get home."

Shane raised an eyebrow. "I don't think you have anything to be worried about," he murmured.

Reagan felt herself blush. She couldn't think of anything to say and thankfully, at that moment, the door opened. It was Dane. He quickly locked it behind him.

"Hey, buddy!" he said, going to Danny and scooping him up. "How was dinner?"

"Good," Danny said, locking his arms around Dane's neck. "I got ice cream for dessert."

"Any luck?" Reagan asked.

"Yes and no," Dane said. He set Danny down on the bed. "Moni's down in the lobby, by the way. Her brother, Gustav, got me the airport surveillance tapes."

Reagan looked at him in confusion. "*Gustav?*"

Dane smiled and shook his head. "Long story for later," he said. "Anyway, we saw—uh, the person we were looking for leave with someone in an unmarked black SUV. No plates or other markings." Reagan glanced at Shane and knew he understood that Dane didn't want to bring up Sara in front of Danny. "I need to get online and check out some things and then see where we go from there." He walked over to the closet and got his equipment out. "Until I have more answers, we don't have anything to go on."

Reagan felt her eyes tearing up. "My sister is out there with— God knows who, and we don't have any way to find her?" Her stomach was tied in knots.

"I'm working on it, Reagan," Dane said.

"Daddy, can I go see Mr. Rogers?" Danny piped up.

The three adults looked at one another. "What do you mean, Danny?" his father asked.

"You know, Mr. Rogers from TV. Miss Sara gets to see him. Can I go, too?"

Dane dropped what he was holding and quickly moved to the bed. He sat and pulled Danny onto his lap. "Tell me about Miss Sara going to see him," he said calmly.

Danny frowned. "Well, I hided behind Miss Sara's big suitcase, and that man came up to her. He told her that Mr. Rogers wanted to see her. I like Mr. Rogers, Daddy. I want to go see him, too."

Reagan's heart began to pound. Danny couldn't know that *Mr. Rogers from TV* had been dead for several years, and the man had to have been talking about another Mr. Rogers.

Reagan knew exactly who it was. And by the look on Dane's face, he knew it, too.

## 22

*LATE WEDNESDAY NIGHT*

**SARA**

SARA WAS SO tired, and scared to the bone. She'd been up early that morning to catch her flight to Miami. She thought about everything she had been through over this long day. There was little chance that she'd make her flight to Orlando tomorrow morning. *There goes my second chance with Disney,* she thought. *And I'll never get a third.*

Would someone raise an alarm if she missed her flight? A sliver of hope needled its way into her heart. What would happen at Disney when she didn't show? Would Lance Petrie call Caitlyn? Just like that, her spirits fell. Probably not. He would be disgusted with Sara for not showing up and probably just dump her audition tape in the trash. And even if he did call them, none of her family knew that Sara had flown to Miami instead of Orlando. They'd think she was missing. Her stomach twisted painfully at the thought of causing them that kind of heartache.

*What am I going to do? I have no way of getting out of here.*

Sara looked around the room for the thousandth time. If she

479

had to be a prisoner, she supposed this was better than any place she'd seen on TV where people were held hostage. By all accounts, this was an outrageously sumptuous hotel that catered to the ultra-rich. The room was decorated in gold and scarlet with its own fireplace. The sitting area was comprised of a large sofa and two elegant chairs. There was a desk at the other end of the room with a desktop computer and a credenza with a printer and some other equipment. The pictures on the walls and other accoutrements were tasteful and sophisticated. One entire wall was covered with gold and scarlet brocade draperies. Sara guessed that windows overlooking the ocean, and probably a balcony, were behind them.

Sara felt entirely out of her element. Her bodyguard sat stoically staring at her and only checked his phone occasionally. He ignored Sara when she asked his name.

She looked over at the glass-topped dining table at the congealed food in the wrapper that he had brought an hour ago. It was some kind of burrito, but Sara had only picked at it. Other than that, she'd only had a few sips of water.

The man's phone beeped, and he answered it. "Yeah?" He sat and listened. "Got it. Okay." He stuck the phone back in his pocket and looked at Sara. "Mr. Rogers can't get here tonight. He'll be here tomorrow."

"What does that mean?" Sara said.

"That means you stay here tonight." He stood and looked around, and his gaze settled on the bed. "You can sleep there. I'll be leaving soon and one of my associates will take my place."

Sara suppressed a shiver. She couldn't imagine being able to fall asleep with a strange man in the room.

As if he could read her thoughts, the man spoke. "It will be a woman."

"Oh." Sara nodded, and a wave of relief washed over her, although she still didn't think she'd be able to sleep.

"You have information that Mr. Rogers needs. Once you've

answered his questions to his satisfaction, well then, he'll decide what to do with you."

Sara didn't like the sound of that. It almost sounded as if once she had imparted this information to Mr. Rogers, if she was no longer needed..." Sara forced herself to leave that train of thought.

It didn't matter anyway. Reagan might know the information Mr. Rogers wanted, but Reagan wasn't here, and Sara had no way of figuring out what it was, or of reaching her sister. What would Mr. Rogers do to her once he figured out that she wasn't Reagan?

Sara felt a tear slip out of one eye, and turned her head. She took a deep breath. *You can't cry. Reagan wouldn't cry.*

# 23

**DANE**

DANE COULDN'T BELIEVE it. Reagan was right. Squeaky clean Florida Governor Rick Rogers was very likely involved—if not running—an operation to smuggle anti-cancer drugs into the US from Cuba in order to conduct illegal trials.

To her credit, she wasn't gloating. She understood the ramifications this would have on their state. She also understood that they still had a lot of work to do to find Sara and secure her safety, which was paramount.

Shane seemed to realize that something was seriously wrong, and had no doubt had guessed who "Mr. Rogers" really was. He moved alongside his brother. "How can I help?" he asked softly.

Dane was setting up his laptop. He glanced at Danny. "Keep him occupied, read to him, get him ready for bed. Reagan and I are going to have to leave soon."

Shane squeezed his shoulder. "I'm on it."

"You two will be safe here. Thanks." Dane jumped online as Reagan pulled up a chair next to his.

"Now what?" she said, her brow furrowed. "We still don't have any leads on where my sister is."

Dane nodded. "I know. But now we know that Rogers is up to his neck in this, and on his way here. So we let *him* lead us to her."

Reagan's eyebrows shot up. "Oh! You're right. That's brilliant. But what'll happen when he gets here? If he thinks she's me and starts asking her questions she can't answer? She might look like me, but she won't be able to hold her own with him."

Dane shook his head as he typed. "It won't get that far. We're going to find him, follow him to where they're holding her, formulate a rescue plan, create some kind of diversion to stall, and do a bait and switch."

"Bait and—? Oh, I get it," Reagan said. Her face lit up. She lowered her voice to a whisper. "Slip me in as Sara, she and I switch clothes, I put on the brunette wig, and I'm me again, and she gets out as herself. Oh my gosh, it might work."

"It *will* work," Dane said emphatically. "Oh, I thought of something else. We don't know for sure if she was wearing a wig under the baseball cap. Do you think she would have dyed her hair?"

Reagan shook her head vigorously. "Absolutely not. Her hair is her pride and joy. I'm sure it's a wig."

Dane felt a measure of relief. "Okay, good. That's one point in our favor." His fingers flew over the keys. "All you'll need to do is get Rogers on tape admitting to his part in the operation."

"On tape?"

"You'll wear a wire."

Reagan frowned. "What if they search me?"

Dane shrugged. "Why would they? They picked 'you' up in the airport. You've been their prisoner since." He leaned in and whispered even more softly. "*Sara* as you wouldn't have had any opportunity to get a tape recorder or anything out of her suitcase." Reagan nodded and he pointed to the screen.

"We need to track his texts and phone calls going back to noon today, from the time Sara landed in Miami—no, from when she hit the streets as you, this afternoon. Somebody had to have been assigned to watch for you. I'm sure they had your building and the *Herald's* office under surveillance. I can't figure out why they didn't take her in Miami. I mean, that would have been so much easier than letting her come here. It doesn't make any sense. And now, he has to come here, too." Dane frowned. "If he's on his way here, he won't fly commercial."

Reagan consulted her notes. "He won't come on one of the state planes," she murmured. "He'll make Navarro fly him here on one of his private jets. Yep, he has three of them. Do you have the call numbers?"

"I will, in about fifteen seconds," Dane said. He looked at Reagan. "Can you handle this? You remember how I showed you to get a data dump off a phone?" Dane went to the closet and dug around until he found what he was looking for.

"Sure. What are you doing?"

"Putting together our posse," he said with a smile. "We're going to need eyes and ears on the ground the minute Rogers hits Jardinian soil. I'm going to see Uncle Louie." He gave Danny a hug and kiss goodnight and headed out the door.

Dane quickly walked to the front lobby. It was time to come clean with Rose and Ike. His son and brother were here at the resort now and the owners had a right to know that. Dane would do his best to keep all the nefarious activity away from here, but nothing was guaranteed.

When he got to the lobby, Moni was sitting by herself, playing on her phone. She hopped up to greet Dane.

"Hello, sir Trey! Do you need some more help?"

"As a matter of fact, I do, Moni. I—ah, I need to talk with your Uncle Louie."

"I will take you to him!"

Dane smiled. "Great. But first, I need a minute with Rose and

Ike." He didn't want to reveal his identity to Moni, yet. "I'll be right back."

He went to the front desk, where a young woman whose nametag said *Haley* greeted him. "May I help you?"

"Yes, I need to see Rose and Ike. It's important," Dane said.

"Sure, they're in their office," Haley said, pointing to a pink door across the lobby with a sign that read *Manager*.

The door was ajar. Dane knocked lightly and peeked in. "Hi, could I come in?"

"Of course!" Rose and Ike both stood to greet him. "How can we help you, Trey?"

Dane closed the door. "Well, I need your help, but first, I need to tell you who I really am." He opened his cred pack that he'd gotten out of the closet. "I'm Special Agent Dane Corsica with the DEA, based in Miami. I'm undercover on a case and needed a place to hide." He swallowed and leveled his most apologetic gaze on the elderly couple. "I didn't mean to deceive you, but it was an urgent matter," he said. "And I can assure you that no one here at the resort has ever been in danger," he added.

Rose and Ike exchanged a glance, and Rose took Dane's hand in both of hers. "And we assume that the young lady with you is not your wife."

Dane felt his face flush. He didn't want to reveal Reagan's identity just yet. "You're correct," he said. "She's a—a colleague, and we're not, you know, together, or anything. We're just here doing our jobs."

Ike patted Dane's arm. "You don't need to explain it to us, Dane," he said. "Or should we still call you Trey?"

"Yes, I think that'd be better until we get this wrapped up," Dane nodded.

"Well, Trey, sometimes these things work out," Rose said pleasantly. "You come to a romantic island like this, and suddenly, the one who's meant for you is at your side."

Dane resisted the urge to squirm. "Well, ah—I just need to get this case solved, and wanted to let you know that Moni is here to take me to her Uncle Louie. I need some local support, and I think he's the one to help me."

Rose and Ike both nodded vigorously. "Oh yes, Louie knows everyone on the island," Rose said.

"The little boy who was here earlier is my son, Danny."

"Oh yes, we know," Rose beamed up at him. "He has your eyes."

"Ah, well, thank you. My brother brought him here. They'll be staying in the room with—Sara, for the time being. I'll be glad to pay any extra charges for them being here, and of course, for their food."

Rose laid her hand on his shoulder. "Oh, don't worry a bit about that, Trey. Just go catch your bad guys!"

"And if we can help in any way, you let us know," Ike added.

# 24

**REAGAN**

*PAY DIRT!* REAGAN plugged in her ear buds and concentrated on the cell phone conversation between Governor Rogers and Doug Navarro that took place only a few hours ago.

*"What happened? How did the St. Clair woman get past your guys?"*

*"I'm sorry, sir, they've been doing 24-hour surveillance for almost a week with absolutely no sign of her. She was already on the plane to St. Jardin before we could confirm the sighting. They just got sloppy."*

*"Sloppy is right. Fire all of them! I expect better from you, Navarro."*

*"I'm sorry, sir. I'll fix it—"*

*"No, you won't. I'm going to St. Jardin to talk to her myself. They got her at the airport, didn't they? You managed not to screw that up?"*

*"Yes, sir. We've got her at a hotel owned by a guy who we've done business with in St. Jardin.*

*"Who's that?"*

487

*"Bobby Olivier."*

*"Bobby O? Great. Another thug for me to run the chance of being seen with."*

*"He's out of the country, sir, so there's no chance of that. His hotel is at the north end of the island, very secluded, and they have a new wing they haven't opened yet. That's where we've stashed her. We can get you in and out of there without being seen."*

*"Well, that's the first thing you've gotten right."*

*"I have a jet standing by to take you to St. Jardin whenever you're ready, sir."*

*"Good. I'll let you know when I can get away. One more thing. Not one hair on her head is to be harmed, you got that?"*

*"Yes, sir."*

*"You make sure you communicate that to your people. Not one hair."*

The call disconnected. Reagan's heart took wing. She knew where her sister was! And it looked like Sara wasn't in any imminent danger. She dialed Dane's burner phone and was relieved when he picked up. "I know where she is," she said in a rush. "It's a secluded hotel on the north end of the island. I'm sending you a text file of a conversation between Rogers and Navarro. And the best thing is—she's safe. They're not going to hurt her. Not unless they discover she's not me."

"That's fantastic," Dane said. "Moni and I are almost to the Boogie Shack. I'm going to talk with Uncle Louie and see what he knows about this hotel, and put together a plan."

"I have a few more things to follow up on," Reagan said. "I wish I could figure out *why* Rogers is involved in this. It still doesn't sync up."

"Okay," Dane said. "Get ready to go. Bring my computer with you." Reagan heard Moni chattering in the background. "Moni will come back for you. Can you be ready in twenty minutes?"

"Yes," Reagan said. "I'll meet her out front. See you soon." Her mind was already leaping ahead. She just knew she could figure out why Rogers was involved. There had to be a compelling reason. All of this was completely out of character for him. It didn't sound like he and Navarro were partners, with Navarro calling him "sir" in every other sentence. The tone of both men's voices established Rogers as being in charge, and Navarro subservient, which had to be a new role for Navarro. Rogers was clearly disgusted at being associated with him.

Reagan closed her eyes and jumped when she felt a soft tap on her shoulder. She removed her ear buds and looked at Shane. "I'm sorry, I didn't mean to scare you," he said. "How's it going?"

"It's okay. Well, I'm making headway." She glanced over at the bed. "Is Danny asleep?"

Shane nodded and leaned against the back of one of the upholstered chairs, his long legs crossed at the ankles. "It's been a long couple of days for him." He fought a yawn and hooked his thumbs in his belt loops. "I may be joining him. Are you going to be leaving soon?"

Reagan nodded. She knew she could trust him. "I'm just missing one big piece of the puzzle, why Rogers has gotten involved with these reprehensible people. It's completely out of character for him. His whole career is at stake."

Shane looked deep in thought for a moment, and tilted his head at her. He stroked his chin with one hand. "Put yourself in his place. If you're a person with high moral character, what would make you do something that goes completely against your values? Or get involved with someone who you would *never* normally associate with?" His deep brown eyes bored into Reagan's. "What's the one thing that would drive you to risk your reputation and everything you've worked your whole life for?"

Reagan heard the faint sound of the ocean waves from the open patio door. As she stared at Shane, the answer suddenly became crystal clear. *"Family,"* she whispered.

Shane nodded.

Reagan's hands flew over the keys. She quickly navigated the back-door paths that Dane had shown her, and soon, she had her answer.

Rick Rogers' seventeen-year-old daughter, Jill, was battling cancer.

Reagan jumped up and before she knew what she was doing, she threw her arms around Shane's neck. "Thank you, Shane! Thank you so much!" Then she pulled back, moved her hands to rest on his shoulders, and realized that his were settled lightly around her waist.

He looked as flustered as she felt. "You're welcome, Reagan," he said softly.

They just stood there for a couple of seconds, but it felt much longer to Reagan, and she couldn't tear her eyes from his. Finally, she stepped back, and tucked a strand of hair behind her ear. "Well, I—um, I need to get going." Shane nodded silently.

Reagan ran into the bathroom, gathered her hair up into a ponytail, and threw a few things into her purse. Then she went to her suitcase and retrieved something that was going to come in handy. She went back to the bedroom and pulled on her windbreaker, zipping it up.

She kept her eyes off Shane as she packed up the laptop and shoved it into its bag. "All right then, that's it," she said, looking around.

"You might need this," Shane said with a smile, reaching for her burner phone that was on the table.

Reagan blushed and held out her hand. "Thanks."

He held onto the phone. "How about I put my number in here? In case you need to get a hold of me."

Reagan nodded and reached for the phone when Shane held it out. Their fingers touched, and Reagan felt a tingle. *This is crazy. I mean, I thought maybe Dane and I....* She stepped away from Shane. She had to get a hold of herself. Sara was still out there under the control of Navarro's men, and even though things were looking up, it wasn't over yet. This wasn't the time to think about either of the Corsica brothers.

"Stay safe, Reagan," Shane said softly. "I'll be praying for you."

## 25

**DANE**

BY THE TIME Moni dropped Dane off at the entrance to the Boogie Shack and roared off to retrieve Reagan, he'd read the text of the phone conversation and collected his thoughts. He entered the restaurant and gave his eyes a moment to adjust. Then he did a sweep and located Louie behind the bar.

The man grinned at him. "I knew you would be back! What'll it be? I will make for you the special of the day!"

Dane returned the smile. "I'm still going to have to take a raincheck on that. I'm here on business. Can we talk in private?"

Louie nodded and put down the glass he was drying. He gestured to a dark-haired youth working at the other end of the bar. "Amir! You're in charge." He gestured to Dane. "One of Moni's brothers. Come on."

*Moni's brothers? Gustav, and now Amir?* Dane glanced over his shoulder at the young man. He looked kind of Middle Eastern. But Dane couldn't think about that now. He followed Louie through the saloon doors and through the busy kitchen into an office. Louie shut the door behind them, sat down at his desk, and indicated a chair for Dane.

"You FBI, CIA, or DEA?" Louie asked.

Dane looked at him evenly. "Who said I'm any of those?"

A slow grin took over Louie's tanned, weathered face. "I've been running this place for over thirty years, amigo. I know an American fed when I see one."

Dane didn't move for a second. Then he pulled his cred pack out of his waistband and flashed it. Louie nodded but didn't comment.

"The alias I'm using is Trey Armstrong," Dane said, putting the cred pack away. "That's how Moni knows me. I'd like to keep to that for a while."

"Fine," Louie said. "So, how can I help?"

"Do you know a hotel on the north end of the island owned by Bobby Olivier?"

Louie's eyebrows knit together, and he nodded. "Everyone in the Caribbean knows Bobby O. He's bad news. What business you have there?"

Dane quickly outlined what was going on. "An American— official is on his way here tonight or possibly tomorrow to meet with a reporter being held there in a new wing of the hotel that hasn't opened yet. That reporter is my partner, but it's her sister who was taken hostage through a mix-up. We need to get my partner in, and get the sister out, before the man arrives. I don't have any resources here, but you do."

Louie stroked his chin. "One of Moni's brothers works there. Let me call him." He grabbed his cell phone and punched in a number.

*Another brother?* Dane thought. *Just how many are there?* His phone buzzed and he looked at the screen. It was from Reagan. *I have more info, and a plan. Moni and I need to make a stop. Be there in half an hour.* Dane squirmed in his seat. He needed to get his laptop set up to keep monitoring Navarro's and Rogers' conversations and/or texts to nail down precisely when Rogers would arrive on St. Jardin. His whole plan hinged on that.

"Fernando? You working tonight?" he heard Louie say. "Good. The family's gonna need some help later." He looked at Dane as he spoke. "I'll be in touch." He stood. "I just got a text from Moni. She be here in a while. Let me fix you the best drink in St. Jardin—no alcohol. You on duty."

Dane smiled and followed him back into the restaurant and sat at the bar, looking around at the authentic décor and the lights strung across the second-story balcony that looked over the main floor. "This is no shack, Louie," he said. "It's a great place."

Louie smiled and set Dane's drink in front of him. He gestured over his shoulder with a thumb. "The original shack is through there," he said with a broad smile. "It's our poker room now."

While Dane was waiting, he put the finishing touches on his plan. Even though Reagan said *she* had a plan, this was Dane's operation, and he would call the shots. He carefully walked through the steps to get Reagan in and get Sara out. He would need a few things to pull it off, but it would work. And, he'd need about a dozen strong, young men. He hoped Louie could corral together that many.

Dane took another sip of his delicious drink and heard a voice over his shoulder. "Good evening, Trey."

His eyebrows lifted. "Gustav, hello." The two shook hands, and Gustav swung up on an adjacent stool. "What brings you here?"

Gustav shrugged. "When Uncle Louie calls, I come." His eyes flicked over Dane's shoulder. "Ah—here are some more brothers. Meet Minh, Carlos, Nico, and Ray." Dane shook each hand as they smiled and nodded to him, and his confusion grew. This was an interesting family, to be sure. The four young men followed Gustav and sat down at a large, round table. It looked like a gathering of the UN.

Dane was thinking about joining them when Moni breezed in. "Hello, sir Trey!" she said, stopping to stand beside him. "You meet my brothers?" Dane nodded. "Hello, boys!" she said with a jaunty wave, and they all waved back and grinned at her.

Dane looked around. "Where's—um, Sara?" His eyes grew wide as Reagan followed her in. At least he thought it was Reagan. She was dressed in Sara's clothes, but wore her damp hair in a long, brunette braid. Dane blinked. He was so confused.

She stopped at his elbow. He looked into her eyes, and knew it was Reagan. "Yes, it's me. Moni and I stopped for hair dye. It's time to be me again."

Dane shook his head. This completely wrecked his plan. "What are you doing? How will we do the bait and switch?"

Reagan smiled. "We won't need to." She patted the laptop case that rested over one shoulder. "Can you and I go somewhere private?"

Dane stood, and looked around until he found Louie. "Louie, could we—"

"Of course. My office is yours."

Dane led Reagan through the kitchen to Louie's office and closed the door behind them. He put his hands on his hips. "I sure hope you know what you're doing, because you've completely shot my plan to—"

Reagan was already at Louie's desk, opening the laptop. "Dane, I have it all figured out. I know why Rogers is involved. One of his kids has cancer." She spoke with calm assurance.

Dane's mind went blank. "Which one?"

"Jill. She's seventeen."

It had been a long time since he'd seen the Rogers' three children. It must be the youngest one. Dane had a vague memory of a little girl with blond pigtails.

"He's contracted with Navarro to get the Cuban anti-cancer drugs to him in exchange for turning a blind eye to bringing them into the US to conduct illegal trials. And the drugs are working on his daughter—like *really* working. Rogers is risking everything, including his career and his freedom, to save his child's life."

Dane let the implications of that sink in. He sat at the computer and pulled up what he needed to do another data dump of Navarro's and Rogers' phones. He set it up so everything would come through as text on his screen in real time. As Reagan outlined her plan, he had to admit that it made sense.

"I know I can talk him down, Dane. Let me do this," Reagan begged.

"But we'll still need backup. You and I can't do it alone."

"Absolutely. We need a show of strength at the airport when his plane lands. And another group ready to go at the hotel."

Dane thought nervously about Moni's brothers and squeezed his eyes shut. A half-dozen young people wasn't much in the way of a show of strength. If this didn't work, he'd be the laughingstock of the DEA. He would probably need to start over somewhere else in a new career, something far removed from law enforcement.

There was nothing further on either Navarro's or Rogers' phones. Dane set an alarm to go off when something came in. He looked at Reagan's hopeful eyes. "All right, go get Moni. Tell her to bring Louie and her brothers in here."

Reagan quickly left and was gone for only a few seconds. When she came back, Dane was astonished when almost twenty people crowded into the room.

"Moni, how many brothers do you have?"

"Eleven. And five sisters," she said happily.

*What? How is that possible?* Dane couldn't believe it. He looked around the room filled with teens and early-twenty-somethings. The look on his face must have given him away.

"Oh! You think we are a regular family? Ha, ha. You are funny, sir Trey," Moni said. "Uncle Louie and Aunt Evie adopted us all. We're orphans. I love my family. You already know Gustav. This is Minh, Carlos, Nico, Ray, Mikhail, Amir, Tony, Heinrich, and Pierre. Our brother Fernando and sister Lucy work at Bobby O's hotel and are ready to do whatever you say." She nodded to the young women standing next to her. "And these are my sisters Carmen, Lily, Sabrina, and Kat. We are just as strong as our brothers. We want to help." The women smiled and nodded, just like Moni.

As he looked at the eager group, a thought hit Dane with the force of a sledgehammer. Rogers was willing to risk it all for his family. Reagan was like family to him, and Sara and the St. Clairs by extension. Families came in all shapes and sizes. Moni's unlikely group of brothers and sisters came tonight without question when Louie called.

An alarm went off on Dane's computer, and he and Reagan instantly looked at the screen. "They land at seven tomorrow morning," Dane said to the group. He looked at Reagan. "Go ahead, tell them the plan."

# 26

**REAGAN**

REAGAN STOOD ON the tarmac just outside one of the airport gates where private planes came in. Her windbreaker snapped in the early-morning breeze. To the east, fingers of rosy golden light crept into the indigo sky. But Reagan's gaze was focused to the west.

She looked at her phone, which read 7:07 a.m. *Come on, come on,* she coaxed, as if she could will the plane to get there any faster.

Reagan looked behind her through the floor-to-ceiling glass windows into the terminal where her team waited: five of Moni's brothers and two of her sisters, all dressed in dark clothing. It was all smoke and mirrors. They were supposed to look like a tactical team, and in the early-morning darkness, would probably pass muster. All of them had older rifles that Louie had produced back at the cantina just before they left, half of the group going with Reagan to the airport, the other half with Dane to the hotel.

But none of the weapons were loaded, except for Amir's. Reagan had no idea how Dane had gotten approval from airport management to even bring them on the property, but Louie had made a phone call and announced that everything was set. Reagan greatly admired him and was glad he was in their corner.

498

She kept her eyes trained on the western sky and suddenly, she saw the lights of a plane, and then she heard the smooth engines of the Gulfstream V as it grew closer in the sky. She turned and gave a thumbs-up to Amir, whom Dane had assigned as her team lead. Reagan walked forward on the tarmac as the group filed silently through the door and lined up in two perfectly straight lines behind her, standing at attention, their rifles at the ready.

The jet landed like a bird on a placid lake and rolled smoothly toward them, stopping in the middle of the tarmac. The engines powered down, and the forward door of the jet opened. A stairway glided noiselessly down to the pavement, and Reagan heard it lock in place.

*This is it.* Reagan took a deep breath and willed her heart to stay calm. *Lord, I know I haven't been good about staying in touch, but if you see me here, I'd appreciate your help, for Sara's sake. Amen.* It was the first prayer Reagan had prayed in years, and it should have felt awkward, but didn't.

A few short seconds later, she recognized the tall, athletic form of Rick Rogers as he appeared in the entryway and began to descend, alone. Reagan walked confidently to the bottom of the stairs and waited for him. As soon as he stepped onto the tarmac, she spoke. "Welcome to St. Jardin, Governor." She held up her press pass. "I'm Reagan St. Clair." She did not offer her hand.

Confusion knotted his features. "Reagan St. Clair? I don't understand."

"I'm sure you don't. You think I'm being held captive at the Golden Ruby Hotel. But as you can see, here I am, in the flesh." Rogers stuck his hands in his pockets as the wind whipped around them. Reagan looked straight into his eyes. "The woman at the hotel is my sister, Sara. Through a mix-up, Navarro's men grabbed her." Rogers' eyes grew wide. "Yes, I know your connection to Navarro. I also know about Jill." She clamped her lips shut to let that sink in.

Rogers hung his head, and then his Adam's apple bobbed as he swallowed. "Ms. St. Clair, I never meant for any of this to happen, for anyone to be harmed." Reagan watched his eyes fill. "I—my only intent was to save my daughter's life. I got in over my head."

Reagan recognized true contrition in the man's eyes, but her voice stayed hard. Her sister's survival depended on it. "You're going to do exactly as I say. I'm here with an armed squad authorized by the DEA." That of course wasn't true, but those were the exact words Dane had told her to say. "My partner is a senior DEA agent and is at the Golden Ruby with another armed squad. You're going to call Doug Navarro right here, right now, and tell him to call his men at the Golden Ruby and tell them to *stand down*, and immediately release my sister to my partner." She took out her cell. "I'm going to get on the line with him. Once I know my sister is safe, I'll take you to talk with my partner, and see what kind of deal he can make for you." Rogers didn't say anything.

Reagan pinned him with a hard stare. "If you don't comply with these orders," she said, looking over her shoulder, "you'll be taken into immediate custody and turned over to the DEA, and my partner and I will go straight to the prosecuting attorney and tell them everything we know. You're on foreign soil now, so this is a federal case. The DEA is outside Navarro's present location, front and back, right now. If he doesn't follow our orders, one call to them from my partner, and he'll be in cuffs in about ten seconds." Dane had assured Reagan that Navarro was going to be taken into custody either way, but Reagan wasn't going to tell Rogers that.

The governor nodded vigorously. He took out his phone. "Yes, of course, I'll—I'll make that call now."

Reagan activated her burner phone and called Dane. "Yeah?" he answered.

"He's calling Navarro now," Reagan whispered. She kept her eyes on Rogers.

"It's me," he said crisply into the phone. "I'm in St. Jardin. The woman at the Golden Ruby isn't Reagan St. Clair, it's her sister. Your guys screwed up *again*. You have to call them right now and tell them to release her. The DEA is here with me, and they're at the hotel waiting, and they're outside your place ready to take you into custody if you don't make the call." He took a breath. *"Do it now*, Navarro, or I swear I will use every resource at my disposal to hunt you down and you'll never see the outside of a cell." Rogers' voice shook and Reagan was mildly impressed by his intensity.

Rogers nodded to her, and Reagan whispered into the phone, "it's a go."

The next thing she heard was Dane shouting, "go, go, go!" and then the line went dead.

## 27

**DANE**

"GO, GO, GO!" Dane shouted. He shoved his phone in his pocket. The adrenaline flowed the way it always did during a raid, and he loved it. It didn't matter that he was with Moni and her ragtag family instead of a highly trained tactical team. After they had arrived at the Golden Ruby and gotten into place with the help of Fernando and Lucy, they had plenty of time while they waited for the call from Reagan. Dane versed his team in how things needed to go down—if Navarro's men complied, and if they didn't.

Now, they marched down the thickly carpeted hallway of the new wing. Dane was in front, followed by Gustav, who he'd designated as team lead, with the others in two flanks behind him. They were a little haphazard, but Dane felt in his gut that they would be sufficient. He rested his hand on the grip of a gun that Louie had given him, ready to pull it from its holster if needed. Only his and Gustav's weapons were loaded.

They reached the door to the suite where Sara was being held. The double doors stood open, and two muscular men stood on either side of it. When they saw Dane, they raised their hands. Dane glanced over his shoulder. "Take them into custody," he said to Gustav.

Dane rushed into the suite, with half of the team behind him, as planned. A female guard stood by the couch, her hands raised. "Cuff her," Dane ordered. Moni quickly moved to obey. "Secure the perimeter," he called out, and two of Moni's brothers carried out his orders exactly how he had instructed them.

"We're clear," they called back. Dane immediately pulled out his phone and got Reagan back on the line. His only concern was for Sara. She sat on the bed, her arms wrapped around her middle. Tears ran down her face. Dane flashed his cred pack at her and smiled. He felt like he already knew her. "Hi, Sara, I'm Special Agent Dane Corsica, DEA." He put his phone on speaker and held it out. "Go ahead, Reagan."

Reagan's voice shook as it came through loud and clear. "Peanut?"

"Reagan, is that you? I'm okay," Sara said with a sob. "Where are you?'

"Oh, thank God! I'm at the St. Jardin airport. I'll see you soon. Dane is—he's my best friend." Dane heard Reagan sniff. "He'll take good care of you. I love you, Sara."

"I love you, too, Reagan. I'm so sorry I got in the middle of this and messed everything up for you."

"Honey, none of this was your fault. It all worked out. We'll talk about it later. Dane, don't let her out of your sight."

"I won't, Reagan, I promise." He took the phone off speaker and held it to his ear. "Everything secure on your end?"

"Yes," Reagan said. "Rogers is ready to cooperate, completely."

Dane walked away to have some privacy, but didn't take his eyes off Sara. "I just got a text message from Miami. Navarro is in custody."

"Good. You did it, Dane! You got Navarro."

He smiled. "*We* got him. Couldn't have done it without you. And our team," he added.

Reagan laughed. "Our team! Who would have thought? Oh

Dane, Moni took me to their—house to dye my hair. It's just a concrete building with two big dormitory rooms. I know Louie and his wife are doing everything they can, and it's more than a lot of people on the island have. It's so amazing that they've opened their hearts to these orphans, but I'm thinking we can help them—"

"We'll definitely make it happen, Reagan. Okay, we're going to lock everything down here. The St. Jardin police are going to take all these folks into custody, and I want to interview Rogers somewhere private, so let's meet up back at Rose and Ike's office." Dane had already called them and arranged this, and he gave Reagan further instructions. "Then you and Sara can get some sleep or go relax on the beach or something."

"Yes, I want to spend the whole day with her. See you soon."

Dane walked back over to Sara. He felt awkward towering over her, so he squatted down in front of her. "Are you okay? Can I get you anything?"

"I'm ready to be rid of this thing." She pulled off the brunette wig, the nylon cap came with it, and they fell to the floor. Her golden hair tumbled past her shoulders. Sara ran her fingers through the tangles and then swiped at her wet eyes. "Yes, I'm—I'm—" she began to shake. Tears poured out of her beautiful brown eyes, and Dane did the only thing he could think of to do.

He sat down next to her and opened his arms.

And Sara fell into them.

# 28

**SARA**

THE LAST TWELVE hours had been a nightmare, and it was finally over.

Sara was embarrassed that she couldn't stop crying, and that she'd flung herself into the handsome DEA agent's arms. Still, she hung on. It felt so good to have someone to lean on. For a moment, she tried to pretend that it was her dad or one of her brothers.

But being held by them had never felt like this.

Finally, she pulled back, and swiped at her face with her shirtsleeve. "I'm sorry," she whispered, her head down.

He didn't say anything, and after several seconds, his finger gently tipped her chin up. "You don't have anything to be sorry for." He wore a crooked smile that was very endearing, and his brown eyes searched hers. Something about him seemed a little familiar, but for the life of her, Sara couldn't figure out what it was.

She reached out and touched his shirtfront just below his shoulder. "Oh…I'm sorry. I got your shirt wet," she said with a grimace. Her face burned with embarrassment.

He laughed. "It's okay, Sara. Believe me, I've had *much* worse happen to me. Are you okay staying here a little while longer? I can't leave until the police arrive."

Sara blew out a breath. "Yes, I'm fine. I'd like to go wash my face."

He stood. "Let's go." Sara's eyes widened. "Hey, I promised Reagan I wouldn't let you out of my sight." He gave her a full-on grin now, and Sara felt her heart trip. She crossed the room to the elegant bathroom and let the cool water sluice over her tear-stained face. It felt wonderful. In the mirror, she saw the DEA agent leaning against the door jamb, his arms crossed in front of him.

She dried her face and turned to face him. "I'm sorry, what was your name again?"

"Dane."

*Dane. It fit him perfectly.* Sara smiled at him. "I'm sure my sister would let you off the hook to let me use the bathroom."

Dane grinned and started to pull the door closed. "I'll be waiting."

As soon as it clicked shut, Sara put her hands to her cheeks, which had suddenly grown warm again. *Gosh, he's so attractive.* She finished her business, washed her hands, and tried to finger-comb her hair. "It's a lost cause," she muttered to herself. She took a breath and opened the door. He was standing right where she'd left him.

"Hi," she said a little breathlessly. She didn't mean for it to come out that way, and wanted to kick herself. *He'll think you're fourteen.*

Dane gave her that crooked grin again. "Hi." He uncrossed his arms and slid his hands in his pockets. "I'm sorry we have to stay here in this room. It's probably the last place you want to be. Do you want to sit down?"

Sara shook her head. "It feels good to stretch my legs." They walked back into the main room.

Dane looked at the wall covered in rich draperies and walked toward it. "I think there's a balcony behind these drapes somewhere." He went to the far right and found a panel of buttons on the wall. He pressed one, then another, and different parts of the drapery parted. It appeared that the entire wall was floor-to-ceiling glass. "Wow, that's pretty cool," he said with a sparkling smile. "My apartment sure doesn't have anything like that."

The balcony faced north to the ocean, and the sun was streaming through. He opened the sliding-glass door and motioned for Sara to go through. She went to the railing and leaned on it. As far as she could see, the ocean waters sparkled under the morning sun, every hue of blue and teal imaginable.

"It's gorgeous," she murmured.

"Yes, gorgeous," Dane echoed. Sara glanced at him, and he was staring at her. He looked away, and so did she.

"I don't see many beaches in the Midwest," Sara admitted. "Well, Lake Michigan. But it doesn't look like this."

"I'm from Florida," Dane said. His eyes were on the ocean view now. "I never get tired of it."

They stood there for a long time, drinking in the beauty of the morning. The rhythmic crashing of the waves was like a soothing balm. She liked that Dane seemed content to just be there with her.

"How long have you known Reagan?" she asked.

"About four years. We work together on cases sometimes. She's a good investigative reporter."

Sara nodded. "I know, but I worry about her. She doesn't have much of a life outside of work."

Dane smiled. "That may be about to change." Sara was going to ask what he meant by that when his phone rang. "Hold on." He listened for a moment. "That works. I'll touch base with your officers when they get here, and then wait for you. Thank you." He turned to Sara. "That was the Chief of Police. He's coming personally to oversee the transfer of these folks into custody, but he won't be here for about an hour, and he needs me here. Do you mind waiting until I can leave and take you to Reagan?"

*Not if I can pass the time with you,* Sara thought. "I don't mind at all."

"I'll be right back."

Sara stared out at the mesmerizing ocean again. Her flight to

Orlando had already left, and since she didn't have her phone and it was likely dead by now, she had no way of getting a hold of Lance. Her second chance with Disney had slipped through her fingers, and she knew she'd never get another. It should have upset her more than it did. For some reason, Sara felt that this was all a part of God's plan.

She heard voices and turned her head toward them. Four local officers had just arrived, and they all shook hands with Dane and his second-in-command. After a few moments, Dane came back to the balcony.

"They have everything under control," he said. "How about you and I go get some breakfast? Or at least some coffee?"

Sara looked back toward the beach, which was quickly becoming awash in the golden morning light. "You know what I'd really like? A walk along the beach."

Dane's face lit up. "That's a great idea. Come on." He laid his hand lightly on her arm, and they went back through the room. "We'll be back," Dane said to the group. He spoke to the tall, dark blond man. "Gustav, call me if you need me."

Sara followed Dane into the hallway. It felt good to be out of that room. He looked both ways. "Let's go left," he said. "There's probably a stairwell at the end of the hallway."

He was right, and he opened the door for her that led into the stairwell. When it closed behind them, it was completely dark, but Sara felt safe with him. "Wow, they must not have the lights installed yet. This whole wing is brand new, still under construction," he said by way of explanation. He clicked the light on his phone and a small puddle of light appeared in front of them. "You ready?"

"Yes," Sara nodded.

"Here, take my hand," Dane said. Sara laid her left hand in his right, and by some unspoken agreement, they laced their fingers together.

And then it happened.

# 29

**DANE**

DANE'S HEART BEGAN to thunder, and his breath caught in his throat. He looked at Sara, and knew she felt it, too.

He felt his face break into a grin, and she smiled back. Dane had an irresistible urge to sweep her into his arms, but something held him back. He held his phone out in front of him, shining the light on the stairs as they descended.

Holding Reagan's hand hadn't felt like this, and Dane couldn't remember much about the good times with Sally Ann, the early days of which were buried under an alcohol-induced fog.

They got down the three flights of stairs, and Dane wished it was three hundred. The zinging from their clasped hands raced up his arm, and he felt like he was holding one of those fourth-of-July sparklers.

They reached the bottom stair, and a closed door. Dane figured it led into a hallway, but didn't know if it was in a construction area or if it would be filled with people. He reluctantly let go of Sara's hand. "Hold on, let me look," he said softly. He carefully pulled the door open and peeked out. To the right was a hallway that looked like it might lead to a lobby area. Immediately to the left was a glass door leading outside.

He opened the door wider, pointed left, and ushered Sara through. He hung back for a moment, and then joined her in the early-morning tropical breeze.

Sara lifted her face to the sun, lifted her arms, and spun around. "Oh, this feels fantastic!" she said with a laugh. Then she stopped. "You probably think I'm crazy."

Dane thought his smile might split his face open. He could have stood there all day watching her. "No, I don't. You're not crazy at all." He laughed. "Come on, let's go!" He started jogging through the grass toward the shoreline and she trotted alongside. The grounds of the hotel were actually on a rise above the ocean. When they reached the rocky edge, Dane could tell it was an easy enough jump down. "I'll go first," he said. As soon as he landed on the sand, he turned around and held his arms out for her. She put her hands on his shoulders and he easily lifted her to the ground.

And time stood still. He didn't want to let her go.

Finally, she lowered her hands. They quickly shed their footwear, rolled their jeans up, and went to the water's edge. Sara squealed when the first wave cascaded over her feet. Her eyes sparkled at Dane. "Oh, this is heavenly!"

*This* is *heaven,* Dane thought. They began to walk along the sand, laughing and talking. Once when Sara ventured out a little, a wave knocked her off balance, and Dane caught her, which made them both laugh even more. He wanted to hold on to her, but held himself in check.

They kept walking until Dane looked at his phone and decided they should go back.

"You're with the DEA, so is this whole thing about a drug case?" Sara asked.

He nodded. "Reagan and I were both working the case undercover from different points, and ended up at a meeting together. We met up later to compare notes, and someone shot at us. They didn't hit us," he was quick to reassure her. "So basically we went on the run and needed a place to hide, and ended up here."

Sara didn't say anything for a few moments. "A little while ago, you said her life outside work might be about to change." She looked up at him expectantly. They were back to where they'd left their shoes, and put them back on. Then Dane looked around and spied a sort of rocky path where they could climb back up to the hotel grounds.

When they got back on even footing, he looked at Sara and shrugged. "My brother ended up coming here, and I think they kind of hit it off."

Sara looked at him incredulously. "Reagan hasn't been interested in a man in...forever." They were back at the door now. She grabbed his arm. "Dane! What if it's locked?"

He couldn't hold back his grin. He opened the door and peeled off the little piece of adhesive that he carried in his wallet for times like this.

Her beautiful brown eyes went wide, and she gasped. "Just like James Bond!"

Dane laughed and swore his chest expanded six inches. He took her hand and opened the door to the stairwell. "Come on, let's go."

# 30

**SARA**

WHEN THEY GOT back to the room, Sara lowered herself into a deep scarlet silk chair and watched Dane greet the police chief of St. Jardin and the other officers. It was clear that he was in command, yet respectful of everyone else around him. The officers got the three guards secured with their own handcuffs and returned the other ones to the people who were with Dane. They seemed a little scruffy and she supposed they were undercover operatives.

Sara couldn't keep her eyes off Dane. It felt like there were a thousand butterflies in her stomach. She still couldn't shake the sense of why he seemed familiar to her. There was no doubt in her mind that some of his interaction with her was pure flirting, but it was different—not like the way the college guys flirted, for no reason or just to see how far they could get with a girl. When his fingers had slipped through hers at the top of the stairs, and their palms met, Sara felt little electric shocks all the way up her arm, and she knew he felt the connection, too.

She couldn't believe how much fun she had walking and talking and laughing with him. He seemed incredibly mature, but of course that made sense. For someone with a successful career in the DEA, he had to be several years older than her.

He lived in Miami, which would make having a relationship impossible. Sara's head was swimming. She had never thought about leaving the Midwest. Could she live in Florida? She gave herself a shake. *Stop. You're moving too fast.*

She stood, and Dane's eyes connected with hers. She wordlessly pointed toward the bathroom and could tell he got the message.

As she stood at the sink washing her hands, Sara looked at her reflection. Even though she was exhausted both physically and mentally, her eyes looked bright and her cheeks were flushed. Dane's handsome face filled her mind. *After today, you'll probably never see him again.* Her heart deflated like a balloon.

She went back into the room and curled up in one corner of the couch, and promptly fell asleep. She dreamed of walking on the beach with Dane hand-in-hand at sunset, and of a glorious, romantic kiss.

# 31

**DANE**

THE PAPERWORK WAS signed, the prisoners were gone, and Fernando and Lucy had assured Dane that they would put the suite back in order. He shook everyone else's hand and promised to catch up with them later. He wanted to talk with Reagan and figure out a way to show their appreciation to their "team."

He'd been up all night, but had a lot to do before he could sleep. First, he had to interview Rick Rogers. That was going to be an uncomfortable conversation, but Dane was a professional and was confident he could handle it. He was certain someone much higher on the chain of command would make the recommendation about whether and how to charge the governor.

Then he would need to get back on grid with the DEA, complete reports, and make sure everything was wrapped up with Navarro's gang. Dane didn't want any procedural slip-ups that would jeopardize their case when it went to trial.

He knew this case would be a huge feather in his cap, and in Reagan's. It was already early in his career to be a special agent, and this would most assuredly propel him to the next level. Right now, his head should be filled with the possibilities on the horizon for his career.

But he couldn't think about any of that now, because his mind was filled with Sara.

She completely captivated him. Holding her had brought out every protective instinct in Dane, and when she slipped her soft, feminine hand into his, he felt fireworks exploding in his hand up to his heart. He could have walked on the beach with her for hours, just communing with nature and engaging in easy conversation. He couldn't wait to spend more time with her.

The officer who introduced himself as Sergeant Aubert was going to drive them to the resort in a cruiser. Everyone else had left. Dane walked over to where Sara was sitting and realized that she'd fallen asleep. Whatever she was dreaming about brought a beautiful smile to her heart-shaped face, and he wished he could kiss her awake.

He gently shook her shoulder. "Sara," he said softly.

She opened her eyes and blinked, then yawned. "Oh gosh, I feel asleep."

"I'm sure you're exhausted. I'll take you to Reagan now. She's out at a resort where we're been staying."

The moment her hand touched his, the zinging started again. She smiled as she rose. "Oh, good. There are my bags."

"I'll get them," Dane said. He went to grab a handle with each hand to set them upright, and they almost pulled him off his feet. "Wow—what do you have in here?" he exclaimed with a laugh.

Sara turned pink and giggled. "Oh—just mostly—well, everything I own."

Dane got one bag up and Aubert, the other one. "At least I won't have to go to the gym today," the sergeant said under his breath. He and Dane both stifled a laugh.

They got down to the hotel entrance, and the brawny man deposited the baggage into the trunk of the cruiser. Dane held the passenger door for Sara, and she climbed into the backseat. He wished he could sit back there with her, but didn't want to make Aubert feel like a chauffeur.

It took about forty minutes to get to the resort, and the time passed quickly as the sergeant pointed out landmarks and answered Sara's enthusiastic questions.

Dane texted Reagan when they were almost to the resort, and she was standing at the front door when they pulled into the circular drive. As soon as the car came to a stop, Dane got out and opened Sara's door. She ran straight into Reagan's arms, and they stood there clinging to one another, rocking back and forth.

Dane and Aubert lifted Sara's bags out of the cruiser and Dane shook his hand and thanked him for his help. As the car drove away, he turned back to look at the two women, who were now arm-in-arm, smiling and drying their tears. "Wow," he said. "Seeing the two of you together—really, if it wasn't for the hair color, the resemblance is uncanny."

They looked at one another and laughed. "It's pretty weird," Reagan said. "You saw how much Landon and Brandon look alike, too. But they don't look like us."

"He met them? When?" Sara looked surprised.

"Right after Brandon and Morgan's wedding," Dane said.

Sara narrowed her eyes at her sister. "Yeah, I heard you were there." She looked between them. "I need to hear the whole story sometime."

Dane recalled the image that was burned into his memory of Sara at the wedding in her flowered sundress, talking and laughing with the other guests. The first time he'd laid eyes on her.

"I know I have a lot of explaining to do, and we'll get to that." Reagan said. She started to pull Sara toward the garden path. "Are you hungry? They're still serving breakfast on the patio."

Sara nodded. "Yes. I really haven't eaten much since yesterday afternoon."

"I'll get your bags upstairs," Dane said. Sara and Reagan began to walk away, chattering.

Suddenly, Reagan stopped and turned around. "What am I thinking?" she exclaimed, and ran to Dane. She threw her arms around his neck and almost knocked him over. "Thank you so much for rescuing my sister!"

# 32

## SARA

SARA STOOD AWKWARDLY while Reagan and Dane embraced. His laughter floated through the air, and his arms came firmly around her sister. Something on his left hand glinted in the sun, and Sara couldn't believe her eyes. He was wearing a wedding ring! *Married? He's married? How is that possible? How did I not see that before?* Her heart jumped into her throat, and she felt her stomach plummet to her feet.

Reagan skittered back and looped her arm through Sara's, and Dane left with Sara's luggage. "Come on, let's go. The food here is out of this world," her sister said.

Sara's appetite had vanished. Now she just wanted to go curl up in a ball and cry her eyes out. What Dane must think of her, acting like an adolescent girl while he flirted with her and held her hand! Suddenly, her heartbreak turned to anger. *What a slimeball!* How could she have been so naïve and trusting? Sara took a deep breath and swallowed the bitterness down. She didn't want Reagan to start asking questions.

"Wait!" Reagan exclaimed. "Aren't you flying to Orlando this morning?"

Sara shook her head. "I missed my flight. I guess it wasn't meant to be. Again."

"Peanut, I'm so sorry. Are you sure? Have you called them? I could talk with them, tell them what happened—"

"No, I got my phone back, but it's dead and until I can charge it, I don't have any way to reach them." Sara wasn't ready to tell Reagan that she had a very strong sense that she wasn't supposed to go to Orlando. She was still trying to figure that out in her own mind. Suddenly, it was all too much. She swiped at a tear. "I just— I just want to be with my sister right now."

Reagan wrapped her arms around Sara. "I called Landon to let him know you're safe."

"Was he mad?"

Reagan pulled back and looked confused. "He was relieved. Why would he be mad?"

Sara looked down. "Because I took off on my own and didn't tell anyone where I was going. And I concocted this stupid plan to try to get my passport back." She clamped her teeth over her lower lip. "Do Mom and Dad know about any of this?"

"No. Just us four kids and Kelsea and Morgan." She looked into Sara's eyes. "You're not to blame for any of this. You had no way of knowing that I was being watched. If anyone is to blame, it's Dane and me for agreeing to the plan for me to travel on your passport without telling you."

"Was it your idea, or his?"

Reagan started walking. "It was actually Brandon's, at first. But Landon put all the wheels in motion." Sara nodded. That's what Landon did. But she was still annoyed at her siblings for not including her, not giving her adult status.

The sisters arrived at the patio. "I'll tell you about it later." Reagan's eyes lit up. "Oh good, there's Shane."

*Shane?* Sara followed Reagan's gaze to a corner table, and felt the blood drain from her face. It was Danny and his dad! What were they doing here? How did Reagan know them?

Danny looked up as they approached. "Miss Sara!" the little boy squealed. Sara thought he must be looking at Reagan, since the "Miss Sara" he sat with on the plane had a dark braid, but instead, he ran straight to her. She bent down and scooped him up.

"Danny, hi! How did you know it was me, since I looked like her on the airplane?" She pointed to Reagan.

"I just knew it was you, Miss Sara," he said, and threw his arms around her neck.

Shane was staring at Reagan, and then his gaze flicked to Sara. "I'll bet you're surprised to see us." He held out his hand. "I'm Shane Corsica."

"Oh..." Sara nodded. *Dane's brother! That explains a lot.* As she shook his hand, she tilted her head at Reagan. "Shane and Dane?"

Reagan and Shane laughed and shook their heads. "Yeah, we think it's hilarious, too," Reagan said. Her eyes were bright and her face a little flushed. Sara glanced at Shane, whose attention was entirely on her sister. *Well, it looks like Dane was right.*

Reagan looked between Shane and Sara. "Didn't you two meet on the plane?"

Shane smiled at Sara. "Well, ah—Sara and Danny got around to names, but we didn't."

Danny laid his head on her shoulder. "I'm so happy you came here, Miss Sara. I missed you."

Sara's heart swelled. "Aww, I missed you, too, Danny."

"Hey, everyone," Dane's voice came from behind Sara, and she felt herself stiffen.

Danny began to wiggle, and Sara set him down. "Daddy, Daddy!" he squealed, and launched himself into Dane's arms. Sara's eyes went wide. *What in the world?*

Sara looked at Shane in confusion. "You mean, you're not—"

"Oh, no. I'm not his dad. I'm his uncle. I was bringing him here, to Dane." *Good heavens, he's not just married, he's a father. Unbelievable.*

Danny bounced in his dad's arms. "Daddy, Daddy, Miss Sara's here!"

"I know," Dane said. "I'm glad that makes you happy. It makes me happy, too." He looked straight at Sara as he said it, and she forced herself to hold his gaze with the iciest one she could conjure up. She hoped he got her message.

Sara tapped her sister's arm. She wanted to get away from Dane. "Reagan, can we get some food now?" It looked as if Shane and Danny had already eaten.

"Yes, yes, of course," Reagan said. "Let's go."

"Where's Rogers?" Dane asked Reagan. Sara was glad that he seemed to be avoiding looking at her. He set Danny down and the little boy ran back to where he'd been sitting.

"In a small conference room off the lobby, thanks to Rose and Ike." She pulled a cell phone out of her pocket and handed it to him. "I took his phone. He can't contact anyone. Amir is standing guard outside the door until you get there, just like you asked."

"Good work," Dane said, and squeezed her shoulder. "I'm off to interview him." He looked at his brother and tipped his head at Danny. "Do you mind?"

"No, not at all," Shane responded.

"Thanks. Did you eat all your breakfast, buddy?"

Danny kept coloring, and Shane spoke up. "He ate a banana and half of his pancakes. And all his milk."

Dane gave his son a thumbs-up. "That's good. See you guys later."

"What about breakfast?" Reagan asked. "You haven't eaten, either."

He waved a hand as he walked away. "Later. I'll grab some coffee in the lobby."

Sara went with Reagan to the buffet. She was glad to get away from the Corsica brothers. They were entirely too...distracting. She felt oddly drawn to both of them, which was totally unlike her. Shane was too old, and seemed enamored of Reagan. Dane was far more handsome, in Sara's opinion, but he'd shown his true character and even if by some strange turn of events he became available someday, she wanted nothing to do with a man like that. She tried to put him out of her mind as she filled a plate with scrambled eggs, an English muffin, and fruit.

When they got back to the table, Reagan sat down next to Shane, and Danny looked up from his coloring. "Sit by me, Miss Sara."

"Please," his uncle prodded.

Danny looked at Sara with an impish smile. "Please, Miss Sara."

Sara's heart melted. She would do anything for this little guy. But where was his mother? The one who'd put the gold wedding band on Dane's finger?

# 33

**REAGAN**

AFTER BREAKFAST, REAGAN, Sara, Shane, and Danny went to the lobby. Reagan wanted to check on Dane's progress with Rogers. She saw him coming out of a room, and crossed to him. He closed the door behind him and nodded to Amir. "Two DEA agents are coming within the hour to take him back to Florida," he said. "I'll be around until they arrive to sign off on the transfer."

"I will stay here as long as you need me, sir," Amir said formally.

"Thanks." Dane shook his hand. He led Reagan back to where Sara and Shane were standing. "Well, I'm done with that."

"Done? I thought we were going to interview him together," Reagan said.

"Nope. DEA business only. No reporters allowed," he said with a wink.

Reagan crossed her arms in front of her. "I can't believe it. I'm the one who figured everything out. You're really going to freeze me out?"

Dane looped a friendly arm around her shoulder. "I know, and the DEA appreciates it. And you'll get the exclusive. How's that?"

Reagan uncrossed her arms. "That's more like it, Corsica," she answered.

Dane turned and looked at Sara tentatively. "Maybe we could all do something this afternoon," he said, including Reagan and Shane. But it looked to Reagan that he only had eyes for Sara.

Sara crossed her arms in front of her chest. "No, count me out," she said. She gave no explanation, but her voice could have bent nails. Reagan frowned. *What in the world is wrong with her?*

"Good morning!" a voice trilled. Here came Rose, with Ike trailing behind her. Reagan and Dane exchanged a glance. They knew they had some explaining to do.

"Good morning," they said in unison.

Rose laid her hand affectionately on Dane's arm and looked up at him. "Did you catch your bad guys?"

Dane laughed. "We sure did, Rose." He nodded to both of them. "Thank you so much for your help."

"Oh, we didn't do anything," Ike said. "Just provided a place for you to grill your suspect. Is that what he is?"

"More or less," Dane said. "We should wrap things up there pretty soon and be out of your hair."

"Oh, it's no problem at all," Rose said. "So, what are you calling yourself now, Trey or Dane?"

Dane smiled, "I'm back to Dane, and staying there."

Rose looked at Shane. "This must be your brother."

"Yes," Dane said, and made the introductions.

"Thank you for letting us stay here," Shane said. "This is a beautiful resort."

"We're happy to have you," Rose said.

Ike looked at Sara. "And who is this pretty young lady?" Reagan hadn't noticed that Sara was hanging back behind her.

"Oh." Dane's mouth opened, and he and Reagan exchanged another glance. Sara looked at her sister expectantly.

"Well," Reagan began, "this is actually my sister. It's kind of a complicated story." She wasn't looking forward to untangling it. "Her name is Sara. I kind of—borrowed it."

"We know," Rose said brightly. "She's Sara St. Clair, and you're Reagan."

Dane and Reagan's jaws dropped in sync. Dane's eyes narrowed. "How did you know?"

Rose sniffed. "My dear boy, we knew as soon as we met your wife. After all, Landon was the one who called and arranged for you to come here. Oh, he didn't say a thing, but it was obvious to us, wasn't it, Ike?" Her husband nodded.

Sara looked between Dane and Reagan and speared her sister with a look. "Wife? Wait—you and he—are married?"

"Oh no, they're not even in love," Rose said emphatically. "You weren't very convincing," she muttered.

Dane's face turned red, and Reagan wished the ground would swallow her up. She couldn't bring herself to look at Shane. "No, we're not," Reagan said, swallowing a laugh. Rose was just too much. "We just—we came here to hide, and since this is a honeymoon resort, we had to go undercover as a newlywed couple." Reagan glanced at Sara, who looked positively furious. Reagan could read her sister's mind as if she'd shouted it: *just how "undercover" did this thing get??* "So of course, we—we had to stay in the same room," she went on, "but we didn't—ah—" *Oh dear. Why did I go down this path?*

"Reagan had rules," Dane interrupted. His voice cracked on the last word, and he looked like he was trying not to laugh. "There was a pile of pillows down the middle of the—" Dane glanced at Danny. "You know, like a concrete barrier." Reagan wondered if the little boy was understanding any of this.

"Daddy, can we go look for seashells?" Danny asked innocently. Relief stole over Dane's features. He leaned down and touched his son's red hair.

"I can go in a little while. I have to wait for some friends to come."

"I'll take him," Shane offered. "You can catch up." Reagan admired his easygoing way with his nephew.

"Thanks, that'd be great," Dane replied.

One of the resort's employees approached Rose and Ike with a question, and they left with a promise to see everyone later. "Head west when you get to the beach," Ike said to Shane. "That's where the best shells are."

"Miss Sara, will you come look for seashells with us?" Danny said. The little guy sure had attached to her. Reagan knew she was exhausted and was surprised at her response.

Sara still looked tense, but smiled at Danny. "Sure, I'd love to see the beach. I just need to go upstairs and change. I've been in these clothes for almost twenty-four hours."

"I'll go with you," Reagan said. Her words were directed at Sara, but she was looking at Shane.

"Um, Sara, could we talk for a moment?" Dane asked.

*What was going on with the two of them?* Dane looked miserable, and her sister looked like she was about to blow a gasket.

Sara didn't say anything for several seconds. Then she spoke a single, terse syllable. "Sure." They walked over by the stairs and began a whispered conversation. Sara had her back to Reagan and Shane, but Dane was visible in profile. Reagan could tell by their body language that Dane was trying to be agreeable and Sara definitely was not. Did t

Reagan moved to stand next to Shane. "Do you know what this is about?" she whispered. He shook his head. Then Sara abruptly turned and marched up the stairs. Anger punctuated every one of her staccato footfalls.

# 34

**DANE**

*WELL, SO MUCH for that.* His heart felt like it had been torn out of his chest, stomped on, and stuffed back in.

He stuck his hands in his pockets and ambled over to his brother and Reagan.

"What's up with you and Sara?" Reagan asked.

Dane shook his head. "Ask her," he said tersely.

He saw a look pass between Reagan and Shane. "I'll be down in a few minutes," Reagan said.

Shane waited until she was out of earshot. "What's up?" he asked.

Dane didn't say anything for a moment. "I don't understand women."

Shane threw back his head and laughed. He laid his hand on Dane's shoulder. "Said every man who ever walked the earth." He squeezed Dane's shoulder. "I'm sorry."

Dane looked at his brother, who was watching Reagan go up the stairs. He recognized that *take no prisoners* look in Shane's eye.

"You're going to go after her," he said.

Dane expected Shane's face to break out in a grin, but he

looked serious. "You bet I am." Shane crossed his arms in front of him and leaned against the back of a couch, crossing his feet at the ankles. "She's the one I've been looking for all my life. I could never put it into words, but I've always been certain that when I found her, I'd know. Make sense?"

Dane nodded. "Completely." He shook his head. "I've known her for a few years. You've got your work cut out for you."

Now the smile that Dane was expecting came, and Shane rested his hands on his thighs. "No, this is God's work." Then his countenance got serious again. "You know I would never marry a woman who didn't love God more than she loved me. Reagan needs to find her way back to Him first. I'm going to stick by her every step of the way, and be there with open arms when she arrives."

Dane couldn't believe that just a little while ago, he was trying to figure out how to work a long-distance relationship with Sara. "Well, at least you're both from Miami. Maybe you can ask her out when you get home."

Shane shook his head and smiled. "You've been with Reagan in disguise for too long. Come on, you know that won't work. We had an opportunity to talk for a long time this morning while we were waiting for you and Sara to get here, but even before that, I invited her to come tour the Miracle Center, and she accepted."

"Nice," Dane said with a grin.

Shane stood and clapped a hand on Dane's shoulder. "Is there anything I need to know about...well, about your *pretend* marriage? Let's clear the air now."

Dane shook his head and made an X on his chest with his finger. "Just one tiny kiss on the cheek. There was a little spark there, but only when she looked and acted like—well, Sara."

Shane grinned, and then his expression grew serious. "What's going on with you two?"

Dane blew out a breath. "Well, there was this, like, instantaneous combustion when we met. Like, sparks *everywhere*. I wasn't sure if it was because I rode in on my white horse and rescued her, but man, it was something else. We spent a couple of *incredible* hours together this morning. I thought there was real potential for it to go somewhere. And then suddenly, after we got here, she went as cold as an iceberg. Just now, she thanked me for rescuing her, and then said goodbye. I asked her what happened earlier today, and she said that it was a mistake and to leave her alone. And then she walked off."

"I think she's attracted to you," Shane said. "But she's fighting it. Want to hear my theory?" he grinned.

"Do I have a choice?" Dane muttered.

Shane ticked his points off on his fingers as he spoke. "First, she didn't realize you had a child. Second, she thought you were married to her sister. Third, because you have a child, even though you're *not* married to her sister, now she thinks you're married to someone else, because you're wearing a ring." He pointed at Dane's hand.

Dane looked down at the gold band, and wanted to kick himself. *Why didn't I realize that Sara would have noticed it?* "I put my ring in a drawer when Sally Ann left me for good. But when I started wearing this one for this assignment, I didn't even think about it." He slowly twisted it off and dropped it in his pocket. "You got all that from watching Sara for, what? A few minutes? You're crazy." His mind spun with the implications. Could his brother be right?

Shane shrugged and smiled. "I've been told I'm especially perceptive when it comes to people.

And I've never seen you look at a woman like you look at her."

Danny was sitting on a couch over the by the window, looking out at the garden and singing to himself. Dane lowered his voice. "I've only been a widower for two days."

Shane clapped a hand on his shoulder. "Legally, yes, but that marriage was over a long time ago." He squeezed. "I know you had your reasons for not ending it, and even though you took the ring off, you honored those vows, even when your wife probably didn't." His eyes were serious. "I respect you tremendously for that. Ninety-nine-point-nine percent of men wouldn't." Dane let that sink in. "God just may be rewarding your faithfulness. He's literally dropped a beautiful Christian woman in your path. The timing is aggressive, to be sure, but God's ways are not our ways. She and Danny are already crazy about each other."

Dane sighed. "You're serious, aren't you?"

Shane nodded. "I've seen stranger things."

"Tell me the truth, Shane. Was there a spark between you and Sara, even a tiny one, when you first met?"

Shane smiled and held his thumb and forefinger a little ways apart. "About this much, when I thought she was Reagan." They both laughed. Shane shook his head. "Sara's too young for me, and too sweet."

"I like sweet," Dane admitted.

Shane made a face. "I can take it, but only in small doses."

Dane laughed. "Then you're definitely going for the right woman."

Danny came bouncing over to them. "Can we go, Unca Shane?"

Shane stood. "Sure can." He looked at his brother. "Maybe Reagan will straighten her out, and then you can talk again."

Dane saw two DEA agents entering the front door. He'd try to figure out how to fix things with Sara later. "I can't think about that right now, Shane. I have a job to do."

## 35

### SARA

SARA TOOK A deep breath and filled her lungs with the salt air. The beach was gorgeous, and what little of the gardens she'd seen were incredible. She wiggled her toes in the pristine white sand. Every shade of blue and aqua surrounded them. The golden sun smiled down on her, and with every breath she took, she felt the tension ebbing away. There was a unique, sweet scent to the tropical air that Sara thought she would never tire of. Danny skipped along beside her, and Shane and Reagan were ahead of them with their heads together. Whatever they were talking about claimed their full attention. Every once in a while, she saw one or both of them in profile smiling at the other.

Sara thought back to the conversation she and Reagan had up in the room. Sara couldn't hide her annoyance. "So, which brother do you have your eye on?"

Reagan's eyes grew wide. "Whoa! Who says I'm interested in either one of them?"

"Oh, Reagan, I'm not a child," Sara retorted. She stepped out of Reagan's clothes and took the other set out of her suitcase. "Here," she said, gathering them up and handing them to her sister. "I'm done with these."

Reagan took the clothes and shoved them in a drawer. "Which one are *you* interested in?"

Sara aimed her sharpest look at her sister. "Neither. One." She rifled through her suitcase, found a tank top and shorts, and headed for the bathroom.

As she closed the door, Reagan shouted, "Dane's not married to me or anyone else, and he and I are just good friends. He's completely available and you can hear all about it from him."

Sara leaned against the coolness of the bathroom door and blew out a breath. *Dane isn't married? Maybe it was all a big misunderstanding.* She closed her eyes and the memories of that morning filled her mind. Sara replayed every smile, every look, and especially the feel of his hand in hers, and how safe and cherished she had felt in his arms, even though she'd literally just met him. There was definitely something very powerful between them. *Please, God,* she prayed. *Could you help fix this?* A sliver of hope blossomed in her chest.

Danny's voice brought her back to the present. "Miss Sara, look!" He ran up to her with three shells. "Feel how smooth this one is!"

Sara ran her finger along it. "Wow, that's awesome. Which shell do you like best?" She smiled as he chattered about each shell's best points. Then he announced that he liked them all the same.

Sara sighed. Even if he was single, Dane was a package deal, and Danny was adorable. But Sara lived in Wisconsin and they lived in Miami. It was ridiculous to even think about it. They couldn't even date. It felt like her life had fallen apart in the last three days, and she had no idea how to put it back together. The Disney deal was dead in the water. She didn't really want to go back to Chicago with Brandon and Morgan and their family, but at least she could be useful there. The prospect of going back to school in Michigan held no appeal now, either.

Sara looked out over the endless ocean, and the important

lessons she learned since childhood filled her mind. Lessons about faith and trust. *Help me, Lord,* she prayed.

They walked a little further, and Danny wanted to stop to make a sand castle. "It's too bad we didn't have any pails or shovels to bring along," Reagan said.

Shane was on his hands and knees, scooping out big handfuls of sand, and Danny imitated him. "We don't need anything but our bare hands, right, buddy?"

"Right, Unca Shane." Danny was concentrating so hard, his eyebrows furrowed together and his little tongue peeked out of his mouth. He was adorable.

Sara and Reagan got down on the sand with them and twenty minutes later, they had an awesome castle to be proud of. "Let's get a picture," Shane said. He took his phone out and they took care of that.

"Where's Daddy?" Danny whined. "He said he was coming."

"I don't know, maybe he got tied up with work," Shane said. He pointed out toward the northwest. "Looks like a storm might be brewing." At that exact moment, his phone pinged with a text, and he read it. He looked at Sara and Reagan. "He said he'll meet us for lunch in thirty minutes. He hit a snag and he'll tell us about it then."

They took more pictures of Danny with the sand castle and assured him that they'd show them to Daddy. Then they began the walk back. Danny wanted to jog, and he and Shane went ahead. Sara and Reagan fell into step together.

Sara nudged her sister. "Looks like you and Shane are getting cozy."

Reagan looked up at her with hopeful eyes. "We'll see. You know I'm not good at relationships."

"Why do you think that is?"

Reagan didn't say anything for several seconds. "I built walls around myself after the debacle with Paul. It was just easier."

Sara couldn't believe it. "Reagan! That was ten years ago. Are you not over him yet?"

"Oh no, I'm completely over him." She shrugged. "I guess I haven't met anyone since who was worth taking a chance on."

"Not even Dane?" Sara wanted to kick herself the moment the words popped out.

Reagan smiled. "No, Dane isn't the one for me. For one thing, he's too young. But that's not really it. I'm too independent for Dane. He's a protector. The right woman will be his partner, but he'll still have that instinct, and she'll embrace it." Her gaze was earnest. "Think about it, Sara."

Sara was so confused, and didn't want to think about any of that right now. "And you think Shane is worth taking a chance on?"

Sara recognized that fierce determination in her sister's eyes, usually reserved for one of her news stories. "Oh yeah, I sure do."

# 36

**DANE**

DANE WAITED ON the beach near the path leading up to the patio for the others to get back. He'd gotten his shower and a change of clothes, and felt much better. He thought he'd be leaving St. Jardin later today, but now that plan was nixed. Maybe it was for the best. He'd just heard some folks in the lobby saying that a storm might be moving in. Dane paced nervously. He'd texted Shane about the snag he'd hit, and also asked him to somehow get Reagan and Danny away from Sara so he could talk with her alone.

He knew now that it would never work between him and Reagan, and he also didn't think he'd ever wanted it to. First, there was the age difference, which wasn't a deal breaker by itself, but there were other things. Reagan was so strong-willed. She always needed a cause, and Dane was more quiet and content to stay behind the scenes. He was a nurturer, and needed a woman who needed him.

And his brother needed a woman *exactly* like Reagan by his side in ministry. Dane shook his head to himself. *Wouldn't that be something?*

He paced back and forth. How could he convince Sara to give

him another chance? He looked toward the direction he knew they'd be coming from, and pretty soon, he saw them, talking and laughing. Sara looked beautiful in a simple blue tank top and white shorts, and her golden hair shone in the sun. Danny rode on Shane's shoulders, and shouted when he saw his dad. "Daddy! We made a sand castle!" Shane lifted him off and set him on the sand, and Danny ran the rest of the way.

Dane ruffled his hair. "I'm sorry I got stuck working, buddy. I'm all done, though. We can play together all afternoon, but it looks like it might rain, so we'll figure something fun to do inside."

"Are we gonna have lunch now? I'm hungry!" Danny exclaimed.

Dane exchanged a look with his brother.

"Yes, we are," Shane said. "Let's go up to the patio and get a table." He held his hand out to Danny. "You can choose." In one smooth move, Shane's eyes connected with Reagan's, and she fell into step with him.

When Dane sensed that Sara was about to follow them, he stepped into her path. His heart began to beat faster. "Sara, please, could we talk?"

Her cheeks turned pink, and she had trouble meeting his eyes. "Um, sure," she said in a voice so soft, he could barely hear her.

He took a deep breath. "I'm so sorry about the misunderstanding. I didn't mean to hurt you. The ring was for show only." Her dark brown eyes were bottomless pools, and he felt terrible for any pain he'd caused her. "I'd really like to start over." He stuck his hand out and gave her what he hoped was his most engaging smile. "Hi, I'm Dane Corsica. Pleased to meet you."

She looked relieved and put her hand in his and giggled. "Hi, I'm Sara St. Clair. I'm pleased to meet you, too."

Dane took both of her hands then, and the zinging returned. "I—ah—I'm a Florida native, I work for the DEA, and I'm a single dad to an amazing little boy named Danny." Her smile got bigger. Dane swallowed. "Technically, I'm a widower, but we hadn't been together for a long time before that, um, happened." A sympathetic shadow crossed over Sara's features, and she squeezed his hands. He looked at her solemnly. "Someday soon, I'll tell you everything about that, I promise." He took a breath. "I'll be twenty-eight on June 20, and I love long, romantic walks on the beach." Sara threw back her head and laughed, and Dane joined her. "Okay, now it's your turn."

"I'm from Baraboo, Wisconsin. I was a vocal performance major for two years at the University of Michigan, and left there a year ago to help my brother take care of my two little nieces. Family is *everything* to me." Dane nodded his agreement. "But he's remarried now, and I'm…not sure what I'm doing. I'm— well, I'm at a crossroads in my life," she said. "I'm just waiting for God to show me, I guess." Dane rubbed his thumb over her knuckles. "I'll be twenty-two on July 7." Her perfectly-shaped eyebrows knit together. "Is that—am I too young?" Her voice trailed off.

Dane shook his head. "No, it's perfect," he said softly.

"Oh, good," she said, and let out a nervous breath. "And I love long, romantic walks on the beach, too—well, at least the one from this morning. That was my first." Her face flushed pink again.

Dane smiled. "I hope it's the first of many to come," he murmured. His heart swelled when she squeezed his hands and nodded. "But for now, will you be my date for lunch?"

She giggled. "Yes, but my stomach is fluttering so much, I don't know if I'll be able to eat much."

"Me, too," Dane replied. He took a breath, stepped a little closer, and moved his hands down to clasp her waist. A thrill shot through him when she wrapped her arms around him and looked up at him. "Sara," he said softly. He stared into her beautiful eyes. "I was married for almost six years and we weren't together most of it, but I never broke my vows." He paused. "I just—I would never do that."

"I know, Dane."

He tilted his head at her? "How? You don't even know me."

She nodded her head slowly. "But I do. My heart knows that you're a good man."

Dane felt the breath leave him. He drew her to his chest and wrapped his arms around her. After a moment, he released her and took her hand. "You ready?"

Her eyes shone with a promise of good days to come. "Yes."

# 37

**SARA**

SARA COULDN'T BELIEVE it. She wanted to pinch herself. *I must be dreaming.* She felt like she'd just come through a hurricane. Six hours ago, she'd been in captivity and was completely alone. Then she was rescued, reunited with her sister, and saw her summer plans go up in smoke. And then, in one pivotal moment, an amazing man opened his heart to her. Sara felt like she was walking on air.

She and Dane arrived at the patio, and she saw Reagan, Shane, and Danny at a round table in the far corner. Dane walked in front of her and wove through the tables. Her heart fluttered as she looked at their clasped hands.

Suddenly, a woman's voice came from their right. "Sara! Trey!"

Dane led her there and put his arm around her. "Cassie and Drew, hello."

*How cool. That's his way of telling me their names.* Sara easily slipped into her role and smiled at the couple. "Hi, Cassie, Drew. Nice to see you."

"What have you guys been up to?" Cassie asked.

Dane and Sara exchanged an amused look. "Oh, you know,

just enjoying our honeymoon," Dane said. He pulled her a little closer, and Sara leaned into him, resisting the urge to sigh.

Sara felt Cassie studying her. "Sara, you look fantastic, much better than you did earlier in the week. Did you go to the spa day?"

"Yes, she did," Dane quickly answered. "She loved the seaweed wrap, didn't you, sweetheart?" His eyes sparkled at her.

*Sweetheart.* Sara nodded, never breaking her gaze with his. "Yes, yes, I did." She bit the inside of her cheek to keep from laughing.

"Have you been to the Queen's Garden yet?" Drew asked.

"Ah, no, we haven't made it there," Dane answered.

"Oh, you *have* to go. It's amazing!" Cassie exclaimed. "They're not doing a marriage ceremony there this week, but you can sign up for a tour."

In a flash, Sara's emotions went from panic to relief. That must be the symbolic marriage ceremony that Landon and Kelsea had participated in that had resulted in a legal marriage. Sara knew she wasn't ready for *that* step. She glanced at Dane and saw the same emotions flit across his features.

"We'll probably do that," Dane said. He took Sara's hand again. "We're joining our—ah, friends for lunch. Enjoy your afternoon."

"Bye," Sara said with a little wave, as Dane pulled her away.

"Bye," the couple echoed.

"Good job," Dane whispered. "You're a natural at this undercover stuff."

"Thanks," Sara giggled. "That was hilarious. Let's not tell Reagan the part where they said I looked so much better than I did earlier in the week!"

"Definitely not," Dane said with a laugh. They reached the table and Dane let go of her hand and put his arm around her, resting his hand lightly on her waist.

Shane and Reagan were sitting next to one another, and looked at them expectantly. "Hi, guys, how's everything?" Reagan asked brightly.

Dane looked at Sara, and their faces wore identical grins. "Great," Dane said.

"Yes, great," Sara echoed.

Shane and Reagan exchanged a glance. "Well, that's great!" Shane said with a grin of his own. Everyone laughed.

There was an empty seat next to Danny. "I want Miss Sara to sit by me!" Danny said. Dane held the chair out for her, and claimed the one on her other side. He scooted in, reached for Sara's hand under the table, and threaded his fingers through hers.

Sara met Reagan's gaze, and couldn't tell which of them was happier.

"Hello, everyone! May we join you?" It was Rose and Ike. Sara's gaze immediately went to Rose's feet, which were encased in pink Converse. The rest of her matching ensemble was pink as well. She and Ike were as cute as Kelsea said they were.

"Of course," the others replied in unison. There was plenty of room at the round table, and Shane and Dane fit two more chairs in. Sara picked up the menu. It looked like a regular restaurant menu, but there were no prices, since it was an all-inclusive resort.

Reagan's phone pinged, and she looked at it. "Oh, look, Sara!" she exclaimed and handed the phone over. "Here's our new nephew! Brandon and Morgan adopted a baby boy," she said to Shane.

"Oh, he's so adorable!" Sara exclaimed. She showed the picture to Dane and then passed the phone around.

"What did they name him?" Ike asked when the phone made it back to Sara.

Sara scrolled down. "Andrew James, for Morgan's dad and our dad." Her eyes grew wide. "AJ. They're calling him AJ." She handed the phone back to Reagan.

"That's the name April and Shelbie always wanted to call their little brother," Rose said.

"They came up with that before Brandon and Morgan even dated," Sara said in awe.

"Yes, back when they first met, when they couldn't stand the sight of one another!" Rose said, and everyone laughed.

The server came to get their drink orders. Once she had left, Rose looked at Shane. "What do you do, Shane?"

"I'm a pastor."

"Oh, that's nice," Ike said.

Dane raised his eyebrows. "He's *not* just a pastor." He told Rose and Ike about the Miracle Center, which of course they had heard of. Sara had, too. She couldn't believe Shane was its founder. They spent several minutes asking him all kinds of questions, and he seemed to always deflect the spotlight away from himself. Sara also noticed that her sister couldn't keep her eyes off him.

Their food arrived and everyone dug in. Dane remarked how much he and Reagan had enjoyed all the meals, which led to a long, fun story from Rose and Ike about how many mediocre chefs they'd suffered through before landing on their present outstanding one.

Shane spoke up. "Dane, you said you hit a snag with the case. Can you tell us anything about that?"

"Well, some. At first, the DEA said they wanted the—our witness back in Miami today. But our station chief is out of the country and can't interview him until Monday, and they'd rather he stay here, away from the media. He also said that I would have to be the one to bring him back." He looked at Sara. "They told me they would fly me home today and back on Sunday night, or I could stay here over the weekend if I wanted to, so I decided to stay."

Reagan's eyes narrowed. "Where's that *witness* now?"

Dane smiled at her. "That's DEA classified information, Ms. St. Clair. Don't worry, you'll get your exclusive when we get back to Miami on Monday."

Reagan glanced at Sara. "Actually, I'm flying home this evening. I need to get back to work." Sara resisted the urge to smile. *On a Thursday night?*

"Me, too," Shane said. "I have a full weekend coming up."

Dane slid a glance at Sara and winked. She swore she could hear his thoughts. *Yeah, they're about as subtle as a freight train.*

"What are your plans, Sara?" that question came from Rose. "You really should stay, too. After all, Trey and Sara Armstrong have reservations here through the weekend. The Carsons and some of the other couples and staff would wonder if you just disappeared. It would be so awkward for Trey."

Sara felt her face heating up. She took a breath and looked at Dane's beautiful, hopeful eyes, and knew the next words would change her life. "I could do that. I don't have anywhere to be."

"Good! That's settled," Rose said. She smiled at Danny. "Some of our staff have children who stay in our community room sometimes while they work. Danny can play with them."

"Cool!" he exclaimed, and smiled up at Sara. Her heart tripped.

One of the young men who worked the front desk came up to the table. "That storm we've been watching all morning is tracking south," he said, looking at the Goldmans. "The airport is closing in a couple of hours. I thought you'd want to know. The staff is already making preparations."

"Thank you, Luc," Rose said.

"Is it a hurricane?" Sara asked as the young man hurried off. Rose and Ike shook their heads. "No, these storms flare up and move through quickly this time of year," Ike said. "We thought this one was going to stay north of us. The airport will probably be open by tomorrow morning."

Rose looked at Shane and Reagan. "Looks like you'll have to stay with us another day," she said. "We had a last-minute cancellation for this week, so we have an extra room available."

Sara saw the brothers exchange a look. "Shane and Danny and I can stay there," Dane said. "Thanks so much Rose, Ike."

Rose stood. "It's no problem at all." She pulled at Ike's arm, and he stood. "Well, since the weather has turned on us, we need to get busy and prepare for our Rain Dance night. It's *very* romantic." She looked around the table. "Not a *rain dance*, but just a dance to keep everyone occupied inside since it will be raining. This is what we do when it rains."

Ike seemed to have a deer-in-the-headlights look. "We do? I mean, yes, we do." He cleared his throat and nodded.

Rose took his hand and dragged him away. "Toodles! See you tonight at the dance!"

After they had gotten well away from the table, Sara giggled. "They're so cute! Just like Landon and Kelsea said."

Reagan rested her arms on the table. "I get the feeling Rose cooked all that up for our benefit. But I'm not going to any dance. I'll just go to bed early."

"I'm with you," Shane said. Then his face grew beet red. "I meant that I'm not going to the dance, either—not, ah, not the other part."

Dane grinned. "My brother has so many amazing gifts and abilities," he said to Reagan and Sara. "But dancing is definitely not one of them. Think bull in a china shop." They all laughed, Shane hardest of all.

Reagan's eyes lit up. "They have a game room with a pizza parlor." She shot Dane a mock frown. "We haven't been near it."

Shane's expression relaxed. "That sounds great."

Sara sighed. "I think the dance sounds wonderful," she said. Her heart skittered as Dane rested his arm along the back of her chair.

He slid a smile her way. "Hey, Danny, what do you want to do tonight?"

"Game room and pizza!" he exclaimed. All the adults laughed.

"How about you and Uncle Shane and Reagan do that, and I'll take Miss Sara out on a date?"

"What's a date, Daddy?" Danny asked.

Dane laughed. "It's when grown-ups who like each other a whole lot get dressed up and go somewhere together."

Danny seemed to mull that over. "Do you like Miss Sara a whole lot, Daddy?"

"I sure do." He looked at Sara with a gorgeous smile.

"Good. So do I, Daddy."

Dane leaned down and whispered in Sara's ear. "I can't wait to hold you tonight on the dance floor."

Sara began to tingle all over. She couldn't believe it, and her eyes connected with Reagan's. Even though a storm was coming, the hurricane had moved on, and left behind the beginnings of a whole new life for both of them.


The wind and rain arrived about an hour after lunch, so they spent the afternoon inside. The guys moved their things into their room, and agreed to meet in the game room.

When Sara and Reagan got there, they found Shane and Danny. "Dane had a phone call to make. He'll be here soon," Shane explained. When Dane got there, they all played Uno, and then Danny got out his Legos and other toys he had brought. Reagan and Shane left, and Sara and Dane sat on a couch by a window, watching the storm, holding hands, laughing, and talking. They were the only ones in the game room. Sara was sure all the honeymoon couples were in their own rooms.

"Hello, everyone!" In came Rose, wearing her usual bright smile.

Danny looked up from his playing. "Hi, Miss Rose!"

She looked at Dane. "I was hoping Danny could come and help us decorate in the dining hall. I could use a good helper."

Danny jumped up. "Could I, Daddy? Please, please?" Sara smiled. He was so cute and hard to resist.

"Sure, but you stay with Miss Rose and do everything she says."

Rose took Danny's hand. "I'm sure he'll be fine. I'll bring him to your room around 5:30, if that's okay."

"It's perfect. Thanks, Rose," Dane said.

After they left, Dane looked around. "We're alone," he said in a loud whisper. Sara thought his lopsided smile was adorable. He pointed at the spot right next to him and wiggled his eyebrows. He pointed to a footstool near her. "Bring that, too," he said.

Sara's heart began to pound, and she giggled as she scooted down next to him. His arms went around her, and they put their feet up. Sara thought this might just be the best moment of her life.

Dane rested his forehead against hers. "I'm so tired," he whispered, "and I need to take a nap or else I'm going to fall asleep on the dance floor tonight and really embarrass you."

Sara laughed. "Me, too. I don't think I slept at all last night."

"But I really, *really* need to kiss you before I fall asleep." Sara stared into his beautiful eyes, and everything went into slow motion. She lifted her lips to his, and his arms came around her. The kiss was soft and unhurried, with the promise of much more, when the time was right.

Dane slowly broke it off, and sighed. It was the most perfect first kiss Sara could imagine. She settled in and laid her head on his chest, and he pulled her close. She couldn't believe how utterly content she felt in his arms. Within minutes, she was asleep.

The next thing she knew, Dane's phone was ringing, and they both sat up and yawned. It was Shane, telling him that it was 5:30, and time to get ready for dinner.

Dane pulled Sara to her feet and they left the game room, hand in hand. His room was on the first floor, and he walked her to the stairway. "See you soon," he murmured, and pressed a quick kiss on her cheek.

Sara ran up the stairs, although she was sure her feet didn't touch the floor. When she got to her room, she went straight to the closet. She knew exactly what she was going to wear.

She heard her phone ping, and looked at it. It was fully charged now. She had several messages, but didn't want to take the time to read them all now. But one—*oh, no. This came just a couple of hours ago.* Sara swallowed and put it on speaker.

"Hi, Sara, this is Lance Petrie from Disney. I just had a call from a special agent at the DEA with a wild story about you being kidnapped. He assured me that you're okay and gave me a number in Miami to call to verify it." He paused. "I made that call, and I'm so sorry that you went through that. Listen, we'll hold your spot if you can get here first thing tomorrow. We'd still love to have you. Please let me know. Thanks, and take care."

Sara sat down on the bed in disbelief. *How in the world had Dane known who to call?* In the next breath, it became clear. He and/or Reagan had called Landon, who contacted Caitlyn. *He did that for me? What do I do now? I have a* third *chance to sing with Disney, but I've just met Dane, and don't want to jeopardize that.*

She showered, got dressed quickly, and put on her makeup. There was a tiny little vial in her makeup bag with a handwritten label on the top that said *Joy*. Reagan had given it to her earlier that day when she was packing. "It's one of those oil blends that Kelsea's always talking about," she'd said. "It's too flowery for me. But some of the other ones, I'm really starting to like." Sara opened the vial and took a deep breath. *Oh, that's wonderful,* she thought, and dabbed some on her pulse points and behind her ears. She hoped Dane would like it.

Then she sat on the bed and began to pray. And ten minutes later, she had peace. Sara knew exactly what she was going to do.

# 38

## DANE

DANE ARRIVED AT Sara's door and straightened the lapels of his suit jacket. He couldn't believe how much had happened in this one short day. He had planned for their first kiss to happen at just the right romantic moment on the dance floor tonight, but once they'd been left alone this afternoon—thanks to Rose—Dane couldn't hold back one more minute. And he was glad he'd given in. Their first kiss had been perfect.

Deep in his heart, he knew Sara would probably be on a plane for Orlando in the morning, and he dreaded saying goodbye. But he felt that he needed to pave the way for her to follow her dream if she still wanted to. He'd prayed about it and deeply believed that it was the right thing to do. And if he had anything to say about it, the *goodbye* wouldn't be for long.

He knocked and the door opened, and there she was, a vision of beauty in an off-the-shoulder dress that floated halfway to the floor. The filmy layers were all the blues and teals of the ocean. His body ran cold, then hot. He stepped into the room and closed the door.

To his surprise, without saying a word, Sara stepped up to him, pulled his head down, and pressed her lips to his. Once Dane got over the shock, he wrapped his arms around her and kissed her back. Her lips were velvety smooth, and her hair was like silk in his fingers. Whatever her perfume was set his senses reeling, and she felt like heaven in his arms.

He wanted the kiss to go on and on, and it did.

When they finally came apart, he felt his face split wide open in a grin. "What was that for?" he murmured. "Whatever it was, I'll do it again, a thousand times."

Her eyes were shining. "You called Lance."

"I did."

"Why?"

He rubbed his hands on her arms. "I wanted him to know that you didn't just blow them off, that there was a valid reason that you didn't show up." He paused. *This was it.* "I wanted you to have the chance to still fulfill that dream if they would agree. They still want you. He made that very clear."

"And I want to go. It's been my dream. But now, there's only one thing that would keep me from it." She stared into his eyes. "You," she said softly.

That one word hit Dane with the force of a tornado. He had to make sure he'd heard her right. He swallowed. "Me?"

"Yes, you and Danny. I'd like to sing with Disney, just for the summer." She took a breath. "But if you won't wait for me, I'll come with you now."

Dane decided that sometimes, actions spoke louder than words. He moved his hands up to gently bracket her face and kissed her, slow and sweet. He didn't know how each kiss could be better than the last, but it was.

Then he touched his forehead to hers. "I'll wait for you," he whispered. He raised his head and took her hands. "In fact, I have a lot of vacation time banked, and I'll get an extra week off after this case closes." He grinned at her. "Danny and I will be your groupies."

Sara laughed, a melodious sound that wove its way straight

into Dane's heart. "I've never had groupies! I have a feeling this is going to be the *best* summer!" she exclaimed. Her beautiful eyes sparkled.

Dane couldn't resist. He leaned down and brushed his lips across hers. "Go ahead, call Lance now, and then we'll go on our first date." He lowered his voice. "By the way, you look *amazing*."

"So do you." Sara rubbed her fingers across the knot of his tie. "Very James Bond," she said with a flutter of eyelashes. "Save every dance for me tonight."

Dane kissed her again. "Count on it."

# 39

*FRIDAY MORNING*

**DANE**

SARA LEFT ST. Jardin on one of the first flights out early that morning. Dane borrowed one of the resort's vehicles and took her to the airport. Their last kiss was filled with longing for the next time they'd see one another, in about a week. But they agreed that this was going to be a fantastic opportunity for Sara, and they'd get through it.

Memories from the night before filled Dane's mind. He felt that Rose and Ike had orchestrated the shimmering, romantic evening just for him and Sara.

Now, he helped load Shane's and Reagan's bags into Sadie-belle's trunk. Moni was delighted to be taking them to the airport.

"I like your car, Moni!" Danny exclaimed. "It's so cool!"

Shane murmured in Dane's ear, "You sure this thing will get us to there in one piece?"

Dane smirked. "Time to exercise those prayer muscles."

Shane laughed. "I'm working on a plan to get her a better vehicle," Dane said. "You know, to thank her for all her help."

Reagan was chatting with Moni, so Dane had a few moments

of privacy with his brother. Shane nodded. "That's nice. How are you and Sara going to do the long distance thing, if it works out?" he asked.

"Well, I have a ton of vacation time banked, and I get an extra week off after this case closes. So—we'll see what happens. I have a couple of plans in mind."

Shane smiled. "I can see the wheels turning."

Dane felt a tug on his elbow, and turned. It was Reagan. "Excuse me," she said to Shane. "I need a few minutes with my good friend." They walked across the grass and stopped under a tree. Reagan looked up at him earnestly. "You break my sister's heart, Corsica, and you'll have me to deal with."

Dane smiled and nodded. "I have every intention of taking care of Sara's heart, and every other part of her, for a very long time."

"Good. Hold out your hand." Dane frowned and did as she asked, and she laid the engagement and wedding rings on his palm. "You may need these again someday."

Dane smiled, slipped the rings in his pocket and hiked a thumb over his shoulder. "And speaking of hearts, you be careful of his. He's waited a long time for the right woman. Remember, I told you to hold out for the best of the best. That's it, right there."

Reagan's eyes clouded over. "I'm not sure I'm the right woman, yet. I have some soul-searching to do, and I need to work on my relationships with my family." Then she smiled. "For now, I'm enjoying cultivating a friendship with him, and I *really* want to learn more about the Miracle Center. I'm fascinated by it."

Dane was certain she wanted to get in there and see how it all worked. "It's an amazing place." He began walking back to where Moni was waiting. "It wouldn't have worked between us, you know."

Reagan smiled. "I know. You're still one of the best friends I've ever had, and I hope that'll never change."

Dane pulled her to his side and squeezed. "You were a great partner, Reagan."

"Thanks."

When they reached Shane, Reagan punched Dane lightly on the arm. "Call me on Monday the minute I can do an interview with Rogers."

"Yes, ma'am," Dane barked with a salute. He and Shane laughed.

Reagan rolled her eyes at them. "After I get this story filed, I'm taking some vacation. I want to see Sara on the road and then go visit our brothers and get to know their families. And spend some time with Mom and Dad."

"Danny and I are going to all of her weekend shows," Dane said. "You can come with us sometime."

"We need to go," Shane said.

"Goodbye, Unca Shane and Miss Reagan," Danny said. He hugged his uncle, and Dane was surprised but touched when Reagan leaned down to give Danny a hug.

Shane grabbed a hold of Dane's hand and pulled him into a hug. "Our women pulled off the greatest bait and switch in history, didn't they?" he whispered in Dane's ear.

*Our women.* Dane laughed and nodded. "They sure did, brother. They sure did."

# 40

**DANE**

AFTER DANE ESCORTED Governor Rogers back to Miami, top leadership of the DEA took over, and Dane's involvement decreased dramatically. In exchange for the governor's testimony about Doug Navarro and others involved in the Cuban anti-cancer drug conspiracy, no charges would be filed against him. He was taking some personal time away to be with his family, and Dane had learned that he was considering resigning from office.

Reagan got her exclusive, and it catapulted her already successful career to the next level. She was able to pick and choose her assignments, and had backed way off on her hours. She had a new passion now, volunteering at the Miracle Center and spending time with Shane. They weren't officially dating, but Dane thought they may as well be.

The summer months were the best time of Dane's life. He and Danny made countless trips back and forth to Orlando, and it was worth every mile. They drove to other cities in Florida where Sara's group performed, and Dane loved making memories on the long car trips with his little son.

The first time he saw Sara on stage, he knew he was completely in love with her. Everything about who she was as a person came out when she was performing in front of a crowd, and the first time she sang solo, Dane almost fell out of his chair, her voice was so pure and beautiful. He was so proud when she introduced him as her boyfriend to her fellow performers.

Weekends were packed with performances, but the first time Sara was able to get a few weekdays off, she came to visit them in Miami, and Dane loved showing her where he had grown up. Nick and Julie Corsica were already wildly hopeful about the prospect of having Sara as a daughter-in-law. Dane hadn't brought it up, but his parents had, and he was thankful for their blessing, although he didn't want to rush things. He and Sara hadn't talked specifically about their future. They were just enjoying being in love and living in the moment.

Sara's contract with Disney went till the end of September. She could have opted out early in order to begin the fall semester, but she was still weighing her options and decided to wait. After her final concert, she and Dane decided to drive to Wisconsin on what Sara dubbed the *St. Clair Family Tour,* and Dane took Danny out of school to go with them. Their first stop was St. Louis to spend a weekend with Landon and Kelsea and the twins. Danny loved the little ones, and it cemented the desire in Dane's heart to give him brothers and sisters someday.

Dane enjoyed talking with Landon, and told him about Moni's Gremlin and how he wanted to get a better car for her. They couldn't have pulled off Sara's rescue without everyone, but Moni was special. "Do you know anything about how to get a car onto the island, I mean, the legal hoops to jump through?" he asked Landon. "I was thinking of getting something in Miami and shipping it over from there. Maybe a good used VW bug. That seems to fit Moni."

Landon let out a moan. "Dane, you're the answer to my prayers." He grinned. "My wife has a VW bug from her single days that's obviously not a good mode of transportation for our growing family, but she's emotionally attached to it and won't let it go. She says it has to have *exactly* the right owner, someone who will love it as much as she does." He sighed. "It's in storage and I'm shelling out money every month for it. If you could take that off my hands, I'll be in your debt. I'll give you anything you ask for."

Dane bit his tongue. *Your younger sister's hand in marriage?* He really did hope that Landon would be his brother-in-law one day. He thought about Moni's affection for Sadie-belle and laughed. "Did Kelsea name the car?"

"Myrtle, as in Myrtle the Turtle," Landon said with a chuckle. "It's green."

"Moni will be the perfect owner, I assure you," Dane replied. "I hope she and Kelsea can meet the next time you go to St. Jardin." He knew the St. Clairs visited the resort at least once a year, usually for their wedding anniversary in January.

"I'm not sure when that'll happen, with more babies on the way, but we'll meet her someday," Landon said. "I'll check into the legal stuff and let you know. And I'll take care of getting Myrtle to Miami—well, once I convince Kelsea to agree."

"A nice piece of jewelry might grease the skids," Dane said.

Landon laughed. "Jewelry doesn't work on Kelsea," he said. "Now Sara—that's a different story. The bigger the bling, the better. Have you figured that out yet?"

Dane laughed in response. "Yeah, that was apparent pretty quickly. But thanks for the tip."

"Anytime," Landon said. "Happy to help you out, Dane. I mean that." Something in Landon's eyes told Dane that he had a real ally.

Their next stop was Chicago, at Morgan and Brandon's beautiful country home. Dane could hardly believe that it had been just a few months since he'd been there at their wedding, when he and Reagan were hiding out. It felt like he and Sara had been together forever.

It took about five minutes for Danny to become best friends with April and Shelbie. The three of them were inseparable and spent hours playing outdoors. Dane didn't feel that he knew Brandon very well compared to Landon, with whom he had spent a full day making arrangements for his and Reagan's escape to St. Jardin, and several phone calls when they were there. He felt like Sara and Brandon had a special bond, as Landon and Reagan did, and enjoyed spending time with Brandon and getting to know him.

Reagan was on her own "St. Clair" tour, but in reverse. She had started at their parents' in Wisconsin, and showed up at Brandon and Morgan's the evening before Dane, Sara, and Danny planned to leave, so they stayed an extra day. Dane felt completely comfortable with their friendship, and had a chance to bring her up to speed—off the record—with what had happened with Governor Rogers.

Sara spent a lot of time with both Brandon and Morgan, and held baby AJ at every opportunity. The first time Dane looked at her face when she held the baby, he realized more than ever that he wanted to build a life with her, have children with her, and grow old with her.

That made it easy to have *that conversation* with Jim and Janice St. Clair on their last night in Wisconsin, after a wonderful few days of getting acquainted and visiting some of the area's attractions, including Danny's favorite, a spectacular indoor water park. Fall was in all its glory now, and Dane had never seen the colors. That was one of his favorite parts of the trip.

Sara had gone to have coffee with her friend, Caitlyn, so it was the perfect opportunity to talk with her parents privately. With a full heart and great humility, Dane told them that he knew that Sara was the woman God had chosen for him, and they joyfully and tearfully gave him their blessing. He told them that he wanted to wait until Christmas or New Year's to propose to her, and they promised to hold his confidence until then.

He and Sara hadn't talked specifically about what would

happen with their relationship now, and it was time to have that conversation. A couple of times, she'd said that she was still trying to make up her mind about going back to school, and Dane wanted to give her all the space she needed to make that decision.

But now, he was ready to take a big, important next step that might help her decide. He got Danny ready for bed, read to him and said prayers, and went to sit on the front porch to wait for her.

# 41

SARA AND CAITLYN hugged one more time. "Bye, boo, love you," Caitlyn said.

"Love you, too," Sara replied. They'd had such a wonderful time catching up. Caitlyn was so thrilled to hear everything about Sara's great time touring with Disney. She was anxious to meet Dane and Danny, and Sara promised her that would happen next time they came north. She *knew* there would be a next time.

She texted Dane when she left the coffee shop, and he was waiting on the porch when she pulled into her parents' driveway. Her heart swelled at the sight of his lopsided grin. Sara still couldn't believe that she could love someone so completely, so deeply, and feel that same love in return. She was ready to take the next step in their relationship, and couldn't wait to tell him her surprise.

He got up and trotted to the driveway, and opened her door when she turned the car off. Sara greeted him with a warm kiss, and he took her hand. "Go for a walk?"

"Of course," she said. "Hold on." She slipped her phone in her pocket, and put her wallet back in the car. They set off and turned left at the end of the drive. She knew exactly where they were going—where they'd gone every night since they'd been there—to the little gazebo overlooking a private lake that sat within the subdivision. They went to "their spot" and sat down. The stars were out in all their glory, and an almost-full moon shone down. The autumn breeze whispered across them like silk, carrying the scent of woodsmoke and leaves. Dane put his arm around her, and Sara snuggled in. She thought she could stay here for the next hundred years.

They sat there for several moments, and then Dane looked into her eyes. "I want to talk about the future, Sara. Our future." Her stomach began to flutter, and he took her hand. "For a long time, I wondered if I would be alone for the rest of my life to raise Danny." She could see his expression in the moonlight, and she'd never loved him more. "It's ironic, you know? I was reckless when I was young, but the biggest mistake of my life led to the biggest blessing of my life." His eyes teared up. "Danny brings me so much joy, every day." Sara squeezed his hand. "You and I haven't known each other that long, but I'm sure God sent you to me, and this summer—well, it's been the best time of my life."

Sara leaned up and kissed him. "Mine, too. I'm crazy about you and Danny."

"I want to get to know you even better. That's going to be hard from fifteen hundred miles away." Sara's heart began to beat faster as his chocolate brown eyes melted into hers.

"Now that I have Danny full-time, it's a much bigger decision. The most important thing is to provide stability for him. I'm not sure how to make a long-distance relationship work. Wisconsin or Michigan is a long way from Florida."

Sara nodded. "I completely agree," she said. She could hardly contain her excitement, and her hand inched toward her pocket. "Oh, Dane—"

He smiled and silenced her with a quick kiss. "I'm not finished yet."

"Okay," Sara said, willing her heart to slow down.

"So, like I said, making a long-distance relationship is hard work." He took a deep breath. "There's an opening in the Detroit field office, and also one in Milwaukee. The Milwaukee job is a better fit for my skill set, but if you decide to go back to Michigan, Danny and I will move there." He swallowed. "I love you so much, Sara."

For perhaps the first time in her life, Sara was at a loss for words. "You'd do that for me?" she whispered. "You'd leave Florida? Leave your parents and your brother, take Danny away from them? They're your support network."

Dane nodded. "Oh yeah, I would, sweetheart." He leaned in and kissed her tenderly, and she held him tight and kissed him back.

Her eyes were moist when they came apart. "I can't believe it, Dane." She pulled her phone out of her pocket and opened it. "I'm so happy that you're willing, but it's not necessary." His expression was anxious as she handed it to him.

His eyes scanned the e-mail that she'd received just this morning. "You're—you're *transferring* to Miami University?" His face was incredulous.

Sara bounced up and down with excitement. "Yes, I've been accepted! They have a top-notch early childhood education program, and they've agreed to apply most of my credits. That's what I want to do, Dane. I'll start in January, but I want to move to Miami now. Reagan said I could stay with her for a few months and see how it goes. I—I want to get to know my sister better, too." She couldn't tell what he was thinking.

Dane pulled her to her feet, lifted her up, and spun her around, his laughter mixed with hers. When he set her down, she put her hands on his shoulders and looked up at him.

"Thank you," he whispered, and covered her lips with his. He raised his head and smiled, his gorgeous brown eyes crinkling. "Now I don't have to learn how to live in the snow!"

## 42

*THE FOLLOWING YEAR, DECEMBER 23*
*ST. JARDIN*

**SARA**

"I REMEMBER THIS island!" Danny exclaimed as he looked out the window of the plane. They were on their final descent into St. Jardin. He looked up at Sara with big brown eyes. "I was just a little kid then." Sara smiled at Dane who was on her other side, and squeezed his hand.

This was Dane and Sara's first trip back to St. Jardin. In two days, they would marry on Christmas Day, and she would officially become Danny's mom. Her heart was so full, she thought it might burst.

They had a smooth landing and quickly got through customs and trundled all their baggage out to the curb.

"I'm heeeeeeeere!" A jolly voice exclaimed, and there was Moni with her trademark smile. She gave jubilant hugs to everyone. "I brought Myrtle the Turtle with me! I never can thank you enough!" she said as she laid both hands on the car and leaned in like she was hugging it.

Sara wondered how they were going to fit themselves and all of their baggage into Myrtle, but Moni had already thought of that. Gustav was parked behind her in a four-door sedan that was in surprisingly good shape. Dane and Sara greeted him warmly. "I will bring all your luggage, and you can ride with Moni," he said.

"Oh goody! I get to ride in Myrtle!" Danny exclaimed.

The plan was to go straight to the Boogie Shack for lunch with Moni's family. All of them had been invited to the wedding, but Dane and Sara wanted a chance to visit with them first. And they had a special gift for Louie and his wife, Evie.

When Dane had gotten back to Miami after their trip to Wisconsin last year, he had received unexpected news of monumental proportions. His first wife and Danny's mother, Sally Ann, had never had much in the way of worldly goods, but Blayze, the international supermodel, left behind a fortune. Some of it was placed in a trust for Danny that he would inherit on his 25$^{th}$ birthday, but the bulk of it, she left solely to Dane. She had penned a poignant letter of apology to him that answered a lot of questions and helped him achieve closure regarding their marriage and the events that led to her downward spiral and eventually, her death. Sally Ann also said that she wanted her earthly fortune to make a real difference and provide a better life for people who needed it, and that she trusted Dane more than anyone else to make that happen.

Dane and Sara didn't want any of the wealth for themselves. Dane thought he would want to leave the DEA someday, but wasn't ready for that yet, and Sara was working hard to complete her college degree. They wanted to save to buy a house and add more children to their family once they were married. They had agreed to just park the money and not make any life-altering decisions. They were praying about the best ways to honor Sally Ann's wishes.

But one thing they had agreed that they wanted to do as soon as possible was to provide a better dwelling for Moni and her family. Landon had done all the legal legwork and today, Dane and Sara were about to reveal the plans for a project that would kick off in the coming year, and they were beside themselves with excitement.

When they entered the restaurant, the noisy group broke out into applause. Dane and Sara greeted everyone with hugs, even the ones whose names they couldn't remember. Then Evie and some of her children came out of the kitchen with a delicious lunch, and they all ate and laughed together.

After that, they brought out a large, beautiful cake and Dane and Sara cut it and fed it to each other. "You need practice for the real thing!" Moni exclaimed.

Dane looked at Sara, and she knew it was time to make their announcement. "Louie and Evie, it's time for you to sit down and relax," Sara said. They had both been bustling around getting food and drinks for everyone. Once the couple was settled with pieces of cake and something to drink, Sara went and stood by Dane.

"Sara and Danny and I are so happy to be here with all of you," Dane said as he looked around the room. "I'm not much at making speeches, but—well, I guess the simplest way to say it is that I received a pretty generous inheritance recently, and the person who left me the money only asked that I use it to help others to have a better life."

He turned to the parents of this most unlikely family. "Louie and Evie, you've given your hearts and everything you own to make a family and give them a better life, and we'd like to help you with that." He walked over to Louie and handed him an envelope. "Here's a little something to start the year off right," he said.

Louie looked at Evie and back to Dane. He looked like he didn't know what to do. "Go ahead, open it," Sara said. She was so excited she would hardly stand it.

Louie pulled the back flap open and looked in the envelope. His eyes went wide, and he let out a sob. "Fifty—fifty thousand dollars? You're giving us a check for fifty thousand dollars?" Evie screamed and covered her face as the room erupted in pandemonium. Tears streamed down hers and Louie's faces, and they embraced.

Sara couldn't help it, and she began to cry. She looked at Dane and saw that he was tearing up, too. Louie and Evie stood and held out their arms, and drew Sara and Dane into them. "Thank you, thank you so much," they exclaimed.

When everyone had composed themselves, Dane held up his hand. "This is just the start," he said. "We've drawn up plans for a brand new home for your family, and I'll go over all that with Louie and Evie later." He looked at them affectionately. "So you can make it just the way you want it." Sara was so proud of Dane. He had put the whole plan together with his father, who owned a construction company. Because of the size of Sally Ann's estate, it had taken over a year for everything to move through the legal system. Landon was advising Dane and had put him in touch with a good attorney in Miami who was setting up a foundation, which Dane and Sara had decided to call *Sally Ann's Hope*.

As the room erupted in more cheers, Sara looped her arm through Dane's and reached up to kiss his cheek. "I love you so much, Dane. I can't wait to be your wife."


"I can't believe that by this time tomorrow, we'll be married." Dane squeezed Sara's hand and stared into her eyes. It was the next morning, and they were walking along the shoreline just as they had on the morning they met.

"This is perfect, having the wedding here and having it all to ourselves," Sara said. The Goldmans had closed the resort for the entire week. She looked around worriedly. "But I won't relax until Reagan and Shane get here. What time is it?"

Dane put his arm around her. "About two minutes later than the last time you asked. Sweetheart, they'll be here. Shane texted that their flight left on time."

Sara's left hand rested on Dane's chest, and her spectacular princess-cut engagement ring sparkled in the sun. Dane had sold the bridal set Reagan wore when they were undercover so Sara could have something all her own. "I can't get married without my sister," Sara said. Rooming with Reagan had worked out great and brought them much closer. "And you can't get married without your brother," she added.

Dane stopped and locked his hands behind her waist. "They'll be here." He lowered his voice. "Can I help you get your mind off them?" He touched his lips to hers.

Sara smiled and gave herself over to his kiss. "Have I told you today how much I love you?" she said.

"Yes, but I never get tired of hearing it," Dane said. He took her hand and they walked up the hill and through the gardens to the resort's main building. They crossed the vacant lobby and entered the main dining room, where the rehearsal dinner was to be held that evening.

"Oh Dane, look!" Sara exclaimed. Both their parents and Sara's brothers and their wives were turning the room into a winter wonderland. "It's beautiful!"

"Here's the bride and groom!" Sara's dad shouted, and everyone stopped what they were doing to applaud.

Danny came skipping over to them with April and Shelbie. They had turned into the Three Musketeers. The smaller children, Rose and Isaac, AJ, and Landon and Kelsea's younger twins, Faith and Emma, were being kept under their mothers' and grandmothers' watchful eyes.

"Daddy! Mama Sara! Come look at what we're making!" He took their hands and dragged them over to a table where Morgan had all kinds of art supplies set out for them. Danny and the girls chattered excitedly about the decorations they were making for the reception tables.

"Morgan, this is great," Sara said.

"One of the perks of being an artist," Morgan said with a laugh. "I would have filled an entire suitcase with my 'art clutter,' as Bran calls it, if I could have talked him into paying the extra baggage fees."

Sara hugged Morgan. "How's he doing?" she whispered. Brandon was sitting at a table near the front of the room untangling miles of red and white lights being hung throughout the room by his and Dane's fathers.

Morgan sighed. "As usual, trying to overdo. Doctors make the worst patients."

"I'll go keep him company," Dane said, and set off in that direction.

"Thanks, Dane," Morgan called after him.

Sara studied her brother. "He looks better even since you got here yesterday." Brandon had been diagnosed with early-stage prostate cancer earlier that year and was undergoing a new treatment regimen.

Morgan nodded. "It's good to get him out of the Chicago winter," she said. "The sun and sea air have already done wonders for him." She sighed. "I wish I could just keep him here, but if I bring that up, he'll just feed me his 'I'm a city boy' line. He's itching to get back to work."

Sara looked at Morgan intently. "And how are *you* doing?"

Morgan's eyes welled up, and she swiped at them. "Fine. Of course I worry about him. I worry about everything."

"But his numbers are looking real good, and the doctors are optimistic, right?" Sara said. She squeezed Morgan's hands.

Morgan nodded. "Yes. They caught it early. But cancer is so scary." She closed her eyes. "I love him so much," she whispered. "I can't—"

Sara drew her sister-in-law into a hug. "I know." She drew back after a moment and blinked her tears away. "He's going to be fine, Morgan. In fifty years he'll still be driving you crazy."

Morgan gave a shaky laugh and wiped her eyes. "I'll take it," she said.

Kelsea came up on Morgan's other side, holding little AJ. Morgan held her arms out and he let out a squeal.

"Did you want to decorate the cake?" Kelsea asked her sister.

"Mom and Janice offered to do it." Today was Brandon's birthday and they were going to celebrate tonight after the rehearsal dinner.

"They can do it," Morgan said. "You know what? On second thought, I want to." She kissed her son's cheek. "You want to help Mommy decorate Daddy's cake?"

"Cake!" AJ squealed.

Suddenly, there was a commotion by the door, and Sara realized that Reagan and Shane had just arrived. "Reagan!" She cried, and ran to her sister. When they embraced, Sara whispered into her ear, "Your hair looks great!" Then she hugged Shane, and everyone else arrived to greet them. Sara moved out of the way to make room.

Her brothers were the first ones to bring it up. "Your braid! You cut off your braid?" they exclaimed. Reagan's dark brown hair was fashioned into a smooth, shoulder-length bob.

Reagan glowed. "It was time for a change."

"It looks fantastic, Reagan," Kelsea said.

Morgan nodded. "I'm not sure I would have recognized you if I hadn't known you were coming."

"You look years younger, Reagan," Dane called out.

Her eyes narrowed. "Watch it, Corsica," she said with a grin, and everyone laughed.

Dane whispered to Sara, "I'm glad Reagan has gotten over her phobia of hugging."

Sara smiled up at him. "It wasn't a phobia. She just isn't an affectionate person."

"Make that *wasn't*," Dane said. "I think my brother has done wonders for your sister."

"Him and God." Sara squeezed his hand and moved to stand by Reagan. She looped her arm through her sister's. "Ok, everyone, we have an announcement." She waited until everyone was quiet, and tried to look sad. "Reagan is *not* going to be my maid of honor."

No one said anything, and Sara took in their confused faces. Then she looked at her sister. "Right, Reagan?"

Reagan gave a curt nod. "Yes, that's right. I'm not going to be Sara's maid of honor." She paused. "But I *will* be her matron of honor." She held up her left hand that had a gold wedding ring. Shane held his up to reveal a matching band.

There was a moment of stunned silence, and then everyone started talking and laughing and hugging again. Reagan and Shane were embraced and congratulated by everyone.

"This is fantastic!" Kelsea cried. "And after tomorrow, you two girls will have the same last name again!"

Reagan smiled. "Actually, it *won't* be the same after tomorrow. I kept St. Clair."

Shane put his arm around his wife. "One of the many concessions I had to make to get her to marry me," he said. Everyone laughed, and Shane planted a kiss on the top of Reagan's head.

"When did you—where did you get married?" Landon asked.

"On Thanksgiving Day," Shane said. He and Reagan exchanged a loving glance. "We just—we love all of you, but it was something we wanted to do quietly. It was just the two of us and a pastor friend of mine, down at the beach with Dane and Sara as our witnesses."

Reagan's face shone. She looked around the group. "You all know that I wouldn't have been a very good traditional satin-and-lace bride." Everyone laughed.

Shane took Reagan's hand. "And after the ceremony, I had the privilege of re-baptizing Reagan in the ocean."

"That's wonderful, Reagan," her mother said, and the others nodded in agreement.

"Did you know about this, Mom and Dad?" Landon said.

Jim and Janice exchanged a look. "They called us about a week ago, but we promised to keep it to ourselves," Jim said. "They wanted to tell all of you in person."

"Peanut kept a secret all this time?" Brandon said with an incredulous look. His eyes were sparkling and Sara knew he was teasing.

"Where's your diamond ring, Auntie Reagan?" demanded little Shelbie. "My mommy and all the other ladies have one."

Morgan grimaced. "I'm sorry, Reagan. She's so inquisitive."

"It's okay." Reagan smiled at her niece. "I didn't want one." Sara noticed that her sister was looking at Dane.

Dane laughed. "When we were fake married, I got her a diamond, and she said the engagement ring wasn't her style."

"Saved me a bundle," Shane muttered with a smile. Reagan elbowed him, and he put his arms around her, and everyone laughed.

Dane drew Sara close. "I told her then that it was the *real Sara's* style, and I was right," he said. "I definitely got the right St. Clair sister."

Shane's eyebrows lifted. "So did I."


The long, oblong dining tables were arranged in a large square for the wedding rehearsal dinner in the main dining room. Dane and Sara had chosen this arrangement over separate round tables because they wanted everyone to be able to see everyone else.

The babies and children were being cared for by some of Moni's sisters who were now working at the resort, in the next building. Their parents were looking forward to having a "date night" and a few hours' reprieve.

The tables were covered with white linen with beautiful red and white flowers and greenery. Silver and crystal sparkled in the candlelight, and sparkling white lights lent a magical atmosphere.

Rose and Ike stepped to the microphone. "Would everyone take their seats, please?" Ike said.

After everyone had located their place cards and gotten settled, Rose smiled at everyone. "We're so happy to have everyone here on the eve of Dane and Sara's wedding," she said, smiling at the couple. "We'd like to have a blessing before the meal is served. Pastor Shane, would you be willing to do that?" she said sweetly.

Shane stood and made his way to the mic. "Happy to," he said. "It's at the top of my job description, you know: *offer prayer at all events.*" Everyone laughed.

After the delicious meal had been served and cleared, Landon took the microphone and carried it over to where Rose and Ike were seated.

"We have an announcement to make," Ike said. He reached out and squeezed his wife's hand. "I'll let Rosie do it, since she's the talker in the family." Everyone laughed.

Rose smiled at the assemblage. "As you know, Ike and I have owned this resort for about eight years. Some of you may not know that we lived in Brooklyn our whole lives until we won fifteen million dollars in the lottery and ended up here on beautiful St. Jardin, and bought this resort." Sara already knew this, as did Dane, and they enjoyed seeing amazement on his parents' and brother's faces.

Rose looked at Ike, and he took over. "We never had children, and didn't have any family in Brooklyn when we left. And now, all of you are our family." His voice wavered, and his eyes grew bright. He smiled and reached for Rose's hand again.

She spoke in a clear, loud voice. "God has given us more than we could ask or think! And I'm not talking about the money. I'm talking about all of you dear people whom we have grown to love. Jim and Janice, and your four wonderful children." Her gaze turned to Kelsea and Morgan's mother, and the Corsica parents. "Beth, you and your two beautiful daughters, and Nick and Julie, whose wonderful sons are now forming new families with the St. Clair sisters—now that they've all figured out who belongs with whom—with a little help." Everyone burst into laughter.

Rose looked at Ike and took a breath. "I think most of you

know that we were planning to turn the honeymoon resort into a family resort, but after conducting some feasibility studies, it's become clear that we can support both, so we're going to add the family resort. But we're not getting any younger, and this business is growing. We've decided to turn the reins over to someone younger who can devote the time and energy to carry this dream forward. So, to help that happen, we've put everything into a trust, and effective March first, the new owner/managers of the St. Jardin Honeymoon and Family Resort will be—" she paused.

"Landon and Kelsea St. Clair."

It felt like all the oxygen left the room, and then everyone began to talk at once. Many questions arose out of the chatter, and once it died down, Landon stood and walked behind Rose and Ike. He placed a hand on each of their shoulders.

"To answer everyone's main question, yes, we're moving our family to St. Jardin. This was a decision made with a lot of prayer and planning." His gaze connected with his wife's. "We think it will be a great place for our children to grow up." He looked around the room. "Of course, the down side is that we'll be farther away from all of you."

"So you'll just have to come and visit!" Kelsea called out.

"Well, if you insist!" Jim St. Clair said. Everyone laughed. "Will you be giving up your law practice?" he asked his older son.

Landon nodded. "I'll sell my equity in JJS," he said, referring to the law firm where he was a partner. "I'm ready for a change, and since St. Jardin is a trade partner with the US, I'll still be able to keep my law license and maintain my skills through all of the administrative and legal tasks associated with owning a business here."

"What kinds of things do you have planned for the combined resorts?" Brandon asked. "I assume you'll be adding more services."

Landon nodded, and looked at Kelsea again before turning his attention back to Brandon. "I'm glad you asked, bro," he said with a smile. "First off, we'd like to add on-site medical services. What's available on the island isn't really adequate for what we need." He paused. "You wouldn't happen to know a doctor who'd be willing to relocate here and take charge of that, would you?"

Silence hung over the group. Brandon looked at Morgan and took her hand. As close as her brothers were, Sara suspected that this wasn't the first that Brandon was hearing of it. "I might," he said with an enigmatic smile. Morgan's eyes filled and she laid her head on his shoulder.

Landon looked around the group. "Kelsea and I have talked about all sorts of other things we'd like to do." He looked at Morgan. "An art gallery, and an arts and crafts center for all ages." His gaze then moved to his younger sister. "A daycare/preschool for our staff children with programs for the children at the family resort."

Kelsea looked at Beth, who had just retired after a long career as an elementary educator. "There'll be a place for you, too, Mom, whenever you want to come. And Jim and Janice."

Beth's face brightened. "I'll sacrifice the northern Illinois winters for starters," she said.

"Hear, hear!" Jim said. Everyone laughed.

"I'm not ready to retire yet," Nick Corsica said. "But I'd love to talk about partnering with Corsica Construction when you're ready to start building. It will be easy to manage projects between here and Miami." He looked at his wife. "We'll give you the family discount," he said with a smile, and everyone laughed.

"That's fantastic, Nick, thanks." Landon turned his attention to Dane. "I'm not sure what we can come up with to rival the excitement of the DEA."

Dane held up both hands. "I've had enough excitement," he said, and put his arm around Sara. "Actually, I've been thinking about leaving. I'm ready for a new challenge. As soon as my wife graduates, we'll talk about it." Sara's heart skittered at the possibilities.

Landon gestured to Shane and Reagan. "Maybe you could open a branch of the Miracle Center here, and of course, a newspaper."

Reagan laughed and shook her head. "I'm still doing some freelance writing, but that's it. For now, anyway." She looked at her husband. "My place is by Shane's side in ministry."

Brandon looked at her incredulously. "Words I thought I'd never hear out of you!" The group laughed. His gaze softened. "Sis, that's fantastic."

Reagan reached for Shane's hand. "I guess this is as good a time as any to let you all know that…this family will be growing."

Once again, there was a beat of stunned silence, and then the room erupted with noise and cheers.

Shane grinned and held up three fingers.

"Triplets? You're having triplets?" Sara shrieked, and the room got even noisier.

Reagan shook her head back and forth. She was laughing so hard, she could hardly speak. "No—I'm not—" She looked at her husband. "Shane, you have to explain."

"All right." Shane let out a breath. His smiling face turned serious, and everyone got quiet. "A couple in my—our—church, that I've known for years, was killed in a small plane crash about six months ago." Silence dropped down on the room. "We—we've started proceedings to adopt their three sons." He reached for Reagan's hand. "They're terrific boys. They're—eleven, nine, and six. We're so honored that God has chosen us to be their—parents." He choked up on the last word.

Landon squeezed the bridge of his nose. "Wow," he said. "This just keeps getting better and better. Shane and Reagan, that's fantastic." He looked at Sara and Dane. "You two are about to enter into the most sacred relationship that God created." He held out his hand to Kelsea, and she came to his side and their arms went around one another. "Almost six years ago, Kelsea and I were about to be married—to other people—and we both got jilted at the last minute. That heartbreak led to us meeting, in a most unlikely way, right here on St. Jardin." He looked at Rose and Ike tenderly and smiled, and then moved his arm in a wide arc across the room. "And look what happened because of a little matchmaking!"

"I'm still willing to serve as the island's matchmaker!" Rose exclaimed, and everyone laughed and cheered.

Landon looked at the clock. "It's getting late. Let's go get the little ones and meet back here for dessert." He looked at his brother. "It's time for a birthday party."

# 43

**REAGAN**

REAGAN WALKED OVER to where her parents were sitting. She'd wanted to have this conversation with them for the past year and a half, but her heart wasn't ready yet. She knew that now was the time. "Mom, Dad, could we talk for a few moments, privately?"

"Of course, Reagan," her mother said. They rose and followed her out a side door and through a garden to a couple of benches set at right angles. Jim and Janice sat down at one, Reagan at the other.

"I—whew," Reagan blew out a breath. "This is harder than I expected." *You can do this.* "Mom and Dad, I want to ask your forgiveness for all the things I've done over the years. I know I was such a big disappointment to you—"

"What are you talking about, Reagan Joy? You've never been a disappointment to us!" Janice exclaimed. She and Jim wore twin expressions of confusion.

Reagan's eyes filled with tears, and she swiped at them. "Oh, I know I was. All my drama in high school. Leaving the youth group and the church, and not following the path you wanted for me—"

Her parents frowned at one another. "All we've ever wanted for you was to be happy, Reagan," Jim said. He took her hand. "You had to find that path on your own. No one could choose it for you."

"More than anything, Reagan, we wanted you to have a right relationship with God, whatever that meant to you." Janice said. She scooted to sit next to Reagan and put her arm around her. "We made that vow to Him when we had you dedicated as a baby. We've prayed that for you every day of your life." Her eyes welled up. "And we're so glad that you've found your way back to Him."

Reagan fell into her mother's arms, overcome with tears. "But—I was so stubborn, so headstrong," she hiccupped.

To her surprise, her parents laughed. "Oh, you sure were!" Janice said, wiping her own eyes. "You burst into the world two weeks before your due date, after only four hours of labor." She smiled at Jim and looked back at Reagan. "When we took our first look at you, we knew that you were going to live life on your own terms."

"They called it *strong-willed* back then," Jim added.

"But the boys weren't strong-willed," Reagan said. "They were perfect all the time and did everything you wanted them to."

That elicited a huge laugh from both of her parents. "Oh, they certainly did not!" Janice exclaimed. "I'll admit, they were more compliant than you, but they weren't perfect."

Jim moved to sit on Reagan's other side. "Honey, God gave you your temperament and your strong will. We just tried to shape that and channel it in a positive way so that you would do great things in the world."

"And you have, and still are," Janice said, and kissed Reagan's temple. "We're so proud of you, Reagan, and always have been." She ran her hand over her daughter's hair. "We couldn't be happier for you. We know you're going to be a wonderful wife for Shane, and a wonderful mother to those boys."

Tears ran down Reagan's cheeks. She felt so safe and secure

and *loved* in her parents' arms. "I love you both so much," she whispered. "But I still need to have your forgiveness. Please."

"Consider it given, Reagan," her dad said.

Her mom whispered, "of course, Reagan, we love you so much."

Reagan looked at them with new eyes. "Now I'm embarking on the biggest challenge of my life. I'm going to be a *mom.*" She felt her eyes filling up again. "I have no idea what to do. It's all happened so fast. I haven't had nine months to prepare."

Janice laughed. "Believe me, Reagan, it doesn't matter. This is one job that you can only learn *on the job.*" Jim nodded his agreement.

Reagan looked between her parents. "Would you two—would you consider coming down after the boys move in? Maybe stay a few weeks or a month? And just tell me what to do?"

Jim laughed and put his arm around his daughter. He looked at Janice. "I think we can work something out. We'd love to spend some time getting to know our new grandsons, and our new son-in-law. But remember, you're not in this alone. Don't you think Shane should have something to say about it?"

"Oh!" Reagan covered her mouth and giggled. "I almost forgot!" All three of them laughed.

Suddenly, Shane came around the corner and stopped in front of them. "Hi, everyone. There you are, Reagan. I was wondering where you were," he said. "Forgot what?"

Reagan popped up and went to him, slipping under his arm and wrapping hers around his waist. "I forgot when it was the boys are moving in with us permanently," she said innocently. "Would it be okay if Mom and Dad came to visit after they've gotten settled in?"

"I think that's a fantastic idea. I think it will be around the first of February." He smiled warmly at his in-laws. "That's a great time to come to south Florida for an extended visit. Mom and Dad would enjoy that, too."

Janice shivered. "You don't have to invite me twice."

Jim stood, and Janice followed. "We'd like to pray for you two," he said. They came and wrapped their arms around the younger couple, praying that God would have His hand on the adoption proceedings, and everything would go smoothly, for His wisdom on Shane and Reagan as they prepared for parenthood, and His blessing on the new family.

When her dad said *Amen,* Reagan's heart felt completely at peace.

**DANE**

DANE LOOKED AROUND this group of incredible people that
God had brought together. *What an amazing family.* His beautiful
Sara was at his side, and Danny's little arms were wrapped around
him. Dane's heart was full to overflowing.

Dane loved that the St. Clair family always had a big birthday
celebration for Brandon on Christmas Eve, separate from
Christmas Day, so he wouldn't feel cheated. Dane loved all of
Sara's family, but had come to have a stronger bond with Brandon.
It was obvious that he and his wife were deeply in love, that he
was a man of great faith, and a devoted dad.

After all the gifts were opened and the cake and ice cream
were consumed, Dane was surprised when Shane stood and
cleared his throat. "Everyone, I'd like to lay hands on Brandon
and pray for him. Would you all join me?"

Everyone gathered their children and they moved in close to
form a circle around Brandon, who held little AJ on his lap. April
and Shelbie stood on either side of him, and Morgan stood behind
him next to Shane, their hands on his shoulders. Dane was next to
Sara, with Reagan on his other side.

Dane's eyes filled with tears as his brother prayed with

eloquence and great faith on Brandon's behalf, and he heard others crying, too. He stood between Sara and Reagan, their arms wrapped around one another. When Shane finished his prayer, a hush settled over them.

Next to him, Dane felt Sara take a deep breath, and then her clear, angelic voice filled the room. *Praise God from Whom all blessings flow. Praise Him all creatures here below. Praise Him above ye heavenly hosts. Praise Father, Son, and Holy Ghost.*

Her *Amen* echoed through the room, carrying everyone's collective prayers heavenward. Dane blinked back tears. *Thank you so much, God, for this family.*

# AUTHOR'S NOTE

In the world of fiction, many books include a disclaimer stating the characters are figments of the author's imagination, and any similarity to a real person, living or dead, is coincidental or non-intentional. The same holds true for places and things that the author uses when building a fictional world.

I want to make a clarification about Shane Corsica's *Miracle Center*. When I began writing about this fictional ministry, I had a vague recollection of something called *The Dream Center* started in Southern California by a pastor named Matthew Barnett quite some years ago. I read Barnett's book about his journey almost a decade ago, and was still impacted by it.

While writing this manuscript, I purposely did not go back and re-read the book, nor did I conduct any online searches about the *Dream Center*. I didn't want to be influenced by any of it, and didn't want to have to change details about that ministry so that I wouldn't be getting too close to it.

The fictional *Miracle Center* is loosely based on *The Dream Center,* and any similarities are coincidental and non-intentional.

# ABOUT THE AUTHOR

Writing is like breathing to Erin. Stories are running through her mind during most of her waking hours, and by the time she sits down at the computer, the words flow and time ceases to exist.

Erin was raised in Illinois and has lived in many places in the U.S., including on both coasts, but is a Midwest girl at heart. She spent many years as an educator from pre-school through college levels, and currently works in training and internal communications for a major global corporation.

When she's not writing, Erin loves spending time with her children and grandchildren, and playing in the garden (which equates to mostly pulling weeds) at her central Iowa home. Her secret indulgence is plain M&Ms.

Connect with Erin!

Email: ESQwrites@gmail.com
Website: www.ESQwrites.com
Facebook: Erin Stevenson Quint
Twitter: @ESQwrites

www.ingramcontent.com/pod-product-compliance
Lightning Source LLC
Chambersburg PA
CBHW020622020726

47494CB00001B/3